Married BLIND

MORGANA BEVAN

Cover Design by: Lily Bear Design Co.

Editing by Dayna Hart

ISBN: 978-1-916719-45-3

DISCLAIMER

Although *Married Blind* was inspired by an existing reality TV show, it is entirely fictional. I work in television when my characters allow, so I know that certain portrayals within *Married Blind* are over the top and would never take place in the real world. That's the beauty of fiction: we can manipulate concepts, characters, settings and situations into something totally unique.

I am a British author, and the concept of this book is British and the hero is Irish. Therefore, you'll find British English ahead. For my Americans readers, that means there will be s's where you expect z's and an extra u in certain words. All vocabulary used by Abi is however Americanised to fit her upbringing and experiences.

*To my determined editor, Dayna. Thanks for battling Word and helping
me meet my deadline. X*

Married BLIND

MORGANA BEVAN

PROLOGUE

FINN

"C'mon, Charlie. You can't be serious."

"I'm sorry, Finn, but you knew the consequences." My agent sighed on the other end of the phone. "I don't enjoy playing the bad guy. Honestly, I don't."

"Then don't."

Ordinarily, I would work to keep the slightest hint of desperation from my voice, but all bets were off in this situation. I needed out, ASAP. Otherwise, I'd be putting a ring on a stranger for America's reality-TV-loving masses in just two weeks.

Finn McCarthy didn't do reality TV.

Finn McCarthy had multiple awards under his belt, and he didn't stoop to cheesy gimmicks.

He also didn't talk about himself in the third person.

Jesus. I'm losing it.

"You knew the deal, Finn. I warned you the last time, and you still—" A hushed voice cut him off, and I sank deeper into my sofa while he argued with his assistant.

"Take your time, Charlie. It's not like you've tied my life to a ticking bomb or anything."

He sighed again. "How long have I looked after your best interests in this town?"

"Five years, but clearly you've lost your damn mind. Making me marry a gold-digging stranger and broadcasting it to millions is not looking after my best interests."

My heart pounded and sweat beaded on my forehead. The longer I let the situation spiral, the more it made me panic. How could a TV show require you to legally marry someone? The entire industry had gone insane, right alongside my agent.

"Seriously, Charlie, what if they pair me up with a right eejit, and she tries to fight the prenup?"

Not to toot my horn, but multi-award-winning actors raked in the cash.

When they weren't caught in the bathroom with the studio head's twenty-year-old daughter.

Okay, so I'd fucked up royally, but did that mean they should punish me with potentially life-altering consequences because a pretty woman offered herself to me?

Hell no.

"Next time you decide to make an ass of yourself in public, you'll remember the next three months," Charlie said. If his voice held so much as a grain of remorse, he hid it well. "I'm doing everything I can to make sure you have a long career, Finn. How about you get on board and help me?"

"Okay." I blew out a breath, a small fizzle of hope springing to life inside of me. "What about one of those survivalist shows? That's got to be better for my rep than this."

Charlie chuckled. "I like the image, bud, but the world already knows you as the macho man."

I'd even eat a spider if that would help me get out of tux fittings and ring shopping.

"It's not good for a well-rounded career actor." Charlie let those words drop like the dagger they were. "You told me you wanted to be the next Ryan Reynolds. Is that still true?"

I chewed my lip and wished I hadn't picked Charlie for a second. I should have picked a ruthless American. Someone born in LA. Hell, keeping my British agent might have worked more to my favour. Instead, I went for a Canadian transplant.

The second passed fast, unfortunately.

"Yes," I grumbled.

"Then trust me to do what's good for you."

I dragged a hand through my hair, biting back the desperate 'no' sitting at the tip of my tongue. I did trust him. Usually.

The thought of marrying someone for damage control put a sour taste in my mouth. Add cameras, producers, and undoubtedly awkward questions to the mix, and I would turn feral.

I'd seen the original of this show. After working extra hard to keep my personal life as personal as possible in this business, I did not want it painted all over billboards.

"I hate talking to reporters, Charlie. How am I meant to handle the producers?"

My best friends were taking bets on how fast I tanked the whole thing; honestly, they weren't wrong. I'll be standing at the altar, feet tapping and my eyes on the wrong door while I worked out my fifth exit strategy.

The point is, it made me feel dirty, and I was not in the business of doing things that aligned me with the lowest tier of Hollywood scum.

"Like you do everything else, Finn." Charlie's faith in me rang loud in his words. Given my knee's uncontrollable bouncing or shaky hands, I didn't deserve his misplaced faith. "It's a role."

Everything froze: my breath, my frazzled thoughts, my hands. "Say that again."

"You're an incredible actor. Just pick a persona and give

them that. There's no reason they have to see you unless you want them to."

Pick a persona.

Just another job.

"Let's say, hypothetically, I can do that," I whispered, a temporary calm flowing through my body.

"There's that confident Irish attitude I expect from you."

I snorted. "And there's that full of Canadian bullshit I expect from you." Shaking my head, I collapsed back against the sofa cushions. The leather whined beneath me. "There's really nothing I can say to talk you out of this?"

"You'd need a time machine, my friend. Suck it up and take your punishment, McCarthy," Charlie said, a thread of steel in his tone. "Next time a pretty woman comes on to you, you might think better of fucking her in a very public bathroom."

"What if my new wife is one of those pretty women?"

Charlie's heavy sigh rattled the phone.

ABI

New Email.

Subject: The solution to ALL your problems.

I snorted. Solutions to my problems wouldn't fit in an email. I needed a time-turner and a fourth job to help my sister clear her medical debt. It didn't matter how many pretty vintage garments I flipped or how much commission I made as a travel agent; we needed a miracle.

Despite my doubts, I clicked on the email, a tiny grain of hope worming its way to the forefront.

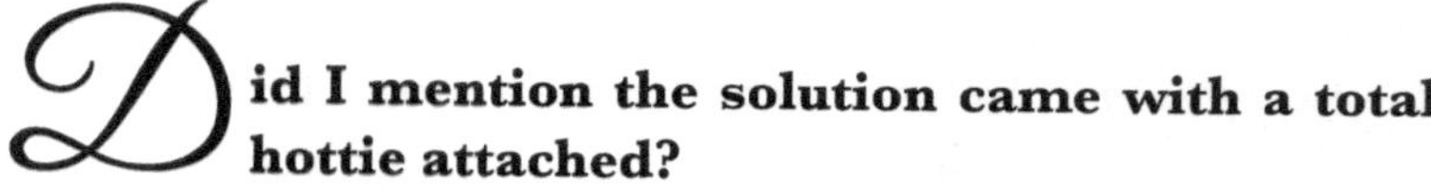

id I mention the solution came with a total hottie attached?

Click the link and thank me later... with all the details.

Ros x

I frowned at the glaring neon blue web link. *Why did Ros think Infinity Productions could help me?* A small thread of common sense shouted at me for even thinking about clicking on a strange link in an email.

Maybe someone had hijacked Roseline's account... although she usually communicated in links and memes.

Throwing caution to the wind, I hit the link. The page loaded and my head cocked to the side, considering the brightly coloured advert before me.

TV SHOW SEEKING BRIDES FOR A BRAND-NEW MARRIAGE EXPERIMENT.

She can't be serious.

I had my cell in hand in a blink. *What the hell are they after?*

"Abi! Did you get my email? Omigod, isn't it amazing?" Roseline said, her words merging into one excited whoosh of breath.

"Uh, possibly, but Ros, I don't know what I'm reading." I chewed my lip, scanning the limited details again. "What is it?"

"You know that TV show, *Married Blind*? I used to force you to watch before I moved out."

"Yes..."

"They're making a celebrity edition." She paused, expecting a gasp of awe, I imagined. We'd been best friends since college. We were predictable to each other at this point. "And they want perfectly normal people to match them with..." She waited again, and this time I smirked, sensing her frustration. "Get a little excited, Abi. They'll pay you to marry a celeb and take part in the show for three months. It's perfect."

"What's the catch?"

Roseline snorted. "No catch beyond the obvious, honey."

"The obvious being what? Spell it out for me."

"Well, for starters, you'd be marrying a stranger."

"Got that part." I brushed it aside as if she could see. "Next?"

"They're celebs, so you'll probably have to move for the duration of the show."

I swallowed hard at that.

Sure, Eva had been back on her feet for nearly a year now. She'd even returned to her job, and her gorgeous red hair had grown back. She was happy, almost like before the diagnosis and chemo, but did that mean I stopped worrying?

Of course not. I'd nearly lost my sister and my best friend. The thought of leaving her now, of vanishing to the other side of the country, even to help pay off her substantial medical bills... How could I?

"Stop the internal debate," Ros said. All the excitement drained from her voice. "You can talk to your sister, Abi. She'll understand. Heck, I think she'll beg you to go."

"You don't know that."

"Hmm..."

"You already talked to her."

"Maybe..."

Maybe? "Ros!"

"Alright! She sent *me* the link."

I gasped. Every eye in the travel shop shot toward me, customers and colleagues alike. Roseline always had the worst timing. My boss's brows rose in question, genuine concern flickering across her face. I shook my head at her and pushed back from my desk.

"Why wouldn't she talk to me herself?" I hissed as I rushed to the backroom and away from curious ears. "Why are you the messenger?"

"How should I know?" Her attempt at innocence fell flat,

and she sighed. "Fine! Eva thought you'd feel pressured into saying yes if she asked."

I rolled my eyes. "That's not true."

"Isn't it?"

"No."

Ros sighed again, her exasperation exploding in my ear. "Think about it for a second, Abs. I'm telling you about a fun thing, an exciting experience. Bonus, it just comes with a nice paycheque."

"What's your point?" My brows furrowed.

I sank into an uncomfortable plastic chair, my mind spinning enough that I didn't really feel the pinch of the seat. We only really used the backroom to store our coats and bags, but the bosses had set it up with chairs, a table, a fridge and a microwave. With the lack of windows, none of us ever wanted to spend too much time inside with the door shut. Far too depressing.

"Imagine how you would have taken my pitch if Eva asked."

I would have filled out the form already.

I dragged a shaking hand through my hair.

"So, now that you've listened to the specifics, are you going to do it?" The excitement returned threefold.

I blew out a breath, indecision a heavy weight in my chest. "How much money are we talking about?"

"I don't know. You'd have to fill in the form and hope you get picked to find out."

I nodded, even though she couldn't see me.

Right at this moment, the decision had to be about me. Could I marry a stranger? Did I want to leave my family and friends for three months?

It had been a tough couple of years, and as much as I hated to admit it, New York didn't have the same happy hold on me anymore. Too many bad things had happened within the city, including my sister's battle with cancer. Working three jobs also robbed any of the joy from my life.

Even if I had the hours to fall in love with it again, constant exhaustion didn't allow for much.

Maybe a brief break from the city and my normal life would revive me somehow. I could get in some excitement and shake off the shadows while hopefully earning enough to pay off my sister's debt for good.

How could I say no to that kind of opportunity? The answer was simple. I couldn't.

"I'll do it."

INTERVIEW I

Question: How would you define your type?
Finn: I don't have a type.
Interviewer: Are you sure about that?
Finn: I wouldn't have said it if it weren't true.
Interviewer: So if I googled your red carpet company, they wouldn't all be tall, blonde, and leggy?
Finn: Maybe. I don't remember.
Interviewer (handing over papers): So you didn't date these women?
Finn: Why did you print pictures? Jesus, man, that's creepy… Yes, they're all blonde supermodels. Don't you understand what image control is?
Interviewer: Does that mean none of your past companions were your type?
Finn: They were gorgeous, but I dated none of them. My agent picked them all for whatever publicity stunt he had planned.
Interviewer: So, what is your type, Finn McCarthy?
Finn: Do we really have to do this? Can't you just pick someone and speed this entire ordeal along?

Interviewer: I'm not interested in furthering your acting career, Mr McCarthy. I'm here to find your perfect match.

Finn: You don't really mean that. C'mon, it's all a farce. We'll all divorce in three months.

Interviewer: I can't say I agree. Now, how about you try to get on board with the process, so I can do my job?

Finn: Fine. If you trap me with a starry-eyed fan, I swear I'll make your life hell. Find me a redhead with fire in her eyes and an interesting story.

Interviewer: That I can do.

CHAPTER ONE

ABI

$\mathcal{D}$-Day had arrived, and nerves had claimed me as their bitch. Add in the unbearable heat of Los Angeles, the cameraman and producer hovering in the corner adjusting their equipment, the assistant setting up lighting, and I'd be lucky if I didn't collapse.

Just getting married to a total stranger for TV. No pressure at all.

Eva and Ros gave me awkward thumbs-ups from the doorway. Each of them grinned at me, excitement dancing in their eyes. Side by side, they looked like night and day dressed to match, Eva with her bobbed auburn hair and Ros with her raven pixie cut, in pink, Grecian-inspired bridesmaid dresses — Ros claimed they'd be the next trend. The true angel and devil on my shoulder. Punk-rocker Ros had not been unimpressed when the producer handed her it.

I tried to return their excitement, revel in their support, but it fell flat. Right along with my hair.

The hairdresser had spent a good hour fighting my curls. She'd started all sunny and welcoming. All of that had morphed fairly quickly. Now, I'd catch her glaring at a fizzing chunk.

"How does an updo sound?" she asked, forcing a smile back to her lips.

Her southern accent came through stronger than it had before. My lips twitched at her frustration before I schooled myself for the inconsiderate reaction. Just because her efforts would cause this nerve-racking train to gain speed didn't mean I should be unkind.

"I'm good with that."

"Is that air conditioning unit for show?" she snapped at an assistant.

He skittered away, muttering promises to fix it. She shoved her fringe back with the back of her hand, grimacing at the sweat transfer.

"If you expect her hair to stay put, someone should fix the heat," she shouted, glaring at the producer.

My lips twitched again, and she smirked at me.

"Nothing happens if you don't light a fire under them."

"Is that an inside tip?" I asked. A genuine smile claimed my lips for the first time since I'd set foot in the building.

When we'd arrived outside the bland white hotel, Eva, Ros, and I had looked at each other in absolute confusion. A TV show with celebrities could have sprung for a hell of a lot more.

And then the producer, Tyler, whisked us through a back door and into the most opulent hallway I've ever seen. Colourful art déco moulding outfitted every corner of the ceiling. Intricate pillars lined the hallway.

Then he opened the door to a team of beauticians who plucked and waxed us to the nth degree while they briefed us on the day's events. To say it was distracting would have been an understatement.

The Élysee Atelier lace mermaid dress I'd picked out weeks ago hung in the corner, taunting my sweaty face with its beauty. I worried for all of five minutes back in New York when I tried the dress on that it would be too delicate and the train too long.

What if it came across as over the top? What if all the other brides went for neck-to-toe lace, too? Was the plunging neckline too revealing for national television?

Thankfully, Eva quickly slapped the camera-shy insecurities out of me. She'd reminded me, in no uncertain terms, that everything about this experience needed to be my choice, including my clothing, hair, and makeup. So I chose the dress I loved and quit worrying about it.

"Oh, aren't you an angel?" the hairdresser gushed as a runner set up a fan next to me.

I blinked at her sudden change in mood, but then I spotted an eye roll and her backhanded Southern charm made sense. I needed to spend more time outside of New York.

Tyler clapped his hands when my hair finally took shape and cool air caressed my glistening skin. Then there was a camera in my face again.

"How's everything going here?" He smiled wide, working overtime to put me at ease. Seated as I was, he towered over me, even though he only had a couple of inches on me normally. He pushed his floppy brown hair back from his face, grimacing. "I really should have gotten my hair cut before Bora Bora. We'll both be suffering in the heat soon enough." He flashed me an amused smile. "Mind if I grab a couple of thoughts before you head into makeup?"

He'd done everything he could to help me chill out. Unfortunately, the only thing that would put me at ease was a shot of bourbon. They understandably frowned on that kind of thing at 11 AM.

"Sure." I tried for sunny, but the word came out as more of a croak.

"Some water?" Tyler asked. His gaze already scoured the

room, searching for an assistant. "Ethan, grab Abi a bottle of water from the fridge."

He settled down on a chair across from me, leaning forward with a notebook clutched in his hands and an eager gleam in his eyes. His lightweight black suit creased in the wrong places, but he didn't care.

"Liam here will shadow you until the ceremony." He nodded towards the dark-haired guy hidden behind the camera. "But you won't need to talk to the camera, anymore. Act naturally, and talk to your family and friends. If you're excited or nervous, don't be afraid to experience it."

"Sure."

The word tripped off my tongue, but did I truly mean it? No matter how much he briefed me, or how patient they were, it still felt weird to catch the flashing red dot of the camera from the corner of my eye.

You'll get used to it. Chill.

"Once we're done, I'm going to slip out and check in on your groom." His brows danced, eyes shining with mischief. "Make sure he's looking handsome for you."

I chuckled, and he grinned, nodding at me encouragingly. Some of the tension drained from my body for the first time since they had whisked me into the bridal suite.

"Ready for some quick questions?"

"Fire away." I nodded, shifting in my seat and tightening the tie on my robe.

"Okay, remember what I said, answer in full sentences and count to ten before you respond."

Satisfied, Tyler glanced at the cameraman, lifting his chin. The red light flicked on and Liam nodded.

"Okay, Abi, are you excited to meet your groom?" Tyler asked. He smiled encouragingly as I hesitated.

"I—"

"Take your time if you need to think about the answer."

Was I excited? My hands shook, and a lump kept trying to form in my throat. But was that excitement or terror?

The same cycle of doubts had run through my head for weeks while I went through the process of joining the show. Yet, despite the repeated questions about my sanity, I hadn't pulled out. Could I thank my drive to help my sister for that? The answer should have been an immediate yes, but…

"I'm nervous to meet my groom," I said, focusing on Tyler rather than the camera lens. "This might be the riskiest thing I've ever done. I'd be a shaking wreck if I didn't have my best friend and sister with me." I swallowed hard as my focus shifted to their smiling faces, urging me on.

"You got this," Eva mouthed. She leaned her head against the doorframe, moisture forming in her blue eyes — identical to mine.

I returned my attention to Tyler, and he nodded. Between the two of them, I somehow found a strength I sorely needed.

"But I am excited. Excited to meet him, excited for a couple of months of new experiences and a break from my normal." My smile turned shy, and I resisted the urge to cover my face. "I'm hoping it'll be a refreshing change from what I've gotten used to in New York."

"Perfect." Tyler flicked through his notebook, scanning a list of questions I could barely read. The man had terrible handwriting. "How do you feel about your sister walking you down the aisle?"

I sucked in a breath. I knew the question would come. They'd warned me plenty of times. Yet it still hit me hard in the gut. I'd naively hoped they'd wait a couple of weeks before making me talk about the painful things.

"I'm so grateful to my sister for agreeing to walk me down the aisle today." That lump threatened to choke me again, and I paused, readying myself to say the hard words that usually turned me into a puffy-eyed mess.

I'd argued with Tyler for weeks about leaving my parents

out of it, but sad stories make for great TV. In the end, I'd had to concede defeat.

"When I was a kid, I always thought, when the day came, it would be my dad…" I glanced down at my fists twisting the material of the robe. Another deep breath and I refocused on Tyler. "But our parents died in a car crash a few years ago. A drunk driver ran a red light at a busy intersection and caused a massive pile-up. Eva and I lost them both in one night, and we're all the other has had ever since. We'd do anything for each other." Including embarrassing ourselves on national television. "I'm not sure I could do this without her support, honestly."

"Excellent, Abi. Okay, one more and I'll leave you to finish getting ready." When I nodded, he jumped straight in. "Why do you want to marry a celebrity like this?"

My eyes widened. Talk about starting with the hard questions. My pulse raced at the wildly incorrect assumptions people could make from my answer — from my participation in the show. How the hell did I answer a question like that without sounding like a gold digger?

"I don't know who I'm marrying today, but I can't wait to meet them." My mind raced as I scrambled for more.

You've got this, sugarplum, a small voice whispered at the back of my mind.

It sounded suspiciously like my mother, the last words she said to me before she died, encouragement on my first day at a new job.

Despite the pang of sadness the reminder sent through me, it settled me too.

"It doesn't matter to me they're famous. I'm looking for a genuine person. Some chemistry would be nice, but above all, I hope we get along." I glanced at Eva, desperate for some validation that I hadn't just made a fool of myself. She waved her hand at me, urging me to keep going. "I work a lot in New York. Three jobs, just to keep the bills paid. Opportunities to meet Mr Right have dwindled. I might be naïve to hope for a real connection, but that's what I want more than anything."

I probably shouldn't have admitted that part, opening myself up to rejection and all that. But I didn't want to lie. The prospect of finding someone to truly get *me* filled me with tingles of delight. Gimmicky TV show or not, I wanted this to work, so I'd give it my all.

"That was brilliant, Abi." Tyler clapped, his hazel eyes sparkling with his excitement. "I've got all I need for now. You relax, finish getting ready." He stood, glancing around the room as if searching for someone. "Ethan will be here if you need anything at all. He'll even pop the bubbly in the other room for you."

"How did I miss a bottle of booze?" Ros muttered before vanishing from the doorway.

Tyler left quickly, while Ethan scrambled into the other room after Ros.

"I'm perfectly capable of popping champers, kid." Her disgruntled voice carried, and I bit my lip, feeling marginally sorry for the assistant.

"You all good, Abs?" Eva asked. She crouched down in front of me, her brow creased with concern. "It's not too late to get out of this if you change your mind. I can figure out another way to pay down the debt."

I bit back the 'no' that immediately sprang to the tip of my tongue and took her hands, smiling at her instead. Staring into her almost identical face, I felt like I was reassuring myself instead of my baby sister. Her auburn hair flowed down her back, framing her pale skin and striking blue eyes.

With the amount of concern creasing the skin around her eyes, I'd expect her to be tugging at her hair by this point. Hell, I expected *myself* to be tugging at my hair. With both of us pinned up in some fashion and wearing at least a can of hairspray, it wouldn't be advisable to give in to old habits. The hairdresser still lurked in the shadows, waiting for last-minute touch-ups.

"I know, but I want to do it." I squeezed her hands. "Yes, I'm nervous, but wouldn't you be if you were marrying someone you'd never met?"

Even if I hope it turns into more than an arranged marriage.

At the thought, my nerves morphed into a tremble of excitement.

The love of my life could be just behind those doors.

"I wouldn't be in this position, Abs." She frowned. "You always were the adventurous one."

Once upon a time, maybe. Before our parents died, and I had to take over, making sure Eva made it through college.

Back then, I'd had dreams of travelling. Spending a year in Paris and Milan to continue my fashion studies. Walking in the footsteps of some of the great designers who had left their mark on the best industry in the world.

Reality made it all impossible in the end. I couldn't exactly spend years as an underpaid, overworked fashion intern. I had Eva to support and we lived in one of the most expensive cities in North America.

Maybe the next three months should *be about me, instead of us.*

If I could shove the pang of guilt the thought produced into a heavy-duty box.

"Why the hell are you two not in here consuming champers with me?" Ros shouted from the other room. "We have thirty minutes before the make-up artist turns up. Do you think they'll let us drink after that?"

Eva and I smirked at each other. "No," we called back in unison.

"Exactly. So get your asses in here!" Ros poked her head around the door, her eyes sparkling, and the bottle dangling from her fingers. "Have you seen this expensive shit? I'm going to need to take a bath in it. It tastes that good."

Chuckling, I took Eva's offered hand and stood. We followed Ros back into the other room.

CHAPTER TWO

ABI

I thought the nerves were bad before. I'd been wrong.

Eva and I stood before two enormous doors waiting for our cue from the producer. Liam hovered nearby, his camera fixed on us, while I tried very hard not to fidget. My fingers dug into the handle of my bouquet.

"Remember what we talked about, Abs," Eva muttered, her voice hard but coaxing. Her hands rested on my shoulders, squeezing and forcing me to stay upright. "Say the word and we bounce."

I nodded, but kept my mouth shut. Sure, my voice had skipped off for its own jolly, but that didn't mean I had to follow. No, I'd made a commitment, and I refused to break it.

"I've got this," I whispered, repeating my mother's encouragement. I forced my shoulders back, lifted my chin and relaxed my death grip on the bouquet.

Eva studied me for a second before nodding. She released her grip and turned towards the doors. Beyond them, strings started up and my stomach flipped.

"Then let's get this show on the road." Eva held out her arm, offering me a soft smile.

"Just follow your instincts now, Abi." Tyler approached me, a calm expression plastered across his features. He gathered the veil the show had insisted on, lifting it over my head. "Go knock him dead."

My lips felt strained, trying to hold a smile in place while butterflies ran amok in my stomach.

Tyler leaned in, whispering in my ear. "I'm confident you can handle him, by the way. Don't hide that fire from him and you'll ace this."

My brows drew together at the tip. *What on earth did that mean?*

Before I could ask, the veil fell into place and Tyler rushed out of the way of the doors. Two seconds later, they swung open on silent hinges. The room beyond was bathed in white light. They had set the chairs up to fold around a central altar, which looked like something out of a Greek myth, ornate columns holding up a canopy of greenery. Arched doorways surrounded the entire space, all of them covered with flowing white sheets.

So many faces swivelled toward me, their expressions blurring between the light and my frantic mind. My breath froze in my lungs, but I kept moving by sheer force of will.

"Oh my god, Abi." Eva pinched me. "He's gorgeous," she hissed.

My body tensed up for an entirely different reason.

He stared at me, a small smile tugging at his lips. He'd restrained his black hair at his neck, but rogue curls broke free from the tie, falling around his face and making me think of Jane Austen novels. I swallowed the amusement fast when his piercing sapphire eyes scanned down my body. His hands clenched at his sides, but otherwise, he gave nothing away.

"Yeah, he is, isn't he?" I whispered back, forgetting that

they'd attached a microphone to my dress and the producers could hear every word.

A navy suit and grey waistcoat hugged his trim build while a pink rose sat on his lapel tying him into the sea of pink flowers surrounding us. Not even the pink rose could ruin the rugged edge that emanated from him.

"I call dibs on the blond next to him." She chuckled. "Make sure you tell Ros. She'll be pissed."

I grinned at her, although she couldn't see it beneath all the lace of the veil.

Three guys stood at his side, nearly all of them wearing matching navy suits and navy waistcoats. One of them paired the look with a tartan kilt. Together, they looked like an ad for a tailor. Or a rom-com.

All of them were equally hot and all staring at me with open excitement. *What was that about?*

Ros stood on the opposite side of the altar, rather indiscreetly tilting her head towards the men. It seemed Eva already had a fight on her hands for dibs.

Before I knew it, Ros took my bouquet and Eva handed me off to my mystery man. His hand engulfed mine, smooth but firm, and instead of listening to the officiator, I stared into his eyes, daydreaming about the things he could do to me with those hands.

"Ms Johnson, are you okay?" The officiant asked me.

I forced the images from my mind, grateful for the veil hiding my burning cheeks and the glaze in my eyes. My focus jumped to the officiant, his bushy white brows rising in question.

"Yes, I'm fine. Sorry, carry on."

He nodded to my soon-to-be husband. "You may unveil your bride, Mr McCarthy."

McCarthy. Abigail McCarthy. I let my new name roll around my mind. I liked it.

He reached for me, his hands steady and his focus unwavering on me. His fingers grazed my neck as he drew the veil up and over my head. I barely suppressed the shiver just one sweep of his skin against mine generated.

At least you won't have to worry about attraction.

His piercing eyes roamed my face as the veil settled down my back.

"I'm Finn," he whispered.

Did he have a foreign accent?

I held in my squeal of delight. I'd always loved a good accent. Couldn't get enough of British TV shows. Eva had banned me from watching Game of Thrones in our apartment. Apparently, I ruined it for her.

"What's your name, *dotey*?"

"Abi," I said, my voice croaking.

The corner of his lips twitched. His fingers flexed against the veil, pressing against my bare shoulder.

"Hi, Abi." My name *danced* off his tongue. "Are you ready to get married?"

I nodded, my ability to speak lost to the shiver of need rushing down my spine from one touch. He stepped back, glancing toward the officiant.

Besides that slip of amusement, I couldn't read the man. No matter how hard I studied him, his expression didn't shift. It remained locked in an expressionless mask — a pleasant one, but a mask all the same.

Clearly, they'd given me an actor.

Whether that would be a blessing or a curse remained to be seen.

"Mr McCarthy, have you prepared vows for your bride?"

"Yes," he said.

His friend handed him a small sheet of paper. Finn cleared his throat, glanced at the sheet once, and pocketed it.

"I wasn't expecting to get married, much less to a stranger…"

The vows passed by in a blur while I sank into my head,

my lips moving on autopilot. The production had provided me with vows. Had they done the same for Finn? And if they did, did the lack of emotion in his eyes mean he didn't agree with a word of it?

Why hadn't I realised that a show like *Married Blind* meant nothing more to the celebs than an ego and image boost?

Nothing serious would ever grow between us.

That shouldn't send a pang of regret through me. I just wanted the money and a break from my boring life. Why did it matter to me if Finn only wanted me to further his ego?

Because you're a romantic at heart.

"Do you, Finn McCarthy, take Abigail Johnson to be your lawfully wedded wife? To have and to hold from this day forward, for better or for worse, for richer or poorer, in sickness and in health, to love and to cherish as long as you both shall live?"

"I do," Finn said, his voice deepening and his gaze fixed on me.

The officiant turned to me, and I swallowed hard.

Last chance to jump ship, Abi. Decide quick.

"Do you, Abigail Johnson, take Finn McCarthy to be your lawfully wedded husband? To have and to hold from this day forward, for better or for worse, for richer or poorer, in sickness and in health, to love and to cherish as long as you both shall live?"

I turned, searching for Eva and Ros as if the entire room had frozen. They stood behind me, tears shimmering in their eyes. Both of them wore soppy smiles that made my heart twist painfully.

How could I turn back when they looked that happy?

Simple. I couldn't.

"Abi?" Finn's hand grazed my arm. His fingers closed around my wrist, turning me back to him. "Are you okay?" he whispered, his face close to mine while his body blocked me from most of the prying eyes of our audience. "If you don't want to do this, you don't have to. We can end it right now."

"I'm fine," I lied. I turned to the officiant and Finn backed away, his mask slipping for all of a second. His lips compressed into a thin line, but I had no clue what that meant. "I do."

"The rings, please?" The officiant glanced between Finn's friends and mine.

Ros placed a thick piece of gold in my palm.

"Finn, please place the ring on Abi's left ring finger and repeat after me."

Finn took my hand, the ring poised at the tip of my finger as he listened to the officiant list off the vows, while two cameramen circled us.

"I give you this ring, in token and pledge of my constant faith and abiding love." Finn paused, his lip twitching again.

His friends weren't so circumspect. One covered his mouth, while another outright grinned. Okay, so the words were extreme for a reality tv show.

"With this ring, I thee wed."

The ring slid onto my finger, and despite the absurdity of it, my heart skipped a beat. *Yours would too if you had those eyes gazing into yours.* If I didn't think too hard about it, I could almost trick myself into believing that the flicker of emotion in his eyes meant more than it did.

"Abi, please place the ring on Finn's left ring finger, and repeat after me."

I followed his instructions, pausing when the producers demanded and repeating myself when needed. The entire exchange probably took twice as long because we kept having to stop for the cameras.

"Finn and Abigail, you have given and pledged your love and faithfulness, each to the other, and have declared the same by joining hands, by virtue of the authority vested in me by the State of California, I now pronounce you husband and wife." The officiant turned to Finn, a smirk playing with the edges of his lips. "You may kiss your bride."

Finn's gaze bounced from him to me, to the camera over my shoulder and back to me. His lips tightened, but he stepped forward. His hands glided against the lace bodice of my dress, grazing my skin yet again on their way to my lower back. This time, he stood too close to miss me shiver, and his grip tightened as he lowered his head. My hands skimmed up his chest, desperate for some kind of support. He caught one hand, holding it still against his pounding heart.

Then his lips pressed against mine. My eyes fluttered shut, and I released the nerves coursing through my body. His trimmed beard grazed against my sensitive skin, focusing all of my attention on him. *As if it could be anywhere else.*

His fingers flexed against my back, right at the very edge of the material, bridging the gap between my ass and the dress's open back.

His heart jumped into overdrive as he deepened the kiss. For a second, I got lost in the sensation. The cameras and the crowd faded away. I forgot that I'd only just met this guy. We were just two people, enjoying a mind-blowing kiss filled with possibilities.

And just like that, every nerve evaporated.

CHAPTER THREE

FINN

I should have pecked Abi on the lips and backed away. I kept screaming the same thing at myself, over and over again.

Yet, I couldn't stop.

Couldn't release my grip on her soft skin, couldn't pull myself away. I got lost in the taste of her, in the almost timid caress of her lips against mine. One soft gasp from her as I deepened the kiss, and I needed more. Her hesitation melting away was like catnip.

It consumed all of me. An on-camera kiss never did that. No matter who it was, I always had control.

Jesus. When did I turn into this person?

Cheers and applause invaded, pushing my common sense to the forefront and reminding me of my surroundings. Renewed determination filled me. If a kiss could be that off the charts when it shouldn't, the next three months would be a piece of cake. I'd play the perfect husband for the cameras, rehab my career, and then divorce her and be done.

I broke the kiss and forced my mask back into place. *Nothing to see here. This Irishman isn't the slightest bit affected.* Which would be a lie, but no one needed to know.

And then I focused on her again, and my control almost slipped.

She gazed at me, her lips swollen, her baby blue eyes glazed, and her cheeks flushed. The need to make her look at me like that with her vibrant auburn hair spread out on my pillow, mussed from a good fucking, took me by surprise.

Christ on a bike. What is wrong with me?

Caught in a daze of my own, I took her hand and turned us to face the raucous crowd. I led Abi through them, aiming for the door.

People threw confetti over us, shouting their congratulations with tears in their eyes. *Where did they get these people?*

Aside from Shaun, his fiancée, my friends, and my agent, no one else on the guest list mattered to me. Charlie had better skip the reception. I was going to murder him for inviting the studio execs.

"Are you alright?" Abi asked as we reached the door.

"Fine," I growled.

"Okay…" She hesitated, her fingers twitching in my grip. She leaned into me, and for a second I thought she planned to kiss me again. "You're mumbling to yourself, so if you don't want them to broadcast it, zip it."

The doors opened, and I did just that. I needed to remember they had me perpetually mic'ed. The producers would have zero concerns about using inappropriate comments for their show if it increased the drama.

So, for the next three months, I needed to break a habit of a lifetime and put on a full-time bloody show.

Shite in a bucket. What have I done?

❄

The producers thankfully abandoned us for a couple of minutes. Unfortunately, a camera followed, hanging back in the corner of the room like we wouldn't notice the scrutiny.

I hadn't wanted to be in the situation in the first place, but even so, everything felt awkward. The idea of not knowing what to say to a pretty woman didn't sit right. It wasn't how I rolled.

One look at Abi, chewing her lip, probably thinking the same things, and that weird pang of need returned. I wanted to protect her from all of this. She seemed so innocent, and bizarrely, I wanted her to stay that way.

Hollywood had a nasty habit of gobbling up people like her and spitting them out a couple of months down the line, irrevocably broken.

I wouldn't let that happen to her.

But you plan to spit her out yourself, when you're done with her, jackass, so what does it matter?

I ignored that concerning thought. For the moment.

"I can get the cameraman thrown out for a couple of minutes if you need a second." The offer tripped off my tongue.

"It's okay. I guess we just need to get used to it," she said, her soft voice sweeping over me like the smoothest bottle of whisky.

Shite.

Her fingers pressed against my forearm, urging me to turn around, and I gave in. The guys were going to have a field day with this bullshit. I stared into her eyes, searching for even a tiny sign that she wasn't the gold digger I feared. Or worse, an attention whore hoping to get her five minutes of fame with the gossip rags. How could someone that sweet and innocent-looking hide that kind of shallowness?

Maybe she isn't hiding anything.

I almost snorted at the thought.

My gaze roamed down her lace-encased body. I hadn't been able to tear my eyes away from her when she'd walked through the doors, her veil barely covering the low reveal of her dress and tight fit hugging her body all the way to her knees before it flared out across the floor. It had been a long time since I'd had to worry about getting a hard-on in public, but one glance at her and I lost control.

Christ, did they have to pair me with such a fine thing?

"Are you sure you're okay? You look stressed." She chewed her lip and that damn need sprung up again, only this time I wanted to stop her from torturing her lips. *Fuck.*

"I'm fine. Just a weird, high-stress situation." I shrugged. "Nothing new really." My gaze flicked to the wanker with the camera pointed at us.

"This is weird, right?"

"Abso-bloody-lutely," I grumbled.

"So you don't make a habit of meeting women at the altar?" She chuckled.

"Christ, no."

"So I'm your first wife?"

"I should hope so."

I let her see some of my true horror at the thought. She snorted and scrambled to cover her mouth, her eyes widening. I didn't hold my grin back.

"What about you? Do you make a habit of meeting men for the first time wearing a wedding dress?"

Her expression fell.

The desire to put that bright spark back in her eyes burned hot. All these years in LA and I'd avoided therapy. It might be time to get my head shrunk.

"I guess we should get to know each other before the producers come in and grill us."

"That sounds like a plan." She nodded, an odd note of relief creeping into her voice. "So you're from Ireland."

"Northern Ireland."

Her brow furrowed. "There's a difference?"

I licked my lips, biting back my instant indignation. One day, it would stop surprising me that Americans didn't know that Ireland was divided. Hell, most of them didn't even know that England wasn't the only country in the UK.

"Yes, a big difference, but let's not ruin our wedding day with politics."

"Okay, so you're Northern Irish and an actor. How did you end up in the US?"

"Necessity mostly. I wanted to do big things and there's more opportunity here." I shrugged, hoping that would be the end of it. Her gaze remained fixed on me, eager for more. I sighed and continued, "I moved out here as soon as I graduated from drama school. Met my best friends a few years later. Now, I never want to leave."

Except some days, I craved something more than the fakery of LA. Something more real.

"How old are you?" she asked, her gaze sweeping down my body as if she could read me like a tree.

"Twenty-nine. You?"

"Twenty-six." She smirked when I said nothing. "No quips about someone like me being single at my age?"

My brows climbed. "Do people seriously say that to you?"

"All the time." She nodded and some of the confidence wilted out of her. "Made it kind of easy to stop dating, honestly. Although I never understood what they meant by someone like me."

I chuckled. "Sure you don't."

Her head tilted to the side, eying me with confusion. No way in hell does she not know. It had to be an act... yet the confusion didn't clear, and she didn't comment on it again. Every woman I'd ever met would have used that line to fish for compliments. Abi just turned away, studying the room with interest. How intriguing.

"Anyway, that's pretty much my life story. Yours is probably more interesting."

She chuckled without turning back to me. "I'm not sure that's even remotely true."

"Well, tell me yours, and let me be the judge." I grinned as she tensed. She turned back to me, her brows risen in question. "We can't compare notes unless you share."

She sighed. "You're right. Sorry." Her gaze dropped to the floor before skittering over to the camera and back to me again. "I just don't normally talk about it. It's not exciting."

A beautiful woman who didn't want to talk about herself. The mystery continued to grow. Despite my common sense, she'd piqued my interest.

"I don't need it to be exciting, Abi." I flashed my classic Hollywood smile, the one that usually resulted in a woman wrapped around my finger and on her way to my bed in under a minute. "Just give me the truth."

Not that I wanted Abi in my bed…

Liar.

She stared at me for a while, her throat working, and her cheeks flushed. I fought a triumphant grin. No need to scare her off or give anyone the impression that I could take satisfaction in dirtying her mind.

"Fine. It's not a happy story though, fair warning." She went to drag her hand through her hair but froze before she could damage whatever held everything in place. "I'm a travel agent, and I flip vintage pieces that I find in thrift stores on the side. I don't really have a lot of spare time in New York and when I have any, I'd rather spend it in the flat with my sister and Ros or sorting through new stock…"

I listened as she explained her jobs, the surprising characters who spent their weekends wandering around their local pharmacy where she worked for extra hours. I avidly devoured the sparkle in her eye as she talked about her sister and her love for fashion.

I shouldn't have cared and shouldn't have been filing the information away for some future unknown need, captivated by the sweet curl of her lips, and the slight blush that claimed her cheeks when she talked too fast.

"What did you mean it wasn't a happy story? None of that was sad."

"I..." She pressed her lips together, hesitation written across her face.

I seriously needed to get a grip on the intrigue. The information didn't matter, couldn't matter.

"You what?" I asked, losing the battle of common sense yet again.

"Nothing." She shook her head. "Slip of the tongue."

"Okay."

There would be one benefit to this match, at least. She couldn't lie. Abi was an open bloody book. Sadness and indecision flashed across her face as if lit up by a beacon.

"Do you have any hobbies?" she asked, a forced edge to her voice.

"I don't get a lot of free time, but I dive and surf whenever I can." I pressed my lips together, fighting the polite need to reciprocate. "You?"

"I already mentioned fashion." She shrugged. "I used to enjoy yoga and going to concerts, but mostly I just read now."

"Do you have any favourite bands?"

"A couple. I don't get the chance to go to shows much anymore, but I never miss Marable when they play New York."

A jolt of amusement hit me, testing even my control of my facial muscles. She couldn't have picked a band not fronted by one of my friends?

"So, an actor. Will I have seen anything you were in?" She breezed on.

I shrugged. "Depends if you like action films, I guess."

"Ah. Not really." She grimaced.

A fucking grimace should not have been attractive. I'd well and truly lost my damned mind. Maybe Shaun could recommend someone.

"I'm more of a romantic comedy person. Sorry."

"Don't be." My focus moved to the cameraman camped out in the corner. "Do we need to stay here?"

"I think so." He straightened up and shrugged. "Sorry, man."

Grand, just bloody grand.

"Then can you get a PA in here, or that gobshite Tyler?"

I ground my teeth as I watched him place his camera down, moving at a glacial pace. He picked up a radio, muttering his call too low for me to hear.

"Does it bother you that much that I haven't seen one of your movies?" Abi asked, her voice scratchy with confusion.

I glanced at her, working extra hard to keep my expression neutral.

"No, it doesn't make a difference to me."

"Then why are you suddenly annoyed?" Her brows rose and her tone sharpened.

"They're dawdling and wasting our time." I crossed my arms, the tailored suit jacket pulling at the seams. The faster I could get the monkey-suit off, the happier I'd be. "The less time they have to ask our friends awkward questions, the better."

I didn't want to think about the shit Shaun, Nathan, and Jackson would share just to wind me up. No one knew me better than the three of them. I couldn't imagine anything more dangerous. Especially when the three of them knew how much I hated this situation.

Abi's face paled.

"It's a terrifying thought, isn't it?" I smirked.

She nodded hard before making a beeline for the cameraman.

"Can we get out of here now? I really need to talk to my best friend." A shrill of panic underlined her rushed words.

The cameraman shook his head, smiling in a bullshit attempt to be sympathetic. I could see right through him. There would be a process to this entire thing. Keep us contained, interview the family and friends, interview us, then announce our entrance and get all the angles.

I might have watched an episode or two…

No wonder they scheduled the ceremony so early in the day.

My focus drifted while the cameraman radioed the rest of the crew again, trailing down her exposed back to a biteable ass contained in tight lace. If I didn't want to resist her so badly, I could have found some fucking incredible ways to pass the time. I almost groaned at the mental image of my hands on her.

Why'd she have to choose a tight-fitting torture dress?

I'd bet my Oscar that it had been Tyler's idea. That weasel knew how to get under my skin somehow.

"They're nearly done," the cameraman said, as if that was any consolation. "And Ethan's grabbing you drinks. He should be in soon."

Abi spun to face me, outright panic blanketing her expression.

"They're hardly going to sacrifice you. It'll be fine."

"You haven't met Ros." The panic didn't recede. "She can spin any generic, normal story into something outlandish and ridiculous. I don't even want to imagine the crap she's going to come up with for a TV show."

A twinge of sympathy hit me hard. *Far too innocent for this business.* It must have been nice to not have to worry about people lying about you to get their five minutes of fame.

"You should probably get used to that." I shrugged and shoved my hands into my pockets. "Whatever your friend makes up won't be anywhere near as bad as the shite some random stranger will sell to the tabloids next week. Anyone who remotely knew you growing up will come out of the woodwork by the weekend and morph into your absolute best friend."

She stared at me. "How can you be so blasé about it?"

"How can I be blasé about a disgusting industry built on selling lies after ten years of living with it first-hand?" I snorted. "*Dotey*, you can't be that naïve."

"Did you ever think that not all people are like that?"

"Christ. Where did they find you?" I dragged a hand through my hair and turned away from her.

Question: Tell me about your first impression of Abi
Finn: *snorts* We aren't doing this.
Tyler, Producer: Right now?
Finn: Ever.
Tyler, Producer: Bu - but it's a part of the show.
Finn: And?
Tyler, Producer: You can't - you have to answer our questions.
Finn: No, I don't think I do.
Tyler, Producer: Yes, you do. It's part of the show.
Finn: You said that already. Listen, *mucker*—
Tyler, Producer: Muck what?
Finn: *sighs* Listen, *pal*, I didn't agree to this fiasco, and I didn't agree to have cameras shoved in my face every five minutes. Got a problem with that? Take it up with my agent.
Tyler, Producer: Mr McCarthy! Wait!

Question: Tell me about your first impression of Finn

Abi: Right now?

Tyler, Producer: Please.

Abi: Okay, but can we step away from the ladies' bathroom first?

Tyler, Producer: Of course.

Tyler, Producer: So your first impression of Finn?

Abi: Finn's confusing, honestly. One minute he's lovely; the next he's snapping at people and muttering to himself. I'm not sure what to make of him.

Tyler, Producer: Are you attracted to him?

Abi: Do I have to answer that?

Tyler, Producer: No, of course not. It just gives the audience a good idea of where you stand. Are you happy you got Finn?

Abi: I think it's too early to say whether I'm happy about marrying Finn. I don't really know the man. Is he attractive? I'm not blind, so yes. Are there interesting possibilities there? Sure. But do I think this will be easy? Absolutely not. I feel like I'm missing half the picture and until he trusts me, I doubt I'm going to get far with him.

CHAPTER FOUR

ABI

"For the first time, ladies and gentlemen, Mr and Mrs McCarthy."

The large doors swung open for the second time today, revealing a completely rearranged room. The altar had vanished to be replaced by a dance floor surrounded by round tables, all decorated with pink and white flowers and greenery. Eddison bulbs hung from the ceiling, casting a glow over the room and stealing my breath.

"Did you pick all this?" I asked Finn, leaning into him to make sure he heard me over the crowd cheering at us.

People swarmed in, shaking his hand and offering congratulations as if our marriage were real and we'd done something momentous.

"What?" He glanced at me sharply, then lowered his head. "No, I didn't plan any of it. I thought they'd handed it over to you."

My gaze cast across the room again. I revelled in the shock

of finding the space decorated exactly to my taste. Then I spotted Eva and Ros beaming at me.

I wonder…

Finn led me toward them, or more toward his friends waiting at their sides. All three of his friends dwarfed Eva and Ros and a pink-haired woman tucked into one of their sides. None of us were tall. Until today, we'd considered Ros's five-foot-seven towering over mine and Eva's five-foot-five. Finn's friends were veritable giants. They must have been over six feet, and lined up together, they looked like a colour wheel for Hollywood heartthrobs.

My face hurt from forcing a smile to my lips while strangers invaded my personal space. A quick glance at Finn gave me absolutely zero insight into whether he felt the same awkwardness. If I couldn't learn to see beyond his walls, the next three months would consist of nothing more than me tiptoeing around him, unsure of every aspect of our lives.

Finally, we cleared the crowd, and our friends swarmed us. Finn released his grip on my hand just in time for Eva and Ros to tackle me.

"I can't believe you did it," Eva shouted.

"Please, as if she'd quit once she saw that face." Ros chuckled, squeezing me tight. Then she pulled back. "I can't believe you married Finn-flipping-McCarthy. You lucky B."

"B?" Eva asked.

"Flipping?"

We stared at her, heads tilted.

She leaned in close. "I'm trying not to swear so the producers don't shout at me."

"You? Not swearing?" Eva snorted. "Good luck with that one."

"I know. They're crazy to even suggest it." She shrugged. "At least if I try…"

Eva rolled her eyes but turned back to me with a massive

grin taking over her lips. "That kiss looked scorching hot. Was it?"

"You were gone ages," Ros whined before a devilish twinkle entered her green eyes. "Please tell me you tested out the merchandise."

My face heated. "Of course not."

I glanced over my shoulder, hoping Finn hadn't heard her. Of course, our gazes locked instantly. His expression gave nothing away. His friends, on the other hand…

"Yeah, Finn, you don't kiss someone like that and not follow through," the blond-haired guy with an English accent said. His hair was close-cropped, tidy and controlled, while his crystal blue eyes sparkled with teasing mirth.

At his blank expression, his friends burst into laughter.

"Don't tell me the show's already changing you?" the shaggy-haired, dirty blond with an intense Scottish brogue gasped. He clapped his hand on Finn's shoulder, whistling. "Wow, man, I'm shocked. Didn't think you'd ever turn over your playboy ways."

Playboy?

"I call dibs on that one," Ros muttered as she pointed at the Scot, her voice almost a purr.

"Can you all shut up?" Finn hissed.

He dragged his hand through his hair, making his curls even wilder than they'd been before.

I'd like to say the idea of him being a playboy didn't track, but then I remembered that practised flirty smile back in the holding room. Finn knew exactly what he was doing, in life, in business, and in bed. Stupidly, the last part made my core ache enough that I needed to squeeze my thighs together to stop it.

"Why would we do that, when we can wind you up instead?" the pink-haired woman with a slightly weaker Scottish accent asked. She grinned at him, her brown eyes sparkling with the promise of more to come. "Seems fitting, considering you all messed with me at first."

"Mona," Finn groaned. "Please don't encourage them."

"Oh Finnie-Boy, you know pleading with Shaun's missus will not save you." The blond chuckled, rubbing his hands together with glee. "Now, Abi, anything you want to know about Finn, you come to us. We'll give you the 411 even when this asshole's being all tight-lipped and broody."

I nodded, but every inch of me froze under their rambunctious attention. It was like being confronted with two and a half Roselines in one go.

"Finn, how about you introduce us to your wife?" Mona smiled as she watched me.

Finn hesitated, a flicker of indecision dancing across his face before he locked it down.

"If he won't, I will," the blond announced, exasperation dripping from his voice. "I'm Nathan. Shaggy over there is Jackson." He pointed at the dirty blond and then slapped his hand against Shaun's chest. His dark hair slicked back, his suit cut perfectly to his swimmer's build. "This bastard, styled for a photo shoot, is Shaun and pinkie there is his fiancée Mona."

"Christ on a bike. Bring it down a notch before you scare the lass!" Finn pinched the bridge of his nose.

A pang of sympathy worked through me. Eva and Ros could be a bit much sometimes too, and he had four of them.

They all snorted and continued ribbing him. Eva rested her chin on my shoulder and Ros bumped my arm.

"Pretty sure that was your cue to do introductions, Abs," Eva whispered in my ear.

Did I have to?

"Fine," I sighed. "This is my sister Eva." I tilted my head to the left, then gestured to Ros. "Roseline, my best friend."

A chorus of greetings went around and the next thing I knew, I'd lost my best friend and my sister. Nathan and Jackson whisked them away, leaving me and Finn staring after them, puzzled. Well, I was puzzled. Finn didn't so much as frown.

"Do I need to be worried?" I asked, watching the lot of them laughing on the dance floor, tucked in tighter than strangers should be with limited alcohol in their systems. Ros's raven pixie cut clashed with Jackson's dirty-blond laid-back surfer look while Eva and Nathan almost seemed to pair off well with their clean-cut, ready-for-business appearances.

Finn rubbed at his trimmed beard, considering it. He glanced at Shaun and Mona for help.

"Don't bloody look at me, mate." Shaun backed away, tugging Mona with him. "Should have set some ground rules."

Right. So my sister and best friend were going to spend the night making fools of themselves with two of Hollywood's hottest actors.

"I guess it's a real wedding now."

Finn glanced down at me, the question written plain across his face for once.

"Friends hooking up and regretting their decisions tomorrow. Although..." I trailed off, studying the lot of them. "Aren't people normally drunk when they make poor decisions?"

"I don't know." He eyed me, a slight smirk claiming his lips. "Were you drunk when you signed up for this show?"

"No," I squeaked. "Were you?"

FINN

Thank fuck Mona wasn't around to hear me say that. She'd have scowled at me, even if Abi's shocked face entertained me on some sick level.

"What? It's a fair question."

Did I wish my friends hadn't deserted me? Of course. The bastards probably figured more time with my wife would convince me to just get on with the show. As if a week in Bora Bora with her wouldn't be long enough to test my strength.

"No, I was perfectly sober." She turned to me, her hands falling to her waist. "Why did you agree to do the show?"

I shrugged. "I had a gap in my schedule."

"He didn't have a choice," Jackson called as he spun Ros past us. "His agent forced him."

I scowled after him. "The next time you need a wingman, don't call me."

Jackson snorted. "As if that's a threat, Mr Groom."

He danced away, leaving me alone again with a far too intrigued wife. She studied me like she could pull secrets from my head through sheer determination. The woman had a shock coming if she thought it would be that easy.

"You can keep staring. I'm not going to crack, *dotey*."

"Why do you keep calling me that?"

I froze, realisation hitting me hard in the face. It didn't hit hard enough. Someone needed to knock some bloody sense into me.

What did I think I was doing, using that word as an endearment without thinking?

Why the hell was I using an endearment to begin with?
Fuck.

My Da had used it on my mother ever since I could remember.

"It's just a word."

"Yeah, but what does it mean?"

Bloody hell. I'd made a right mess of this farce of a relationship and we weren't even two hours in.

"I'd really rather not say."

She frowned. "Is it bad?"

"No, but you'll get annoyed."

The crease between her brows deepened. "If it's not bad, why would it annoy me?"

I sighed. "The next three months with you are going to be a right craic."

She crossed her arms, her face smoothing out into a look of pure determination I never wanted to see again.

"Fine, but don't say I didn't warn you!" I scratched my beard and glanced around the room, hoping stupidly that there wouldn't be a camera pointed at us. Which of course there fucking was. Who was I trying to kid? "It means little."

"I'm five-foot-five, that's hardly little."

I snorted. "Lassie, your nose hardly reaches my shoulder. You're short."

My breath stilled as I hoped she'd accept the explanation. She could blow up for all I cared, as long as she stopped questioning me. Thankfully, no one here knew the other meanings. The last thing I needed was Abi realising I'd been calling her adorable for an hour.

"Why do I feel like you're not telling the whole truth?" Abi stepped towards me, stabbing her finger into my chest. "We only just met. Why would you be insulting me?"

I caught her hand before she could repeat the action. A mistake. Something told me I could easily get addicted to touching her. I already craved the fire I'd kept seeing in her gaze. She wasn't as timid as she'd originally let on… why did my brain take that as a challenge?

"It's not an insult, Abi."

"Then why are you being cagey?"

I hung my head, fighting the frustrating urge to bite at her and put an end to the entire thing. "Because the slip embarrassed me."

Her head cocked to the side, studying me yet again. Jesus, all my years of acting and I let it slip on something like that? I seriously hoped she missed my flare of genuine feeling.

"Why would that embarrass you?"

"Jesus fucking Christ, woman." I dropped her hand and stepped back. "Can you stop with the questions?"

If I didn't have the attention of the cameras before, I'd put a bet on every single one in the room being focused on me now. Every bloody head swivelled towards us, so why not?

Shaun slung his arm across my shoulder and leaned in close. "I thought you didn't want to make a flipping scene."

"I don't," I hissed. "But she won't stop and let tiny pissing things go."

Abi chewed her lip, her gaze fixed on me. I couldn't tell if I'd hurt her feelings or just surprised her. I'd leave my future shrink to figure out why the thought of hurting her feelings bothered me.

"I'm going to find my sister and let you guys catch up." She backed away, plastering a subpar excuse of a smile on her lips.

Nathan stopped on my other side, watching her go. He whistled low. "Well, that didn't take long."

"Why do you sound surprised?" Jackson asked, joining us. "Finn doesn't do aftercare. Hell, he's barely had to sweet-talk a woman into his bed in years. I'm shocked you lasted this long without putting your foot in it."

"Thanks for the votes of confidence. Much bloody appreciated, you wankers." I shook Shaun's grip off. "Anyone want to tell me where to find the bar?"

They all crossed their arms, a range of serious expressions bulldozing over their amusement.

"I'm not sure we should tell you," Shaun said. "Alcohol won't make the situation better."

"No, it won't, but at least I'll have something to do with my bloody hands."

Nathan frowned. "Why would you need to keep your hands busy?"

I glared at him. "Because I'm mic'ed up, five cameras caught mine and Abi's first tiff, and you can bet they're going to make a big deal out of it." I scanned the nearby faces, hunting for one familiar, bearded face. "My agent's around here somewhere."

"I'm sure that's not…" Nathan trialled off as I cut him with a dark scowl.

"Don't even bother." My jaw shifted. "I unconsciously gave her a stupid flipping nickname and got slated for not telling her what it means. How's that for reputation rehab?"

"Let me get this straight." Shaun's grim expression cracked and his shoulder shook with laughter. "You wanted nothing to do with this show or your new wife, and you've already given her a nickname with too much meaning to share?"

He cracked up fully as my scowl deepened and the rest of the guys followed suit.

"Oh man, that's too good." Shaun wiped his eyes.

"If you care so much about how you'd come across, why didn't you just tell her?" Nathan asked, confusion deepening his voice. "You could have avoided an outburst entirely."

"What have you been calling her?" Jackson asked.

I grimaced. "Dotey."

Jackson's lips twitched, Shaun snorted, and Nathan glanced between us all, brows furrowed in confusion.

"What does it mean?" he asked.

"I don't know what it means, but I've heard his dad using it with his mom, so…" Jackson grinned at me.

"I can't with you lot right now." I stalked off, determined to find the bar and a bottle of whisky to drown myself in.

CHAPTER FIVE

ABI

"This is your suite for the night," Tyler said, his voice far too cheery when you considered the implications of the moment.

An entire night in a room with Finn, Mr Snappy. His routinely blank expression wouldn't shield me from his grumpy side. Snapping at me over a perfectly reasonable question. Who does that? My husband apparently.

"We'll do some filming of you guys getting ready for bed and then leave you to yourselves for the night." His brows rose on that last part, and my stomach flipped.

When he said suite, he meant an almost open-plan room with far more space than the average hotel room. He led us into a sitting room that flowed straight into a dining room that just consisted of a bench and table set before glass barn doors. The massive bed beckoned me from the entryway, feeding a pinch of foreboding in my stomach.

They'd set a plush sofa in front of the black steel four-poster bed. The sight of it inadvertently eased some of my nerves. Between that and the leather sofa in the living room, we didn't have to share a bed. If I could convince Finn…

"Your bags are in the closet back there." Tyler gestured to the bedroom. Then he glanced at Finn, his lips pinching slightly. "I hope it's to your liking."

Finn snorted. "As if you care." He brushed past Tyler, tugging at his tie. "Am I allowed to get out of this suit now?"

"Actually, no," Tyler called after him.

Finn spun around, a scowl darkening his blue eyes. "Why the bloody hell not?"

"We need to get your reactions."

His brows rose. "To what?"

"The room, of course."

"Can't you do that after we get changed?"

Tyler shook his head. "Sorry."

He didn't look sorry. In fact, it looked like he was enjoying pissing Finn off. He gestured to the sofa in the living room, and his grin grew when Finn stomped back to us with a face like thunder. A surprising break from his calm mask.

Two cameramen set up on the opposite side and Tyler lowered himself into an armchair.

Once Finn and I sat down, he studied us. A glint entered his eye, and I almost groaned.

Why was it that I could anticipate Tyler's antics from one look, but Finn remained an enigma? Seriously, the man could give me whiplash with how fast his emotions shifted from seemingly genuine to practised.

"Can you shuffle in a little more? Need to make the audience think you're at least slightly happy with each other."

Grumbling, Finn shifted towards me. There were still a couple of inches between us. Tyler chewed his lip, tilting his head.

"Hmm, why don't you put your arm around Abi, Finn?"

Every inch of my body froze up. Surely we didn't need to…

Finn sighed but did as asked, shuffling so close our thighs pressed together and his fingers grazed the back of my neck on their way to my shoulder. Goose bumps broke out on my skin, sending a shiver down my spine. Any hope that it wasn't noticeable died with Tyler's next words.

"Ethan," he yelled without taking his eyes off us. "Turn the air conditioning down for Abi, please." He flashed me a sympathetic smile. "Can't have you shivering on camera, now can we?"

I pressed my lips together and kept my head straight forward. I did not need to see Finn's reaction. No need to make the situation mortifying. I could do that without his help.

His fingers didn't retreat from my shoulder, but they also didn't move around. If one graze sent shivers down my spine, I didn't want to know what would happen if he started toying with my skin.

"Okay so, the first question," he glanced down, checking his notes, "how are you feeling about your first night together?"

Awkwardly nervous. *Can I even say that?*

"Sharing space with another person is going to be a bit of an adjustment," Finn said, saving me from having to shape my nerves into something more positive. "We're still strangers, so it'll take us some time to get comfortable." His fingers smoothed across my bare shoulder, robbing me of breath. "But I'm sure we'll get there. Right, Abi?"

Finn squeezed me towards him. I glanced up at him and my mind spun out of control. *What's with the soft look in his eyes?* Between the gestures, his words, and that almost intrigued gleam, he confused the ever-loving crap out of me. For a couple of moments, he turned into the perfect husband.

"Absolutely," I agreed, working extra hard to stop the frown itching to claim my face. I turned back to the camera. "It feels like we're on our first date, except we sped everything up and it's taken an extra serious turn. Of course, we're going to be awkward for a little while."

Finn squeezed me again, the movement feeling almost praising this time around. When I glanced up at him again, his eyes were on Tyler and the softer expression had melted from his face.

"Next question?" Finn asked, his tone bored.

For thirty minutes, we ran through questions in almost a cycle. By the end, patterns started to emerge in Finn's mood changes.

"How important is it that your partner has the same tastes in music as you?"

I blinked at Tyler. Why would anyone care about our music tastes? I snuck a peek at Finn from the corner of my eye. His expression softened, and he chuckled.

"If Abi's going to fill my house with hard rock screamo, we might have a problem." Finn glanced at me, outright grinning, his sapphire eyes twinkling. "But otherwise, I don't care what music she likes. Who picked our first dance song? Fleetwood Mac is one of my favourite bands."

I stared at him, perplexed. The second I thought I had my feet under me, he changed entirely and made my head spin.

"My sister did," I said with absolutely no conviction.

"Remind me to thank her."

We stared at each other, me unable to contain my confusion and Finn… the loving look in his eyes could not be real.

"Brilliant." Tyler snapped us from our staring contest. "Finn, you were perfect. Abi, I'm going to need a little more emotion from you."

The cameras started to reset and Finn eased away from me slightly. The softer edges fell away from him. A lightbulb went off in my head as I finally put it together. My actor played it up for the cameras.

He's not my *anything.*

The shift went on and on as Tyler ran through a long list of questions. I gave up trying to predict Finn halfway through.

"Okay, that was perfect." Tyler shut his notebook and stood. "Ian's going to stick around to get some more shots of you guys getting ready for bed and everything. I'll see you in the morning for the flight to Bora Bora."

Tyler left us, and I did my best to ignore the camera hovering nearby. I followed Finn into the bedroom, my brain focused on getting out of my dress and into a shower. I wouldn't be able to sleep with the number of pins and the rock-solid consistency of my hair.

He stopped dead in front of the bed, making me dodge around him. He stared at the massive thing, chewing his lip.

"You alright there?" I asked, very distracted. I turned my back on him quickly, making a beeline for my suitcase.

"I'll sleep on the sofa if it makes you more comfortable."

"If you want." I pulled my suitcase out of the closet and carefully kneeled.

"Sofa it is," he muttered.

I glanced at him over my shoulder, confused by the odd determination in his voice. I found him staring at me with enough heat in his gaze to set an ache free inside of me.

"What is it?" I patted my hair and my face, certain my eyes were deceiving me.

"Nothing." He shook his head. "Nothing at all. Do you want first go of the shower?"

I shook my head, freeing my toiletry bag from my suitcase. "No, it's going to take me forever to get my hair down, so you can go first."

I regretted those words sheer minutes later when the water turned on and my mind wandered down a path it had no business finding in the first place. Images of Finn naked in the next room set me aflame. I resolutely remained on the floor, with my back to the camera, fussing with my suitcase, even though I'd found everything I needed.

How would I survive a week in Bora Bora with him and not make an ass of myself?

By the time the barn door rolled back and he returned in a puff of steam, my cheeks were red and my body ached in all the places it shouldn't for my fake husband.

Then I turned around and it all got worse. He sauntered into the bedroom, chest bare, cut abs on display and sweat pants hanging low on his hips. My mouth went dry.

"All yours," he said, oblivious to the train wreck happening inside my head.

I rushed past him without a word, my pyjamas bundled close to my chest and my focus fixed on the tile ahead.

"Uh, Abi?"

"Yeah?"

I stopped in the doorway and reluctantly turned back to him. He rubbed his trimmed beard, a sheepish expression playing across his face.

"Do you need any help? With your hair?" His gaze roamed my hair. "My sister used to enter dance competitions. She always needed someone else to fish the last of them out."

"That would be great. Thank you." I led the way into the bathroom and dropped everything on top of the marble countertop between the two his and hers sinks.

Black slate tile stretched across the floor while huge white marble slabs veined with gold patterns covered the walls. A gorgeous freestanding soaker tub stood off to one side, surrounded by a bed of black rocks. A double shower with more nozzles than I knew how to use took up the entire back wall. The space was the size of my New York bedroom.

Then Finn stepped up behind me and the room shrunk, taking my ability to ignore him with it. He started plucking pins from my hair, the burn of his body heat caressing my bare back.

Focus on your hair.

I started dragging my fingers through the almost solid

mass of my auburn hair, digging for the metal pins and breaking up the smooth run of hairspray. Every now and again my fingers faltered as I caught Finn's blue eyes fixed on me in the mirror, or he leaned a little too close and his bare chest pressed to my back.

"I'm sorry about earlier," he whispered, his voice low enough that the cameraman probably wouldn't pick it up, since he'd taken his microphone off.

A flash of his frustrated expression danced through my mind, but I played dumb, raising my brows at him in the mirror.

"For snapping." His fingers caressed the nape of my neck as he stared at me with open regret. "I shouldn't have."

"No, you definitely shouldn't have." I nodded, then pursed my lips, arguing with myself over pushing him again. "Are you going to explain why?"

Finn hesitated for all of a second before shaking his head. "I'm sorry. I'm not great at this."

I waited, hopeful that maybe he'd say more. He continued digging through my hair instead.

"So you're not going to tell me what dotey means, or why my wanting to know set you off?"

"Do you actually care?" he asked. His gaze bore into mine, hunting for the truth. "Or is it just that I got defensive about it?"

I chewed my lip, considering him. He'd told me one meaning, of course, but I couldn't escape the feeling that he meant more by it. But if it really had been a slip of the tongue…

"You're not insulting me?"

His gaze roamed my face in our reflection, his edges softening. "Definitely not."

"Okay, why did you get flustered?"

"You're going to think I'm nothing more than a pompous

celebrity if I answer that." Amusement creased the corner of his eyes.

I turned, a small smile tugging at my lips. "Well, now I definitely need to know."

"Fine," he groaned. "I'm not used to people questioning me anymore. Besides my agent and my friends, and even they can recognise when not to push." He shrugged. "Apparently, it's a button for me, and you wouldn't quit jabbing at it."

"Okay." I turned around, going right back to tugging at my hair.

"That's it?" he asked, his voice raising with incredulity.

"Yup. I'm not unreasonable, Finn. Just talk to me."

FINN

I stared at the back of her head, utterly perplexed by the woman I'd married. We'd have three months together, and I already knew she would drive me insane.

Especially if the producers kept forcing us close on camera. I only had so much self-control. One touch of her against me and it had started to unravel. I shouldn't have offered to help with her hair. Escaping into the living room would have been the safest bet.

Yet I didn't stop, didn't remove my hands from the soft hair or put distance between us so the heat of her couldn't tease me.

When her hair fell around her shoulders, unrestrained, I forced myself away from her.

"I think we've got them all." I took one last glance and then headed for the door. "I'll leave you to it."

"Wait! Can you undo these buttons for me?" Abi asked before I could escape the bathroom. I turned back, my shoulders tensing at the thought of getting close to her again. "They're too small and too low for me. Please, Finn?"

I almost groaned at the sound of my name falling from her lips. Did I shake my head and shut her in the bathroom alone to deal with the dress that had spent the better part of the day winding me on edge?

Of course not. She'd been breath-taking before, her hair tamed and every mouth-watering curve of her body hugged by that torturous dress. But now, with her auburn hair mussed and flowing down her back in soft curls, framing her pale face and making her almost look Irish? Abi had effortlessly stepped into irresistible territory.

I'm a fecking eejit.

Abi presented her back to me and my fingers, the grabby bastards, reached for her without pause. She sucked in a breath as they grazed above the material line. Just three buttons and she should be able to get out of it. I could handle three buttons.

With an intense focus, I worked them free with deft fingers. No matter how fast I went, I wasn't blind. Her gorgeous ass already teased me, but then the material loosened, revealing a white lace thong. My cock hardened for the fiftieth time today and yet again, as the image of all that auburn hair spread out across my pillow hit me hard.

The straps slid off her shoulders, dragging my focus away from her ass. She caught the dress with a hand to her chest before it could fall from her body, leaving her nearly naked.

Shame, a stupid voice moaned in my head.

I straightened up and backed away from her yet again.

"Do you—" I stopped, clearing my throat. "You got it from here?"

Her cheeks were rosy and her blue eyes burned with desire I intended to ignore. She met my gaze in the mirror, nodding.

As I slid the barn door into place, reality knocked me hard

in the face. I'd never run from the promise of an interested woman before, but I was going to spend the next three months in a world of sexually frustrated pain.

We might be married, but Abi Johnson needed to remain off-limits.

INTERVIEW III

Question: Did you have sex?
Finn: I don't see how that's any of your business.
Tyler, Producer: You're going to be married for three months. You don't think intimacy is an important part of marriage?
Finn: I didn't say that. I said it was none of *your* business.
Abi: No, we haven't had sex.
Finn: Don't give in to him. He'll think he can ask even more inappropriate questions.
Tyler, Producer: Thank you, Abi. Why didn't you have sex?
Finn: See?
Abi: If we answer, he'll go away, and we can get to the airport.
Tyler, Producer: Listen to Abi, Finn. She's clearly the logical one in this relationship.
Finn: Christ. I'm going to kill Charlie.
Abi: I wouldn't have sex on a first date. Why would I change that?
Tyler, Producer: You know, our specialists recommend getting it out of the way.

Finn: *splutters* Getting it out of the way?! Get out!
Tyler, Producer: Now, Finn, we need to—
Finn: I said GET. OUT.
Tyler, Producer: We'll continue this in Bora Bora.
Finn: We won't.

··

CHAPTER SIX

··

ABI

My first time in First Class would have to be with a ridiculously good-looking actor attached to my hip. The female flight attendants kept staring at Finn, eating up his every move. I'd sink a little deeper into my book, attempt to tune it all out, and then bam! They're back, hovering over us, brushing past him, inappropriately close.

Of course, I could admit that part of my annoyance might have come from a lack of sleep. Turns out not sharing a bed with Finn might have been more awkward than caving to the inevitable. Every time he shifted on the couch, I'd feel a pang of guilt for having an entire queen-sized bed to myself. Neither of us had looked all that fresh when we'd called it quits not long after the sun rose.

Still, the longer their extreme attentiveness went on, the more I bristled for him. Couldn't they leave the man in peace?

Then they served lunch. I'd never considered lunch to be a revolutionary part of my day before. Just a time with food, nothing special.

"Can I get you another whisky, Mr McCarthy? To go with your lunch," one attendant asked, her voice hopelessly breathy.

If any of them had clocked the rings, I wasn't sure. Although I doubted anyone could truly miss the massive emerald princess cut diamond Finn had slid onto my finger along with a classic gold wedding band. The pair of them glittered no matter the light. The ring Production had given me for him wasn't exactly conspicuous either. It had a spiral pattern running around it, framing emerald stones that matched my engagement ring.

Maybe they didn't care.

Seeing our rings side-by-side definitely robbed me of breath at moments. Never in my wildest dreams would I have imagined myself in this situation, married to a famous actor and flying first class to some exclusive resort.

"That would be wonderful, Gloria. Thank you, love."

He flashed the same smile at her as the one he'd used on me at the reception last night. She tittered as she rushed away without so much a glance at me to see if I wanted anything. Although, I couldn't blame her. I knew how potent that smile was. My anger at them fizzled out. He encouraged them. If anyone deserved the full brunt of my distaste, it should have been him.

"Had to marry a spoilt jackass," I muttered under my breath.

"What was that?" Finn asked, ducking his head towards me.

I glared at him. "Nothing."

His gaze roamed my face, reading me like a book, I expected. He smirked and leaned closer.

"The jealous type, are we?"

"Nope. I'm good." I turned away from him, twisting my body so I faced the window.

"We both know that's a lie, Abi girl." Amusement curled around the words. "I didn't realise I'd married a hellion."

His breath ruffled my hair. Against my better judgement, I turned to face him and found him inches from my face. His amusement faded fast, and his focus dropped to my lips.

"If you want them to stop, you'll have to stake your claim," he whispered. "Or are you too chicken to kiss me without a camera pointed at us?" He smirked.

I slammed my lips against his before I allowed myself to think too hard about it.

Finn's hand dove into my hair, angling my head as he took control of my ill-thought-out kiss. His tongue invaded my mouth, massaging mine and ridding me of all thought. My fingers curled around his wrist, whether to push him away or pull him closer, I had no clue. An electric charge worked through me, building a hunger I had no hope of fulfilling at thirty-six thousand feet in the air.

I could get addicted to this.

A throat cleared above us, but Finn didn't pull away. The kiss gentled, slowed until my panties were soaked through and all of my common sense had nose-dived off the plane.

Finn released my lips. His hand fell away, and he turned to the waiting flight attendant. A blush claimed her cheeks, but she didn't comment.

"Thank you, love." He accepted his drink, grinning at her.

"Can I get you something, Ms…"

"Mrs McCarthy will have a glass of red wine, Gloria. Thank you." His amusement deepened as her attention jumped to me, her eyes widening.

Alright, she hadn't noticed the rings.

She nodded and turned away quickly. I watched as she rushed up to the other attendants. Their heads bowed together as they whispered amongst themselves. Every couple of seconds, one of them would glance at us with puzzlement or surprise written across their faces.

"See, that wasn't so hard, was it?" Finn asked, his voice lazy, almost like he'd also felt the drugging effects of that kiss.

I nodded, glancing back at my book before he could question me further. I failed to block out the way he'd played her.

FINN

We followed the hotel concierge across the boardwalk. He listed off information about the hotel, the amenities, and the restaurant hours, but I couldn't concentrate on a word he said. Abi walked by his side, nodding along, absorbing every word. She appeared happy, and given she had a shite poker face, I was inclined to believe it.

Yet, she'd barely said two words to me since we'd kissed on the plane.

"I can't believe how beautiful it is here," she said, her voice filled with awe as her head swivelled around to take in the open blue water and over-water bungalows lined up in front of us.

The concierge opened the door to our villa and waved her in before him. She gasped before I'd even set foot inside.

"This can't be right."

The man assured her she was in the right villa and her jaw popped open. The bungalow didn't contain more than the necessities — beautiful necessities, but still. A huge bed sat opposite open patio doors that stretched the entire length of the bedroom. A glass cutout at the base of the bed gave a view straight into the glistening blue waters below. One look at it and I knew where I'd be the moment we got rid of the concierge. Honeyed wood covered the floors and vaulted ceiling, adding warmth to the neutral whites and beiges of the furnishings.

"Did you arrange this, Finn?"

For some reason, I kicked myself for not taking an interest in the planning of it all before.

"No." I shrugged before wandering out onto the patio.

The damn thing had an infinity pool and a hot tub. How ridiculous, considering the ocean was a mere foot beneath my feet. Still, I would call the patio a thing of beauty. Steps led down to another platform and then down into the water.

"Well, I think it's gorgeous," she continued to gush.

After giving her a quick tour of the suite's amenities, the concierge abandoned us. I tuned it all out. You'd seen one five-star exclusive resort, you'd seen them all. The fact *Married Blind* had got them to allow filming on the premises surprised me more than the opulently-decorated villa.

We had five minutes of peace before someone knocked on the door. Abi went to answer it, glancing at me quizzically. I collapsed into a chair on the patio instead of following her. *Probably just the eejit producer.*

"Abi, hi. I hope you're settling in okay," Tyler said, his voice far too excited and far too loud for our tranquil surroundings.

"Well, we only just got in, so I'll let you know."

My brows rose at the bite in her tone. Had yesterday's timid act been just that?

"Of course. We just need to grab some reactions to the suite." Tyler's voice grew closer. "Where's Fi…ah, there you are. Welcome to Bora Bora."

He joined me on the patio, two cameramen trailing him with a wheel bag each, full of equipment.

"Everything alright with the flights?" he asked, twitching slightly at the silence.

"The flights were fine," I muttered, keeping my tone bland.

"Great, great."

I glanced around the perfectly normal bungalow, my eyes

narrowed, searching for the slightest suggestion of hidden cameras.

I found none. That didn't mean they weren't here. I gestured at the crisply decorated bungalow. "Is this room rigged? What about the patio? The bathroom?"

Tyler's eyes widened, and then his expression shifted.

I clocked the moment his shrewd producer brain kicked in, connecting the dots between my past and my questions. If he thought I'd talk about it on the show, he had —

"The only cameras we use are the ones the guys are holding."

I nodded, unexpected relief rippling through me.

"So the interviews…"

"Give us a chance to settle in first," Abi said as she joined us on the patio. Her hands landed on her hips, declaring business, while she smiled at Tyler, confusing the entire image. My girl needed tips for playing intimidating.

She's not your *anything.*

"I'm sorry. We need to stay on schedule."

"But if we're both bleary-eyed from a nine-hour flight, what does the schedule matter?"

Tyler glanced between us, his brow furrowing with indecision. The two cameramen covered their smirks, rubbing their jaws or flat-out turning away. What were the chances they found this plonker annoying, too?

"I mean, we can do it, but I *know* I've got black circles under my eyes right now." Her brows rose. "Doesn't the camera emphasise those things?"

If kissing her hadn't already gotten me into trouble, I'd have done it again. The timidness at the wedding must have been nerves. No way would I have rubbed off on her in a day. Either way, I liked what I saw, and I needed more of that snarky fire in my life.

Except she's only your wife for three months.

Why did I keep forgetting that part of the plan?

"Decide whatever you want," I said as I stood. "I'm going for a swim."

I wandered inside, leaving Tyler to splutter his displeasure and ignoring the thrill that the shift of Abi's expression from stern to triumphant sent through me. I'd let them figure their own shit out. I needed to put some distance between us before I did something more stupid than teasing her into kissing me.

I bit back a groan as I dug out my swimming trunks. If the flight attendant hadn't returned, I don't know what would have happened. I'd like to think I wouldn't have dragged her into the bathroom to join the Mile High Club there and then, but I didn't have that much faith in myself. I wasn't exactly known for being sensible.

Abi might be attractive, and I might be craving her something fierce, but she was off limits.

ABI

Somehow, I got Tyler to agree to give us the rest of the day. No thanks to Finn. I couldn't believe it when he ducked out.

I rushed out the back, instantly spotting him face up, floating on his back with his eyes shut.

"Way to show a united front," I called to him.

He peeled an eye open. "You had it handled."

I had, but that shouldn't have given him permission to just abandon me.

"They're gone for the day." I crossed my arms. "But we have to meet them tonight for dinner with the other couples."

"Okay." His eyes shut again and he spread his arms out.

He looked so relaxed.

I took a seat on a cushioned patio chair, sinking deeper

into the chair. With the sun kissing my face and the cool breeze tickling my skin, I took my first deep breath in months.

I lasted a glorious five minutes before worries wormed their way to the forefront. The most pressing of them: our one-bed situation.

Unlike the hotel room, it didn't look like we were going to escape sharing a bed. Not unless he agreed to sleep on the floor and I just couldn't see it happening.

Water cascaded from him as he lifted himself out of the water on the lower deck. My eyes took on a life of their own, devouring every glistening inch of him as he walked up the stairs back to our patio. For an Irishman, he'd definitely embraced the LA lifestyle. I couldn't see an inch of pale skin on him.

My gaze dipped to the waistline of his shorts. *I wonder if his tan runs the entire length of him.*

He collapsed into the chair next to me, a grin toying with his lips.

"What was the serious expression about?"

For a second, he lost me, and then I remembered.

"How are we going to deal with the bed situation?"

He glanced back at the giant bed framed in the doorway behind us.

"I'm not sure we have a choice."

"That's what I was thinking." I covered my face, groaning into my hands. "I bet Tyler set this up."

"I don't doubt it," Finn said, amusement dripping from his voice.

I glanced at him sharply. "If you'd just answered his questions this morning…"

"We'd still have one bed. My answering inappropriate questions wouldn't have changed anything." Finn chuckled. "*Dotey*, they want us to fuck. Better drama."

I didn't know what to focus on first: the nickname slipping

past his defences again or the fact that one muttered fuck tripping off his tongue made me squirm in my seat.

"It's a massive bed. We'll be fine." He bit his lip and fixed wide eyes on me. "Unless you're a cuddler?"

When I didn't answer, Finn grinned at me. "This is going to be fun."

CHAPTER SEVEN

ABI

*S*omehow, we avoided each other for the rest of the day. I went to investigate the spa offerings on site and booked myself in for a day of pampering before we were forced to report for dinner with the other couples participating in the show. Despite my brain's refusal to let me forget that I'd be sharing a bed with a man who could make me ache with just a look, I enjoyed myself. I'd never been pampered before.

My phone pinged as I wandered back to the room. Our group chat flashed across the screen and I stopped in my tracks. Would it be bad of me to dodge their texts?

ROS

Bitch. Spill all the deets. How big are we talking?

My cheeks heated.

ROS

Don't leave me on read and stop blushing.
Share with your bestie.

EVA

She might be busy, Ros.

ROS

Yeah, deep-throating her Hollywood hunk.

Eyes widening, my fingers flew over the screen.

ABI

Oh my god, stop, Ros. We haven't slept
together.

ROS

Why the hell not?

ABI

Because I've known him for a day and I'm
pretty sure he hates me.

EVA

He doesn't hate you.

ROS

You don't need to know him to enjoy that ride.

EVA

That's true.

ABI

I'm ignoring you both now.

My phone continued to ping but I ignored it. I didn't need someone else filling my head with ideas. When it came to Finn, it seemed I could manage perfectly fine alone.

When I returned to the bungalow, Finn had made himself scarce. As much as the silence felt weird, I relished the space and focused on picking out my dress for filming. I might have taken a little extra care than I normally would, plotting all the ways I could get back at him for tricking me into kissing him on the plane.

I could get lost in his kisses.

Just get the money, pay off Eva's debts and enjoy the thrill of it all.

Except that wasn't all I wanted. I wanted him.

With my hair and makeup already done, I was dressed and ready to go pretty fast. Left to tap my foot and wonder if Finn would actually make an appearance before we had to leave. At least if he walked through the door I could bury the over-thinking again and go back to living in the moment.

My cell pinged ten minutes later with a new message. I fished the device from my clutch, still frowning at the blushing horizon as the sunset.

FINN

I'll meet you at the restaurant.

I waited, my breath held as if another text would load and explain his absence. It didn't. We were meeting all the other couples and he wanted me to walk into dinner without him like it wouldn't immediately scream trouble.

Despite my burning cheeks and the ache in my chest, I pushed my shoulders back and made my way up to the restau-rant. By the time I made it to land, the cool breeze had soothed away the sting of abandonment.

Tyler frowned at me as I walked into the hotel lobby, my heels clicking against the marble floor.

"Where the hell is Finn?" he asked.

My acting skills must have improved. I didn't so much as flinch at the accusation in his tone.

"He said he'd meet me here." I shrugged, working to keep my voice flat, pleasant, but emotionless.

No one else loitered in the lobby so I could at least take a second before they pointed a camera at me. Tyler pulled out his cell and lifted it to his ear.

"I swear he'll be the death of me before this show wraps."

He turned away from me, focusing his glare on the front doors.

I chewed my lip, liking that he'd moved on from blaming me but needing direction all the same. Delaying in the lobby like a chicken didn't sit right with me. I never would have hesitated before. In New York, I would breeze into places alone, never waiting for permission or company. Why had that changed now?

"What do I need to do?" I asked, ignoring his grinding jaw. He spun to face me, his brows rising while the cell blared a dial tone in his ear. "Do I just walk in there and get mic'ed after I sit down?"

"You can't go in there without Finn." Tyler's eyes widened in horror.

His expression softened as he considered me. He hung up and pocketed his cell, taking a couple of steps toward me. His eyes scanned the lobby, as if he were checking for eavesdroppers.

"I take it he hasn't told you he didn't want anything to do with the show?" He quirked a brow. I shook my head and he grimaced.

My gaze flicked to the open restaurant doors, beckoning me with the soft light and murmuring music.

"If you go in without him, we have to cover why he's not there in the edit." Tyler crossed his arms. "The last thing his fans would want to see is him standing you up…"

I hadn't thought of how they'd put the story together. Or how much control Tyler had over how the viewers saw our relationship. The thought of anyone misunderstanding it sat weirdly on my chest. All the same, I nodded.

"He didn't say anything about his plans for the day?"

"No. He was there when I left for my appointments. We didn't talk about tonight."

Before Tyler could voice his annoyance, Finn sauntered through the door, his hands in his navy dress pants pockets, his trademark smile curling his lips. He'd a couple of his shirt buttons undone, teasing bronzed skin that made my mouth water. His hair was slightly mussed, like someone had dragged their hands through it while he made them scream. The perfect picture of an unaffected playboy.

My gut twisted at the thought of him fucking someone else.

Why my mind went there, I had no idea. I didn't want to know why I let it send a flicker of hurt through me. I smothered it fast and focused on the task at hand.

"Where the hell have you been?" Tyler exploded before Finn could open his mouth.

His brows rose at the bite in Tyler's voice.

"Out," he bit out. He turned his attention to me, tuning Tyler's muttered annoyance out. "Why are you standing out here? I said I'd meet you inside."

"He wouldn't let me." I tilted my head toward Tyler.

"And why is that?" Finn eyed Tyler. I caught amusement flickering across Finn's face before it settled back into the blank mask.

"Go." Tyler threw his hands up, then turned his back on us. He walked away, muttering to himself. "Fucking celebrities and their overinflated egos. I should quit."

I stared after him, wide-eyed and mildly concerned.

"C'mon, let's get this over with."

Finn brushed past me, heading for the restaurant like we shouldn't discuss the weirdness.

"Where were you?" I asked, rushing after him.

He stopped outside the door, rolling his shoulders back and stretching out his neck.

"Diving."

He held out his hand without even glancing at me. I took it and he threaded our fingers together, a new familiarity that shocked me. I stared at that connection for far too long.

"Why didn't you just say that earlier?"

Finn tugged my hand and my focus snapped to his face. He stared down at me, his lips pinched.

"I didn't realise you needed to know my every movement."

"I don't, but the production…"

His shoulders dropped and his blue gaze softened. "Sorry, I didn't think of that."

He glanced toward the bustling restaurant. Glasses clattered, piano music drifted in the air, and guests chattered loudly, laughter reached us with ease. There was too much noise for us to be filming in the main dining room.

"Ready to face the land sharks?" Finn asked.

I grinned. Maybe he knew the other celebrities.

I nodded and we walked into the room. The cameras were easy to spot. Six cameramen surrounded a table on the patio, shielded by a living wall of vines between them and the busiest part of the restaurant.

"I'd heard rumours that they'd talked you into doing this," a man said, his British accent making me work to understand him. He chuckled. "What do they have on you?"

"Casey Jackson," Finn growled.

For a man with a perfect poker face, he directed a lot of open hostility at the man. *Is he acting even now?* I narrowed my eyes on Finn, taking in the burn of red on his neck and the crush of his hand in mine. *Maybe not.*

"Didn't think I'd have to deal with your ugly mug tonight."

His mousy brown hair stood on end, in desperate need of a cut or a brush. Even so, between his chiselled cheekbones and teasing smile, he could command the attention of everyone in the room.

His wife shifted uncomfortably in her seat, her gaze fixed on a point beyond our table where one of the cameramen stood. Her shoulders were hunched and if her ash-blonde hair hadn't been pulled back in a bun, I got the feeling she would have used it as a shield.

She didn't look happy. Maybe she wasn't adjusting to the show? My gut disagreed. Casey towered over her. I frowned at the sight of it and squeezed Finn's hand. He caught my eye and I tried to silently communicate to him.

Tyler appeared before I could figure out what to do.

"Oh great, you're all together, at last." He clapped his hands while Finn and I took our seats as far from the Brit as we could get. "Why don't you all start with introductions? You could compare notes on how things are going. Your food will be along shortly and your server here will grab more drinks in the meantime."

Tyler backed away and Liam, the cameraman who filmed our wedding, filed into his place.

"Anyone else feel like we've been set up?" A woman with jet-black hair asked from the end of the table. She glanced around the table, wearing a huge, welcoming smile. Her navy-blue halter-neck top hugged her, emphasising her tan. "Like by compare notes does he mean our relationships or this godawful show?"

Finn snorted, but he otherwise didn't react, his focus attached to the couple opposite us. A hulking man with white-blond hair I vaguely recognised as a professional hockey player and a beautiful woman with dark hair and lavender tips. They were absorbed in each other, their faces pressed close together while they murmured to each other, completely lost in their own world.

I want that.

It didn't look like they were acting, either. Maybe the show's matchmakers did know what they were doing.

"They'll want relationships, but we could dissect the show and watch Tyler's face turn red." Casey twisted a glass of dark liquid.

Everyone chuckled at that.

"How about we start with introductions before we wind him up?" An American guy sat next to me suggested. He looked like your typical boy next door — If the boy next door were a surfer with long hair and a sweet smile. "I'm Kyle. Not sure if Aria actually needs an introduction." He gestured to the jet-black-haired woman next to him.

She chuckled. "Not everyone likes country, Sweetheart."

Casey looked her up and down, his smile turning my stomach yet again. "I could learn to like it."

Aria stared at him, her eyes narrowing. "I don't think that'll be necessary."

The hockey player introduced himself as Anders Olafsson, goalie for the Los Angeles Stingers and his wife Haley, another New York girl. Casey's wife introduced herself with a tentative voice that set me on edge. No way should they have paired Nicole with a man like him.

While they all chatted, Finn turned toward me, leaning into me, his face hovering near my ear. Every nerve ending in my body froze, desperately waiting for him to touch me. *What an idiot.*

"I didn't tell you where I went because I didn't want you to freak out." His breath caressed my neck, ruffling strands of my hair. I braced myself against a shiver.

"Why would I freak out?" I asked, turning my face towards his.

To anyone else, we'd look like the picture of a loving couple. My heart squeezed tight with want. That just wouldn't do.

"It was a shipwreck in open water," he whispered.

Finn pulled back enough to assess my expression. Whatever he saw made him shut down. Shit. Despite it, he didn't pull away. He pressed his forehead to mine, maintaining the picture for the cameras.

"I didn't want you to worry."

Logically, I shouldn't have believed him. My heart shouldn't have sighed happily. Nope. That would have been crazy when I knew better than to go soft for a playboy actor. Especially with a camera pointed at us.

But we were being filmed and we were meant to be playing a happy couple.

"I get it," I said, deciding to play along. "But I worried."

Finn's jaw slackened. "Really?"

My eyes roamed his face and I barely restrained myself from frowning at him. For a second, I could almost convince myself his surprise was real.

I nodded. "Yes, but I also thought you were avoiding me."

"Ah." Finn tilted his head, his focus turning inward. He winced. "Maybe I was. Sorry."

"It's fine." I shrugged. "It's not like you need to explain it to me."

Finn pressed his lips together and for a second I thought he would argue. Then he nodded, straightening up in his chair to face everyone else.

"Can you stop looking at Aria like that?" Kyle asked Casey, his voice wavering. "She's not a slab of meat."

Casey chuckled. "Nice one."

"Why are you even here?" Aria asked. She scowled at the musician. "I've heard about you."

"Aria's making a very good point." Finn shifted in his seat while he glared at Casey.

He rested an arm across the back of my chair, his face set in hard lines.

"Where did Tyler run off to? He should be explaining this choice." Finn's gaze roamed the restaurant.

"I already tried," Aria sighed. She crossed her arms, locked in a staring contest with Casey. "They didn't realise he had a history of sexual assault when they locked him in."

That got the attention of Anders and Haley, opposite us. They broke apart, glancing around the table with furrowed brows.

"What the hell are you talking about?" Anders said, his voice lilting with a foreign accent.

"Allegedly," Casey spat through bared teeth.

"Only because your Daddy paid off the victims and forced an entire company to sign an NDA." Finn's voice vibrated with anger.

Nicole stiffened, and her wide eyes flew to one of the cameramen.

"Allegedly," he repeated.

"You can say the word as many times as you like," Finn snapped. "It doesn't change the fact your label dropped you last month after you made a pass at the wrong person."

Finn's knee bounced and his fist pressed against my back while he gripped the top of my chair. One wrong move from Casey and I could see him exploding.

"How the hell would you know that?" Casey leaned forward, any closer and he'd be mounting the table.

"It's not exactly a state secret anymore." Finn shrugged, feigning nonchalance, but the action was far too strained to be truly careless. "You hit on the wrong band manager's girlfriend."

I placed my hand on his thigh, squeezing to get his attention. His focus dropped to the contact. He released the chair and smoothed his hand up and down my back as if soothing me. All around us the outrage continued, but I tuned it out, focusing on only Finn's sapphire eyes.

"Are you okay?" he asked, his voice low but deep with concern.

I almost laughed. I wasn't the one losing my shit.

"Yes. Are you?"

He blew out a shaky breath. "I don't like people like him."

I smirked. "I got that." The lightness faltered a little inside of me. "We can talk to Tyler about it later? I'm worried about Nicole."

Finn nodded.

"Hey Finn, how'd you feel about sharing?" Casey called across the wall of noise surrounding us. "I hear you like that sort of thing."

Finn stiffened beneath my hand. His gaze turned cold within the blink of an eye and his touch fell away from my back. He looked away from me, shooting daggers at Casey.

"Stay the fuck away from her," Finn shouted, his voice shaking.

Casey grinned. *Mark hit.*

"It's okay, Finn," I whispered, pressing a hand to his chest.

"Yeah, listen to your woman, Finn." His voice grated against me, turning me sick. "She wants it."

Finn shot to his feet, his intent clear. I scrambled up, stopping him before he could get too far.

"Can one of you put your fucking camera down and go find Tyler?" Anders demanded.

Someone rushed past me, but I couldn't take my eyes off Finn to follow his progress.

"Move out of the way, Abi," Finn whispered through grinding teeth.

I shook my head. "He's not worth it. Especially not in front of cameras." I stepped into his body, pushing myself against him and wrapping my arms around his waist.

A small part of me worried that he'd reject me in front of the cameras when he wasn't thinking straight, but I had to try something.

I smoothed my hands up and down his back. "You're not the violent type, Finn. Don't let him get to you."

Casey kept talking, his voice rising over the group, trying to dig deeper at Finn. The longer he went on, the crasser his comments became, but Finn didn't move, just kept watching me with a question in his eyes.

"You seriously expect me to let him keep saying this disgusting shit about you?" His brows rose, but then he noticed the camera pointed at us. His expression shifted as soon as he clocked it. His hands moved up my arms, caressing my bare skin like he could protect me from Casey.

He'd just shifted into actor mode faster than I could blink.

"No, I want you to keep looking at me like that." I smiled as his expression softened even more.

His arms wrapped around me, squeezing me to him.

"I'll look at you any way you want," he whispered, the sound almost lost with the ruckus at the table.

He lowered his head, his intent clear in his sapphire eyes. Surprise froze me to the spot.

CHAPTER EIGHT

FINN

"Right, what did I miss?" Tyler asked, raising his voice to crack above the arguing at the table.

His appearance snapped some sense back into my head. I'd nearly kissed Abi with the cameras rolling.

What the fuck was I thinking?

Clearly, I hadn't been. With all the adrenaline firing through me, I got lost in her kind eyes, lost in the fact someone had tried to put my best interests above themselves.

I released Abi and stepped back, turning to find Tyler poised at the end of the table wearing a deep frown. As if the wanker hadn't expected an explosion when he left us at a table with Casey, the serial abuser.

"Why does the show think it's okay to pair a sex offender with an innocent woman?" Aria demanded, her tone scathing. "I'd wager you didn't feel the need to fill Nicole in on his history."

Tyler spluttered, his eyes going wide.

Anders' voice was quiet but seething. "My agent definitely

didn't agree to my taking part in a show that would damage my reputation. I'm up for contract renewal." He gestured down the table at Casey. "Being in a lineup with him will destroy my community credibility."

"Yeah, they sold me this stupid thing on the basis that it would be *good* for me." Aria glared at Casey. "*That* is not good for anyone."

"Fix it, Tyler," I said, far too much joy in the words. "Or we'll all be calling our agents and heading home in the morning."

"Now wait a minute," he sputtered.

All of us settled back against our chairs.

Abi slid back into her seat, her head high but tension radiating through her shoulders.

I liked her. Lying to myself wouldn't achieve anything, but it couldn't change anything. Abi Johnson would be better off without me. Better to escape before I got attached to it all, to her.

"Alright then." I took my phone out of my pocket and hit speed dial.

The others followed suit before I walked a couple of paces away from the table. I turned to watch the chaos while the phone rang. Charlie could have been asleep for all I knew. I didn't know what the time difference was between Bora Bora and LA.

"Wait, you don't need to do this," Tyler shouted, absolutely panic shaking his voice.

"Then fix your mess and get rid of him," Anders demanded.

"And make sure Nicole gets therapy," Aria snapped before her voice gentled, a mixture of horror and sadness clinging to her. "I can't imagine what she's had to deal with sharing a room with him."

"Finn, my man, I wasn't expecting a call from you,"

Charlie said, his typical cheerfulness blaring in my ear. "What's up?"

I filled him in while Tyler continued to panic, and Casey started shouting. For a man who prided himself on being so suave and charming, he lost his cool quickly. It served him right.

He'd worked for his father's record label five years ago, taking advantage of any woman he could in the office. When his father's company crashed, he reinvented himself as Casey Jackson, a singer-songwriter who required far too much legal attention. From what Shaun had told me, he'd graduated from sexual assault to outright attempted murder before it all blew up in his face. He'd tried to put a guitar tech through a window at a soundcheck.

The sight of him made me sick. His name alone silenced Charlie.

"You're bullshitting to get off the show, right?" All the cheer drained from Charlie's voice. "Finn, please tell me you're bullshitting?"

"Can't."

"For fuck's sake," Charlie groaned. "I put you on *Married Blind* to fix your shit. How do you find trouble where there shouldn't be any?"

"Hey, I didn't know he was on it until tonight."

Tyler gave up trying to reason with the others and made his own phone call. All the while, Charlie swore up a storm in my ear.

"What a fucking mess." Something clattered on the other end of the line. "You know the paps will eat this up, yeah?"

I frowned. "The fact the show picked him or…?"

"If you divorce Abi before the show concludes, no matter the reason, it won't look good."

"Charlie," I said, a clear warning in my voice.

"I'm just saying the better option for you is getting rid of that piece of shit Englishman and staying on the show."

Charlie blew out a shaky breath. "Fuck. Don't do anything drastic right now. Let me make some calls and see if I can fix it from my side. Leave it with me."

With that, he hung up, leaving me even more agitated than I'd been before.

I stalked back to the table. Tyler talked in a hushed voice with a livid-looking cameraman while Anders and Haley had moved to an entirely separate table with Aria and Kyle.

Casey paced next to the table while Nicole stared at the tablecloth, pretending to be transfixed. Christ, we were all so focused on saving our own skin, only Aria had even considered Nicole's feelings in all this chaos.

I stopped behind Abi and placed my hands on her bare shoulders. I shouldn't have done it, but the need to keep her safe overruled logic. She startled before tilting her head back to catch my eye.

"Do you want to get out of here while they fix this mess?" I asked.

"Sure." Abi smiled, but then it collapsed. She stood, turning to glance at me as she chewed her lip. "I'm just not sure we should leave her," she whispered, leaning toward me.

"Nicole, why don't you come and join us at another table?"

Her gaze snapped to us, surprise breaking through her fragile mask. She focused furious eyes on Casey. He had all of his attention on his phone call.

Nicole collected her bag and edged around the table, keeping her distance from him. Abi threaded her arm through hers and led her towards the other couples. I collected our drinks and followed them. When Abi went to sit down opposite her, I bumped her shoulder before pressing my mouth to her ear.

"Why don't you sit next to her?" I whispered, working hard to keep the suggestion light and not the protective measure it really was.

With Haley to her right and Abi to her left, Casey couldn't wheedle himself next to her to scare her anymore. It might loosen her up.

"Great idea." Abi turned around, smiling up at me.

One piece of praise from this woman and my heart jolted. I needed to work harder at keeping her at arm's length.

She settled down next to Nicole and I slid her drink across the table. Abi turned in her chair to face Nicole, that easy, friendly smile of hers plastered to her lips, brightening her entire expression.

They'd given me my perfect woman.

Tyler approached us, his panic replaced by a sheepish expression. We all turned to him, brows raised in expectation. Mine were at least.

"The series producer extends his apologies. The background checks weren't updated before filming began and the news about Mr Jackson slipped through the cracks." His gaze moved between Aria, Anders and me, completely ignoring our spouses. "We'll remove him from the show with immediate effect and we won't use any of tonight's footage. Hopefully, you'll all agree that we acted swiftly."

"Try it again and talk to everyone at the table and we might accept it," I said, my blood boiling once again. "You put Nicole in danger."

"Finn's right, of course." Tyler nodded. His attention fixed on Nicole at last. "I've already arranged for Casey to fly out tonight. The staff are packing his belongings now. It was a huge oversight, we never should have paired you with him."

Nicole nodded, moisture glistening in her eyes. Abi laid a hand on her shoulder in quiet support.

"Can I move rooms too please?" Nicole asked, her relief palpable but her voice catching.

"I'll arrange it." Tyler's focus turned to everyone else. "I'm sorry we wasted your time tonight. We'd like to try again tomorrow night. If you're up for it, we'll just grab some quiet moments of you all while you eat dinner separately."

"I don't think that's a good idea." Anders settled back in his chair, scowling at Tyler. "I think we all need time to process."

"Yeah, everything we talk about is going to involve this instance. You'll just waste more of our time." Kyle pushed his chair back and Aria followed him. "We'll make our own dinner plans, thanks."

The pair stalked off ignoring Tyler's protests.

"My agent is going to want all of this in writing by the way." Anders stood too, his hand gravitating to Haley's lower back as she joined him. "If he doesn't have it by tomorrow morning, I'm walking and taking Haley with me."

Hayley smiled at Nicole. "Do you want to eat dinner with us?"

She quickly agreed and the three of them left, leaving me to stare at Abi.

Any moment we shared on camera needed to be a conscious one.

Abi is off-limits. Do not get attached to her.

If I needed to make it a daily mantra, I bloody would.

Question: How did it feel watching Finn get angry on your behalf?
Abi: I thought you weren't using that footage.
Tyler, Producer: We aren't.
Abi: So why are you asking me about it?
Tyler, Producer: It seemed like a pivotal moment in your relationship.
Abi: It might have been, but this interview will be pretty pointless without the footage or story to explain it. So, again, why are you asking me about something you agreed to cut?

CHAPTER NINE

I'd taken my time brushing my teeth, washing the layer of makeup off my face, and changing into a pair of pyjama shorts and a tank top. Now I eyed the bed from the bathroom doorway, out of delaying tactics and unable to ignore the ball of nerves twisting in my stomach.

"C'mon, Abi," Finn said, exasperation mixing with his tiredness. He pulled the covers back and patted the expanse of the empty mattress beside him. "I won't bite, and there's plenty of room. You won't even know I'm here."

He leaned against the headboard, cushions propping him up and his bare chest on display while the sheet pooled in his lap. My gaze wandered despite my brain begging for control, tracing the lines of muscle down to his lap.

"I could make a bed on the floor." My cheeks burning, I glanced at the closet where I'd found a pile of blankets and extra pillows while we unpacked. "Couple of layers, and I'll barely tell the difference."

"Abi," Finn groaned. He rubbed a hand across his face.

"I'm not opposed to manhandling you if you don't get in this bed right now."

Finn slid down the bed as I climbed beneath the sheets. I caught his smug satisfaction from the corner of my eye and instead of calling him on it, I turned away from him, settling down against the pillows to pretend there wasn't a mere two feet of distance between us.

"Thank you for earlier," I whispered into the silence of our room.

"What for?" he asked, his voice hoarse with tiredness.

"Take your pick." I shrugged, smiling into the darkness.

Finn sighed. "You don't need to thank me."

I pressed my lips together and didn't respond. He could deny it all he liked, but he'd played the perfect husband tonight. Laying in the dark, with no one to scrutinise me, I could acknowledge how nice it had felt.

FINN

We'd started on opposite ends of the bed. Loads of space between us.

And then I woke at 3 AM. Rock hard with her body against mine. Not just pressed, she'd flung a bloody leg across my waist and her head on my chest.

My gaze fixed on the ceiling, jaw clenching, and my cock throbbing with a need I had no intention of fulfilling. It felt like torture.

I needed to move her.

My limbs had other ideas. My arm wrapped around her and my fingers smoothed down her arm. I'd sworn to keep her at arm's length.

I hadn't thought resisting her would be hard, but I'd been very wrong.

She sighed, and I lifted my hand, bracing myself for her shocked gasp. Instead, she snuggled closer. Her thigh grazed lower, and my breath exploded from my lungs.

Fuck.

Even in sleep, she teased me. No woman had ever wound me so tightly that an innocent touch set me off. Evidently, I'd underestimated Abi.

I should have fucked a bunch of women before this all started…

As sensible as the idea would have been, I didn't believe it would have helped. I'd lost interest in casual flings nearly a year ago. None of them actually wanted me. Just the money, fame, and connections that came attached to me.

I shifted until Abi settled into the crook of my shoulder and I could study her face. She looked so peaceful in sleep. All of that fire hidden. I didn't want to believe she would be like the rest of them, but why else take part in a show like *Married Blind?*

ABI

I groaned, coaxed from a deep sleep, interrupting the best dream. Flickers of glistening skin and an intense sense of satisfaction clung to me. Bright light filtered beneath my lashes, chasing away the vague memory of it.

"Turn the heating off, Eva," I grumbled.

Oh, no.

Smooth skin pressed against my palm. Hard muscles tensed beneath my thigh. *Please tell me I didn't….*

My eyes popped open, and horror sunk like lead in my stomach. The heat belonged to Finn.

I scrambled upright. The sun blazed in through the patio doors, extra intense thanks to the water glistening beyond our terrace. I slid across the bed slowly, eying Finn for the slightest hint of movement. Instinct said he'd never let it go if he caught me cuddling up to him.

Better if I made myself scarce.

I rushed into the bathroom and focused on showering. Or tried to.

Despite the shock, the dream still clung to me, a toe-curling, hands grasping sheets kind of heated.

I had five minutes to develop a poker face before he saw straight through me.

Shit.

Ten minutes later, I tiptoed back into the main room, a towel wrapped around me and another pressed to my hair. My pulse beat intensely in my throat despite my constant reminders that it would all be fine. He'd been asleep.

I didn't want to look at the bed. Or more, I was too much of a coward to face him in the intense silence. Only the sound of the water lapping against the bungalow's struts filled the room. I would have found it soothing if I hadn't been so high-strung.

"Why are you sneaking about?"

I jumped out of my skin, dropping the towel in my hand and spinning to face him. The picture of sneaky. He lay in bed, propped up against the pillows, watching me with what I was coming to see as his trademark blank expression.

"I — I'm not."

His brow rose and I blew out a shaky breath.

"I thought you were still asleep." I picked up the towel and rushed over to my suitcase. "Didn't want to wake you."

Deafening silence followed me. The skin on the back of my neck itched as if he were watching me.

"Are you going to shower?" I asked as a way of breaking the intense air, but also gauging my next move.

I turned to face him, clothes clutched to my chest, and my eyes far too wide to not be suspicious.

"Maybe," he said, the word popping as amusement

danced across his face. "You're very tense this morning. Didn't you sleep well?"

My heart leapt into my throat again.

Do not react. He doesn't know.

"I'm just trying to get ready before the crew comes knocking again. So you're not showering right now, then?" I rushed past the bed, expecting a denial.

"No, I think I'm going to cuddle in a bit more." His voice dipped on the cuddle. "It's cosy in here, don't you think?"

I kept my mouth shut, fighting the urge to not chew my lip. I might not have a good poker face, well, any poker face, but I would not be the one to volunteer embarrassing information.

The amusement slid off his face, and his brows drew together. His gaze fixed on me intense enough to make me squirm. I tensed every muscle to prevent that.

"If I have to restrain you to keep my personal space, I will."

His tone dropped, grating over me deliciously while convincing me that the threat in his voice was no joke.

It should have horrified me. Instead, my core clenched.

Crossing my arms, I willed the feeling away. Something to pack away and not think about in his presence.

"I don't know what you're talking about."

"Sure, you don't." Finn threw back the covers and stood. "Next time I'll wake you up and you can make your denials while your legs are wrapped around mine." He stopped in front of me, lowering his face to mine before whispering, "I'm sure you'll be able to sell it, love."

He vanished into the bathroom, leaving me to shake off the pulse of warmth in my core.

If only he weren't so hot and cold, I'd —

Something black caught my attention in the glass on the floor at the end of the bed. When I looked properly, my blood ran cold.

"What? What is it?" Finn shouted, rushing back into the bedroom with a towel wrapped around his waist. I stared at him in wide-eyed panic. "You shrieked, Abi. What's wrong?"

I pointed down at the shark thrashing around less than two feet beneath my feet. My vocal cords had frozen up. Finn padded across to me, his brows furrowed. The concern faded into annoyance as soon as he looked down.

"It's just a shark." When my panic didn't ease, he shook his head. "It's a Blacktip reef shark. It's not aggressive, and you aren't in the water with it."

"I'm a New Yorker. We don't do marine life." The longer I watched it the more the blood drained from my face. "You were in the water yesterday. What if it — oh my god."

"Christ, Abi, save the drama for when the cameras are on." Finn scrubbed a hand across his face.

That one sentence cut through my panic better than a cold splash of water. So I hadn't been imagining his odd shifts in behaviour. On camera Finn was nicer, but it set me on edge every time. I much preferred the real Finn, biting tone and all.

"It's a shark. It lives here," he continued, his voice dry and scathing. "You aren't a fish, and man-eating sharks aren't common in Bora Bora."

"How do you know that? It could be one."

I barely heard myself speak. Which Finn was real?

Finn growled. "I live in California. I know what a man-eating shark looks like and that is not it." He turned his back on me. "Pull it together," he muttered before disappearing into the bathroom.

The glass door shut, snapping my focus from the reality adjustment unfolding in my head.

❄

*W*ith an hour to spare before the crew collected us, we rushed to breakfast in what I'd like to call companionable silence. If I ignored the way Finn kept his eyes on anything but me, turning away or grunting in response to any of my attempts to lighten the mood.

The longer it went on, the more my stomach knotted up.

When one of the cameramen wandered into the dining room, trailing Aria and Kyle, his foul mood dissolved. They headed straight for us, smiles on their faces mirroring Finn's. He turned into the perfect husband, reaching for my hand across the table, coaxing me into the conversation with light teasing.

My head hurt trying to see through it.

They stopped to chat pleasantries for a couple of moments before heading to their table at the far end of the room.

The second the camera left Finn, his scowl came right back.

"What's wrong with you this morning?" I poked at my eggs, peeking at his scowling face from beneath my lashes. He grunted but otherwise continued to ignore me.

"Seriously, Finn? You're making me think you're pissed at me, but that would be ridiculous. I can't control my body when I'm asleep."

Again, he grunted.

"Stop acting like a sulking child and talk to me." I pointed my fork at him. "And if you grunt at me again, I swear I'll drive this fork into your hand." I wouldn't, but he didn't need to know that.

"I need to grab something from the room." He pushed his chair back and stood, avoiding eye contact. "I'll meet you out front before we have to leave."

He stalked off, blazing across the open restaurant with his head down.

Oh, no you don't.

I abandoned my half-eaten plate and rushed after him. My sandals clattered against the boardwalk as I struggled to catch up. The man had almost a foot on me. I didn't stand a chance.

"Will you just talk to me?" I called after him.

He glanced over his shoulder, a scowl marring his gorgeous face.

"Go back to the restaurant, Abi," he snapped before continuing towards our bungalow. "There's nothing to talk about."

I continued after him.

The bedroom stood empty, so I continued on to the patio, following a hunch. There I found him collapsed in a deck chair, staring out at the sea.

His gaze met mine as I approached, and his jaw tensed.

"I'm not in the mood to play nice right now. Go."

I shook my head. Call me stubborn, but we had spoken vows, made promises.

"Talk to me. I can help."

His hands stilled where they drove through his hair. Something in his expression shifted, chasing away the agitation and replacing it with a hard determination that made my body tense up.

"I'd rather not."

He shot to his feet and stormed inside. I paused for a second on the patio, shut my eyes and took a deep breath. Logically, I should have left him alone. So why did I feel compelled to do the illogical thing?

I followed him inside. "Then tell me what's wrong."

He spun to face me, growling under his breath. "For Christ's sake, woman, can't you leave me alone for five minutes? I'm stuck with you for three months. Isn't that enough?"

I crossed my arms and glared at him. "I was trying to be nice," I hissed. "You don't need to be an asshole."

"I told you to stay away. Did you listen?" he shouted. "No. When you refuse to listen, I'm allowed to be an asshole." He dragged a hand through his hair, lowering his voice. "Sweetheart, I'm Hollywood's biggest playboy. A ring isn't going to change me."

My mouth snapped shut. Both surprise and shame hit me in the chest, because he was right. As legit as our marriage looked on paper, we weren't in a relationship.

I shouldn't have expected anything from him. He didn't need to share his feelings with me and I didn't need to make allowances for him.

"You're right." I nodded, my hands falling to my side. "We don't owe each other anything but to put on the right face and say the right things to the camera." A smile claimed my lips for the first time since I'd woken up. "I'll meet you at reception."

"Wait. That's not what I — fuck."

Eyes on the prize, Abi.

CHAPTER TEN

FINN

I should have been happy.

Yet I couldn't stop studying her while she stared out the window in the back of the minivan. Guilt gnawed at my gut, directly contradicting the elation I should have felt.

What the fuck is wrong with me?

Agreeing to *Married Blind* in the first place had been a huge mistake.

We stopped at the marina and Abi flung her door open, genuine excitement brightening her expression.

If we'd met under any other circumstance, I might have tried…

No, I couldn't lie to myself. Had I met Abi outside of the show, I would have sweet-talked her into bed and left the next morning. No attachments, no smiling at her singing in the shower or kissing her in public places. No wondering if there might be something real to unearth.

I would have played the perfect, unattached playboy.

Life was safer that way.

"So, what are we doing?" Abi asked as I climbed out of the car.

I slid my sunglasses on and turned my face up to the sun, absorbing that one pleasure without hesitation.

"We'll tell you once we're on the boat," Tyler said.

He ushered us towards a waiting catamaran and the request to wear swimwear started to make sense. For once, the crew didn't mess around. They loaded us onto the boat and headed out to sea.

I tried not to watch Abi soaking in the sun and sea breeze, but with her auburn hair flying behind her and her head tilted back, I couldn't keep my eyes off her. At some point, my goals and my body had to get on the same page. I needed to stop feeling guilty, needed to stop appreciating how well her wild hair complemented her face or how stunning her blue eyes were. She needed to become just another woman, and one I didn't want to sleep with.

About ten minutes later, the easygoing atmosphere changed. Tyler pulled out his notebook, and I knew our time to relax, and wallow, had ended.

"Okay, so we've got something exciting planned for today. Are you ready?" Tyler flashed a smile that failed to be infectious. Abi and I stared at him, the silence stretching between us. "You can strip down to your swimsuits and we'll get started. This gentleman is going to outfit you with some snorkel gear, and show you how to use it." He gestured to a tall, tanned man with a captain's hat perched on his head.

"What are we doing?" Abi asked again.

"You're swimming with sharks!" Tyler's enthusiasm made a resurgence, and he flung his arms out at the glistening ocean.

Abi's face paled. I unbuttoned my white shirt, eying her all the while.

"Do we have to?" She almost squeaked.

"Fun, right?" Tyler said, totally missing the shake in her hands.

Stick with the programme, Finn. Do not engage.

"I wouldn't have used those exact words," Abi muttered. She turned her back on the swim deck and crossed her arms, almost hugging herself.

"Once you're in your swimsuits, we'll ask you a couple of questions, but this should just be natural." Tyler glanced between us, a slight frown finally hitting as he studied Abi's back. "This is a bonding exercise, so relax, have fun and stick close together."

He caught my eye and tilted his head toward Abi. The message couldn't be clear. *What the fuck is her problem, and why aren't you fixing it?*

Sighing, I approached her.

I tapped her on the shoulder. "What's up, *dotey?*"

I needed to *stop* using that word with her.

She turned toward me and my breath caught. Moisture shimmered in her eyes. She bit her lip as she studied me. Indecision flickered in her eyes. Even so, she leaned towards me.

"I can't go in there," she whispered.

"Why not? These people do things like this daily. We'll be perfectly safe."

She pressed her lips together and shook her head.

"What is it about this that you don't like?" I resisted the urge to pull her into my chest. She kept rubbing her arms, seeking comfort where there was none. "The swimming in the sea? The cameras? The sharks?"

She squeaked. I'd forgotten her reaction in the bungalow to the reef shark.

"You're afraid of sharks," I said, purely to get a confirmation out of her. At her nod, something in me relaxed. "What sharks are out there?" I asked the skipper.

"Some Lemon and Whitetips, and the Blacktips of course,"

he said, the words lilting over a French accent. He glanced at Abi and his expression softened. "No reason to worry. They're used to humans, and it's unusual for them to bite. Just keep your eyes open, don't splash around and don't panic."

"What if I *do* panic?" She stepped closer, staring up at me with open trust in her blue eyes.

"Just keep hold of me." I threaded our fingers together. "Tap my hand if you panic, and I'll bring you back to the boat."

For a couple of moments, Abi studied my face, a guarded light entering her eyes for the first time since we'd met. That pang of guilt resurfaced.

"How are you so calm about this?"

"I told you, California has a lot of sharks. Surfing and diving, I've met a lot of them." I smiled, squeezing her hand. "A couple of reef sharks don't scare me."

"Okay, but if I can't handle it…"

"We'll get out."

"Wait —" Tyler snapped his mouth shut at my glare.

He wanted me to be a good husband and handle her. If he wanted it to continue, he needed to shut up and back me up.

"Yes, of course."

"Okay." She nodded and released her death grip on my hand. "I'll try." Her hands still shook as she tugged her summer dress over her head.

My eyes had a mind of their own. My gaze dipped, tracing the lines of her bikini, absorbing details to haunt me later. Her full breasts, slightly rounded stomach, and toned thighs. Add in her long, wavy auburn hair, and if I'd had any concept about my type, Abi had bulldozed it in less than a minute.

Abi approached the swim deck with a determined step. It cracked as the skipper started his safety briefing and she turned to search for me. My hands itched to touch her and despite knowing I shouldn't, I gave her what she wanted. I stopped at her side, my fingers pressed into her waist, reminding her I'd be by her side through it all.

The cameramen went in first, their cameras locked inside plastic underwater casing. One stayed on the surface, while the other disappeared below. Then I jumped off the back of the boat.

When I surfaced, Abi still hadn't joined me. She stood on the deck, staring at the spot where I'd dived.

"Are you coming in, Abi?"

I waited, my gaze fixed on Abi as she shakily climbed down the ladder. She paused on the last rung, her fingers clenching around the metal. I swam to her, closed my fingers over hers, wrapped an arm around her waist and pressed my front to her back.

"I've got you, *dotey*," I whispered in her ear.

With a deep breath, she let go of the ladder and allowed me to pull her away from the boat. For a couple of minutes, we trod water while she adjusted. Her blue eyes shone brighter with the water reflecting off her snorkel mask. She kept trying to adjust it.

"Stop. The mask is fine." I caught her hand, pulling it away from the mask before she could dislodge it. "Take your time. Putting these things on in the water is a nightmare, so don't play around too much."

Abi nodded, but beyond treading water, she felt like an empty vessel. I spun her to face me and she gasped. With her chest pressed against mine, close enough that I could feel her nipples pebbling in the water, I bit my tongue.

"Just breathe, Abi. We don't need to go under until you're ready."

She stared into my eyes while her fingers dug almost painfully into my forearms. Nearly every inch of her brushed against me. Keeping my expression calm and pleasantly blank took more work than it should have.

"Ready?" I asked when her breathing evened out.

"You'll stay by my side?" She chewed her lip, staring at me with a vulnerable light in her eyes.

"Right next to you." I took her hand and lifted it out of the water. "Keep hold of my hand. Squeeze it when you need to, tug on it when you need my attention. I promise you'll have fun if you can relax."

With one last deep breath, she nodded. Then we were off. She squeezed my hand the second she spotted some Blacktip sharks swimming in and out of a black shoal of fish. Others patrolled the sandy seabed.

The fish engulfed us, and after a moment of stunned panic, Abi settled down. Her shoulder periodically brushed against mine, as if she needed more than my tight grip on her hand for reassurance.

We circled in the water, tracking one shiver of sharks. Some passed her by without so much as a pause. She loosened up, tugging *me* in whichever direction she wanted.

The heady rush of relief hit me.

"That was incredible," she shouted when we surfaced at the back of the boat. "Thank you, Finn!"

She threw her arms and legs around me, hugging me as she pressed a kiss to my cheek. One impulsive move, and she unravelled all of my efforts to ignore her body. Holding her felt right, and my dick couldn't agree more, which was a problem considering I wore swimming trunks, and I still had to get out of the water.

"Told you you'd enjoy it." I smiled before disentangling us.

Giddy, she spun around and reached for the ladder without prodding. One cameraman had stayed on board. He stood poised and ready to capture one of the most inappropriate shots of the show as Abi climbed back on board.

"Hold on, Abi." I swam to her, and she turned, her brow furrowing at the edge in my voice. "Let me help you."

She stared at me for a couple of seconds, confusion

clouding her eyes. Then I tilted my head slightly towards the waiting camera, and her eyes widened.

"Oh. Thank you."

She placed her hands on my shoulders and her foot on the bottom rung of the ladder. With a firm grip on her waist, I lifted her onto the swim deck, her back to the camera. Her expression softened.

I'm my own worst enemy.

INTERVIEW V

Question: Why are you so resistant to the show?
Finn: Why do you need to ask loaded questions?
Tyler, Producer: Why do you think it's loaded?
Finn: Because you'll twist any answer I give.
Tyler, Producer: We're not a gossip show, Finn. Your words are your words.
Finn: *Snorts* As if. If you could splice a chunk of an interview specifically to sensationalise the drama on this show, you would. And don't say *you* would never do something like that. You're not the editor or the edit producer. You won't be in the room.
Tyler, Producer: That's true, but it doesn't change the fact that these interviews are here for you to get out any feelings you're not ready to talk to Abi about.
Finn: Why would Abi care if I hate this show?
Tyler, Producer: You're not that obtuse. If someone you were involved with hated the thing that brought you together, wouldn't you wonder if they hated you too?

CHAPTER ELEVEN

ABI

The crew packed up once we returned to the hotel, freeing us to shower off the salt water and enjoy the rest of our afternoon. With the salt drying on our skin, Finn and I spent it in comfortable silence on the patio. For the first time since my parents died, I could actually relax, guilt-free.

I embraced the good life between the sun, the surroundings, my comfortable position on a lounger with a book, my phone on silent to avoid blushing at Ros's inappropriate suggestions. And, of course, the odd dip in the pool.

Maybe this is why people chase fame.

The one blip in my relaxation plans came in the form of six-foot-three inches of pure muscle. Seriously, had Finn McCarthy never eaten a peanut butter cup? The abs on the man made my mouth water, and don't even get me started on the bulge I couldn't help ogling every time he climbed out of the pool or ocean.

Flashbacks wouldn't stop hitting me. Him pressing against me in the water. His long fingers wrapping around my hand.

The way he'd lifted me out, his biceps straining, just so I wouldn't flash my tits to the cameraman. The *feel* of his hardness pressed against me when I wrapped my legs around his waist.

He was hard…

Because of *me*.

That still boggled my mind. If there hadn't been cameras pointed at us, I might have tried my luck.

"What time is it?" Finn asked from the pool, pausing in yet another round of laps. The man couldn't stay still.

I glanced at my phone. "Nearly six."

He studied me for a second, his expression perfectly blank. Then something shifted. A small smile curled his lips, setting my heart off into a patter. What did that smile mean, and why did I wish he'd direct it at me more often?

"Do you want to get food?" He stopped at the edge of the pool and pressed his hands to the deck. "You probably need a drink after today, right?"

He lifted himself out of the pool as he spoke. My mouth dried and I lost control of my eyes. Who wouldn't when confronted with that body? Water cascaded from him, sliding down his skin in tiny rivulets, taunting me to follow their path.

"Abi?" he asked, amusement audible in the one word.

My gaze shot back to his face, eyes widening while my mouth popped shut. He smirked at me, his brows rising, knowing exactly where my head had gone.

"Yup, sounds like a plan." I nodded, my cheeks burning and my stomach twisting with a mixture of need and mortification. I gestured to the shower. "You can grab the first shower."

Finn picked up a towel and patted it against his chest. His blue eyes remained fixed on me, mirth dancing through them. He glanced at the outdoor shower and his expression turned devious.

"Or I could just shower out here…" He stepped towards it, absolute mischief curling his lips.

I shot to my feet and squeaked: "Then I'll use the one inside."

His laughter followed me inside. I shut the bathroom door with a shaking hand while my heart made a bid to escape my chest. I leaned against it, forcing air into my lungs and begging my core to stop clenching at the idea of him touching himself as he showered….

Shit, I meant washing.

"Fuck." My brain short-circuited and threw up a very enticing picture of Finn masturbating.

With the cold water turned to full blast, I braced myself for the worst shower of my life. Something needed to shock some sense into me.

*A*fter a pleasant dinner, I climbed into bed, the tension unwritten by several cocktails. I might have giggled a bit and sighed overly loud when the cool sheets covered me.

"I need to know where they buy these sheets," I muttered into my pillow. "They're so soft."

"You can ask in the morning," Finn said from the other side of the room.

I frowned as I lifted my head from the pillow, tracking his movements. He kept walking back and forth to the bed, dumping more and more pillows on it.

"What are you doing?"

Finn flashed me a smile but didn't answer. Instead, he started piling pillows down the middle of the bed, forming a barrier.

I chortled at the sight of it and his determined expression.

"You really don't like cuddles."

He glowered at me. "I like my personal space."

"Ooookay. You must be fun after a night of fucking."

His fingers stalled and I should probably feel embarrassed about those words.

I didn't.

Finn recovered fast, continuing to pile the pillows down the entire length of the bed. Satisfied, he settled under the sheet without comment, turning away from me.

I frowned at the wall of pillows.

For a couple of seconds, only the sound of the air conditioning unit and the waves lapping the struts below us filled the room. Altogether, I found it oddly soothing. My eyelids drooped.

"Thank you for helping me today," I whispered, losing the silence battle fast.

"No problem."

I chewed my lip, wishing I could see his face. Did he mean it?

"I didn't think I'd freak out that much."

He sighed and the sheets rustled. Rolling over?

"I thought you were brave," he said, his voice so low I had to strain to hear him.

Heat burned my cheeks and the biggest smile claimed my lips. "Thank you."

Silence descended again, but words clamoured through my mind, desperate to get out. My tongue pressed to the roof of my mouth as I tried to stem the flow. *Whose idea has it been to have four cocktails?* I could never hold my liquor.

"I promise I won't cuddle you tonight." Even if it felt amazing.

"Good," he huffed. "Goodnight, Abi."

Why couldn't they have paired me with someone resistible?

❄

FINN

The next morning, I woke to heat and the gentle weight of Abi cuddled into my side again.

The pillows lay all over the place, my barrier absolutely decimated. Yet again, she'd wound herself around me, her leg hooked with mine, her pelvis pressed to my hip and her head resting in the crook of my shoulder. At some point, I'd wrapped my arm around her again, holding her to me.

I rubbed a hand across my face and groaned. *How could I keep her away from me when I couldn't trust myself?*

Biting at her yesterday had been hard, almost painful, and I'd blown all the effort up within an hour. I was running out of options. If I were totally honest with myself, I didn't have any to begin with. Abi needed to be the one to quit.

I needed to get my head on straight and fast.

Abi stretched against me, and her thigh moved higher up my leg, grazing my morning wood with very little effort. I gritted my teeth against the rush of sensation. The intense need I felt for her could not be normal.

Maybe she'd go for a one-time thing…

Talk about stupid ideas. Those kinds of arrangements never ended with one night and they never ended well. Mona and Shaun had started their relationship as a direct result of the "get it out of our system" lie.

Nope. I could hold on.

I just needed to last five more days. Then we'd be in my massive house, sleeping in separate rooms and hardly seeing each other. I could definitely wait.

"Sorry," she mumbled. Her fingers skittered across my nipple and another bolt of need shot through me.

Fuck.

A second later, Abi tensed. She lifted her head from my chest and met my gaze with horror widening her eyes.

"I'm so sorry." She untangled our legs and sat bolt

upright, turning to check out her destruction. "I don't know how I…" She glanced back at me, her teeth sunk deep into her lower lip. I couldn't tear my eyes away, could feel my grip slipping on my self-control. The need to kiss her burned strong. I craved that 'out-of-body, nothing else matters' feeling she inspired.

I hadn't craved someone since Natalie.

"I really am sorry."

My restraint snapped and I reached up, smoothing my thumb along her lip, freeing it. Her eyes widened again, but this time, they darkened with desire. Her tongue darted out, unintentionally caressing my skin. I froze, with my thumb against her soft lips as my cock ached and my brain caught up with my wayward hands.

"It's okay," I said, surprising myself.

I dropped my hand and sat up. She watched me, the need warring across her face.

"Try not to do it again," I muttered before climbing out of bed.

Heading for the bathroom, I didn't look at her. One glance at her confused face, her hair mussed from sleep, and I might crack. Breaking wouldn't be good for either of us.

CHAPTER TWELVE

FINN

The production kept us busy for most of the day, shadowing our every move from breakfast to lunch. Then they bundled us into another minivan with more secretive smirks, predictably keeping their mouths shut whenever we asked for clues about the day's torture.

The minivan wound up into the mountains, bracketed by thick foliage on each side. Abi sat next to me, chewing her lip, while Tyler nattered on. I'd tuned him out pretty fast.

Half an hour later, we stopped in a gravel car park with a steel structure at the bottom end. The team filed out of the minivan. Their cameras went straight onto their shoulders, ready to catch our "surprise" at the activity.

The urge to roll my eyes bit at me hard, but then I'd be breaking character, and I had no intention of giving Tyler an inch of ground.

"Okay, Abi, Finn, can I get you to stand here, please?" Tyler said. His tone would have been perfectly pleasant if not for the glimmer in his eyes. He guided Abi to me, turning us until our backs were to the building. "Excellent. Now, do you know where you are?" He stepped back, outright grinning at us as if his excitement would catch.

Abi shook her head and his focus shifted to me. I just glared at him.

"You're going to tell us, so quit the theatrics and get on with it." My voice dropped, hardening with my annoyance.

"Right enough." Tyler smirked and rubbed his hands together. "Today you're zip-lining over the gorgeous Bora Bora forests. Isn't that cool?"

He paused, expecting something more than the stone-cold silence he got.

"I said, isn't that cool?"

"Do we have to?" Abi squeaked.

"It'll be fun, I promise." He grinned, his eyes on fire with excitement and missing the fact we weren't mirroring him.

Abi paled and took a step back, bumping into me. Her back pressed against my arm, the heat of her body burning against me despite the warm afternoon. My fingers itched to touch her, to wrap my arm around her and console her.

"Are you afraid of heights?" I asked her, keeping my voice low while Tyler waxed poetic about some psychological mumbo jumbo theory about couples who took part in terrifying situations forming tight, lasting bonds.

I knew the answer before she turned her fear-ridden gaze on me.

Who was I fucking kidding? I didn't stand a chance faced with her watery blue eyes.

I wrapped an arm around her, tugging her against my chest. Her fingers curled in my shirt, white-knuckling it.

"We're not doing this, Tyler." I kept my voice firm and stared him down. "I'm pretty sure you have a duty to not traumatise your contributors."

Tyler offered Abi a sympathetic smile. "It's perfectly safe. You'll be well strapped in and it'll be over faster than you can say acrophobia." He chuckled at his joke. "This is part of the show." He held his hands out, trying and failing to claim his helplessness in the face of the system. "This is the last thing on the list for the day. We get through this and you'll be able to relax without the cameras."

"You can't be serious with that bullshit."

"I'll do it," Abi croaked. She pushed away from me, turning her pale face to the cameras.

ABI

As sick as I felt at the thought of being thousands of feet in the air, I was grateful when they strapped us together. *At least I don't have to face my fears alone.*

That didn't mean I relaxed though.

Oh no, the closer they tied us, the harder I clung to Finn. He continued to rub his hands over my arms and back, soothing me as best he could. My fingers twisted in his shirt, wishing I could get closer.

"Thank you for trying to stop them," I whispered, my throat far too tight to project my voice.

"There's still time for me to try again." He squeezed me against him and my heart fluttered. "If you want."

Oh, how I wished it were that straightforward.

"Thank you, but no." I shook my head, forcing a smile to my lips. Finn frowned at me, seeing through my bravado. "I'll just hide my face in your chest and hope it ends quickly."

The instructor appeared at our side. "Okay, Abi, turn around and I'll lock the last clips in place."

Every muscle in my body locked up. He gripped my arm,

probably assuming the harnesses made moving difficult rather than seeing the fear crippling my body. I shuffled around, my heart pounding at an alarming rate.

"Can't she stay facing me?" Finn asked, fighting for me still.

The instructor smiled kindly. "Sorry, it's safer this way."

Resigned to my fate, I let him strap me in. In any other situation, the heat of Finn's body cupping mine would have made me feel safe. Facing the endless run of a zip-line and a metal platform that did nothing to hide the drop, the close press of our bodies barely registered.

"Close your eyes, okay?" Finn said, his breath caressing my ear. His arms wrapped around me, squeezing tight around my waist. "When we get out of this, I'll book you into the spa for the rest of the afternoon."

I smiled at the promise but kept my mouth shut.

"And the production will pay, won't they, Tyler?" His tone promised painful consequences if he denied it.

Tyler readily agreed.

They strapped the cameramen into their own harnesses and rigged their cameras around them, ready to catch every second of my terror for the viewing pleasure of millions of strangers.

The instructor called something, and we started moving. The edge flew at me faster than I could handle. I squeaked and the air lodged in my throat. I slammed my eyes shut before we could get too close, leaning into Finn and putting my faith in his promises.

Air blew through my hair and my stomach dropped. The scream tore from my throat, resisting my every effort to squash it.

Finn's grip never faltered, even when the drop jostled us painfully together.

❄

inn smoothed my hair down as we stood by the minivan, waiting for the camera crew to decide their next move. He tilted my face up, forcing me to meet his concerned gaze.

"Are you okay?"

I blew out a breath. "I think so."

My heart still pounded wildly and my pulse throbbed in my temples, but I'd survived. I needed to lie down for a week to recover.

"A stiff drink would be good about now, right?" His lips quirked, a glimmer of the real Finn shining through. He coaxed a breathless agreement from me. Then the tiny glimmer of amusement faded, replaced with a dark look that made my stomach drop for an entirely different reason. "Do you have any other fears I should know about?"

I bit my lip.

"You told them you were afraid of sharks and heights, right?"

I nodded. I'd given them every detail. They'd said I should be honest, that it might affect the results if I wasn't.

He glowered at Tyler's back, swearing under his breath.

"It's okay." I stepped closer to Finn, placing my hand on his forearm. "I got through it."

"Yes, you did. After they scared the shit out of you." Finn frowned at me, that unusual concern darkening his eyes. One look and my heart warmed. "You don't need to accept that shit, Abi. You can put your foot down if they're pushing you too much."

"Honestly, I'm past it now." I squeezed his arm, smiling. "Thank you for looking out for me again. Next time, I'll push back." Then I rolled my shoulders and winced. "Although I'm definitely going to need a massage. It feels like I went a full-on hour at the gym.

"What are you afraid of?" I asked, catching Finn off guard.

Something about our closeness made this moment seem private, a grain of time just for us. Probably thanks to adrenaline from the fear I'd just been forced to face.

Finn's expression shut down, the light and concern slowly fading until the robot of an actor stared down at me.

"So we know what else they might throw at us."

Finn nodded and his face smoothed out. "They can't throw my fear at you. You'd have to learn to dive first."

He took a step back. I caught his arm, following him. "What is it?"

He studied me with a critical eye, assessing me for something, but hell if I knew what.

"Drowning," he finally said. "And I don't mean simply losing control in the water."

I frowned. "Then what do you mean?"

He sighed, rolling his eyes to the clear sky before narrowing them on me. "This stays between us, right?"

"I promise."

Despite my reassurance, he still hesitated. His fingers twitched and his body twisted away from me, bringing us closer but also convincing me he'd turn away from me.

"I'm scared of *something* drowning me." He glanced towards the crew again. "There's no logic to it, and the animal doesn't matter. It's just the lack of control. Tyler and his accomplices have no way of manufacturing that situation to put us through it, which is why he's focusing on you." His sapphire gaze pierced through me.

"Why do you dive and surf if you're scared of that?"

"Why do you get in a car if there's a chance it'll crash?" He shrugged, staring into my eyes with a singular focus. "Fear is no reason to miss out on life. I love diving and surfing. I'm not going to avoid the sea because of irrational fear."

It made a twisted kind of sense. Not a sense I had any intention of applying to my fears.

Finn stepped back, breaking my hold and our close connection. Seconds passed and already I missed our little bubble of trust. We stared at each other, an awkward air weaselling its way between us.

What the hell just happened?

INTERVIEW VI

Question: How do you feel about Finn now?
Abi: I'm not really sure. It's all a bit muddled.
Tyler, Producer: In what way?
Abi: One minute, he's snapping. The next, he's… sweet. I don't know what's real, I guess.
Tyler, Producer: That's understandable when you meet someone new, right? You don't know how to read him yet.
Abi: Yes, but it's also the actor thing. Or more, I can handle his game face now, I can almost see it coming. But when the cameras are around, he's… different, and I can't tell if that's real either sometimes.
Tyler, Producer: Have you talked to him about it?
Abi: Why on earth would I do that?
Tyler, Producer: Communication is kind of important in a marriage, Abi.
Abi: Yeah, but I've known the man for less than a week. In the real world, by this point, we might have gone on one date, and I'd be sat at home second-guessing whether I should call him or text to arrange a second. None of this is normal, so why would the normal rules of marriage apply?

Tyler, Producer: It's a sped-up process, granted, but every relationship falls apart when communication breaks down, no matter how progressed it is.

Abi: *shakes head* He was a sweetheart when I needed him to be. What if I question that and he never does it again?

CHAPTER THIRTEEN

FINN

Hours later, we'd nearly escaped when they pulled Abi back for a one-on-one interview. I couldn't stand being alone in the bungalow with my thoughts.

The call connected before I could formulate any kind of reason for ringing. The Welshman loaded on my phone screen, wearing a massive grin. Shaun Martin and I had become friends very early in our careers. I'm not sure how I would have turned out without him acting as my sounding board.

"Hey, mate. How's the honeymoon?" Shaun asked. Amusement shone in his green eyes while his dark brown hair looked unkempt for once.

I twisted my lips into a wry smile. "A little more challenging than expected."

Shaun snorted, dragging a hand through his hair.

We all had problems, secrets whispered to the wrong person at the wrong time that could destroy us. Shaun had gotten out in front of his before it took him down. It probably helped that he had sweet, smiling Mona on his arm to distract his fans.

Unfortunately, I hadn't needed to develop a problem for someone to take advantage of me. I got good at being the honey-lipped player who could talk any woman into lifting her skirt no matter where we were or who could see.

"Wow. That's…" Shaun shook his head, shock and mirth shining in his eyes. "Unexpected?"

"Laugh it up, asshole," I grumbled, shifting further back on the bed. "I know you're all enjoying my pain."

"You make it too easy." Shaun shrugged without so much as an ounce of apology. "But in all seriousness, maybe you should just give it a chance."

"Give it a… Bloody hell, what have you been smoking, and does Mona know?"

"It's not crazy to suggest you give someone a chance, Finn." Shaun glanced behind him and then lowered his voice. "What do you have to lose by giving Abi the benefit of the doubt and putting some faith in the show's systems?"

"A renewed media shitstorm. The loss of my remaining shred of credibility. Studio execs being reminded of the 'reputation' my ex gifted me before fucking off with a boatload of money for selling me out. The loss of future jobs." I ticked them off on my free hand, tapping my fingers as I ran through the list. "And maybe a bit of heartache," I whispered.

"I agree, it's a hell of a list, but what if Abi *is* different?"

"Shaun," I groaned, covering my face. "I. Don't. Want. To." I bit out the words, acting every bit like a petulant child.

"I didn't want to stop drinking, but I did it." His face hardened. "I didn't want to go back to acting, but you lot forced me. You can't just hide forever."

Why the hell not?

"We're worried about you, man."

"Beyond my current situation, there's nothing to be worried about."

Shaun stared at me, his deadpan expression telling me exactly how much he believed me.

"I need a drink." I dragged a hand across my face.

"Alcohol's not the answer, Finn."

"Yeah yeah, I know, but it's at least fun for a couple of hours."

Shaun frowned at me, and I bit back the apology before it could slip off my tongue. He hated it when we apologised for living. Besides, his frown had nothing to do with my talking about drinking.

"Look, at least if I'm in the bar, she's nowhere near me, right?"

"You're lusting after her and you don't want to." Concern deepened Shaun's Welsh twang, making his words trip over themselves. "How is getting drunk going to help the situation?"

"I'll forget for a couple of hours."

"It's not a good idea."

I nodded. "Possibly."

"No possibly about it. All common sense goes out the window when you drink."

"I don't want to think so much anymore."

"Think! For a second, just think." Shaun growled, his expression turning frantic. "Where will you go after you get drunk, Finn?"

I'd go to bed.

"You'll go back to your room where Abi'll be waiting for you and you'll make a fucking mistake."

"That won't happen."

Shaun snorted. I shook my head. "Christ, have some faith in me." Shaun glanced over his shoulder. He leaned forward, almost like he hid the phone from someone.

"I'm getting married in a couple of months," he whispered. "And my wife-to-be seems to be attached to the idea of *your* wife."

I stopped, my head spinning with all the unconnected shit.

"She has her heart set on befriending her, Finn. I'm under strict orders not to get involved."

"Mona is choosing my wife over *me?*" I shouted, absolutely outraged. "Put that bloody Scot on the phone."

Shaun chuckled. "I've tried. Don't waste your breath."

I sat back on the bed, the blood draining from my face as my shoulders sagged. "Okay, so I've lost Mona… I think I can deal with that?"

Silence followed my question and I glanced down at the screen, expecting the connection to have dropped. Instead, I found Shaun staring at me like I'd lost my mind.

"Some wingman you are," I grumbled. "Clearly, I should have called Jackson."

"Good luck with that. Pretty sure he's busy trying to talk his lawyer into fucking him." Shaun tilted his head, realisation flickering through his eyes. "On second thought, yeah, call him."

I'd hoped talking to Shaun would help clear my head, but muddled, conflicting wants still confused the ever-loving shit out of me. Should have known calling the sensible one of the four Kings of Screen would backfire on me.

"Thanks for nothing, asshole."

"Don't be a reckless tosser, Finn." With that parting warning, Shaun hung up.

I stared at the glowing patio and setting sun for less than ten seconds before the devil on my shoulder chipped in.

Fuck it.

"What is an Irish coffee?" Abi asked, her nose scrunching up.

Abi leaned against my side, almost falling off her stool at the bar. Don't ask me how it happened. I'd been on my third glass of whisky when she walked in, looking far too delicious in her low-cut sundress and sandal heels.

"*Dotey*, you don't like coffee."

She grinned up at me, her head lolling against my shoulder. A giggle slipped past her lips.

The barman might have surrendered the bottle to us and we might have emptied it. Distantly, I knew tomorrow would be painful, but I couldn't make myself regret it when that happy buzz thrummed through my veins.

"So not a good idea?"

"You'd hate it, so definitely not."

"Okay," she sighed.

How a sigh could sound happy, I had no fucking clue, but I needed to hear it again.

Her eyelids fluttered shut and she sagged further against me. Instinctively, I wrapped an arm around her waist, saving her from a painful fall to the marble titles. I could just imagine the accusations of abuse the tabloids would levy at me if a photo of her with so much as a bruise on her arm surfaced.

No negative shit allowed.

I squeezed her against me, enjoying holding her far too much. Tomorrow I'd blame the booze.

"Abi?"

"Hmm?"

"This isn't the best place to fall asleep."

"Okay," she sighed again as she turned her face more firmly into my shoulder.

I blinked at the row of brightly lit liquor bottles lined up on the wall in front of me. All of them danced.

Maybe Abi has the right idea.

I gestured for the bartender's attention. He wandered over, his brows rose as he spied the empty whisky bottle.

"Can you add this to our room?"

At his nod, I slid out of my seat carefully, turning to catch

Abi before she face-planted into my seat. She groaned as I slid an arm beneath her legs.

"Where are we going?" she mumbled, one word flowing into the next.

"To bed."

"Hmm… yes, please." Her voice deepened, grating across my skin like nails down my back.

Two words and she had me hard. Un-fucking-believable.

I carried her back to the room while her fingers toyed with the buttons on my shirt and she pressed open-mouth kisses to my neck and shoulder. Concentration eluded me, putting one foot in front of the other proved difficult.

"You need to stop, *Dotey*." I frowned at the boardwalk leading out to the bungalows. I remembered it being wider. "We'll be going for a swim if I'm not careful."

Mercifully, or unfortunately, she stopped. Her fingers dug into her clutch, hunting for what I hoped was our room key. The reprieve didn't last long. She clutched the old-school key in her hands and went right back to nibbling my neck.

"Abi," I groaned.

I knew this was a bad idea. Now if only I could remember why, so I could reason with my idiot self.

"Yes?" she hummed against me.

Our bungalow appeared out of nowhere. Grateful, I stopped at the door and waited for her to unlock it. She didn't even notice that we'd stopped, her teeth and lips continued wreaking havoc on my shredded self-control.

"Can you get the door, Abi?" The words came out strangled.

Just like my cock felt. It pressed hard against the zipper of my shorts. Every step I took, bumped Abi against me, both teasing and torturous.

She lifted her head. Her lust-filled gaze met mine and she licked her lips. The final thread snapped on my control as her focus dropped to my lips. I don't know who moved first, but our lips crashed together, need overriding everything else.

Our tongues duelled. Teeth nipped. Her hands roamed. Desperation won out over sense and sensations overloaded me.

"Open the door," I panted, breaking the kiss long enough to press her to the door. She dragged her kiss-swollen lips between her teeth and I groaned. "Abi. Open the door before I fuck you right here for anyone to see."

Her eyes widened, interest flickering across her face. She slotted the key in the lock before my whisky-addled brain decided a little exhibitionism would be a good idea.

The door swung open and she wrapped her arms around my neck again. Her sinful mouth returned to torturing me before I'd even taken a step.

"About time you carried your bride over a threshold," she mumbled. Her lips caressed my neck again, grinning I assumed.

I snorted. "That a secret kink?"

"Nope," she said before sucking on my throat.

I almost doubled over as lightning shot down my spine. *One foot in front of the other.*

Kicking the door shut, I rushed across the room and lowered her to the bed. She sprawled across the sheets, a dazed look in her eyes and a smile curling her lips.

"The tying me up thing though…" Her eyes fluttered shut on a sigh. "That might be one."

"That can be arranged," I said, my voice hoarse.

I lay down on my side next to her. She rolled into me, her fingers driving into my hair. Her lips crashed against mine, stealing my breath with her eagerness. My hand rested on her hip, clutching her dress in a tight fist, before gliding down her thigh, searching for the hem.

"Please," she whispered against my mouth as I grazed her bare skin.

Before I could follow through, Abi threw her leg over my hip and pushed me back against the mattress. She shifted until she sat on top of me, her bite-able ass resting against my cock and her hands holding me down. She rocked against me, unleashing a strangled gasp. A knowing grin overtook her features.

"Fuck," I gasped as she did it again.

My fingers pressed against her hips, urging her on. Her sundress covered nearly every inch of her, but I couldn't make myself care when pleasure thrummed along my nerve endings. Then I blinked and missed the moment she tore it over her head and launched it across the room.

She giggled at my slack-jawed expression.

"Careful, Finn. You'll make me think you genuinely like me." Abi grinned before rolling her hips again.

"Can't have that," I ground out while my gaze dropped to her pussy.

That should have been my cue to stop.

I didn't. Need bit at me, urging me to move the show along, but I just wanted to revel in the feel of her soft skin beneath my fingertips. Then she twisted her hips and robbed me of the ability to breathe.

I shot upright, pulling her tighter against me. Her gasp turned to a pleased sigh, skittering across my neck while my hands roamed her body. I caught her lips, enjoying the way she melted against me far too much for my own sanity.

Thankfully, the buzz of whisky masked the warning inside my head.

With a quick snap of my fingers, I freed her from her bra and leaned into teasing her. I traced a line from her lips to her nipples, taking great pleasure in every quiet cry to fall from her lips. Her fingers tightened in my hair and her back arched as I sucked on a nipple.

"Finn, please. Oh my god." Words spewed from her lips, almost lost in a string of gasps and moans.

I grinned, my lips curling against her tit. If she never stopped making those sounds, I'd...

Do nothing. Because we shouldn't be doing this.

The warning bounced off me and I turned us, lowering Abi onto the bed. Her grip on my hair loosened as I kissed my way down her body, learning every inch of her like a starved man. I slid off the bed, my fingers hooking in her lacy underwear and dragging them down her legs without delay.

She draped her legs over my shoulders, her toes curling into my back before I could do more than skim my hands up her thighs. After nearly four days of resisting her, all of my chill evaporated. The teasing had gone on long enough.

I grazed a knuckle through her wet folds and her hips jolted.

"Careful, Abi. I'll think you're eager for me."

Her head thrashed to the side as I circled her clit. I licked my lips at the wetness coating my fingers, her folds soaking for me.

"You'd be right," she whispered, a vulnerable edge to her voice I must have imagined.

I lowered my head, desperate to taste her.

I'm in perfect control. I can stop whenever I want.

Then I tasted her.

She writhed beneath me at the first lap of my tongue, her hips shifting, both trying to escape and urge me on all at once. My fingers delved inside of her, crooking to drag against her inner walls. She clenched around me, flooding my mouth with more sweet liquid. Her fingers twisted in my hair, but I could barely feel the painful bite.

Her hips rocked against me and I pressed a forearm across her stomach, holding her down while I tortured her with a mixture of slow and hard strokes. My cock strained against my shorts, begging for release, but I couldn't make myself rush. I enjoyed the sounds of her cries, my name falling from her lips, one minute an expletive and the next a benediction. I worshipped her, taking her to the brink of orgasm twice before letting her fall over the edge, craving those little sounds far more than sober Finn would.

She cried out, her hips bucking against my hands. Then she relaxed into the bed, sighing with a sound of contentment I could get addicted to. I couldn't get enough of her sweet taste, couldn't stop lapping up at her.

Her tight grip on my shoulders relaxed. I pressed a soft kiss to her hip before climbing back onto the bed and laying a trail of kisses along her stomach, her breasts, her neck as I went. She hummed and stretched with every caress. Each sound shot straight through me, teasing me with a light feeling I craved far more than I'd ever let anyone know.

Her long lashes framed her closed eyes, the picture of perfect innocence and not the woman who effortlessly rammed at my defences to keep her at arm's length. Her lips parted slightly, making me want to devour her all over again. Then her breathing evened out and my stomach sank.

"Abi?"

No response came.

My gaze roamed her face, finally taking in the sight of her wild auburn hair sprawled out beneath her, haloing her sweet sleeping expression. No one would suspect her of being an addictive hellion when she looked like that. My cock ached, but I ignored it and tugged the sheets back. I picked her up again, tucking her into bed and kissing her forehead like the sappy, drunken idiot I was.

Tomorrow I'd slam myself over it.

CHAPTER FOURTEEN

ABI

I stretched in bed, a sense of relaxation filling me. I almost missed it under the screaming headache stabbing behind my eyes. It had been a while since I'd felt so relaxed. I soaked it in, enjoying the caress of the sheets against my bare, sensitive skin.

Then the memories crashed in, flickering before my eyes and heating my face.

I turned my head slowly, grateful that for once I hadn't woken wrapped around Finn. He lay on his side, facing me, his eyes thankfully closed. I didn't know what I expected to find: the spitfire glaring at me or a blank schooled expression. I'm not sure which would have been worse.

Five days ago, Finn wouldn't have let me maul him, drunk or not. I'm not even sure he would have carried me back to our room or sat in the bar with me for hours sharing a bottle. He would have turned his back on me before I'd even sat down. Well, at least that's what I thought he would have done.

Aside from a couple of weird moments, he'd never actually been mean to me.

Maybe we did have a chance after all.

Before I could get too comfortable, his eyes snapped open, fixing on me. Pinched lines formed on his forehead and around his eyes. He covered his face, groaning at the light streaming in.

"Should have shut the fucking curtains," he growled into his pillow, his voice strangled with pain.

My head hurt, but I could stand the light without it making it all worse.

"I can grab some painkillers."

"No, I don't need your kindness right now."

I frowned at the brutal snap of his voice. After last night, I expected some kind of shift.

"I don't mind," I said despite the urge to press my lips together and say no more.

Why does he have to be so confusing?

Finn groaned, the sound muffled by the pillow. "You're overthinking shit right now, aren't you?" He turned his head slightly, catching the surprise dancing across my face. He frowned. "We were drunk. It didn't mean anything."

Something in my chest squeezed painfully tight at those words. "Is that what you say to every woman you share a bed with?"

Despite a slight tic of his jaw, his gaze roamed my face perfectly blank. If I didn't have memories of him desperate beneath me, I'd think he'd used me. I couldn't believe that he had, even though it would make resisting him so much easier.

Silence stretched between us, filled only by the rocking of the water beneath us. I stared into his sapphire eyes, refusing to be the one who looked away. If he wanted to pretend he'd felt nothing, I'd make him work for it.

"Let's forget it happened," Finn said, his voice sharp in the tranquil silence of the bungalow.

What if I didn't want to forget?

"**W**here are we going now?" I asked, barely restraining a pained groan.

The fact they'd loaded us into four-wheel drives didn't bode well, honestly.

A guide drove the car while Tyler chatted with him in the front seat. Liam sat in the row in front of us, his camera resting on the seat next to him. They'd rigged GoPros around us to capture who knew what. Finn had barely looked at me since this morning. Nothing but awkward silence filled the back seat.

Then again, after Finn's suggestion that the show intended to use our fears to heighten the drama, I couldn't help but look for the possible sting points.

What do I fear that could come from remote, bumpy terrain?

Turned out, I didn't need to think hard. They pulled off the main road, taking a narrow lane buffered by trees. Branches slapped against the open sides as we barrelled down a dirt path. Some might have called it a road, but seriously, if another car came at us, we'd all be screwed.

"There's a private beach at the end of the track," Tyler called back to us. He turned slightly, grinning at us. "Finn's taking you for a sunset picnic."

I sided-eyed Finn. "Is he now?"

Finn rolled his eyes. "Sure," he drawled. "Because I get any say in this farce."

I chuckled and Finn smiled. It lit up his sapphire eyes and gifted me a very real peek into the real Finn. My heart warmed at the sight.

Then a small black and red bug landed on the ledge of my door and the moment passed. I squeaked. For a second, it was nothing but a bug. Then my brain caught up and I scrambled into Finn's lap with a barely muffled shriek.

He stiffened beneath me, but I didn't care, I wrapped my arms around his neck and tucked my legs tight to my body.

"Get it away from me," I cried. My eyes widened as it crawled along the door. It got no closer, but it was already too close for comfort. "Finn, please." I didn't even care that I sounded whiny and pitiful, begging him to rescue me from a tiny bug.

"Get the camera on her, Liam," Tyler snapped from the front seat.

Liam scrambled for his camera, shifting in his seat. Not an easy feat with the car jerking down the dirt path.

I really fucking hate spiders.

Finn's arms wrapped around me at last. He rubbed my back, squeezing me to his chest.

"Shh, Abi. It'll go away now."

"No, it won't." I whimpered as the spider crawled towards Liam. He didn't pay it any mind. Tears burned my eyes while my heart pounded. "It looks venomous"

Finn placed a finger beneath my chin and forced my head back to meet his gaze. It freed me from staring at the spider, but equally, it made my fear spiral.

"How do you know that?"

"The hourglass. Know thy enemy," I muttered, surprised Finn had to ask. I'd always thought it was common to learn everything you can about the things you feared. How else was I meant to avoid them? "I've hated spiders since I was six, when one bit my mother in our kitchen. I developed a slightly obsessive interest in learning about them after that."

I shuddered at the memory of the false widow climbing out of a bag of bananas while I distracted my mother with some inane question or another. I couldn't even remember the question.

Finn studied me, his expression softening in complete

contrast to the rock-solid tension riding my body and face. He smiled, his sapphire eyes shining with something gentle for the first time all morning.

"You're full of surprise, *Dotey*."

I frowned at that but a motion in the corner of my eye caught my attention before I could figure out his meaning.

"Finn," I whispered, his name drawn out as horror stabbed at me.

"You might want to move, Liam." Finn continued to stroke my back and arms, despite the spider crawling towards the cameraman. "Of course, you could get the shots but I'm pretty sure even you value your life above this orchestrated bullshit."

"I resent that," Tyler shouted from the front.

"Oh really?" Finn drawled.

If I turned my head, I'd find him smirking. I didn't look to confirm. Fear froze me in place while Liam hadn't so much as shifted away from the car door. He continued to lean against it, his face pressed against the viewfinder.

"Yes. I didn't orchestrate anything."

"Oh, so you aren't knowingly bringing Abi into a mountain range knowing she's terrified of spiders?" When Tyler didn't answer, Finn's voice hardened. "Yeah, that's exactly what I thought." He patted me on the thigh. I'd assumed he meant to comfort me, but then he turned my face towards him. "I'm going to have to put you down on the seat for a second."

I shook my head hard. The urge to beg and plead with him thumbed through me.

"You don't want anyone to get bitten, do you Abi girl?" Finn asked, his voice low and honey-sweet. I shook my head. "Good, then let me get rid of the spider and then I'll put you back in my lap, okay?"

Finn broke my grip on his neck with ease. He gently placed me in the seat next to him and then he unclipped a

GoPro, over Tyler's protests. I shuffled into his seat, getting as far from the spider as possible. My entire body shook and my breathing started to hurt. I couldn't take any more of these fright exercises.

"Shut up, jackass. I'm not touching the thing with my hand."

A clunk sounded followed by the plop of something hitting the seat in front and clattering to the ground.

Then Finn's spicy scent engulfed me again.

"It's gone," he whispered near my ear.

His hand forced its way under my clenched legs and his arm came around me back. I released my death grip on my legs and glanced around. He lifted me with ease from the next seat, then shuffled us into the middle, pressing me to his chest.

Liam still had the camera pointed at us. Honestly, I couldn't tell if he'd even reacted to the spider. The spot for the second GoPro stood empty, but I wasn't surprised Finn hadn't put it back. One less camera to capture my meltdown.

"We need to have words about your tactics, Tyler," Finn called, a threat thrumming through the words.

Despite the anger vibrating in his voice, he smoothed a hand down my hair and back with gentle care. I lay my head against his chest and shut my eyes, exhaustion sweeping over me.

Just take a minute.

I sagged against Finn, trusting him to look after me.

FINN

For the first time since we'd turned off the main road, Abi relaxed. Did I wish she'd relaxed in a seat on her own and not curled up on my lap with her irresistible heat burning against me and her head in the crook of my neck? Abso-fucking-lutely.

Would I move her?

Listen, I wasn't that much of a jackass. I knew my strengths and abandoning her when terrified was not one of them.

"It needs to stop, Tyler. You're dancing dangerously close to psychological abuse here."

Abi shifted, her head tilting back until she rested against my shoulder. Her previously panicked expression smoothed out, relaxing in sleep. Without thinking, my hand rose from her side, gliding along her jaw and into her auburn hair, clenching. The strands wrapped around my wrist, silky soft.

I couldn't tear my gaze from hers. Tyler shouted at me from the front but I barely heard him, too focused on the sleeping woman in my arms. How could she sleep after the fright she'd had?

Why couldn't I push her away? I felt like a broken bloody record, pushing her away and caving the second she showed me even an inch of need. With the dinner, the sharks, the zipline and now this.

I needed to be stronger.

And then she smiled, nuzzling her face against my shoulder like I was the only person she trusted to keep her safe. My chest squeezed tight, an ache forming that I had never experienced with a woman. Not even my family.

Forget stronger, I needed to be careful.

Tyler, Producer: Things looked very cosy in the back seat today.

Finn: Is that why you keep exposing Abi to her biggest fears?

Tyler, Producer: That was only a coincidence.

Finn: Nice line change. It was a purposeful action that could have resulted in your cameraman going to the hospital or Abi hurting herself while she freaked out. If you keep going, Abi'll be able to sue you for psychological damage, you do realise that, right?"

Tyler, Producer: How about we talk about you instead? You're very quick to comfort her. I'm surprised.

Finn: Unlike you, Tyler, I'm not an unfeeling asshole. Stop trying to hurt her, or I'll make sure any line in your contract you think protects you gets voided.

Tyler, Producer: Before you go, you might like to know that there are no venomous creatures in Bora Bora.

CHAPTER FIFTEEN

FINN

"Oh, Christ!" I shouted the moment I opened my eyes the next morning. My entire body jolted at the surprise. "Abi, why the fuck are you staring at me while I sleep?"

She sat beside me, her legs crossed and her hands pressed together, barely restraining her excitement. That grin did not help the whole look. Even if her blue eyes looked incredible, lit up with that much joy…

Or was it mischief?

"I had an idea and I think you'll love it."

"That does not explain the staring." I rubbed my heavy lids and shuffled up to lean against the headboard. "Seriously, it's bad enough we're living together. Don't make it creepy."

Her grin collapsed.

It was just a smile on the face of a woman who shouldn't still be my wife. What did it matter in the grand scheme of things?

Still, I missed it.

"Do you want to avoid the crew or not?"

My brows rose. The distracting war for logical action inside my mind quieted.

"How?"

"Exactly as I thought." She nodded, her excitement slipping through again.

Abi scrambled off the bed and started pacing. I bit my lip on a groan when my gaze tracked down her body. She wore an oversized white man's shirt, *my shirt*, buttoned to her cleavage, and nothing else. It barely covered her ass and her pacing did not help the material stay in place.

My eyes narrowed on the shirt. *Why is she wearing my shirt?* The damn thing looked good on her.

Or maybe it wasn't the way she looked but the fact she'd dressed in *my* clothes, *my* scent. My cock hardened at the sight of it.

She stopped pacing at my silence, turning slowly to study me with an arched brow. "Are you listening, McCarthy?"

No. Who the hell would be able to?

"Carry on," I said, forcing the gravelly notes of arousal from my voice.

My gaze tracked down her shapely legs while she continued talking. I caught snippets, but not enough to make any of it make sense.

"You have a serious attention problem, don't you?" Abi muttered, exasperation reducing her voice to a growl.

She glided towards me, those intense blue eyes fixed on me while the little minx swayed her bloody hips. I swallowed, my mind well and truly in the gutter while the voice of logic faded.

Her fingers gripped my chin, forcing me to meet her gaze as she leaned over me. Amusement clashed with annoyance, her lips pinched but her eyes smiling— if eyes could even smile.

"Are you going to listen to me now?"

I nodded and her fingers danced across my skin.

"They want us to be intimate, so let's make them believe we are." She kept her voice low and soft, barely above a whisper. "If we stay in the bungalow, they can't force a camera in our faces. If they knock, we make them think we're…*engaged*. We'll order room service for every meal and actually enjoy a day without Tyler questioning us or forcing adrenaline-producing activities on us." Her brows quirked when I said nothing. "Any questions?"

"You want us to bunk off filming together?"

She tilted her head, confusion scrunching up her nose. "Bunk off?"

"Skip."

"Oh! Yes, that's exactly what I want to do." She frowned. "Don't you?"

A day locked in a bungalow with the woman turning my common sense to mush? Sure. What could possibly go wrong?

ABI

For a moment, I didn't think he'd agree. He seemed reluctant and a little skittish. He gave in with a tight nod and then vanished into the bathroom without another word. For all of ten minutes, I worried that he'd rather face the cameras than be trapped in the bungalow with me all day.

Then the first knock came.

I sat up straight in bed, panic squeezing my voice box. Finn's brows rose at me when he stepped out of the bathroom, water dripping from his hair and a towel wrapped around his waist. His sapphire eyes seemed to dare me to follow through.

My eyes dipped, tracing the glistening lines of his six-pack. *Follow through with what?*

He cleared his throat, and then I remembered.

I'd said we'd make noises. I'd meant sexual noises and, by the smirk curling his lips and the glimmer of a dare in his eyes, I was pretty sure he knew that.

Our gazes locked and my face heated. Another knock, and this time, Tyler called our names.

Finn crept towards me, indecision warring across his face.

I'd wanted the experience of the show, a break from my mundane life, but I'd also been hoping for more. It would be far too easy for me to fall for Finn.

He almost reached the bed, and panic gripped me.

A loud moan fell from my lips and the knocking stopped. Finn's gaze fell to my lips, avid interest in his eyes. I did it again and again, louder, throwing in his name for good measure. Through it all, our gazes locked, his burning with what I hoped was desire.

His hands clenched at his sides, almost as if he wanted to reach out and grab me… maybe he would if the expanse of the bed didn't separate us?

It could have been a trick of the light, but I thought his towel tented.

None of it helped keep my mind from replaying our short-lived night, the way he'd held me, watched out for me and then made me come all over his face.

Minutes passed before we heard the distant sound of the boards bouncing on the boardwalk. By the time they gave up, my face burned and my pussy ached while Finn's eyes had darkened.

I scrambled off the bed and into the bathroom, shutting the door on Finn before he could say anything.

❄

FINN

I'd been wrongfully sceptical. I'd expected a day of boredom and torture agreeing to remain locked in the bungalow with Abi. Instead, we spent our time on the patio, reading in companionable silence, laughing over one tiny thing or another.

After five days of second-guessing and stressing about how I'd appear on camera, I could relax for once. Maybe that would come back to bite me one day soon, but in the moment, I couldn't care less.

"Why would you get up that early for a show?" I asked, wincing at her.

A tingle of laughter escaped her, the sound wrapping around me like a hug. "Ros is obsessed with the Sanderson brothers. When she found out the three of them would be on Jimmy Michaels's show that week, I didn't have a hope in hell of escaping." Her lips twitched and her eyes shone as she lounged back on the sun lounger, stirring her rapidly melting daiquiri. "She asked my boss for time off before I even knew about it. I had zero excuses left."

I shook my head. "I've never been that dedicated to something."

"Yeah, I'm not surprised." Abi snorted. "You don't look like the fangirling type, Finn." Her brows rose and she leaned towards me, her gaze sweeping up and down my body. "Or are you hiding it?"

I swirled my beer bottle, watching the dregs of the liquid dance. Anything to avoid her eyes and keep the grin off my face.

"Oh, you're so hiding it." She chortled, throwing her legs over the side of her lounger and shifting onto mine. She bumped against my thigh, pushing it aside to make room for herself on the edge. "Out with it. What or who have you fangirled over?"

I sighed, throwing my head back like she'd forced it out of me. "When I first got to LA, I might have lost my cool when I bumped into Bryce Reid at a restaurant." I grimaced, remembering how out of control and cringy I'd been. "He was great about it, but I can't look the man in the eye without feeling a trickle of mortification now."

"That's brilliant." Abi slapped my thigh, her face lit up with amusement. "So you are human like the rest of us. Good to know."

Before I could comment, a knock sounded at the door. I groaned and let my head fall back against the lounger, biting my tongue against the profanities desperate to slip out.

After hours locked in, we had a routine by now. If we were expecting food, one of us would get almost completely undressed and muss up our hair. If the knock was unexpected, we faked sex that left me hard, aching, and at the very edges of control.

"I'll go," I sighed when the knock came again.

"Let me." Abi patted my chest, pushing me back down.

She climbed to her feet, silencing my protests with a look and a finger to her lips. I couldn't sit still when she disappeared into the bedroom.

I followed her in, catching her as she tugged her dress over her head. I stumbled in the doorway, breath trapped in my throat.

"Just a minute," she called to whoever was beyond the door.

All the while my gaze devoured every bare inch of her body, from the black lace cupping the firm ass I'd had my hands all over days ago to her smooth, bare back. How hadn't I noticed her lack of a bra?

She scooped my shirt off the unmade bed and shrugged it on, quickly buttoning it up on her way to the door. She glanced over her shoulder, catching me staring with a smirk.

"Hide," Abi mouthed.

Then she gave me exactly two seconds to follow her command. I jolted away, racing towards the bathroom just as she pressed down on the handle.

"Hi, Abi. Everything alright?" Tyler asked, his voice slow and too rough.

A jolt of possessiveness shot through me. No one else would be ogling her bare skin today. Roughly, I shoved the shorts off my hips and tugged my t-shirt over my head.

Before I couldn't stop to think, I rushed back into the room. I schooled my features into the smarmy look of a well-satisfied man.

"We're great," Abi said. "Just a little busy." Her voice rose, taking on a giggly edge.

"And we're not done yet," I growled as I wrapped my arm around her waist and pulled her into my side.

Abi shivered, glancing up at me with wide, lust-filled eyes that added perfectly to the image of two people completely lost in each other.

"I'm glad to see you're making progress." Tyler grimaced. "But we need to film."

His gaze raked down Abi's length as he spoke, pausing on her bare legs for far too long. It made my blood boil and my fists clenched with the urge to break his fucking nose.

"Sorry, mate, we've got other plans." I grinned at him, forcing the anger back and the lust forward. "Excuse us."

I bent and threw Abi over my shoulder. Before he could do more than splutter, I had the door shut. The second it clicked shut, Abi giggled.

"That was incredible, Finn," she huffed around her laughter.

Her fingers skittered across my back, searching for somewhere to hold. Really I should have removed my hand from her ass and put her down. Instead, I found myself standing in the middle of the room, breathing a little too hard.

"Finn?" Abi asked, her giggles dying and her tone turning tentative. "Are you alright?"

Abi wiggled in my grip and my hand tightened on her ass. She squeaked in surprise, but she didn't fight again. No, instead the little minx let her hand drift to my ass, gripping me in what could be an innocent move.

My body didn't care.

And that was a problem.

With jerky movements, I paced to the bed and lay her down. Her face was flushed, her auburn hair sprawled out on the white sheets, and her blue eyes sparking with desire I had no business feeding.

"Sorry," I muttered, backing away. I made a beeline for the bathroom and my abandoned clothes, squeezing the nape of my neck and willing the burn of need to fade.

"Wait," she cried.

"I need a minute, Abi."

Whether she heard the struggle in my voice or not, I couldn't say.

CHAPTER SIXTEEN

ABI

*H*alf an hour later, I heard the bathroom door click open. Unfortunately for Finn, he'd given me twenty minutes too long to soak in my confidence.

Room service delivered our food and drinks, and the blush burning my cheeks chilled out. I took the executive decision to set everything up by the hot tub we hadn't used once.

It would be a shame to leave without testing it out...

I repeated that line to myself as I changed into my bikini, turned the tub on, and slipped into the heated water.

At no point did I think it would be a bad idea. That is until Finn stepped onto the patio and froze.

"What are you doing, Abi?" he asked, suspicion rife in his tone.

"What does it look like?" Somehow, I pulled off nonchalant.

Or I thought I did. Finn didn't relax and he didn't climb in.

"Drink?" I pushed his new bottle a little closer to the hot tub entrance.

His jaw ticked and his fists clenched at his sides. The actor breaking character.

"I'm not getting in there."

"Okay." I picked up my refreshed cocktail and took a sip, watching him all the while over the rim.

"I'm serious."

"Okay."

Amusement bubbled beneath the surface but I held tight to it. No need to let him know I didn't believe him.

He spun on his heel, stomping back inside with a huff. My shoulders shook with silent laughter. I didn't want to question why I enjoyed testing him. He rarely reacted so it couldn't have been because I enjoyed the reaction.

When he returned moments later wearing swimming trunks, joy burst through me and I barely restrained it. I bit my lip, sinking lower beneath the water.

He climbed in, grumbling under his breath and glaring at me. I just smiled back at him sweetly. *Nothing to see here.*

"Happy?" he grunted.

I lifted my brows in question, keeping up the innocent routine. He sank beneath the water, glaring at me, and my grin broke free.

"At least I know you're not acting with me now."

"Is that right?"

"In front of the cameras, you're all lovely and sweet. Perfect doting husband material." I chuckled to myself, thinking about the shocked look on Tyler's face when I opened the front door. "I don't think you're as convincing to the crew as you think you are. But I can tell." I gestured at his scowling face. "This is the normal I expect when we're alone."

His expression smoothed out and his shoulders relaxed beneath the water. I eyed him with suspicion, searching for clues as to whether he'd slipped back into character.

"Don't shut it down on my account." I feigned boredom and sipped my drink.

"What does that mean?" His eyes narrowed on me, scanning every inch he could see both above and beneath the bubbles.

Playing with fire would not keep my heart safe from Finn McCarthy, but then safety was wildly overrated. I'd joined the show for a break from the mundane. Maybe I needed to take a couple of risks along the way.

Finn lifted his head, catching sight of me next to him. He studied me, his sapphire gaze darkening the longer he traced my features. His focus dropped to my lips and I instinctively dragged the bottom one into my mouth.

His hand coasted out of the water and up to my jaw. He rubbed a thumb across my lower lip, freeing it from my teeth.

One second, he stared at me with indecision. The next, our lips slammed together. His arm wrapped around my waist, tugging me into his lap to straddle him. I jolted at the hard press of his cock against my eager core. His other hand slid from my jaw and into my hair, gripping it tightly and tilting my head to his liking.

Nerves fluttered in my belly, but they had nothing on the empty clench of my pussy.

Five days in close proximity to Finn had not been easy on me. I could push the need away when I thought he didn't want me, but he kissed *me*.

Our tongues danced and my hips jolted almost with a mind of their own. We groaned at the delicious motion. His fingers gripped my hips, urging me to keep grinding myself against him.

Time lost all meaning. Dolphins could have jumped from the water in front of me and I wouldn't have noticed. Every fibre of my being focused on the enigma of a man beneath me.

Finn's hands coasted up my torso, cupping my breasts. He

teased me through the bikini top, toying with my peaked nipples through the fabric of my top, tearing another groan from deep in my throat.

The strings loosened and the top went flying to who knew where. I couldn't focus on anything more than the thrum of pleasure coasting through me, chasing the buzz of pressure against my clit.

Then he broke the kiss, his head dipping. His bearded jaw grazed against my skin, scattering goose bumps across my chest. The heat of his mouth latched onto my breast and any air I'd pulled in exploded from my lungs.

As delicious as the friction felt, it wasn't enough.

"Finn," I moaned. My fingers delved into his hair, holding him to me, desperate for more and for nothing to change all at the same time.

He hummed, the sensation vibrating through me as he sucked harder on my nipple. His free hand glided down to my ass, palming me more firmly against him.

"It's not enough." I hated how needy I sounded, but fuck.

Finn lifted his head, smirking at me before capturing my lips again. Still not what I needed.

Then he shuffled forward. I frowned, confused by the movement, but unwilling to break from the kiss. His rock-hard heat pressed against my core, burning through the bikini bottoms, unhindered by fabric.

When the strings on my bottoms loosened, it all started to make sense and I wasted no time, teasing him as I rubbed myself along his cock. The pressure built fast, coiling until I couldn't feel much more than a mindless sensation.

Finn gripped my hips, forcing me to rock faster and faster against him while his tongue danced with mine, stoking the fire.

My release snapped into place, locking up my muscles until I couldn't do more than cry out. Finn didn't stop. He pressed me harder against me, rocking his hips and dragging me against his cock. He broke the kiss and I fell forward, burying my face in his neck.

With each glide of him against my swollen clit, little flutters of aftershocks went off, stealing my breath and making me groan against his burning skin.

"Oh, fuck," he grunted as his body tensed up beneath me and he stilled.

Finn's fingers dug into my hips, holding me still. His heart beat wildly against my chest, almost matching my own.

For countless moments, neither of us moved or spoke. My muscles trembled against him while the shock of what we'd done settled in my mind. *At least he got off this time.*

He released a ragged breath and stiffened beneath me. The tiny flutters of happiness fizzled out, replaced by trepidation that turned my stomach. Hesitantly, I straightened up, leaning back to assess his face.

My heart dropped at the sight of his closed-off expression.

"This can't happen again," he whispered, his voice devoid of feeling.

I could only nod as he pushed me away from him and scrambled out of the hot tub. He rushed inside, leaving his shorts floating in the hot tub.

Mindlessly, I gathered our discarded clothing and climbed out. My hands shook as I wrapped a towel around myself.

Rejection stabbed at my heart and for a second self-doubt crept in. *What did I do wrong?*

Cold logic slapped me and my jaw clenched.

He knew what he was doing when he reached for me. Yes, I tempted him, but he didn't have to say yes, he didn't have to strip me bare and dry fuck me.

CHAPTER SEVENTEEN

FINN

"Absolutely not," I growled at the producer. "It's five fucking AM. I don't care what you have planned. We're not doing it."

I went to shut the door, annoyance swirling dangerously inside of me. After screwing up with Abi last night, I was already on edge. Didn't matter how many times I reasoned with myself, it didn't change the fact I'd given in to the allure of her again.

And we weren't even pissing drunk.

"Wait, Finn."

Tyler placed his foot in the doorway, catching the door before it could slam shut. It bounced back, slamming against the wall. The noise couldn't disguise Tyler's wince of pain. *Serves him right.*

"I'm sure Abi will love it and you're already up," Tyler said, his tone soft and pleading.

He smiled and I narrowed my eyes.

"Will she actually love it, or is that code for another hell trap designed to force her to face yet another fear?"

Tyler shrugged. "Her questionnaire suggested she'd enjoy it."

The need to slam the door in his face again stabbed at me, but if she really would enjoy it… I owed her.

I couldn't explain my actions without giving her more of myself, and I wasn't willing to do that.

I still couldn't say for certain that she wasn't after my money. Why else would someone agree to marry a celeb and bare their lives to the criticism of strangers? Surely it wasn't just for the thrill of it all.

The faster we got home and I could put space between us, the more in control I'd be. It wouldn't matter how much she drew me in, there would be plenty of things to distract me, plenty of distance.

I sighed. "Fine, but you're going to have to give us a minute." I glanced over my shoulder, taking in Abi's serene form. "Abi's still asleep."

ABI

"Next time you knock on my door at stupid o'clock in the morning, I'll slam it harder," Finn muttered, his tone low and threatening as he glared at Tyler.

"I don't know what you're talking about." Tyler's barely restrained smirk belied his nonchalance.

"Fucking couples yoga." Finn fumed as the instructor told us to change positions.

I could understand Tyler's smirk. Finn McCarthy doing yoga was a sight to behold. For someone with so much muscle, he couldn't balance for shit.

"None of your training for action films involved yoga?" I

asked, turning my head away so he couldn't see my gleeful amusement.

"No," he ground out. "Surprisingly, bending at inhumane angles isn't a requirement."

I chuckled at his pained groan as his hamstrings stretched out and he wobbled.

"Laugh it up, sweetheart." He glared at me. "You're never getting me to do this again."

"Well, I didn't ask you to, but sure, let's point the blame at me."

For the next thirty minutes, I blocked him out and focused on my body and our incredible surroundings. The pink of the rising sun painted the sky, glistening and bouncing off the open water before the patio. An expanse of lawn swept up to the main hotel building set on the hill behind us.

Aside from the rustle of the crew's clothing, Finn's occasional grunt and Tyler's muttered orders, peaceful silence surrounded us. With money and time being so tight in New York, it had been a while since I'd done a sunset yoga session. I'd forgotten how much I enjoyed it. How much I'd missed it and the myriad of other hobbies I'd had to sacrifice when Eva got sick.

When the instructor called time, I stretched out, my body deliciously loose. Finn straightened up with a pained groan.

"Where are you going?" I shouted after him.

He ignored me and continued to stomp across the lawn. I threw Tyler an apologetic smile before racing after him at almost a dead run.

"You know, this doesn't look good, right?" I asked as caught up, huffing and puffing.

"I don't care."

"I don't believe that." I gripped his arm, throwing all of my body weight into making him stop. He spun around, shaking me off as if the touch burned. "Wipe that look off your face. You're the one who doesn't want the cameras to see the real you. You care about how the show makes you look to the American public." I pointed at his glare. "That does not give the impression of a man falling for his wife."

"I'm not," he growled.

My brows rose. "I know! But you want *them* to think that." I jabbed a finger towards the film crew gathered on the waterfront patio. "What the hell's gotten into you?"

"Nothing." He crossed his arms.

"Try it again without the scowl."

His agitation melted away before my eyes. His brow smoothed out and his lips curled into a pleasant smile. If it weren't for his sapphire eyes burning with annoyance, I'd think he'd morphed into a different person.

"Okay." I blew out a breath. "Do you want to give them the united front they expect today?"

I held out my hand. He stared at it, making no move to get closer. Instead of reaching for me as I expected, he took a step back, and then another and another.

"I can't, Abi."

My brows shot up. "Let me get this straight." My voice rose as annoyance and embarrassment twinged in my gut. "Grabbing me in the hot tub is perfectly fine, but god forbid, you have to hold my hand in front of the cameras?"

A flicker of true emotion sparked in his eyes. Regret.

"Don't push me, please? I can't do this right now." He backed away, a pleading light entering his eyes. "I'm sorry."

With that, he took off and this time, I let him go. I could feel the burn of Tyler's gaze against the back of my head. He'd ask me a thousand questions and demand an explanation. What on earth would I tell him? I couldn't exactly admit that yesterday had been fake…until it wasn't.

❄

FINN

I'd like to say I didn't know what had gotten into me, but that would be a lie.

Abi had gotten into me, and I needed to get far far away from her before I made more bad decisions. Guilt, lust, and annoyance mingled inside me, churning together until they created a volatile mixture.

Even free diving couldn't quiet the chaos inside my head.

Over a hundred and fifty feet below the surface, surrounded by sharks and the calm of the sea and I couldn't push her out of my head.

By the time I walked into our bungalow after 5 PM, I felt more hopeful.

It quickly died when I caught sight of Abi standing before the mirror wearing a dress that flared out at her hips. Sunlight danced around her while she brushed out her auburn curls.

For a second, words caught in my throat and the awkwardness reared its head again. I squashed it fast. "Why are you dressed up?" I asked, keeping my voice neutral.

She met my gaze in her reflection, her eyes narrowing as she assessed me.

"You ran off before Tyler could drop his latest task in our laps."

My muscles twitched, ready to tense up at the thought of another experiment. I couldn't honestly say I'd keep it together and that was concerning.

I forced my shoulders to remain relaxed as I walked past her, aiming for the shower. Salt coated every inch of my skin and hair.

"We're meeting all the other couples on a sunset cruise. You have half an hour to get ready." The whip of her voice snared me and I turned against my will to find her watching me with her hands on her hips. She looked too damn fuckable with her blue eyes spitting fire and her body bristling for an argument.

"Don't worry. I'll be ready."

An apology formed, desperate to get out, to smooth the tension between us.

I bit it back.

ABI

Forty-five minutes after departure, the yacht weighed anchor as the horizon began to blush with the setting sun. Soft pastel colours lit up the sky, painting yet another beautiful picture.

If not for the changeable actor, I'd miss Bora Bora.

I couldn't lie to myself. I'd miss it because I got to be so close to him.

"Abi, hey," Haley said. She and Anders gathered around me with smiles.

She'd restrained her black lavender-tipped hair in a tight top knot. A pang of envy hit me in the gut for that speck of foresight. I'd taken extra care with my curls, but the moment the yacht got underway all the effort went out the window. If I could avoid the bathrooms, I wouldn't have to know how badly the wind had destroyed it all.

"No Finn?" She glanced around the deck as if he would miraculously appear.

"He's inside grabbing a drink."

I sipped my champagne and tried not to think about the fact he'd gone in for a drink as soon as we boarded and hadn't come back.

"How have you found it all so far?" Haley chuckled, the sound a little strained. "We heard whispers about you and Finn playing hooky yesterday. Tell me you got to have your way with that fine man."

"In a manner of speaking."

"Did they push you as hard as they did us?" Haley asked, changing the subject with an awkward smile.

"In what way?"

She shrugged. "They just seem to relish orchestrating situations we'd hate."

"Like things that would terrify you?" My head tilted, scrutinising their reactions.

"Exactly that." Haley's eyes widened. "Did they do it to you too?" She tapped Anders's arm, inexplicable excitement dancing across her face. "I told you it was planned."

Finn chose that moment to put in an appearance. He settled at my side, a tentative arm around my waist while he greeted Anders and Haley.

I snuck a glance up at him, working hard to keep the surprise from my expression. He smiled and laughed with them, sharing notes about our own brushes with my fears.

The perfect image of a happy couple.

Then I caught sight of Tyler, watching us through a window. His arms were crossed and his focus drilled into Finn. *Had something happened between them?*

"We should ask Aria and Kyle too," Haley said, the excitement draining from her face and voice. "We're already in a high-stress situation. Surely they can't knowingly add to it like that."

"As if they'd care." Finn snorted. His fingers twisted in the material of my dress, grazing my hip in distracting circles. "But you'd be surprised what they can get away with. We signed contracts."

Anders and Haley paled.

Anders tugged Haley closer to his side. "I'm going back to LA with a full training schedule. Life is going to be stressful enough without our producer manipulating us like that."

"It'll be okay." Haley patted his chest. "At least we know what's coming."

Anders hummed in agreement but he didn't look too convinced. At least they seemed genuinely happy together.

I dreaded to think what would happen to us once real life entered the picture.

"Let's go check with Aria and Kyle." Haley stepped back, catching Anders's hand. She rocked back on her heels, her balance shot with the shifting of the yacht. "Maybe they've had a different experience."

The hope leaking from her voice made me wince. I squashed it while they said goodbye and turned to head down the side deck.

For a second, I enjoyed the peace and the heat of Finn's body against mine. Then I remembered we hadn't started the day well and I was still pissed at him.

Maybe I should go inside too…

I pushed away from him, took a tentative step, and the boat rocked extra hard. My heels slipped out from under me with a ripple of sharp pain. My gaze locked on the darkening waves. Other than a thin rope, there wasn't much to stop me from going overboard.

I threw my arms out and squeezed my eyes shut. *Please be strong enough to hold me,* I silently begged the rope.

Heat engulfed me, a hard band wrapping around my waist and throwing me backwards. My eyes flew open as I slammed into Finn's chest. His arms tightened painfully around me, but I had no interest in complaining.

I smoothed a shaky hand along his forearm, patting it while my heart pounded, and a wave of gratitude shook me to my core.

"Are you okay?" Finn asked, his voice hoarse.

"Only thanks to you." I tried to regain my feet and a shot of pain went up my leg. I whimpered, returning all of my weight to him without a moment's thought. "Or maybe not."

He swore and then swept me into his arms without so much as a pause. He took off down the side of the boat, more surefooted than I would have been. I scrambled to wrap my arms around his neck. He might be fearless in the face of the moving yacht, but I really didn't want to take that dip.

"Get me some ice," Finn shouted the second he swept inside. He sat on a sofa, holding me in his lap. "Where does it hurt, Abi?"

His fingers stroked down my calf, brushing lightly over my ankles. I frowned at the side of his head.

"Abi," he growled, cutting me a dark look. "Tell me where it hurts."

Anders dropped a bucket of ice on the sofa and started piling cubes into a tea towel.

"It's just my ankle." I wiggled my toes experimentally. No pain. The second I rotated my ankle, I winced. "Yeah, just my ankle."

Finn's strong fingers engulfed my foot, holding me still. Anders handed him the makeshift ice pack and he gingerly rested it against my skin. I hissed at the sudden cold but held still.

Concern burned in Finn's eyes, his brow creasing with it. I couldn't tell if any of it was real. Hope that he meant it, that he really did care, bit into me, digging its claws into my heart, determined to never let go.

He held me against him, his free hand gripping my side tightly. So tightly, I could have sworn I felt him shake.

"You could have gone overboard," he muttered, emotion riding his voice, deepening his Irish accent. "There are sharks beneath us. You would have panicked."

I narrowed my eyes at his disturbed yet accusatory tone.

"I didn't make the boat rock, Finn."

"I know." He blew out a harsh breath and pressed his forehead to mine. "You scared me," he whispered.

I studied him, the single grain of hope tangling with suspicion. He wouldn't say these things to me now if he truly meant them.

Would he?

The cameras were rolling. The show would milk every second of this display of weakness. I barely watched TV, and I knew viewers would eat this situation up.

But I couldn't tell if he was real.

Swallowing the need to question him, I relaxed in his grip and just enjoyed it. If it all flipped again when we got to LA, at least I had this moment to hold on to.

INTERVIEW VIII

Question: What did it feel like playing Finn's damsel in distress?
Abi: I wasn't playing.
Tyler, Producer: Oh, I know, love.
Abi: And I resent the implication.
Tyler, Producer: Sorry, but for the show, what did it feel like?
Abi: It felt like my ankle was on fire.
Tyler, Producer: Right. You're focusing on the wrong thing.
Abi: Am I?
Tyler, Producer: Yes. Tell me how it felt to have Finn sweep in and rescue you. How did it make you feel having his muscular arms wrapped around you?
Abi: I have a better question. Why do you insist on forcing me to do things I made very clear in my application that I don't want to do?
Tyler, Producer: Uhm…
Abi: Not so fun when it's turned back on you, is it?

CHAPTER EIGHTEEN

ABI

The flight back passed slowly while I wallowed in the post-holiday blues. Although, I guessed the holiday wouldn't end for another two and a half months. It wasn't like I'd be living my normal life in LA.

Finn barely said a word to me the entire time, absorbed in one script or another. I'd tried to get lost in a book, but no romance could hold my attention. Not when the star of my own sat so close, a total enigma I didn't have a hope in hell of keeping.

I didn't know what his normal looked like, but I couldn't imagine it included women like me. Eva had sent me a couple of photos from his red-carpet walks, and I looked nothing like the leggy blondes he paraded around. Especially not with my swollen, bruised ankle.

All the more reason to forget about it …

We passed through the airport quickly, with Finn hiding his face between dark-tinted sunglasses and a baseball cap pulled low over his face. Whenever celebrities pulled that move in movies, I always laughed, but it got us to our pick-up without anyone hassling us, so maybe I'd need to rethink my opinions.

The second we turned the corner to what I assumed would be Finn's house, chaos broke out. A herd of cameras surrounded the guard gate while a crowd of young girls with signs declaring their love to Finn lined the street.

Flashes went off. People shouted and rushed the car.

I jolted back as a sign hit my window. It went by in a blur, but I'm pretty sure it said 'Marry me instead.'

Who the hell were *these people?*

I tried to calm down, knowing there was a camera in the front and smaller cameras rigged all around us.

Another took its place. 'I'll love you better than her.'

Then the cameras came. The flashes blinded me. The windows were tinted, but did that matter with a bright light going off that close?

"Shit," Finn muttered before his hands landed on my face. "Look at me, Abi." He gripped my chin, forcing me to focus on him. "Ignore everything out there."

Staring into his eyes didn't make them all disappear, but it helped, though the banging got worse behind me and people crowded in on his side too.

"Is this normal for you?" I asked, my voice weak.

"Sometimes." He grimaced. "Normally when I've screwed up and caused a scandal. I guess they consider us getting married out of the blue a scandal." Mirth creased his eyes. "Might be the first positive media frenzy I've caused."

The car moved through the gate and the noise died away.

"That's better." His hands fell away and he settled back in his seat. "I hate being one of those Hollywood assholes living in a gated community, but it's worth it for the peace when they're like that."

His voice drifted around me, registering but not. I couldn't shake the fact he'd assigned the word *positive* to us. The man could give me whiplash sometimes.

We stopped outside a massive grey stucco single-storey house before I could shake the optimistic haze from my mind. Finn threw his door open while the cameraman worked his way out of the front seat and the driver beat me to mine.

I winced as I stepped out of the car but smothered it quickly. There had been enough pitying glances at the party and the airport as I hobbled through, refusing to let Finn help me. I could look after myself, I'd done it for years.

My eyes must have been round as saucers as I stared up at the house because Finn chuckled at me.

"It's monstrously big, I know."

"Uh Finn, give us a second to catch up," Tyler called from his open window. Their car had barely stopped when the second cameraman flung his door open.

"If you want the shots, you move at my pace," Finn said, scowling at Tyler. "We already discussed this after your screw-ups in Bora Bora."

Tyler wisely kept his mouth shut. Finn had taken great delight in throwing the show's errors back at him the last few days. I couldn't say I didn't agree with him.

Finn's eyes narrowed on me. I had a second to feel the pressure of concern before he came straight at me. He scoped me into his arms before I could question him.

"I can walk you know," I muttered, indignation dripping from my words.

"I'm aware." Finn continued towards the house at a clipped pace, assuming the cameras would follow.

"Then put me down."

He ignored me and kept moving forward. Scowling, I gave in and wrapped my arms around his neck. No point making myself feel unstable if he wouldn't see reason.

"What about the bags?"

"Frank will handle them."

The driver popped the trunk just as Finn reached the door. He unlocked it and whisked me inside within seconds.

I gasped the moment he crossed the threshold. The ceilings stretched at least nine-foot. White walls contrasted with dark mahogany floors and bright prints on the walls. The front door led into an open plan living room, dining room and kitchen, flowing straight out to a full wall of glass doors that framed the Hollywood Hills. It might have been luxe and ridiculously large for one man, but no one could argue that it wasn't beautiful.

It didn't escape my notice that he'd unintentionally carried me over the threshold like a normal married couple might have done. I squashed the flutter of softer feelings the unconscious gesture inspired. Bora Bora should have taught me not to read into the small things. I'd learn one day.

"There's not a lot to explain. Main living area." Finn gestured at the expanse of space five times the size of my New York apartment.

"Is that a fireplace?" Awe overtook me as I caught sight of the free-standing, oval-shaped black iron. The chimney corkscrewed into the tall ceiling, drawing the eye out the doors to the patio and view.

"Yep," he muttered, his tone rushed and void of emotion. I must have missed him shutting down.

He gingerly put me down, keeping a hand close while I found my feet. An ache twinged in my ankle but I ignored it. Liam used the opportunity to get in front of us. Then Finn wandered off down a hallway leading off the living room without checking that I'd followed.

"All the bedrooms and bathrooms are down here." He stopped at the first door, flinging it open. "This is your room."

A pang of loss that we wouldn't be sharing a bed anymore stabbed at me, but logically I knew separate spaces would be better. Better for my heart and my resistance.

I wandered in, mindful not to move too fast for Liam who had to walk backwards to catch my reaction.

The walls in the bedroom were as white as the main space. All of the furniture carried a shade of deep blue that reminded me of Finn's eyes. Almost like the designer loved them as much as I did. A huge wooden four-poster bed stood proudly in the centre of the room.

If I have to restrain you, I will.

Finn's words echoed in my head while I took it all in. My face burned, but I still turned back to him, smiling.

"I love it."

"Great," he said, his voice soft while he schooled his reactions for the cameras. "You've got your own bathroom and those doors open." He nodded to the wall of glass behind me.

I spun around, my eyes widening at the key feature I'd missed beyond my little sitting area. I had a view! The doors opened directly onto the patio and the pool, stretching out over LA. I resisted the urge to pinch myself. None of it could be real. First Bora Bora and now this? And they were paying me? I had to be dreaming.

"I'm glad you like it," Finn said. He scratched his neck and backed toward the door. "I'll let you get settled in. I need to…" He glanced around at the cameras focused on us. "I have a meeting with my agent. I'll be back for dinner. Order anything you want."

He rushed out of the room.

Liam lowered his camera, frowning at the door. "That wasn't on the schedule."

FINN

"You need to help me," I shouted the second I walked into Shaun's house.

Shaun stood in the kitchen, stirring a pot while Mona chilled at the breakfast bar surrounded by frilly things.

"How did you even know we'd be here?" he asked, incredulity soaking his tone.

"Where else would you be when your next project doesn't start for a week?" I rushed across the open space, dodging the sunken lounge. I waved the whole thing away. "None of that matters. Help me."

Shaun sighed. "I'm not helping you chase Abi off."

Mona gasped. "Absolutely not."

"See?" Shaun pointed at her. "I told you you'd piss *my* wife off."

"She's not your wife *yet*." I collapsed into the seat next to her. "At this rate, you'll have to make Abi a bridesmaid."

I covered my face when Mona squeaked excitedly at the idea.

"Christ woman, it wasn't a suggestion."

"But it's a good suggestion."

Pen scratched across paper.

"What the hell is that?"

"My wedding journal."

I glanced at Shaun, horror widening my eyes. "Tell me she's joking."

Shaun shrugged.

"Sweet Jesus, I'm friends with mad people." The two of them just stared at me, enjoying my pain far too much. "Abi can't be a bridesmaid, Mona. She'll be back in New York by the time you two tie the knot."

Mona laughed.

"I'm serious."

"Sure you are." She went back to glueing things together.

"She can't stay."

"Didn't she move in today?" Shaun asked.

"Yes. That's a problem too."

"I have a perfect idea," Mona said without taking her eyes off the lace.

"To help me get rid of her?" The words came out a little breathier than I'd like to admit.

"Of course not." Mona frowned at me before turning her attention to Shaun. "Put that in the fridge. We're having dinner at Finn's tonight."

"You're what?" I shook my head hard. "No. Absolutely not."

Mona smiled.

Shaun turned the stove off and focused his full attention on me. "Tell you what, I'll help you—"

"Shaun," Mona growled.

"Under one condition." Shaun paused, raising his brows at his fiancée.

"Anything."

"Give us a good reason why you can't see it through."

I stared at him. He couldn't be fucking serious.

"You're not even going to try?" Shaun asked, shock raising his voice.

"Just give me a bloody minute." I held my hand up, staving off more questions.

He knew my history with Natalie, he knew what she'd done to me. Why the hell wouldn't that be enough?

"She's only involved with me for money. She probably wants some kind of fame, they all do." I ticked them off, becoming more and more desperate as Shaun's face remained blank. "I'm not a Hollywood whore, even though the press like to believe it."

"None of that is why she scares you," Mona said, dead serious.

"She doesn't scare me."

"Yes, she does." She grinned at me. "You're terrified she's perfect for you and you'll have no way to stop yourself from falling for her over the next few months."

Shaun's eyes widened. "Is that true?"

"Definitely not."

He frowned. "She's not Natalie, man. If she were, we would have seen it at the wedding." He smirked. "She would have dumped your ass before the bouquet toss for one of the Sanderson brothers."

I scowled at him. My mouth went dry at the very idea.

"See you don't like the thought of her with someone else, do you?"

I gritted my teeth, but kept my mouth shut. I'd underestimated the pair of them.

"So, you're not going to help me?"

Shaun snorted. "Come back to me when you fuck it up and you need help learning how to grovel."

"That's not going to happen." I pushed out of my seat.

"Suit yourself." Shaun straightened up, shrugging.

"I'll call Nathan next time," I muttered, stalking towards the door.

"She's not Natalie, Finn."

"Yeah, yeah, you keep saying that," I called over my shoulder. "I'm still not believing it."

"Natalie would have sold photos of you in Bora Bora to the paps." His words stopped me at their front door. A cold sweat broke out on the back of my neck at the reminder. "You've been off the radar for a full seven days. No new pics until you landed today."

"That doesn't mean anything." I turned to face him, my skin itching. "Maybe she's waiting until I get comfortable."

Mona glanced between us, confusion screaming on her face. "What am I missing?"

Shaun rose a brow. "Do you want to tell her or shall I?"

"Neither of us will." I shot a warning look at Shaun.

"That's not how it works in this house." He shook his head. "Maybe it's time you stopped hiding from it."

Easy for him to say. "No, I think I'm good."

I rushed out of the house fast, grumbling to myself with every step. Shaun knew better than to force that fucking topic on me.

Twenty-year-old Finn trusted far too easily and didn't bother to check for cameras where there shouldn't have been any.

The thought of Abi knowing I'd been stupid enough to let a sex tape get out into the world made me sick. I had no plans to figure out why.

CHAPTER NINETEEN

ABI

The doorbell rang almost two hours after Finn left. I dithered for a couple of seconds, wondering if I should answer it. What if a camera flash went off in my face or one of the fans at the gate had come to make sure they got their shot at Finn?

But then I remembered I lived in a gated community now and the only people able to get to the door had clearance.

Plus, I didn't exactly have anything else to do with my time.

Maybe I should ask Finn for a sewing machine.

I chewed my lip as I padded through the sprawling lounge to the door. The idea had merit, but it felt weird to ask him for things. I could just wait until my first pay cheque from the show and buy my own.

A screen next to the door lit up with a greyed-out video image of a couple on the other side. A short woman smiled into the camera, making it easy to recognise her and the hunk of a man behind her.

Why are they here?

I opened the door tentatively and Mona's smile went up a notch.

"Hey, Abi." She asked, her accent just as interesting as it'd been at the wedding.

"Yes. Finn's not here."

She turned to Shaun, frowning. "He left ages ago."

"Probably sulking in his car somewhere." Shaun shook his head.

Why would he be sulking? His panicked expression when he'd rushed out came to mind. Clearly, I'd done something. I couldn't say what besides walking into a bedroom he directed me to.

"Oh well, can we come in and wait?" Mona asked. "Since it's your first night, we thought we could have dinner together."

I opened the door and gestured them in. "I don't know where anything is, but make yourselves at home."

"Tell me he didn't duck out on you without a proper tour?" Mona gasped when I hesitated. "Shaun."

He sighed. "I'll talk to him."

Mona wandered into Finn's kitchen, her black halter skater dress swaying with each step. She opened a drawer and pulled out a pile of takeaway menus while Shaun opened the fridge and unearthed a big bottle of water.

Did that man ever dress down? He wore a black shirt and cream linen pants, almost casual but not when combined with his perfectly styled hair. I guessed it came with the territory.

It shouldn't have surprised me that they both knew their way around Finn's kitchen. They were his friends, not inter-lopers like me.

"What's your favourite kind of food, Abi?" Mona asked as she shuffled through leaflets. "We can order while we wait for the Irish sod to turn up and face the music."

I hesitated. Something I'd never do over ordering food,

but what if I ordered something Finn hated? Should I even care?

"We should wait. I don't know what Finn likes."

"That's his fault." Mona shrugged. "No reason for us to suffer because he can't communicate or be present."

I studied her smiling face as her logic sank in. If he'd cared, he could have shared the mundane basics of his life. He hadn't. He'd also ditched me in a massive opulent house with nothing to do, but even if I had something to do, I probably wouldn't through fear of ruining something.

"Do you have a menu for Mexican there?"

"Of course." Mona grinned. She pulled a yellow leaflet out with barely a glance at the pile. "This is the best one in the area."

"That sounds great." I bit my lip on the urge to ask if Finn liked Mexican.

It doesn't matter.

"Shall we grab a seat while we decide?" Shaun placed a glass of water on the counter in front of me. He nodded towards the plush deep blue sofas framing the fireplace.

"Yes, sorry." I flushed as I picked up the water. "I'm a terrible host."

Mona laughed. "I would be too in your situation."

"We know our way around better than you do right now." Shaun smiled before collecting his and Mona's drinks. He led the way to the living room area. "I promise we won't hold it against you."

We settled on the sofas opposite each other, sipping our waters while I scanned the menu. Nerves twisted in my stomach. We hadn't talked, beyond the couple of minutes I'd spent with them at the wedding.

What if they didn't like me?

I took a deep breath and pushed it away. It didn't matter. They'd like me or they wouldn't, and there wasn't a lot I could do about it aside from being my normal self.

And my normal self would not be worrying her lip over other people's opinions.

"How did you both meet Finn?" I forced my shoulders to relax and settled back against the sofa.

Making myself feel comfortable in this place went against the grain, but if I didn't start now, I never would. I tucked my feet under me, settling into a corner of the sofa with a huge pillow at my back. Much better.

"On the set of an action film. He was the cocky fucker the assistant director spent a lot of time manhandling back to his mark." Shaun grinned, his blue eyes shining with remembered mirth. "Considering he went to acting school, he should have known better."

I considered Finn's relentlessness with Tyler, he fought to never give him much ground and always with such a serious expression. I couldn't imagine him being cocky, but it was an image I liked far too much.

"Was that here in LA?"

Shaun shook his head. "Nevada. All of us were just background artists at that point, finding our feet in Hollywood." The amusement faded to be replaced with something close to wonder. Appreciation maybe. "Somehow, we stood out in that film. All four of us started landing bigger and bigger roles. Always together."

I needed to do a deep internet search on Finn.

"By all four, you mean the other guys who were with you at the wedding?" At Shaun's nod, I tried to recall their names. "Jackson and…"

"Nathan." Shaun grinned. "The Kings of Screen. A weird title for the American industry to dub four Brits but we're not going to complain any time soon."

"I still find it weird how that happened," Mona said, settling back against Shaun. He wrapped an arm around her, his fingers smoothing slowly up and down her arm.

His expression softened as he gazed at her and a pang of

want shot through me. Not for Shaun obviously, but for the look.

"Americans love our accents. Of course, they'd keep us together if they could."

He couldn't be more right. Everyone I'd ever known had been fascinated by a foreign accent. I hadn't plucked up the courage to ask where theirs came from.

"You can ask, you know?" Mona smiled at me. "We won't bite. I'm Scottish and Shaun's Welsh. Our accents have probably gotten a bit mangled though living together and over here." She winced at that, and I chuckled, relaxing even more.

"Jackson is Scottish and Nathan's English too."

"Except Jackson's from Aberdeen so his accent can be a lot stronger than mine when he's had a couple of drinks or just isn't thinking straight." Mona leaned forward, reaching for her phone. "Let's get this order in before Finn comes back and demands we change our minds."

"Order him the spicy soy tacos. It'll serve him right." Shaun smirked as he sipped his water. He had a devious glint in his eyes I recognised far too well. Ros regularly flashed it at me before she got herself into trouble.

Despite my nerves, I found myself liking them both. Enough to make the gigantic house feel a little homier.

❄

*W*e were just making a start on our tacos when the front door opened almost an hour later. Finn sauntered in, his eyes on the ground instead of us. I studied him, searching for signs of whatever he'd spent the last few hours doing. His hair stood a little on end, but otherwise, he looked normal.

He puttered around the front hall, putting this jacket and shoes away. All the while Shaun, Mona and I shared incredulous looks. How in your own head could you be not to notice a second car outside or the extra eyes on you?

Finn paused in the entryway, his eyes on the hallway leading to the bedrooms. His brow furrowed and I found my gaze glued to him. Why would he hesitate to walk to his own bedroom?

Shaun cleared his throat and we all chuckled as Finn startled. He whipped around to face us, a light flush burning into his face. Fascinating. He'd always been in such control, his mask either firmly in place or dropped by design. I'd never seen him blush. Or jump. It almost made him more human than celebrity for once.

"About time you turned up," Shaun called across the open plan space.

Finn scowled at him. "I said no to this."

I turned back around in my seat, sharing a grin with Mona.

"Too bad. Abi's been enjoying our company." Shaun flashed me a mischievous grin. "Haven't you?" His eyes urged me to play along, but after spending an hour with them, I didn't need the encouragement.

"Definitely. We should make this a weekly thing."

I could feel Finn's gaze itching against the back of my head. The need to turn around and soak in his reaction burned through me but I held firm. He'd see the teasing immediately and ruin the fun.

"Oh, we'll need more than a weekly catch-up." Mona grinned at Finn. "Abi's agreed to be my bridesmaid. Isn't that great? You can walk down the aisle together again."

I bit my lip. We had talked about it and I agreed. With one caveat: she couldn't rely on me. Their wedding would take place after the show ended. I couldn't delude myself enough to think Finn and I would still be together, but the idea of having something solid like that in the future felt amazing.

"Mona," Finn groaned.

I glanced over my shoulder.

"We talked about this." He stomped towards us, dragging a hand through his hair.

"And I ignored you." Mona smirked at him before picking up her taco. "Besides, I don't think you'll be divorcing in three months."

Finn spluttered. She took a bite of her taco, her eyes dancing with mirth. Mona enjoyed torturing him and I could get on board with it. Maybe he'd think twice before abandoning me in a strange place next time.

"We're not talking about that," Finn said. His sapphire gaze drilled into her.

"No, we're eating." She pushed his container across the table. "Sit down. Eat. Show us the nice guy you've been trying to hide from Abi."

His jaw shifted but he pulled out a chair all the same. He sat next to me while Shaun covered his lips with a hand, but not fast enough. He couldn't disguise his smirk.

"He has a nice side? I thought it was an act." I tried to keep it serious, but couldn't stop a chuckle from slipping out. I'd seen plenty of evidence to prove Finn could be more than a nice guy. It always made me crave more.

I flicked a glance at Finn, expecting a glare. Instead, he eyed me with a curious look in his eyes. Almost like I terrified him. *Interesting.*

Mona's eyes widened before she burst out laughing. "I can see why you'd think that. I can't imagine what he tried on you." She hooked a finger at Shaun. "This one dragged me running at sunrise on my day off."

"I didn't do that to chase you away," Shaun muttered. His amusement vanished as he turned in his seat to face her.

"Oh really?" Mona's brows rose. "Shall we ask Abi how she would have reacted?"

"No need." He shook his head.

"No, no. We should settle this argument." She glanced at me, a small smile curling her lips. "Abi?"

"If a man makes me run, period, I'm out." I could feel Finn's gaze burning against my skin. I turned my head, narrowing my eyes on him pointedly. "Don't get any ideas."

"See!" Mona shouted.

"Hey! I also took you to aerial silks and flat hunting." Shaun's voice rose but he couldn't quite pull off the annoyed demeanour. His expression kept softening every time he laid eyes on Mona. "Neither of those things would have chased you away."

"Anyway." Mona rolled her eyes and turned back to us. "Finn can be an absolute gem if he wants to be. When I first moved out here and Shaun was busy on a film, he took me to get all my paperwork sorted. He sat in the DMV with me for six hours! Would an asshole do that?"

"Mona," Finn groaned again. "Can we just eat?"

He tucked into his food while Mona and Shaun frowned at him. Seemed neither of them believed his denials. If I thought too hard about our honeymoon, I wouldn't either.

And that would be a massive mistake.

How could I keep my distance from him if I thought he could be good for me?

"Are you going to Jackson's premiere tomorrow night?" Shaun asked. He placed his arm along the back of Mona's chair, a shadow of a smirk on his face.

Finn nodded. "As if I could get out of it."

"Have you sorted Abi's stylist yet?"

Finn eyed me from the corner of his eye, freezing with a taco clenched between his fingers.

"You can't go alone, you plonker." Mona tutted at him. "It wouldn't look good if you turned up to your first red carpet since getting married without your wife."

"I don't need to go. I'm sure it'll be fine."

Mona shook her head. "You do not want that kind of

speculation on the doorstep." She shuddered. "Trust me. The less we do to draw the attention of rabid paparazzi the better."

"You're right." Finn's shoulders sagged.

"I'll text Marie and get her to pull some things together for Abi." Shaun pulled out his phone. He glanced up at me from beneath his lashes. "I'm going to need your measurements, though."

Mind spinning, I rattled off the details. Finn continued to eat his taco, his entire body tense. Within five minutes, I had an appointment with Marie, as well as a hairdresser and makeup artist to make a house call, and a delivery of jewellery because my lack was apparently bad for the wife of an A-list star.

It felt like I'd stepped into a new world, where diamonds were the norm, and people waiting on you hand and foot should be expected. I guess it was a new world. The Holly-wood world.

CHAPTER TWENTY

ABI

*R*elax.

No matter how many times I muttered that word to myself, I couldn't do it.

I'd been plucked and waxed to within an inch of my life. My skin *still* tingled. The hairdresser and makeup artist had made quick work taming my frizzy curls and covering the spattering of freckles on my nose. And the dress…

Sigh.

All of the fashion magazines had been plastered in the same basic style, since multiple designers presented their takes on it in Paris in January. Rose gold with vertical lines of narrow sequins and a cape. *A cape*! I felt like a princess. Material pooled at my feet, making me sweat ever so slightly at the thought of tripping over it on the carpet.

The neckline plunged though, making a bra impossible. For the second time in a month, I found myself strapped up with boob tape. I'd hoped to never experience someone else putting the stuff on me again, but that had evidently been wishful thinking. It didn't get any less awkward. At least I didn't have Eva and Ros smirking at my squirming.

I looked incredible though, and I should have been brimming with confidence.

Even so, nerves plagued me. I guess it made sense. First red carpet. All I knew about them came from movies. I'd prepared myself for a ruckus—lots of noise and bright lights—but my hands shook and the longer the drive took the more I started to freak out about the stylist's choice of shoes.

I didn't do heels often. With my ankle recovering from the sprain, I really shouldn't have agreed, but Marie had insisted and, sure, it made sense. Put me next to six-foot-three Finn in flats and we'd look odd. I'd argued for at least an hour over the need for them to be four inches.

It seemed like overkill.

Overkill that could break my neck and embarrass me for the entire country to see.

I lost that argument and Marie handed me a bottle of painkillers before she strapped my ankle up tight.

"Stop fidgeting," Finn said, his voice harsh in the silence that consumed us.

He sat beside me in the limo, pinching the bridge of his nose.

"Sorry."

I pressed my shaking hands hard against the leather seat at my side and focused on taking a deep breath. Nothing bad could happen. I just had to walk. Didn't need to answer a single question.

"It'll be over in a flash, I promise." His fingers glanced over mine, the softest of brushes that sent tingles up my arm.

His tone had gentled, and I dared a peek at him from the corner of my eye. He'd turned his head, his frown smoothing out in favour of a reassuring smile.

Why did he have to be so handsome? It's not fair.

While I got ready, he'd had his own treatment. His beard

had been trimmed. His black baby curls rested against his shoulders, slightly more tamed than usual. Add that to his grey tailored suit, emphasising his broad shoulders and the hands that made me whimper in Bora Bora and had a bit of trouble concentrating.

"I only need a second to fall." Despite the horror of it, my cheeks twitched at the thought of proving him wrong, resisting the smirk trying to take over my lips.

"It won't happen. I'll be holding onto you the whole time."

I studied him, hunting for signs of the guy who snapped at me on our honeymoon or abandoned me in his house. He appeared earnest. I appreciated his reassurance, but the pang of happiness in my chest concerned me.

"And you didn't need to wear heels," he grumbled. His eyes narrowed on my hidden feet. "It must be agony."

"I'll be fine." I suppressed the smile itching to break free.

"Fine, but if it becomes too much, tell me. We'll leave." His fingers clenched around mine. "I'll bloody carry you out if I have to."

I lost the battle with the smile.

The noise level exploded, even with the car door between us and the outside.

"Are you ready?"

His gaze roamed my face. At my nod, he squeezed my hand and flashed another of those calm, suave smiles.

"It really will be fine."

His expression morphed before my eyes, smoothing into the perfect collected smile. The picture of beautiful and unaffected. The actor coming out to play.

The driver opened the door, and a wall of noise hit us. Lights flashed and people screamed. White spots danced before my vision, and I hadn't even made it to the carpet yet.

Finn got out first.

He waved at the crowd of fans gathered near the car.

Then he turned back to me and held out his hand. With a tremor, I took it, sliding out to join him, grateful that the length of my dress made it impossible for me to flash any of the onlookers. I did not need *that* photo on the front page of any gossip mags.

With a firm grip on my hand, he led me down the carpet. Snippets of questions emerged the further we went. Reporters eagerly waved to Finn, desperate for an interview.

"How did you meet?"

"Why was it a secret?"

"Are you in love?"

"Is it a publicity stunt?"

"Give us a kiss?"

"Finn! Look this way."

On and on they went. I very quickly tuned them out. I didn't need to know what they were speculating about me. I'd already had to field questions from Eva almost daily, and that would only get worse once I convinced her to visit.

At some point, I got too comfortable. I could see the end of the carpet and elation at my lack of embarrassing stunts overtook me.

Then it all went to shit.

My heel caught in the train of my dress and I tugged hard at Finn's hand as I tilted towards him. He turned. I had a second to register the widening of his eyes before gravity took over.

I can't believe I'm going to faceplant on a fucking red carpet.

Stupidly or not, I squeezed my eyes shut. My stomach whooshed. My eyes fluttered open at the heated press of Finn's chest.

His face hovered above mine. He studied me, concern glimmering in his eyes. *For the cameras or just me?* My heart thundered in my chest even with the doubt, and it had nothing to do with my near miss. His fingers twitched against my back while his other hand gripped my arm.

He'd saved me from making a fool of myself. Not that this little display would go unnoticed but at least I didn't have a bruise on me or a bloody nose.

A chorus of voices rose above the chaos, a chant spreading through the crowd. "Kiss her. Kiss her. Kiss her."

Finn's brows rose. *How can I deny them?* his expression seemed to say.

My gaze dropped to his soft lips. The smirk transforming his face caught my attention before our mouths touched. He wasted no time with a tentative peck. His tongue swept along the seam of my lips. I didn't have the will to resist him.

Oh, I should have.

Instead, I got lost in the taste of him, in the heat of him pressed so close to me. I'd missed the feel of his body against mine in the night.

I barely had the presence of mind to hold in my groan.

Finn jolted when someone wolf-whistled. He broke the kiss, stiffening against me before pulling back. Again he studied me, only this time, his lips parted, his chest rose and fell erratically against my hand, and his eyes darkened with desire.

I watched as his mask slid back into place, replacing the real, raw need with an artificial smugness. I missed the glimpse of the real him, but with so many cameras around, I couldn't begrudge him wanting to hide before the rest of the world.

With a graceful move, he righted me. My breath caught as my feet almost left the ground and then his arm wrapped around my waist, his hand gripping my hip firmly. With that smug smile in place, he urged me back into motion.

Tomorrow, there would be pictures of Finn kissing me plastered across the internet and every newsstand in the country.

When I agreed to *Married Blind,* I hadn't prepared myself for this. Of course, I knew I'd be participating in a tv show and strangers would see my face and watch my every reaction to this strange situation, but this, all of it felt like another level.

It could roll out of control so fast.

"*I* thought for sure he'd hide you from us," an English accent sounded behind me, cutting above the chatter of guests.

After the premiere, we moved on to an exclusive after-party. I'd never been ushered past a red rope before. The night held so many firsts, I couldn't take them all in.

Tiny lanterns hung from the ceiling of an otherwise black venue. Plush burgundy and royal purple cushions decorated every seating option, be it a barstool or an overstuffed sofa. A rich dark oak wooden floor blanketed the room while huge copper drop lights illuminated the bar.

The place screamed expensive just as much as the perfectly made-up people surrounding me.

Despite my incredible dress, I couldn't help but feel out of place. Even with Finn's hand resting lightly on my hip.

Finn turned at the sound of that voice, spinning me with him. His face lit up at the sight of Jackson Levi, decked out in his deep blue three-piece suit. Unlike at our wedding, he'd tamed his dirty blond surfer locks, tying them back at the nape of his neck. Despite the four-inch heels, he still managed to tower over me.

"I'm not a monster," Finn said, amusement curling his lips. He slapped Jackson on the back. "Nice showing tonight, man. I did not think you could pull off the romantic hero."

"That's me. A natural talent." Jackson grinned, his gaze jumping between me and Finn. "Whether you need a battle-hardened soldier, a private investigator, a vampire, or a love interest, I can do it all."

Finn snorted. "Easy there. We don't want your head exploding."

"Too late." Jackson chuckled. Then his eyes sharpened on me, a mischievous smile tugging at his lips. "I hope he's been treating you right, Abi. You can tell me if not, and I'll use it to drive him off his rocker."

"Stop being obnoxious, Jackson." Finn shook his head. "He's tried to drive me insane every single day since we met, and fails every time."

"Maybe I haven't had the proper ammunition." Jackson lifted a beer bottle to his lips, smirking as he eyed us both. "My luck might be about to change."

I chuckled at the devious mischief painted across his face.

He reminded me so much of Ros. She could be just as unpredictable and enjoyed teasing me whenever the opportunity arose.

"We're figuring things out," I said, bringing them back to the original question but dodging it all the same.

A handsome older man passed behind Jackson, his grey hair styled in controlled waves. He glanced at us and away quickly, then stopped in his tracks to look again. His eyes widened with recognition.

"Finn McCarthy! I was hoping I'd run into you here," he said, his voice soaring above the chatter and low-level music. "I know I thanked you over the phone, but with the size of that donation, I have to do it in person." He stopped at Finn's side, slapping his hand down on his shoulder.

Finn shifted, his neck flushing as he snuck a glance at me. "It's no problem at all. The least I could do."

"Don't undervalue it, my boy." The man boomed happily. "That money will do incredible things for the Institute. There are so many selfish people in this business, it's a pleasure when I come across gems like you." He flashed me a smile, beaming with an inexplicable pride. "You've got a good one here. Hold on to him."

With that, he patted Finn on the shoulder one more time and vanished into the crowd, leaving me with a swirl of questions. Jackson and I turned to Finn with raised brows almost at the same time.

"Finny boy, when did you do it, and why didn't you tell me?" Jackson asked, his face lighting up with delight.

"It's not that big a deal."

"Don't play me. We both heard the man." Jackson shifted into the man's position, wrapping an arm around Finn and pulling him into a sideway hug. "How much did you give away?"

Finn glanced away, shifting in absolute discomfort. "Quarter of a mil to a cancer research charity," he muttered, his lips barely moving.

Jackson whistled in appreciation. "My best friend, the secret philanthropist. Did not see that one coming."

Neither had I.

Did he do it for me? No, he couldn't have.

I hadn't told him about Eva.

CHAPTER TWENTY-ONE

FINN

Eventually, Jackson fucked off to mingle more with his co-stars and every glitzy name in Hollywood. He left us grinning like the Cheshire Cat with his new fodder. I'd never hear the end of it.

I'd donated anonymously on purpose.

I didn't want people to know.

You'd think people knowing would elevate it somehow, make the magnitude of it hit harder. It didn't. Somehow, it cheapened the whole thing. People would just speculate about my motives.

Christ knows, I needed all the help I could get with my image, but I hadn't even told my agent about it.

With Jackson escaping, I collected more drinks for us and led Abi into a darkened corner. We settled on a sofa in an alcove, sheltered from the ruckus of the party.

I sank into the cushion, letting my head fall against the sofa and my eyes shut.

"Are you okay?" Abi asked. Her thigh brushed against mine, teasing me with things I couldn't have.

"Fine," I sighed. I didn't open my eyes. Didn't need to to know she probably chewed her lip. One look and I'd kiss her again. "These things just take more energy than I have sometimes."

"I can understand that."

Silence lapsed between us while I focused on relaxing. Honestly, I enjoyed our quiet moments, breathing in her floral scent, feeling the heat of her body next to mine.

That could get addictive fast.

My eyes snapped open at that. Addictive? No, thank you.

"You did well tonight."

She sniggered. "At which point? When I tripped on the carpet or when I dropped a glass of red wine in your lap?"

I rolled my head to look at her, soaking in the carefree smile lighting up her entire face. They had to pair me with an absolutely stunning and sweet woman. Couldn't give me a grain of a chance at keeping her at arm's length.

"I think the carpet one worked out well."

Truth be told, I'd have kissed her even if the fans hadn't been chanting for it. The shock and wonder in her eyes had been too much to ignore. Add the flush creeping into her cheeks and her parted lips, I didn't stand a chance.

Weak. That's me. Too fucking weak to stay strong.

"You didn't even tense up when I kissed you."

Why the fuck am I praising her?

Abi glanced at the couple leaning against the wall next to us. She leaned toward me and my gaze dropped to her lips without thought.

"How much chaos will that cause?" she asked, her voice low and careful.

"There's probably already some articles up and maybe a segment running on a celebrity gossip show about my sudden behaviour change." I took a sip of beer, shrugging the whole thing off. "Honestly, it's nothing new. As far as the world knows right now, we're happily married. That kiss probably helped my image."

She dipped her chin and the tension drained from her. She relaxed against the sofa cushions, her body irresistibly close to me. If I shifted across an inch or two, my arm would brush against her tit.

"Finn!" An eerily familiar voice shouted from across the room.

Heads turned toward our alcove while a raven-haired viper barrelled across the room at us, dragging along a scowling guy who looked like he'd stepped out of a GQ magazine. The fakest smile I'd ever seen stretched her lips.

"It's been ages," Natalie said as she stopped in front of us. "I can't believe we ran into you."

Why the fuck did she look happy about it?

"You look great." She raked her gaze over me, unmistakable interest in her eyes.

I ground my teeth. "What do you want, Natalie?" I asked, my tone making it perfectly clear her latest game wouldn't work.

The heat faded fast, her pleasant socialite mask slipping into place. The guy wrapped his arm around her, laughably trying to stake his claim.

"This is my fiancé, Zeke." She tilted her head towards him, that sickly fake smile fixed in place while her eyes hardened. As if I cared. "How amazing that we both got engaged at the same time."

A click sounded in my head and a smirk claimed my lips. I slid a hand along the back of the sofa, resting it on Abi's neck.

"What a coincidence." I closed the remaining inches between us, pressing Abi tight to my side and resting my other hand high on her thigh. She caught it, twining our fingers together. "But Nat, you've got your facts wrong. I'm married."

I picked Abi's hand up and pressed a kiss to it, the emerald stone glinting beneath the club's low lights.

Natalie's gaze dropped to the rock. I took great joy in watching her nostrils flare. I needed to send Charlie a thank you card for the beast of an engagement ring.

She recovered fast, moulding herself to Zeke, the poor guy. Her plastic smile slammed back into place. Apparently, we'd gone from people who sued each other to people who had a pissing contest over jewellery.

"I heard." She puckered her brow, tutting as if she truly cared about me. "Didn't think you were dating anyone seriously."

I shrugged. "I haven't heard any more scandal about you stealing from people and leaking their personal shit for a quick payoff, so I guess we're even."

Zeke stiffened next to her, and a thrill of triumph rippled through me.

"What is he talking about, Nat?"

She patted his chest. "Oh, nothing. Nothing at all." She shot me a warning look and led him away. "He's only joking."

"Am I?"

She took a panicked step back. "We'll leave you to your evening." Another step.

"Good idea." A menacing grin overtook me. I didn't consider myself the vindictive sort, but I would gladly tear her to shreds in front of an audience. It would be a public service. "Wouldn't want me to spill too many of your secrets."

She spun on her heel, tugging her frowning fiancé after her. My heart rate slowed as she vanished into the crowd. I hadn't seen her in years, and I'd pretty much assumed she'd quit LA.

What were the fucking chances?

"Who was that?" Abi asked, her tone tentative.

Christ, I didn't want to get into it.

"No one important."

She scanned my face, hunting for a truth she wouldn't find. If she really wanted, she could find all the sordid details online. The fact she hadn't recognised Natalie suggested my wife hadn't gone digging into my past. For some reason that filled me with hope.

"An old girlfriend?"

"Unfortunately," I grumbled.

Abi continued to stare at me, her scrutinising expression gradually softening.

"There you two are," Mona shouted before collapsing onto the sofa opposite us, freeing me from Abi's attention. "For a minute, we thought you'd skipped the party."

Shaun sat down next to her, eying me with a guarded look. "Did I just see…"

"Yep." I nodded. "Don't ask me why."

"You can't be that oblivious." Abi's brows rose at my blank expression. "How could you miss the 'my achievement is bigger than yours' vibes?"

Shaun chuckled. "Remembering how artificial Natalie was, your wife's got a point."

Despite the amusement creasing his face, Shaun watched me with a glint in his eyes. Anticipation rolled off him in waves, and I could understand why. That one word would have been enough to send me to the bar a week ago. Add in the run-in with Natalie and I should definitely be deep into a bottle of whisky by now.

Nothing but calm rolled through me. Calm and an insane awareness of Abi's skin beneath my fingertips and the pads of her fingers grazing circles around my knuckles.

So no, I didn't rise to the bait. I also didn't shift away from Abi.

"How's your sister doing with you away?" Mona asked. She leaned forward, her gaze avidly fixed on Abi. "Did you ask her about visiting?"

"Not yet." She shook her head. "I'm going to wait until

the first show payment comes through and book the flight for her. Flights aren't cheap so I don't want her to be able to say no."

"Good idea. I didn't think about that." Mona nodded, sinking into Shaun's side. Her eyes narrowed as she stared off into the corner. "I bet she'll be relieved when it's all paid off."

I glanced between them, the dread eating a hole in my stomach. "When all of what is paid off?"

Please don't say debt.

If I couldn't spot the money-hungry whores, how could I avoid them?

Abi hesitated, her mouth opening and closing. My heart sank.

"My sister had cancer," she said, her voice cracking. She cleared her throat while my brain scrambled to adjust. "She's in remission now, but she wracked up a pretty hefty medical bill getting treatment."

"Did you know Abi worked three jobs trying to help her pay it off?" Mona asked, the awe in her voice merging with the devious glint in her eyes as she studied me. "Honestly, you're so brave, taking on the show to help her. You must have been terrified."

My eyes narrowed on Mona while my grasp on reality shifted.

"I think Finn's got the point now, Sparky." Shaun laughed as he squeezed her hand. He shuffled forward on the sofa and for the first time ever, I desperately hoped that my best friend would leave. "You've hit Finn with enough of a bomb, let's get a move on."

They abandon us as fast as they appeared, leaving everything upside down.

"You didn't tell me about your sister," I said, my tone soft… and maybe a little miffed.

Would I have treated her differently had I known?

Possibly, but I couldn't say for certain.

"I didn't think..." She trailed off, chewing her lip.

"What?"

She sighed. "We're having a good time, let's not ruin that with this."

I stilled, my gaze roaming her pale face. "Why would telling me about your sister's cancer ruin this?"

"Fine," she muttered, her tone hardening. She pushed her shoulders back and locked eyes with me, determination riding her. "I didn't think you'd care."

It should have hurt.

This close, I could make out the moment she braced for my mood to change. Her cheeks lifted and her lips flatlined. The sight of it drove a dagger into my heart.

Maybe I'd been wrong.

I couldn't get addicted to her because I already was.

I relaxed into the sofa, turning so my body angled toward her. "That's a fair assessment. I might not have when we first met." My gaze dropped to her lips which parted slightly on an almost inaudible gasp. "No one stays the same though, *dotey*."

With the tip of my finger, I drew circles around the nape of her neck. I gave myself permission to get lost in her eyes for the first time. My heart pounded as I considered how I could make it up to her. It would take a while, but there was one thing I could share, one thing that tore me open, maybe not as much as her sister's battle with cancer had her, but it felt like a personal trade.

"That woman, Natalie," I paused, waiting for her to acknowledge the change in conversation. When she nodded, I blew out a breath and forced the words out. "We were together for five months. Not a huge amount of time in the grand scheme of things, but for the damage she did, it could have been decades."

As the story spilt from me, I kept my gaze fixed on hers, absorbing every wince, grimace and trickle of sympathy.

"I'd just won the first award of my career when I met her.

We were like a bonfire rigged with explosives, burning up slowly and exploding in a thousand directions in a shower of debris when it ended." I toyed with her ring, circling the emerald and dragging the straight edges along the pad of my finger. "I didn't sense a shift. She went from being all over me to avoiding my calls and messages in the blink of an eye. I couldn't figure out why and then my agent called…"

I thought I'd put it all behind me, but the shame rose, ramming into me. Abi squeezed my hand and her quiet support messed with my voice.

"She's the reason I don't trust people," I said, my voice gruff. "Most of the time, she pushed me out of my comfort zone, ready with one line of reasoning or another for why there'd be no consequences." I winced as the memory of Charlie's scathing voice rang in my ears. "She worked me like a pro, urging me into incriminating positions and then she… then she sold it to the tabloids."

"Oh Finn, I'm sorry," Abi whispered. Moisture shimmered in her eyes.

"She took advantage of me. Used me to orchestrate a huge payday for herself." My face hardened. "And in the process, she convinced anyone who would listen that I had forced her into half the shit. That I," I swallowed, "manipulated her, hurt her. Didn't matter that she lied, didn't matter that the thing she sold showed that she knew what she'd done."

"What did she sell?"

"Doesn't matter."

Christ, the idea of Abi *knowing* terrified me more than it should have.

"It took years to rebuild and at some point, I stopped trying. I leaned into the playboy image the media had forced onto me." I shrugged. "Why bother, when everyone wanted something from me anyway? The studio execs wanted the cash my face would generate. The women wanted to brag that they'd fucked me or try to take my money. The media wanted another story, more eyes on their pathetic gossip rags."

"So you shut everyone out," Abi whispered.

She watched me with more sympathy than I deserved. I'd perpetuated the myth, fed it, rolled around in it until the real me couldn't be seen. Everything I'd done since that moment had been a choice. I didn't deserve her sympathy.

CHAPTER TWENTY-TWO

ABI

We left the party early.

I sat next to Finn in the limo, my hand still locked with his, his thigh pressed to mine. I'm not sure I could have let him go even if I'd really thought about it.

It felt natural.

And after he opened up to me, showing me the soft, scared man beneath his facade, every defence I had against him crumbled.

That should have scared me, but I felt curiously hopeful.

And filled with a need that burned.

First, I wanted to jump his bones, but after that? Then I'd convince him that not everyone wanted to use him. I didn't. If I could make him see that, maybe he'd never look at me with that gut-punching sadness again.

The limo pulled through the guard gate, making the ascent to the house through the quiet, tree-lined streets.

I tugged on Finn's hand when the car stopped outside his front door and he didn't react. His sapphire gaze clashed with mine for the first time since we left the club. My breath caught at the intensity of his focus.

Something had changed between us. The walls he forced between us had dissolved somewhere between the club and his house.

Before I could react, the driver opened his door. Finn squeezed my hand and slid out of the car. He hovered outside, waiting for me.

He held his hand out to me when I cleared the car, clear expectation painting his expression. He didn't expect me to hesitate or refuse. A week ago, he wouldn't have opened himself to the rejection.

I slid my hand into his and let him lead me into the house. He called a 'thank you' to the driver but didn't turn around. He also didn't increase his pace, seeming content to take our time. Another shift.

"I'm absolutely knackered," Finn mumbled after he locked the door. "I'd stay up but I think I'll fall asleep on you." His expression turned sheepish as he silently apologised.

"That's okay, I'm going to head to bed too."

We walked across the foyer, hand-in-hand still, nothing but the dark silence of the house surrounding us and the tap of my heels on the hardwood.

When we reached my door, he turned me to face him. Muted moonlight cast his face in shadows, but I could still make out the spark of hesitation in his eyes.

"Thank you for tonight," he whispered, swallowing hard. "For not running after I told you about Natalie."

"I couldn't blame you for one woman's vindictive actions." I smiled, rising a hand to rest on his jaw. "It wasn't your fault."

He nodded, but he didn't believe it, which saddened me. One day, I'd convince him.

"Well, good night."

He leaned down pressing a kiss to my forehead. My stomach twisted at the chaste move after our scorcher of a make-out session on the carpet. Then I firmly shut the worry down. I couldn't coax him into giving us a real chance if I didn't take risks.

Finn stepped away, trying to release my hand. I held on tight, moving with him.

"Wait, Finn. I…"

"What do you need, *dotey?*"

A shiver ran down my spine as that word tripped off his tongue. I knew he wanted me.

So ask.

"Will you stay with me tonight?"

"Okay," he whispered, his voice hoarse.

Words froze on my lips. I scanned his face, both surprised and elated.

Smiling, I led him into my room, nerves babbling away in my stomach all the while. I couldn't look at him while he stripped and turned my back to pull out a pair of pyjamas and unhook my dress.

The whoosh of the fabric sliding off me screamed in the silence. The catch of breath in his throat shot through the room, ringing in my ears.

I tugged the oversized t-shirt over my head, smirking to myself as I dropped the leggings back into the drawer.

Slowly, I made my way to my bed. Finn already lay beneath the covers, facing me. His gaze roamed my body with the help of the moonlight shining through the open curtains. The cool air burned against my bare skin like a touch.

I lifted the covers, sliding under to lie facing him. A couple of inches separated our bodies and nerves began to own me.

Calm the hell down.

I hadn't been nervous about sleeping with a guy since I lost my virginity. Why the hell should this time be different?

Finn's fingers grazed across my cheek and goose bumps prickled across my skin. From an innocent caress.

Fuck.

He leaned forward, brushing his lips against mine in a sweet move completely at odds with our unstable beginnings. I kissed him back, ratcheting up the pressure and coaxing him into giving me the demanding guy I'd glimpsed in Bora Bora.

His fingers delved into my hair as he shuffled closer. As his tongue invaded my mouth to tease mine, his solid chest pressed against me, engulfing me in the best kind of heat.

Finn broke contact and I moaned. He leaned away, smirking while he studied me.

"Not going to fall asleep on me this time, are you?"

"Definitely not." I shook my head, then grinned. "Are you?"

"Nope, you've woken me right up," he whispered, lowering his head.

He grazed his lips along my jaw, then mercifully returned his lips to mine. Our hands wandered, learning every divot and crease. His fingers slid lightly down my torso while mine mapped the lines of his back and side.

Finn made circles against my hip, the gesture so soft it focused all of my attention, anticipating the next brush.

"Open for me, Abi," he whispered against my lips. He tapped my hip, pushing a little to force me onto my back before his hand redirected, skimming across my stomach.

I rolled onto my back and Finn followed, closing the gap between our bodies. Wasting no time, his fingertips danced down my outer thigh. My core ached with pulsing need and my hips shifted restlessly.

He scattered kisses across my jaw and down my neck, swirling his tongue and scraping his teeth until I wasn't sure which torture affected me more. His fingers continued to tease, running up the inside of my thigh and stopping short of where I desperately needed him.

"Finn," I groaned. My hips lifted, chasing his retreating touch, desperate to urge him on.

"Yes, Abi?" he asked, his voice gravelly but filled with laughter.

"Stop. Torturing. Me."

He smiled, his lips curling against my collarbone.

"Are you sure that's what you want?"

"Definitely."

His touch shifted, running light circles around the lips of my sex, barely touching but setting off pulses of pleasure all the same.

"Better?"

"Finn," I growled.

"So needy." He chuckled.

"Stop teas— Oh!"

He dragged two fingers through my folds, circling my clit with a focused determination that made my head swim. Leaning up on his elbow, he watched me as he drove me out of my mind with nothing more than two digits.

When I came, a smug smirk claimed his lips, only this time, I didn't have the urge to slap it off his face. Floating in bliss, I decided it looked good on him, especially when my pussy fluttered with aftershocks.

"Going to let me take all the time I want in the future, aren't you, Dotey?" He slammed his lips down on mine, stealing my breath for a second before he started moving down my body. "You're going to trust that I know what your body needs, aren't you?"

The way he said it, sugary sweet, but coated in no-argument steel...liquid heat flooded me and my core clenched, desperate for round two.

"Yes," I hissed on a breathy sigh.

He worked his way down to the bed, nipping, kissing, licking… sucking. He latched on to a nipple, bathing the taut nub in the warmth of his mouth. My breasts had never been particularly sensitive, but with all of Finn's attention fixated on them, I didn't stand a chance.

He hovered above me, the hard tip of his erection grazing against my core, tantalisingly close. While Finn drove me out of my mind, rolling my nipple between his fingers and lips, I rocked my hips up, pressing myself firmly against him. His tip dragged through my soaking folds, skittering against my clit and making my eyes roll back at the tiny flutter of pleasure.

"Patience, Abi," Finn growled. He pulled away, sitting back on his hunches. "If you want my cock, you need to be a good girl." He gripped his length, pumping his hand up and down, captivating me. With his smouldering gaze taking me in, he smiled and released himself.

He reached into the bedside table, his gaze never leaving mine while he felt around inside the drawer. While he retrieved a condom, I propped myself up with my elbows as I watched him with bated breath.

"Do you have any idea how much you've messed with my head?" Finn asked as he rolled the condom on, slow and torturous, winding me up as much as he did himself. "I was meant to hate you."

His sapphire eyes darkened and cleared in the blink of an eye. His lips curled, smug and knowing, making me want to wrap my hand around his nape and drag him back down to me.

"But how could I resist you when you look at me like that?" He shifted forward, leaning over me again, holding himself up with his forearms at either side of my shoulders. Minuscule inches separated our bodies, teasingly close. He ghosted his fingers across my jaw, smoothing a thumb across my lower lips. "Such sweet, innocent trust. It's bloody addictive."

My stomach flipped while my heart took a lap of victory. *Finn McCarthy thinks I'm addictive.* It filled me with a strong sense of control. Feeling brave, I darted my tongue out, swirling it around his thumb. His eyes darkened again and this time, I wanted them to stay that way.

"You're my good girl, aren't you, Abi?" he whispered, dragging his lips along my jaw to my lips.

I nodded and he tutted.

"Say it." His cock pressed against my pussy, achingly close.

I studied his hard, watchful face, chewing my lip. It seemed I had an endless list of firsts for Finn to claim. My cheeks burned at the thought of saying something like that to him. Yet, as foreign as it was, my core clenched.

"Abi," he whispered, a warning in his hoarse voice. He rocked against me, teasing us both and making my body shake with need.

"Yes. I'm your good girl."

His sapphire eyes lit up and his expression softened. I had a second to take in the sheer beauty of him, the unbelievable fact I had all of his attention focused on me and me alone.

Then he pushed forward, filling me inch by inch and my ability to think straight evaporated. Within seconds, he reduced me to nothing more than moans, groans and whimpers. His measured, slow thrusts stretched me, brushing against all the best places.

At some point, he pinned my arms above my head, gripping my wrists with one hand. Something about the action wound my body tighter, bowing my back as shivers of pleasure danced up my spine.

"Fuck, don't…" Finn trialled off with a breathless sigh as my core clenched around him.

His fingers dragged down my thigh, a soft caress against feverish skin. Then he hooked my knee and tugged it up. He pressed it into the mattress, forcing me wider. At the first stroke, my eyes fell shut, soaking in the mind-numbing fizzle of pleasure winding me tighter and tighter.

Finn picked up speed, pounding into me, grinding against my clit with each thrust. My toes curled into the mattress and my fingers hunted for something, anything to hold on to. He released my wrists and weaved our fingers together, filling my chest with the warmest sensation.

"Eyes on me, Abi," he ground out, his breathing laboured.

I forced my heavy lids to lift, meeting his intense sapphire gaze.

"Good girl," he muttered as the pressure spiralled, tightening until it didn't matter how hot those two words made me.

The coil snapped and my muscles locked up, squeezing tight as lightning shot up my spine and consumed everything. Finn swore as he came, burying his face in my neck, sucking in deep shaky breaths.

Minutes ticked by as we came down from the high. He released his grip on my hands and knee, caressing my face, hair and arms with soft touches that heated my blood for an entirely different reason.

In the silence of my room, shadowed in the soft glow of moonlight, with his body cradling mine, I felt loved. The words rushed to the tip of my tongue.

I bit them back and relaxed into the mattress.

CHAPTER TWENTY-THREE

ABI

I woke to the press of Finn's chest against my back and sighed. He smoothed circles on my hip, rising goosebumps and awakening an insatiable need for more.

"How are you feeling?" Finn asked, his voice groggy behind me.

"A little sore, but otherwise great." I turned over, sighing happily at the delicious ache in my body. I dragged a finger down his chest, scratching slightly with the nail. I bit my lip for a second before shoving the hesitation away. "How about you? Still happy with your choices?"

He cupped my jaw, a soft smile brightening his eyes.

"Not a single regret." Finn pressed a chaste kiss to my lips.

I recoiled.

"Maybe I should be asking you that question." He chuckled as I scrambled out of bed.

"Sorry, I just have a thing about morning breath." I raced towards my bathroom. "Go brush your teeth and we'll try this again."

His laughter followed me. I rushed through brushing my teeth, splashed water over my face and jumped back into bed.

I lay there, grinning like a loon at the ceiling. Of all the ways I'd expected yesterday to end, that wasn't it. A giddy feeling of triumph trickled through me.

My bedroom door shot open. Finn laughed again as he walked in, carrying a tray.

"That was quite the shriek, *Dotey*." He grinned as he approached the bed. "I'm not that scary, am I?"

He placed the tray between us and lay down next to me. I slapped him lightly on the arm, my heart still racing.

"You scared me."

"I couldn't get the handle." Mirth danced in his eyes. "Sorry."

I didn't believe him.

"Can I bribe your forgiveness with waffles?" he asked, a sly look entering his eyes.

He knew full well he could. I'd made no secret of my love for waffles in Bora Bora.

My brows climbed as he tugged the tray closer. A pile of syrup-coated waffles sat on a plate.

"How did you make those so fast?"

He'd only been gone for ten minutes at most.

"I might have put an order in with my chef last week. He left them in the fridge for us last night." He scratched his scruff-covered jaw, the lightest of blushes colouring his cheeks. "I remembered you saying you loved them and I wanted to help you feel comfortable. This was all I could come up with."

"Rewind." I circled my fingers. "You have a chef? No wonder your kitchen is spotless."

"He's your chef now too." He glanced away, that blush spreading further.

I caught his chin, turning his focus back to me to study him. Funny, how I went weeks accepting his controlled mask of emotions and now I couldn't shake the fascination every time he let me see the real him.

Finn stared back at me, patiently waiting for my next move.

"You're not even slightly comfortable with showing off wealth, are you?"

He shook his head, a small smile curling his lips. He seemed… pleased. But with me or the question?

"I grew up in an Irish Catholic family. Having money is like sin."

"Is that why you donated as much as you did?"

His mouth opened and then his gaze sharpened on me. "I don't know," he whispered, his tone mildly freaked. "Shit. Maybe." Guilt flashed across his face. "Christ, that sounds terrible."

"Why? The charity doesn't care why you did it." I shrugged. "All they'll care about is how it'll help people. It's not like you announced it to the world and made a big deal out of it."

Although, he probably hadn't because of his Catholic guilt. Oops.

"You're right." The concern faded from his blue eyes and he grinned at me. "Thank you."

"For what?"

"Take your pick." He lifted a shoulder, his gaze glued to me. "Talking sense into me. Not caring about the money. Not pushing me when I'm not ready to talk about something."

"You don't need to thank me for that, Finn." I shifted onto my knees and pressed a quick kiss to his lips. He chased me as I pulled away, eliciting a giggle. "It's what you do for the people you…" I swallowed, halting myself before 'love' could traipse off my tongue. Far too early for that kind of talk. "Marry. It's what you do for the people you like."

He scanned my face, scrutinising the blush working its way up my neck and the panicked flare of my eyes.

I can't believe I nearly let that slip out.

"If I can't thank you, what can I do?" His expression morphed in a blink of an eye.

The calculating gleam faded, replaced by a mischievous interest I couldn't look away from. His voice dropped, dragging over sensitive nerve endings, reminding me of all the ways he'd made me scream his name last night. He pushed the tray away and pressed a hand to my shoulder.

"Or shall I surprise you and we can compare notes later?"

My core clenched as he shifted towards me. He pushed me back down onto the bed, tugging the covers out of the way until he straddled me. With my hands gathered in his, he pressed them to the pillow above me. Heat flared in his eyes and a wicked smile curled his lips.

"Definitely need to tie you up sometime," he muttered under his breath.

Then he kissed me and I forgot about everything else. I focused on the press of him against me, the heat of him hovering over me, the commanding sweep of his lips and the tight pressure of his hands around my wrists.

Fuck, I could get addicted to him.

Somehow, the waffles escaped destruction. We moved into the kitchen before I dared try one.

They were the fluffiest, softest, most delicious things I'd ever eaten. Each bite turned into a religious experience, coaxing moans from me.

"If you keep that up, I'm going to fuck you on the breakfast bar," Finn warned, his voice low and deadly serious.

He stared at me from the other side of the counter, a cup of coffee pressed to his chin. His smouldering gaze devoured me.

I should have been sated. The thought of more sex should

have sent me running for the hills. Instead, my clit throbbed and the need we'd tamed intensified. How we'd resist each other until now, I had no clue.

It took effort to swallow the waffle in my mouth without choking.

"Put it on the to-do list," I said, my voice thick with want.

His jaw slackened.

"I want to be all in, give our marriage a real shot. What do you want?" I willed myself not to chew my lip while I anxiously waited for Finn to answer. Thoughts danced across his face, I couldn't read any of them. Damn actors.

"I want to try too," he said, his voice hoarse.

"Terrifying, isn't it?" I flashed a sympathetic smile. "Opening yourself up to another person." At his nod, I pushed the waffles aside. "Come over here."

He tilted his head for a second, trying to work me out. When he stopped in front of me, open curiosity shone in his eyes. I glided my hands up his chest, trying to soothe any doubts.

"We can pretend we aren't married, if that makes it better." The idea of it put a lump in my throat, but I could get on board if he needed it. "Take some of the pressure off and just be a normal couple getting to know each other."

He shook his head. "No. I don't want that." His hand captured mine, playing with the rock on my finger. "As bizarre as it seems, I've gotten used to our weird beginnings. I don't want to brush it under a rug."

My heart swelled as I stared into his eyes. Oh yeah, I needed to be careful if I didn't want to fall head over heels for him.

"Okay, so we're doing this. A real relationship." I couldn't stop myself from repeating it, the words wouldn't sink in.

"A real relationship," he repeated, grinning at me. Then his expression shifted to the mischievous one that set my heart racing and liquid heat flooding through my core. He leaned forward. "Starting with me eating you out on the breakfast bar."

I clenched as heat spiralled through me. *Fuck.* The mouth on him. I needed more.

My fingers gripped his t-shirt, tugging him forward. His lips slammed down on mine, coaxing groans from me in less than five seconds. Lost in the pressure of his kiss, I missed him picking me up. Only the cold press of marble against my bare legs clued me in.

I gasped and he swallowed it. He forced my thighs wide open, shifting between them and closing the distance between our bodies and tugging me to the edge of the counter. My core pressed against his taut stomach while his fingers danced down my thighs. He teased me with light caresses as his mouth devoured me.

Finn's hand slipped beneath my panties, grazing my slit. I groaned, bowing my back to give him better access. He swiped a finger through my folds, gliding through the wetness with ease.

It felt like seconds passed, but already the pressure built. He circled my clit, applying delicious pressure that made my eyes roll back and my toes curl. When his fingers retreated, I whimpered.

"Do that again, Finn," I groaned. "Fuck, please, do that again."

Then the doorbell rang.

"I'm going to fucking kill whoever that is." He pulled away, scowling. "Don't move. I'll get rid of them."

He stomped into the foyer. I heard the front door open and then Finn's voice hardened. I couldn't make out the words, but he'd definitely gone from annoyed to furious.

My chair sat two feet away. Finn had kicked it out of his way to get to me. My feet dangled miles off the ground. With my ankle still healing, I didn't want to have to jump, but I couldn't exactly stay put while Finn had a meltdown at the front door. Who knew what horrors waited out there?

Voices grew closer and then Finn emerged, his face shut down in his trademark clean slate. It flickered when he spotted me, panic flickering across before he rushed towards me.

"We can set up in the living room if you'd prefer, Finn?" Tyler called from down the hall.

My stomach hit the ground. No way in hell could he find me like this. I did not want to be on TV wearing nothing but an oversized t-shirt.

Fuck it. I'd jump. Screw the sting.

I shuffled towards the edge of the counter, pressed my palms to the hard edges. Finn caught me, his arms wrapping around me while his gaze bored into mine. It could have been my imagination, but I could have sworn his eyes screamed at me to be quiet.

I glanced at the hallway, expecting Tyler to appear at any moment. But he didn't. Neither did the crew. Rather than question my good luck, I wrapped my legs around Finn's waist and zipped my lips. He carried me to my bedroom door on swift feet, setting me down and gently shoving me into the room.

"Shower, take your time," Finn whispered. "I'll keep him busy."

With that, he turned away, a grim twist to his lips.

I shut the door and took a second… to catch my breath and mourn the loss of what would have been the hottest head I'd ever experienced.

Damn tv crew.

CHAPTER TWENTY-FOUR

FINN

"I couldn't help but notice your family weren't at the wedding." Tyler walked into the kitchen, a smug smile plastered to his face.

"It was a bit far for a farce wedding." I crossed my arms and stared him down.

The crew set up around us, adding LED lights on stands here and there. Overkill, considering the entire back wall consisted of wall-to-ceiling windows.

"So." Tyler clapped his hands. "Where's Abi?"

I scrambled for an excuse. Call with her sister, shower, sleeping. Thankfully, she appeared before I settled on anything plausible.

"Right here," Abi said. She turned the corner, her eyes casting across the setup, and joined me at the breakfast bar. "What are we up to today?"

Tyler frowned at her hair. She'd thrown it up into a messy bun, some of the auburn strands escaped the hold and cascaded around her face. I thought she looked gorgeous, especially with the morning sun setting her pale skin aglow. Tyler evidently disagreed.

"What did you do to your hair?"

I fought every muscle in my body to prevent it from stiffening, to keep my mouth shut. Abi and I might now be on good terms but that didn't mean I wanted the show to catch the real me. Any more than they had anyway.

"You didn't exactly warn us of your plans." Abi smirked at him, enjoying his annoyance. "Washing my hair is a luxury you didn't afford me. I can go take an hour showering and styling it if you'd prefer?"

Watching her sass Tyler, I couldn't say why I ever believed we wouldn't fit together.

He grumbled to himself but dropped it. Shame.

"Go ahead and mic them up." He nodded to the crew.

"No need to be cryptic, Tyler." Abi held her arms out while Ian clipped her radio mic on, her expression much gentler than mine. "Just tell us what's happening."

"All in good time." He turned away, surveying the room, that smug expression returning.

"Christ, you're annoying," I muttered.

"Is that why you didn't tell us about the film premiere?" For a second, the smarmy calm facade cracked and he glared at me. "You knew we'd want to capture Abi's first red carpet."

So that's what's got his panties in a twist.

"There were fifty cameras." I shrugged. "I'm sure you could source the footage."

"That's not the point," Tyler ground out through a clenched jaw.

"No, you just wanted me to mess with my friend's premiere so you could go right back to manipulating us." I grinned, enjoying his annoyance. "You know the rules, Tyler. You're on *my* schedule now."

He spun away, grumbling under his breath. I wasn't fooled, he'd find a way to pay me back.

Once we were fully mic'ed up and Ian had his camera pointed at us, Tyler's grin returned, growing until it set me on edge. *Maybe the payback's already coming.* I watched him like a hawk as he pressed his phone to his ear, never taking his eyes off me.

"Send them in, Ethan."

Four simple innocent words and yet my stomach churned.

"Send who in?"

The front door opened and he turned, his arms open in welcome.

"Fiona, Saoirse, welcome." Tyler stepped out of the way, giving the camera trailing my smiling smirking mother and sister a clear birth.

If not for my training, my jaw would have hit the floor. Tyler had surprised me. My mother, to her credit, didn't look pissed. Her pale, freckled face bore nothing but excitement, not a red tinge of annoyance in sight. Small mercies.

"Finn McCarthy! Don't just stand there gawking." My mother walked towards me, her arms open and a stern gleam in her blue eyes. "Get over here and hug your Ma."

My sister snorted as I followed her orders, old habits quickly falling into place. I barely stopped my eyes from narrowing at her.

Arms wrapped around me, squeezing tight. "You got married without telling me?" Ma asked, her voice deathly low. "You'd better have a good bloody reason, child-o-mine."

Then she released me, brushing me aside to engulf Abi in a hug. She squeaked in surprise but sensibly didn't resist. Caught in the wrong mood, my mother liked to do the opposite of what people wanted. The wind-up sod always knew how to get a rise out of me.

So can Saoirse.

I eyed my sister from the corner of my eye, awaiting her reaction. Aside from the twenty-five-year age gap, Saoirse and my mother were almost a mirror image. Both had short, raven hair flowing down their backs, pale skin and piercing blue eyes.

Even as she hugged me, I moved with suspicion. I studied her from the corner of my eye, waiting for her happy smile to snap. My sister and I got on perfectly well, but I'd know she would be the wild card when I chose not to tell them about the show.

"You robbed me of a Grecian bridesmaid's dress, Finn," she murmured in my ear, her voice low and hissing. She pulled back, her eyes narrowing on me. "Grecian!"

"I got married without telling you, and you're pissed about a dress?" I asked as she released me, my voice climbing with shock. "Christ. Tell me how you really feel."

"You're my only brother." Saoirse's hands landed on her hips.

"Still doesn't explain the outrage over a bleeding dress."

Saoirse tutted. "Of course, you wouldn't get it." Her gaze settled on Abi. "I bet Abi would get it."

Saoirse had always had a penchant for the dramatics. "How the hell am I the actor in this family?" I muttered to myself as I tugged at my hair.

I'll kill Tyler. And then Charlie for putting me in this shitty position.

"Now, don't read anything into his secrecy, Abi." Ma mostly released Abi, holding her away by her shoulders. She grinned from ear to ear. "He never did learn from every other one blowing up in his face."

Abi smiled at me, her eyes far too wide. That distracted me from the downward spiral of the day. My wife, scared of my mother. Somehow that fit. I bit down hard on the grin tugging at my lips.

"Stop overwhelming her, Ma." I swept in, brushing my mother's hands away and tucking Abi beneath my arm. "Give her a minute to catch up." I glanced towards the empty foyer, finally seeing what I missed when they first walked in. "Da didn't come with you?"

"I'll make tea," Abi whispered. She pulled from my grip and paused. "Tea's right, isn't it?"

She glanced up at me, worrying her lip. I squashed down the urge to free it with the caress of my tongue. Even if she did look adorable in her uncertainty.

"Yes, love. Tea would be brilliant," my mother said before I could do more than smile at her.

Then she latched onto the subject change, just as I knew she would. I guided her and my sister to the sofa while Abi pulled tea bags from the cupboard and set the kettle to boiling.

"Your Da couldn't get off work." Ma sat, her gaze sweeping over the modern open and airy room like she'd never seen it before. She had. They'd spent every single Christmas with me here since I bought it.

"He's what?" I asked, caught by surprise. I scowled. "Why hasn't he retired? I thought we agreed—"

"I tried, love. You know how stubborn he is." Her head tilted as she studied me. "Where do you think you got it from?" Abi snorted in the kitchen and my mother grinned. "Looks like your wife knows what I'm talking about."

Saoirse chuckled. "Of course, she does." She shifted on the sofa, turning so she could watch Abi moving around the kitchen with uncertainty. "How long did it take Finn to kiss you, Abi?"

She stiffened, her hand hovering over the wheezing kettle.

"I kissed her within half an hour of meeting her."

"Other than the required marriage kiss?" Saoirse's brows rose. "Bet it wasn't for days."

Only the buzz of lights drifted around us, as Abi and I stared at each other like deer caught in headlights.

"That's exactly what I thought." Saoirse frowned at me, the sisterly judgement arriving right on cue.

"Oh, let's hear it." Resignation dripped from my voice. I leaned back against the cushions, rubbing a hand across my face.

The shuffle of movement drew my attention to the watching crew. I'd worked so hard at keeping the real me from the show, but how could I continue that with my family? They'd call me on my shit if I hid behind a facade.

Tyler watched me, not even bothering to smother his smug smirk.

"What? I'm just saying I'm not surprised." She shrugged, brushing her dark hair over her shoulder. "You don't do affection easily, bro. Can't imagine all of this,"—she gestured at Ian, holding a camera within five feet of us— "is enjoyable for you."

Thankfully, Abi saved me from having to justify my caution when it came to women. She held a box of tea bags in her hands, her eyes narrowed on the tiny instructions.

"See this right here," I said as I stood, gesturing at myself and making pointed eye contact with my wind-up sister. "This is me being a good husband. Can we move on?"

Saoirse grinned at me and nodded. I rescued the tea bags from Abi.

With tea made, we both settled on the sofa, braced for my mother's next of many volleys. She smiled at us, her gaze softening for all of a second as Abi settled against my side.

"Now Finn, how's about you tell us why you kept Abi a secret." Ma assessed Abi, her eyes shining with approval. "She's lovely."

How many times… *Remember there are cameras.* I bit back a growl of frustration.

"I didn't keep Abi a secret." I forced my voice to assume natural, perfectly content tones. No expiration here. "I kept the show a secret."

Saoirse's brows rose. "Aren't the two mutually inclusive?"

"Unfortunately," I grumbled.

"He tried to keep defined lines." Abi patted my knee, grinning up at me and making my chest ache. I'd ignore the mischief in her eyes. "But turns out, he's not great with lines." She chuckled and my sister joined in.

"Oh, I can imagine." Saoirse leaned forward, resting her elbows on her thighs. "Tell us about Finn's avoidance tactics. We could compare notes."

"No need for any of that right now." My eyes narrowed on Saoirse while I frantically searched for a way to change the subject.

"Yes, let's leave that alone." Ma sipped her tea, her gaze fixed on me over the rim. "Finn's finally come to his senses and given his heart to a woman. We shouldn't question it too much, Saoirse. He might use us as an excuse to change his mind."

Saoirse grunted in agreement, picking up her own cup. My mouth opened to deny them, but then I caught the glint in Ma's eyes and shut it again. I would not get sucked into leading questions.

"Just so we're clear, though." Saoirse held her cup to her lips, her head tilting as she considered me. "You didn't invite us to the wedding because of the show?"

"Yes." My hand unintentionally gripped Abi's. I squeezed hers, hoping she'd believe that my feelings had changed.

"So, I get to be involved with a second wedding?" Saoirse lowered the teacup, her face lighting up. "Like really involved? Bridesmaid, bachelorette, and wedding planning involved?"

I stiffened, my grip on Abi's hand reaching painful. "Let's not get ahead of ourselves."

"I agree with Finn," Abi said. She smiled up at me but wiggled her fingers. I loosened my grip before they could turn blue from lack of circulation. "We've only just moved in together. We've still got ages on the show. Best not jinx anything."

"Agreed," Ma said, placing her teacup on the coffee table. "And now that we've got that all cleared up, why don't we skip to the part you thought you'd escaped?" She pulled her handbag onto her lap, patting it as she grinned at me.

"Sweet Jesus woman, tell me you don't have what I think you have in that Tardis handbag?"

"I know you weren't planning to rob me of my right as your mother to embarrass you, Finn McCarthy." Ma popped the clasp and started digging into the contents. "I raised you right, boy."

"Abi doesn't want to see pictures, Ma."

"Of course, she does. Besides, it's a rite of passage." She smirked as she patted the sofa cushion next to her. "Come sit next to me, dear. Better for you to see all the embarrassing pictures of Finn as a boy."

Abi stood, and my gaze caught on Tyler, his entire face lit up with laughter at my expense. He'd probably talked my mother into bringing baby pictures with her.

"Before we dive into these." Abi tapped the huge photo album in her lap. "Can I ask you a question?"

"Of course, dear." My mother shuffled around to face her, absolute delight plastered across her face. "We're an open book for you."

"Yes, we are." Saoirse leaned around mother, grinning as her gaze flicked to me. "Especially when Finn tenses up like that."

I released the tight clench of my fists as Ma chuckled.

"Go ahead. What do you want to know?" Ma patted Abi's arm.

"What does dotey mean?"

"It depends on the context," Ma said. Her eyes flicked between us, her head tilting as suspicions danced across her face. My mother was no fool. She might stall but she knew the context.

"It means adorable," Saoirse chimed in. Amusement lit up her face as she watched me fight to keep my mouth shut. "Has my brother been using it on you?"

"Yes. He didn't want to tell me what it meant." Her lips pursed while she studied me. "He said it meant short."

"That's one definition." Ma smiled before she flicked the photo album open. "I'm pretty sure he means adorable though. His Da gave me the nickname after we met." She ducked her head, leaning close to Abi. "We married two months later. You might have skipped the courting, but I'd say you're right on track for the speed McCarthy men move at."

"Ma!"

"What?" she cried. Her eyes widened with faux innocence. "Both of your uncles married their girlfriends within six months of meeting them too, and don't even let me start on your Granda."

I scrubbed a hand across my face, barely restraining a growl of frustration. Time to prepare for this meeting would have been nice, but even then, I'm not sure I would have escaped unscathed.

"Abi doesn't need to hear about that."

"Is that so?" Ma's brows rose. "I'd think *Abi* would like to know her situation isn't that bizarre in our family, and I'm sure *Abi* can speak for herself." Ma squeezed her arm, smiling at my smirking wife. "Shall we look at some photos and watch Finn squirm?"

Abi eagerly agreed and I spent the next hour eying the three of them with growing trepidation. *Good thing I got my shit together and decided to keep Abi.*

My enabler wife made all the right noises as my mother flicked through photo after photo. Even Saoirse's face turned red as she got caught in a couple.

By the end of it, I could say one thing for certain. My mother had fallen head over heels in love with Abi. If we didn't survive the show, I'd never hear the end of it from my family.

Touche, asshole. Touche.

Time flew by, and before I knew it, my mother and sister

were leaving. They gathered their handbags, muttering promises from Abi to call them whenever she needed a sympathetic ear — I took offence to that one — that she'd stay with them the next time I went home to Belfast.

"Where are you staying?" I asked as I led them to the door.

"We're flying out today, love."

I stopped in my tracks, turning to face my mother with confused horror pumping through my veins.

"Tell me you didn't fly across an entire ocean just for this bloody show." I stared at my mother, fury quietly licking up my spine when she only smiled. "You have got to be kidding me." I turned the full brunt of my ire on Tyler. "You forced them to travel for more than half the day for three hours of footage? What kind of twisted bastard are you?"

"It's okay, Finn." Ma caught my wrist, turning me away from Tyler. "We wanted to meet Abi, and we're glad we came. Right, Saoirse?" She nudged my sister's shoulder, her stern expression urging her to agree.

My sister grimaced instead. "I mean, a video call would have sufficed." She shrugged. "I could have made you a slideshow of embarrassing baby photos and not had to leave my flat."

Ma shook her head at Saoirse, tutting. "Well, it wouldn't have been enough for me."

"You could stay," Abi said, weaving her fingers through mine.

I met her gaze and read the tight press of fingers for the restraint they truly were. So maybe my wife could read me better than I thought. Her shrewd blue eyes begged me not to throttle Tyler as I desperately itched too.

"Unless you have plans," she added, never breaking eye contact with me.

"Unfortunately, we do." Ma edged towards the door, snagging my attention. "You remember Enid, right? Her baby shower's tomorrow and we need to be home for it."

I frowned, searching the recesses of my mind for anyone called Enid.

"She's your cousin's sister-in-law." Ma's brows furrowed. "She was at the summer BBQ. Don't you remember?"

Couldn't say I did, but that wasn't the point.

"You'd rather get on back-to-back flights for a stranger's baby shower than spend a week with the daughter-in-law you claim to already love?"

Saoirse chuckled and Ma scowled at us both.

"That's not what I'm saying at all."

"You kind of are," Saoirse said, amusement making her Irish accent lilt further.

"Christ, there's no reasoning with the pair of you when you're like this." Ma dragged a hand through her hair. "Call us on Sunday, Finn, or next time I get on a plane, I'll stay for my full visa allowance and drive you insane."

My jaw slackened as she flung the front door open. She couldn't possibly mean…

"And drop that terrible tan," she shouted over her shoulder. "You're Irish. Look it."

She left us gaping after her. Saoirse stepped in, throwing her arms around me.

"You should be impressed," she whispered in my ear. "Ma's adapting to the Hollywood lifestyle better than you are. Swanning across the pond without a thought."

One way of putting it.

Saoirse released me, grinning as she turned to Abi. "And you, get my number from this one, and text me. We can start planning your vow renewal." She clapped her hands together, glancing between us. "This thing with you two is clearly going to be around for a long time.

With those shiver-inducing words, she rushed after Ma. If I hadn't had a camera fixed to me, I would have slumped against the wall and hugged Abi to me. The pair of them always could sweep in fast, all smiles, and leave chaotic wreckage in their wake.

I studied Abi, trying to be subtle about it. I couldn't see any sign that they'd scared her further than the fear of wanting family approval.

After last night, I couldn't deny it anymore. I wanted her to stay. I needed her as much as I needed my next breath.

INTERVIEW IX

Question: Did you enjoy meeting Finn's family?
Abi: It was a pleasant surprise.
Tyler, producer: You can be more specific than that.
Abi: Fine. Fiona made me feel like a part of the family and…
I didn't realise how much I'd missed that. Of course, I have
Eva and Ros. They've been my only family for years and
they're always there when I need them. But there's just something about having a mother pushing you, teasing you…
loving you. I missed it.
Tyler, producer: Does it make you feel hopeful for things to
come? After the show?
Abi: I think it's still early days to make plans for after the
show. Finn and I need to settle into daily life. We need to
figure out how we fit together in this weird world of fame…
but yes, knowing his mother likes me, it feels like part of the
battle has already been won and I'm… cautiously optimistic.
Tyler, producer: Perfect.

CHAPTER TWENTY-FIVE

ABI

Tyler and his crew cleared out soon after Finn's family. I kept a firm grip on Finn's hand while Tyler waltzed away, a smug gleam in his eyes. When the door closed on him, we both relaxed.

One glance at the other and we both chuckled. Finn collapsed onto the sofa, sagging into the cushions.

"Not how I expected the morning to go," Finn groaned into his hand.

"I had other ideas too." I joined him on the sofa, fitting myself into his side, hooking a leg over his.

He wrapped an arm around me, pulling me closer, smoothing his hand up and down my bare arm. I pressed my face into his chest, smiling at the 'walking on air' feeling something so small inspired in me.

He hummed in agreement. "Did yours involve the kitchen counter, too?"

"Maybe." I drummed my fingers against his chest, enjoying the momentary peace.

"Nothing stopping us from picking up where they rudely interrupted." Finn sat forward, taking me with him, his eagerness making his Irish accent more pronounced.

I laughed. "There's no rush, McCarthy."

"I just suffered through my mother's best efforts to embarrass me." He tucked an arm under my legs. "I need to prove to you I'm still in charge."

"As if you were ever in charge."

My chuckle died as he speared me with a dark, heated look. It promised retribution for the lie. *Would he tie me up?* Liquid heat flooded me at the idea.

"A reminder it is." He stood, scooping me up with him. I squeaked, scrambling for a grip, throwing my arms around his neck.

I squeezed my thighs together, trying and failing to quell the ache he'd caused.

Finn placed me on the breakfast bar and pressed his hands to my knees. With his eyes fixed on me, he forced my legs open and wedged himself in the gap. He slid me towards the edge of the counter, dragging me forward until my breasts pressed against his chest and the bulge of his shorts grazed my core.

His gaze fixated on my mouth, darkening as I licked my lips. He lowered his head, his intent clear. I held him off with a hand to his chest.

Questions first, then fucking.

"How old is your dad?"

Finn groaned. "I'm about to fuck you and you're asking me about my dad?" He dragged a hand across his face. "What the hell am I doing wrong with you?"

I smiled, channelling my inner vixen. "Answer the question and I'll let you do whatever you want to me."

Finn eyed me, clear interest slackening his expression. "Anything?" At my nod, he gave in. "Fifty-five."

"You looked shocked when your mother said he's still

working." I let my hands smooth down his chest to play with the edge of his t-shirt. "I'm trying to figure out why."

Finn bit his lip, and I decided waiting for him to answer my questions before I got my hands on his skin would be a waste of time. I tugged the t-shirt over his head. He didn't resist, lifting his arms and helping me.

He placed his hands on the counter at either side of me and leaned forward, his lips teasingly close. My fingers took on a mind of their own, ghosting over his pecs, blindly mapping out the lines of muscle. I shook my head, fighting the lust-filled fog.

"I paid off all of their debts when I made my first million — my sister's too." He pressed his forehead to mine, his nose brushing against mine. "Then I set up investment accounts for them so they could comfortably draw off the interest for the rest of their lives. He doesn't need to work. I guess I don't like the idea of him putting unnecessary stress on himself and..."

His entire body tensed as he paused, peeking at me from beneath his lashes. Something about his watchful tension made me think he'd nearly said something bad... or bad in his mind.

I turned his words over again, searching for the meaning that worried him.

"I'm sorry, I didn't mean to..."

I dropped my hands from his glorious chest, placing them over his. I squeezed, willing him to relax.

"It's okay to say the word, Finn." I smiled at his hesitation. "Dying. It's just a word."

"I don't need to." He shook his head. "You got the picture, and I didn't mean to remind you that your parents..."

Warmth flooded me. I wrapped my arms and legs around him, hugging him tightly. He patted my back, the gesture tentative and uncertain.

"I'm so sorry, Abi."

"Shh, Finn. I'm okay." I leaned back, smiling softly at the surprising lug. "My parents died five years ago, and I miss them. I've still got Eva, though. It hurts sometimes, but it doesn't cripple me anymore." I caressed his face, dragging a finger along the crease between his brows. He relaxed beneath my touch. "You can talk about death. You can talk about my parents. I won't collapse into a blubbering heap."

Finn nodded, his gaze softening on me.

"I think I'm done asking questions," I whispered. My brows rose suggestively, but Finn continued to stare at me like he'd gotten lost cataloguing me. I reached up, snagging a hand behind his neck, and dragged his head down. "Kiss me, Finn." I ghosted my lips over his. "Remind me who's in charge."

His lips crashed against mine, snapping out of his daze and going from zero to eighty. He devoured me. His tongue warred with mine while his fingers bunched in my shirt. The material went flying over my head with little preamble.

"I hope you weren't hoping to leave the house today," Finn muttered as his head dipped back to mine.

The doorbell chorus floated around us.

"Fuck off!" he shouted at the door.

Ding. Dong.

"I need to disconnect that fucking doorbell," he growled. He pulled away from me with a severe look. "Do not move an inch. I'll be back."

Finn stomped away, and I collapsed back on my elbows, gasping for breath. The door opened and closed quickly, with nothing more than a brief murmur of voices.

Then Finn returned, carting a heavy-looking black box. He placed it on the counter beside me. A sheepish edge entered his eyes as he rubbed his beard, glancing between the box and me.

"What is it?"

"I got you something." He stared uncertainly at the box. "Ros said at the wedding that you'd like it, and I ordered on our way to Bora Bora." He grimaced when he met my curious gaze. "Now I'm thinking she could have been pulling my leg."

"What did you get?" I asked as I shuffled along the counter towards the box. A flutter of excitement settled in my chest.

Finn McCarthy bought me a present. A non-TV show exploited present. I could scream.

He kept his lips tightly sealed while I tore open the box. When I finally laid eyes on the gift, I didn't stop to wonder if he'd be ready to catch me. I just trusted and launched off the counter.

Air exploded from his lungs as he caught me.

"Thank you. Thank you. Thank you." I pressed kisses to his face, his lips, his neck. "Ros wasn't trying to wind you up. I love it."

He set me back on the counter, a cautious smile curling his lips. "You're sure?"

I glanced at the white sewing machine nestled in its box, waiting for me to put it to work. "It's the best gift you could have ever given me."

His shoulders sagged. "Thank Christ for that." His smile fell as he glanced between the box and my excitement. "You don't want to play with it now, right?"

I snorted, then tucked a finger into the loop of his belt, tugging him *much* closer.

"You need to punish me first, remember?" I whispered, my voice low and sultry.

Finn's eyes darkened. "What am I punishing you for?"

Words collided in my throat as nerves got the better of me. I'd never… I tried to be open to anything with him, but all the sex I'd ever experienced had been very vanilla. Finn awakened kinks for me I never knew I had.

I swallowed. "For questioning your control."

His lips curled and then his mouth slanted across mine. I handed myself over to him, not caring what he did, as long as he made me feel half of what I did last night. Thankfully, I had total faith in my surprise of a husband.

He made quick work of my clothing, but each time I reached for his jeans, he slapped my hands away.

"Lean back on your elbows, Dotey."

Once I obeyed, he took a seat in front of me and my legs automatically tried to close. My cheeks burned, but he forced my knees open. He circled my clit with his thumb without warning, and then his fingers dragged through my wet folds, forcing the slight sting of embarrassment out of my mind.

He leaned forward, ducking his head. His shoulders pushed my legs further apart and then his mouth latched onto my clit, and I shut up.

Between his mouth and his fingers working me, my body started to tense as an impending orgasm gripped me. At the first twitch, he pulled back. His fingers continued to caress my pussy, but the pressure wasn't enough to push me over the edge.

"Finn," I begged.

My hips shifted, shamelessly chasing his mouth. He didn't give in. Instead, he held me down with a powerful forearm across my stomach. The heat of his arm across my abdomen and my over-sensitised body, combined with the freezing cold slab of marble beneath me made for an interesting contrast.

"What are you doing?" Nerves thrummed in my throat, making my voice breathy.

Finn glanced a finger over the lips of my soaking pussy, barely touching, but my core clenched all the same.

"Punishing you." His brows rose. "That's what you asked for, isn't it?"

"Yes, but this isn't what — Oh!" I moaned as he circled my clit again, my head falling back and my eyes fluttering closed.

"I'm going to take you to the edge of orgasm," he whispered, his voice deep and gravelly. "And then I'm going to stop."

My eyes flew open to assess him. He couldn't be serious. Only, one look into his sapphire gaze and I knew he was.

"Finn, no." I frowned at him.

He smirked. "You asked for punishment."

"Yes, but I didn't mean…"

He lowered his head and dragged the tip of his tongue through my folds. I thought he'd finally given me what I wanted, and I sighed as pleasure unwound again. I'd been wrong.

Intense pleasure and no reward? Okay. Carry on.

I don't know how long I lay there, or how many times he stopped me from going over the edge. What I do know is that, by the time he stood up, every muscle in my body shook with need. Sweat glistened on my rose-tinted skin and my hair had worked its way out of my bun to flow across the worktop, no doubt leaving a tangled mess for me to fix later.

"Finn, no," I whimpered. I watched him stand through hooded lids.

"On your hands and knees," he said, surprising me.

"What?" Through some sheer miracle, I managed to lift my head.

I frowned at him, but it had no effect. His sapphire eyes burned with need and his jeans stretched taut with his constrained hardness.

"On. Your. Knees," he ground out.

Gingerly, I shifted, following through without another question. As I moved further onto the counter, Finn unzipped his jeans, pushing them and his boxers to the floor with a relieved sigh. His cock hit him in the stomach, rock hard and dripping with pre-cum. My mouth watered as he rolled on a condom.

"Be a good girl, Abi, and turn around." Finn wrapped a hand around the base of his cock, stroking once as he stared at me. "You've done so well taking your punishment. Don't spoil it now."

My core ached at the feverish light in his eyes. I turned around, barely registering the warning note in his voice.

Despite technically obeying, I kept my head tilted in a direction that would let me watch him. He climbed onto the counter behind me. His hands coasted across my ass and lower back, gentle and loving even as he owned me.

I jolted slightly when he notched his cock against my opening. My hips automatically rocked back, desperate to feel the stretch of him inside me again. I expected him to stop me, even braced for a reprimand.

Instead, his fingers dug into my hips and he finished the job, filling me to the hilt. We both moaned at the tight fit. My arms gave out as he pulled out and lightning bolts of pleasure shot through me. I collapsed onto the counter, ass in the air and only my elbows stopping me from falling face first into the counter. Every inch of me shook.

"You're so fucking tight," Finn groaned as he thrust back into me.

Somehow, his thrusts went deeper, stealing my breath along with my strength. The hard surface bit into my knees but I couldn't care less, as long as he kept driving into me… like… that.

Finn picked up the pace, slamming into me until only the sound of our gasps, moans and bodies filled the house. Everything tightened inside of me and then the coil snapped, finally tipping me over the edge and into the bliss of an orgasm.

"Christ." Finn's arm wrapped around my stomach and a hand landed next to my head as he leaned over me. "You're going to be the fucking death of me, dotey. All I'm going to want to do after this is draw those mindless sounds of need out of you."

He pressed his forehead to my heated back, holding still while my body settled down from the high of coming. Finn pressed a kiss to my neck, gentle and tentative. The complete opposite of the determined way he handled my body.

Then his fingers slipped between my legs and any thoughts of gentleness evaporated.

He swirled his fingers around my clit and I couldn't bite back my cry. Aftershocks danced through me, forcing my pussy to tighten around his hardness. He nipped my shoulder, groaning as my inner walls tried to milk him along with me.

"Next time you want to question control," he whispered, pressing his lips to my ear. "Remember how helpless you are right now."

He rocked his hips, barely leaving my body but still sending shockwaves of pleasure through me. My knees shook and if not for his arm wrapped around my waist, I'd slid to the counter in a graceless heap.

"It's too much, Finn." I pressed my face into my forearms, crying out as he grazed my g-spot on his next thrust. "I can't…"

"Yes, you can, dotey." His teeth grazed my neck, making me shiver. "You're taking it so well. You don't want to stop yet, do you, baby?"

My eyes slid closed as he rocked back into me, lighting me up from the inside out. Teeth gritted, I shook my head.

Finn pressed a kiss to the nape of my neck. "Words, Abi. Tell me what you want."

"Don't. Stop," I groaned as he retreated.

"Good girl." His lips curled against my neck and then he pulled back, straightening up again.

I let him manhandle me, pumping into me faster and faster while every muscle in my body tensed up from fatigue and pleasure. A litany of curse words flew from Finn's mouth as my next orgasm crested. This time when I came, he let go with me.

I must have blacked out, because the next thing I knew I

was lying on his chest on top of the counter. His fingers smoothed up and down my back and through my hair.

"What have you done to me, dotey?" Finn whispered, his voice raw and open. I held still, getting the distinct impression he didn't think I'd hear him. "I wasn't meant to let anyone get close to me and here you are, stealing my heart. Should fight you. Instead," he pressed a kiss to the top of my head and my chest squeezed. "I'm handing it to you with a smile."

CHAPTER TWENTY-SIX

FINN

A few days later, I led Abi out to the patio, finally showing her around the house properly. She gasped at the pool, and one thing led to another, and the next thing we knew, I was throwing her in.

Fuck.

I wanted her anywhere, anyhow. She'd walked onto the patio in her skimpy bikini, and I felt things I hadn't allowed myself to feel in Bora Bora. Arousal being the biggest of the lot, followed quickly by the intense need to hold onto her and not let go.

So I did just that. Until we were both shaking and moaning with our releases.

"Hold on." I caught her waist before she could climb out of the pool. "Put your bikini back on first."

"Why?" Abi's brows furrowed. "It's just a quick run to the towels."

"We don't know if someone's watching." I grimaced

Despite the silence, I glanced up, checking for helicopters.

The skies were clear but that didn't mean a pap hadn't set themselves up with a long-range lens and a clear view of the property.

"I should have waited until we were inside." I dragged a hand through my soaking hair, a ball of lead forming in my stomach. "I'm sorry."

I readjusted my shorts, covering myself while Abi wriggled back into her bikini. She bit her lip, throwing me suggestive looks.

"It's okay. I enjoyed it."

"You wouldn't if they had your sex life on replay for millions of gawkers across the world," I grumbled mostly to myself.

"Is that what happened to you?" She climbed up the pool ladder, casting glances over her shoulder. "Did someone catch you in the act?"

I huffed. "You could say that."

Abi wrapped a towel around herself, watching me with raised brows and a quiet determination. I studied her, the need to keep my mouth shut driving me hard.

But she's your wife…

"Let's go inside and I'll tell you." I wrapped a towel around my waist and led the way, psyching myself up all the while.

It would be okay. She'd given me enough of herself for me to trust her. And if I wanted this relationship to last, I needed to be open with her.

We walked down the hallway towards my bedroom. Abi paused at her door, her hand hovering over the handle.

"I'll just grab a shower and then we'll talk?"

"You can—" The words died as my throat closed up. *You're getting serious, remember?* I shook myself and tried again. "You can shower in my room if you want."

My gaze bore into hers while I silently communicated what my nerves wouldn't let me. *Me, nervous over a woman?* The thought of it made me scoff. I didn't do nerves. I faced diffi-cult situations head-on and with confidence.

"Move into my room." I winced at my commanding tone. "Please."

For a second she stared at me, shocked and my stomach tied itself into knots while I wondered if I'd completely misread her. Then she smiled, unearthing my own.

"You want me to stay in your room?" she asked, her voice tentative.

"Only if you want to." I scratched my beard, feeling oddly sheepish for even asking.

"I'd love to."

In my room, she settled on the edge of the bed, a white towel wrapped teasingly around her damp body. My cock hardened but she continued to stare at me with a raised brow.

"Well?" She patted the space beside her. "Spill the details."

"Didn't you want to shower first?"

"That can wait." Her gaze roamed my face, eyes narrow-ing. "You in a sharing mood won't."

"Okay, fine." I sat next to her, stiff at first while reality hit me. *Why did I agree to this?*

"Why are you hesitating?" she shuffled around until she faced me. "I'm not going to judge you. No promises I won't get angry on your behalf though."

I chuckled at the fierce burn in her eyes. "What Natalie did to me was worse than a pap catching sight of something they shouldn't have." I took a deep, shaky breath and reached for her hand, needing support for the first time in my life. "Without my knowing, Natalie filmed us having sex. I still don't know how long it went on."

Abi paled. "Is that what you meant about her stealing from people?"

I nodded. "She sold it exclusively to one gossip site, but once something hits the internet, it's uncontrollable."

Her eyes widened. "And then it spread and damaged your reputation."

"Bingo." I smiled, not an ounce of happiness on my face.

"Is that why you needed to do the show?"

I chuckled, indecision racing through me at the thought of being honest with her on that. Never mind the fact it felt weird to share my sexual scandals with the wife I wanted to keep.

"No, I recovered from that donkey's years ago." I chewed my lip but ultimately caved to the inevitable. "You could say having the woman I thought I loved betray me like that for money and fame made me a little bitter." I winced. A lot bitter. "They wanted me to be the playboy, so I leaned into it."

Abi tilted her head, her eyes narrowing as she tried to follow. "What does that have to do with the show then?"

"I got caught on camera in a public bathroom with the studio head's daughter."

I studied her closely, braced for the moment she recoiled. Instead, she laughed.

"So your agent thought marriage would make for suitable punishment?" she asked through peals of laughter. Her eyes started to water. "Charlie's got a sense of humour, huh?"

"If you say so," I grumbled.

That only set her off more. Watching her take my failings in stride, I couldn't help but loosen up. I revelled in the feeling, smiling at her all the while.

A month ago, I vehemently refused to get attached to anyone. Now I could feel the first glimmer of hope.

ABI

We didn't make it to the shower. Finn's secret sharing devolved into testing out his bed which devolved into... well, you know.

I had to test the mattress out. What if I hated it and need to change rooms again?

"You must see some bizarre things on sets," I said, my voice overly loud in the silence of the room.

I lay against him, drawing random patterns on his chest while he did the same to my back. It felt… almost too peaceful. Like at any moment a shoe would drop and we'd revert to bickering with and resisting each other in Bora Bora.

"Hmm, you have no idea." Silence fell and that was all I'd get, then he surprised me. "On my… I think it was my third feature film, we — the guys were on it with me — were all excited to be working with this incredibly hot director. He was award-winning, a true powerhouse in mainstream film and the job offer fulfilled an unexpected bucket list item for me."

I smiled as he raced on, his Irish accent rising and falling at speed as he talked with excitement. *I could happily listen to him read the phonebook.*

"Good things aren't always what they seem though." His excitement faded and I lifted my head to study his down-turned expression. "None of us knew that Mike Lewis spent his off moments coercing and blackmailing the female staff into his bed." He whispered the words with such vehemence.

A twinge of unease hit me in the gut as I absorbed his sudden tension. I barely followed names in film and TV, but even I knew Mike Lewis still directed some of the biggest movies on screen. How could that be if he…

"No one knows, do they?"

"Some do." Finn's lips curled in a sad smile. "But he paid his victims off, and the rest of us liked our lives too much to go up against Hollywood's golden goose without proof."

My eyes widened. "That's why you jumped to get Casey off the show."

Finn nodded. "I might have been powerless back then, and I might not have the ability to out Mike Lewis, but things are different on *Married Blind.*" His fingers toyed with my hair while he focused on the ceiling. His brow creased with concentration. "I knew I could count on everyone else being outraged by the potential image damage. If they lost all their celebs, just as they invested hundreds of thousands into weddings…" He shrugged, the motion jostling me slightly. "The series producer wouldn't have let it happen, even if Tyler had."

If he trusts me with this, does that mean he's finally on board with the long-term?

And if so, why did that thought fill me with unease?

My phone pinged before I had to figure out my feelings or how to respond to Finn. I shuffled across the bed, grasping for my device on the bedside table. A message from Eva lit up the screen and I smiled, the unease momentarily forgotten.

EVA

Talked to my boss. Can't make it to LA.

I missed my sister. I knew she wouldn't want to waste money on airfare but the show paid me more than enough to cut a decent chunk out of her debt and fly her to LA for a visit.

ABI

Why not?

EVA

It's just a busy period. I'll try to make it out next month.

I should have been happy with the promise. Instead, I could only focus on the first half of the text. Pre-cancer, my sister had been a workaholic. I'd hoped remission would have changed that. Sometimes, it felt like she worked harder than she did before. *Yes, I realise that's hypocritical of a woman with three jobs.*

It still hurt even knowing we were both working our asses

off to free her from debt. Like did she not want to see me? We hadn't spent this long apart since I left for college.

"Everything, alright?" Finn asked, tone careful. His fingers danced up my back.

Five minutes ago, I would have stretched into the feel of them grazing up my spine. I would have enjoyed the affection.

Now, it felt stifling. Like a touch could be responsible for the distance from my sister. Or the weight of Finn's trust resting on my chest.

It was all too much.

CHAPTER TWENTY-SEVEN

ABI

"Hey Abs," my sister said, her smiling face filling my laptop screen on the coffee table. "I miss you."

"I miss you too."

"I can't wait until you get back."

My stomach dropped as her face lit up.

"Did you think about coming out for a visit?" I slid off the sofa, settling on the rug so I could be closer to the laptop and at the same eye level.

She winced. "I don't think I'll be able to get time off, I'm sorry."

My gut twisted with disappointment, but I fought to keep it off my face. I didn't need to make her feel guilty.

"It's okay. It was a long shot, right?" My smile felt brittle.

Things had been incredible with Finn in the last few weeks. I'd moved into his room after he fucked me senseless on the kitchen counter. The glimpses of his kind heart I'd seen in Bora Bora had come out of the shadows. Unexpected flower deliveries, surprise dates in the most random of places. He made me feel spoiled, and I couldn't get enough of him.

But I missed my sister. We hadn't been apart this long since I'd left home for college.

"Has Ros been driving you crazy?" I asked, changing the subject before either of us could dwell on the situation more. "She texts me like fifty times a day."

"She spends nearly every night at my place." Eva chuckled. "I got home last night and she announced we were having a movie night. Can you see these dark circles?" Eva leaned closer to the camera, pointing at her eyes. "She picked the Lord of the flipping Rings. For a Wednesday night!"

I snorted. "Were they the extended versions?"

"Thankfully not." Eva shuddered. "The sooner you get back, the better. I can't handle all the attention."

What if I don't want to come back?

A pang of guilt hit me hard in the gut. Things were going so well. We weren't pretending anymore and, every day, I could feel myself slipping further and further down the rabbit hole. I think I already loved him. How could I leave him?

"A month to go." Eva grinned, excitement setting her expression alight. "Are you counting down the days?"

"I haven't thought about it," I lied.

Another pang hit me. Lying to my sister. Who had I become?

"Honestly, you're missing—" A deep cough cut her off, shaking her shoulders and turning her face red.

Panic flared inside of me, tightening my chest. We'd been so vigilant while she went through chemo, terrified that she'd catch something and not be able to fight it off. That pressure had eased once she got the all-clear but seeing her doubled over and not being able to touch her? Hell, pure hell.

"Eva! Are you okay?"

She held up her hand, urging me to wait as the coughing fit continued, but how could I? Once it stopped, she lifted a tissue to her nose and blew. Only then did I truly see the signs that she'd caught a cold.

"Is Ros there with you? How long have you been sick?" Questions spewed from me in a stream of gasping panic. "You should be in bed, Eva."

"I'm fine, Abi." My sister grimaced. "Seriously, it's just a normal cold, a little fever and a cough. Everyone gets them."

"You have a fever?" I cried. "Where the hell is Ros?"

I scrambled for my phone, opening the text box with my best friend with shaking fingers.

"She's at work. Leave her alone, Abs." Eva's brow furrowed as she tried to wave me off. "It's a busy week for her with preparation for Paris Fashion Week. She doesn't need the extra stress."

ABI

Did you know Eva's sick?

"Look at me, Abi," Eva said, her tone stern. I glanced up at her, my fingers tapping on the table while I waited for Ros's reply. "I've got meds. It'll clear just like it does for everyone else."

"Not everyone is a year into remission. Everyone else has a support network to fall back on." A network that went beyond an uber-busy but also flaky friend and a sister who stupidly thought she could leave the state for three months and not worry about her only remaining family member.

I scowled at her. A voice deep inside acknowledged that scowling at my sister for being sick probably wasn't the sanest thing, but at that moment, I was beyond logic.

"How long have you been sick?"

My phone pinged while she dithered over a reply.

ROS

Yeah, she's been spluttering every time I've seen her in the last two weeks. She says she's fine.

I glared at the text as my fingers flew over the screen at a furious pace.

ABI

> And you believed her?

"Eh, a week or so." She waved her hand, brushing it all off. "Stop harassing Ros. She's our friend, not my keeper."

No, that had been *my* job.

"A week? Have you seen your doctor?" My voice rose, the panic spiralling it higher. "Does she think you should be working?"

"I'm working from home. Hardly dangerous." Eva smiled, a look of pure patience she'd learned from our parents. Oh, how the tables had turned. The patience role had been assigned to me. I was the eldest after all.

"She thinks I'm recovering fine." Eva leaned forward, a serious light entering her eyes. "Listen to me, Abs, I'm okay. It's just a cold. It will clear."

I chewed my lip, unconvinced.

"I need to go, Abs. Work calls. I'll text you later." She flashed a smile and killed the call before I could even say goodbye.

My gut churned.

Mona sat down opposite me, picking up her cup. She didn't say anything, just sipped her tea and waited me out.

Eva might have recovered from the cancer, but she clearly needed me. Someone with her health conditions should not be working while sick. Logically, I knew avoiding a cold in New York was difficult with all the closed-in spaces and crowds of people, but we'd managed it. For the duration of her treatment, we'd managed.

Staying in LA would mean not being there for her when she needed me, never going to hers on a random evening, never getting a last-minute call to meet her for lunch, or spending an entire weekend, with takeout and an endless binge of Gilmore Girls.

"Are you okay, Abi?"

I nodded. "Great."

Mona continued to study me. She didn't believe me. Hell, I didn't believe me.

"It's hard, isn't it?"

"What is?"

We'd been having so much fun, chatting about Mona's wedding plans and the vintage pieces I'd found in a thrift store in Hollywood. The guilt deepened. How could I be this happy having tea with Mona when I hadn't seen my sister since the wedding?

"Being away from your family." She smiled when my eyes widened. "My parents live in Cornwall, my sister is in Glasgow, and my brother is in London. I haven't seen any of them since we moved out here in January. Five months with just calls."

"How do you handle it?"

"I'd already been pretty separated before I got here so I don't think our situations are identical." She bit her lip, her gaze dropping to her cup. "It can be hard, I won't lie. We do a weekly group video call and have visits planned. They'll all be here for the wedding. But I do miss my sister. She was an hour away on the train before I met Shaun." She shrugged. "I wouldn't change a thing. I love Shaun. Before him, I was lost and pretty flipping sad. I've never been as happy as I am with him."

"So you think I'd adjust?"

"That depends on whether you want to." She leaned forward, her gaze fixed on me. "If you love Finn, you'll do anything to stay with him. And trust me, it's not simple with an actor." She smirked, her shoulders shaking slightly as amusement creased her eyes. "Shaun only accepts roles now where I can work on the production team. He's very forceful about it too, something his agent was not prepared for when she hired me. It doesn't matter where in the world the job sends him, we'll always be together."

"And you don't mind moving about for him?"

"We haven't had to yet, but I'll jump at it when the time comes." She tilted her head, a thought flickering across her face. "But I always wanted to travel. The way I see it, I'll get two of my favourite things. The love of my life and the excitement of seeing new places."

It all sounded perfect, but guilt still gnawed at me. The other thing I loved was pretty fixed in her location. Eva loved her job. She'd never quit to move out West. Rosaline might. She'd always been changeable with her wants and interests.

Two choices sat before me and neither of them made me feel all that great. Lose Finn and get unlimited time with Eva. Or only see Eva every couple of months and commit to a life with Finn, whatever that looked like.

"You don't need to figure it out, right now, Abi," Mona said, her tone gentle. "I'd be sad to see you go, but you have to do what's best for you."

I chewed my lip. "Even if it hurts Finn?"

Her sadness swept across her face, but still, she smiled. "Sometimes we can't avoid hurting the ones we love."

And I did love him.

"Abi, are you here?" Finn called from the hallway later that day.

I released the pedal on the sewing machine and glanced at my closed bedroom door. I rarely came in here anymore, but after Mona left, I couldn't face sitting in the cavernous living area alone with my conflicted thoughts.

My fingers ached as I pushed back from the machine. *What time is it?*

I clicked my phone to life and my eyes widened. I'd been working for two hours straight without a break. No wonder everything hurt.

Finn called again, an edge to his voice that made my brows rise. Where he thought I'd go without him, I couldn't say. I didn't have a car and the thought of using his car service like he told me to, made me uneasy. Only rich people used chauffeurs and I was not one.

I opened the bedroom door just as he rushed back. He spun on his heels, absolute panic on his face.

"There you are," he said, his voice breathy.

"Are you okay?" I stepped into the hall towards him. Concern beat like a pulse in my mind. His hair stood on end and his sapphire eyes were wide. "Did something happen?"

"No, no. I just…" he trailed off, his gaze roaming my face as the panic gradually receded. "I don't know what I thought." He chuckled, shaking his head. "I've got far too active an imagination."

Finn caught my hand, tugging me into his chest. He wrapped his arms around me and rested his chin on my head while his heart pounded beneath my ear.

"What did you think had happened?"

"I don't know." He blew out a breath. "Too many terrifying things went through my head. The front door was unlocked and…"

I pulled back, staring into his exhausted expression.

"You thought someone had taken me."

He pressed his lips together but didn't deny it.

"Is that even a real possibility?" It seemed insane, but what did I really know about his life? "There's a guard at the gate, and the house is plastered with alarms and cameras."

"The alarms only work if you turn them on."

Which I hadn't.

"And the guard?"

He shrugged before a sunny smile swept over his expression. I narrowed my eyes at him.

"I told you, I'm being irrational." He broke from my arms, gripping my hands, he led me down the hallway, towards the main room. "I have a surprise for you."

I let him guide me into the room. How could someone go from panic to excitement so fast?

Someone sat on the sofa, their back to us. Finn just grinned at me when I tried to silently demand answers. Short white-blond hair and broad shoulders, that's all I had. And Finn's ridiculous excitement. Curious.

The guy stood when we were closer to the sofa. He turned, a careless smirk on his lips. Icy blue eyes, striking enough to rival Finn's, fixed on me. I glanced at Finn, my mouth working but no words coming out.

How had he — why had he — Shit, was it real?

Had I fallen asleep at the sewing machine?

"Abi, meet Owen Parry. The —"

"Lead singer of Marable." I blinked at him and gawked like a stunned fan might. *Because you are a stunned fan, dipshit.*

Owen Parry was waiting for me to be normal.

"Why couldn't you warn me?" I slapped Finn on the arm. "I would have changed."

Finn chuckled. "That would have ruined the surprise. Plus, Owen doesn't care what you're wearing. Right, man?"

"Definitely not," he said, that melodic Welsh accent sweeping over me better than any recording could.

"I'll grab us some drinks." He pressed a hand to my back and shoved me forward. "Why don't you and Owen chat, *dotey*?"

I went without protest and miraculously avoided chewing my lip.

"Finn said you're a fan?" Owen asked, his voice gentle. I nodded. "I bet he didn't expect that. We arrived in LA around the same time. It's been a running joke between us that our girlfriends always loved the other."

"Only because you're a careless flirt," Finn said, amusement softening his words. He handed Owen a glass before joining me on the other sofa. "You've got stadiums of screaming fans, you can't leave me one person?"

The longer we chatted with Owen and Finn ribbing each other, the more the surprise and awe cleared. I tried to focus on the press of Finn's thigh against mine or the way his fingers toyed with my hair. Anything to keep my focus away from his panic when he couldn't find me.

Unfortunately, it didn't work.

New York had its issues. I knew that, but New York had never truly hurt me despite all the sketchy corners and crowds of people. Stupid or not, I knew that devil and it had my back.

Whereas here, nothing felt familiar. Not LA, not the culture, not Finn's glamorous life. Eva would have rolled her eyes at his flash of wealth if he'd put her in a private helicopter or whisked her into an uber-expensive and exclusive restaurant at the last minute. And if someone did break in, she'd have said he brought it on himself, flashing his cash the way he did.

But what if someone attacked her to get to Finn?

Nearly losing her once was bad enough and with our parents gone, we were all the other had. We didn't have any other family.

If I decided to stay, she'd smile and pretend to be happy for me, but I knew her too well not to read the truth in her eyes. She'd be heartbroken.

And if I left, Finn might be too.

Fuck, would the negatives ever stop?

CHAPTER TWENTY-EIGHT

FINN

SHAUN

When's Abi free for dress fittings?

FINN

I don't know. Why isn't Mona asking her?

SHAUN

Because I'm asking you.

FINN

The wedding's in December.

SHAUN

Answer the question.

I sighed and let the tablet drop to my chest. "Is Mona pressuring you on the wedding?"

Abi puttered around the kitchen area, making something despite the pile of prepared meals in the fridge. Her hair was piled on top of her head and she wore tiny, lacey shorts, and a tank top that left nothing to the imagination. I cherished the sight.

Abi glanced at me, brows drawn and a question in her eyes.

"Shaun's bugging me to get you to a dress fitting or something?" I picked the tablet back up and flicked through his latest messages. "I keep telling him the wedding's months away and he should chill out. Have you heard anything about this?"

Her eyes widened a fraction, and she went pale. I watched her for a second, mapping my fastest route to her if she passed out.

"Are you okay?"

"I'm fine," she squeaked. She cleared her throat. "No, no pressure. On this end anyway. Maybe Shaun's the bridezilla in their relationship."

ABI

I spent two days avoiding Finn. Guilt consumed me— for avoiding him, for even considering staying in LA when my sister needed me. Take your pick of reasons, I felt guilty for it.

Hell, I wanted every ounce of attention he threw at me. But every time he tried to get close, every time he mentioned an event or plan in the distant future, my body froze up.

I needed to be careful or he'd realise I had doubts. Why I thought that would be a bad thing, I didn't know, but the fear of it consumed me.

A knock sounded on my door frame, distracting me, and I jolted, messing up the stitch on my latest creation: a pleated tartan skirt. I might have taken inspiration from Jackson's kilt at our wedding.

I glanced over my shoulder to find Finn smiling at me with that soft light that both made me ache and squirm uncomfortably.

"I was thinking, we haven't been out in a while," he said as he sauntered toward me. His skin glistened and his t-shirt stuck to his body, highlighting every divot and ridge of his abs. "After I shower, do you fancy going out for a picnic or something?"

My tongue glued itself to the roof of my mouth.

It sounded incredible.

"Or we could do something else?" He edged towards me, a furrow of confusion marring his brow. "A sunset stroll at Venice Beach. You said you want to check out Santa Monica Pier."

"Won't you get mobbed?" I asked, desperation leaking from my voice.

"Probably not, but I'll wear a hat and glasses just in case." He grinned. "C'mon, dotey, bunk off with me for a couple of hours."

My mind raced, fighting for a logical way out that would stop my heart from pining for the picture he painted.

"I already have plans with Mona." I grimaced then pushed my chair back and shot to my feet. "In fact, I'm late."

He frowned, crossing his arms. "And you just remembered?"

"Yep. Sorry." I race around the room, collecting things. "I lost track of time," I said before slipping into the attached bathroom to change.

His scepticism haunted me as I called a taxi and texted Mona to warn her of my imminent arrival.

A hard pressure formed in my chest, settling against my lungs and restricting my ability to breathe freely.

I couldn't keep this up.

It tortured me just as much as it confused Finn. I missed relaxing against him on the couch. Waking up wrapped up in his arms without feeling like I'm betraying someone else. Letting him spoil me with unexpected trips out.

I'd have to make a decision soon. My heart couldn't take

the temptation of having him so close when the guilt begged me to stay away.

FINN

Charlie had argued his case and I conceded defeat. I couldn't put auditions and meetings off any longer.

Abi sat at the breakfast bar, an orange juice and her laptop laid out on the counter. I wrapped my arms around her, squeezing her back against my chest.

"Good morning," I whispered in her ear before placing a kiss on her cheek.

"Morning," she said, her tone hesitant as she patted my arm in a rather awkward manner.

Yet another oddity in a long line of oddities. I shook it off and released her.

"I'm heading into Hollywood for an audition." I slid into the seat next to her, smiling despite the strangeness. "I thought you could come with me and I'll show you around some after I'm finished with business."

She stared at me, chewing her lip. A ball of lead settled in my stomach. *What going on with her?*

"I'm sorry, I can't." She glanced away, focusing on her laptop screen instead. "I have a call with my sister."

The hesitant note in her voice made me frown. "Can't you reschedule?" I asked, now forcing the sunny upbeat note in my voice. "It's not every day you get a guided tour around a Hollywood film studio."

She grimaced and shook her head. "Sorry."

For some reason, I didn't think she meant it.

I might have taken my time opening up to her, but now that I had her, I had no intention of beating around the bush.

Some people might have backed away and left her to it. Not me.

I scooped her out of her chair and into my arms. She protested loudly as I carried her to the sofa, but I ignored it.

"What's going on, Abi?" I asked as I settled on the sofa with her in my lap.

She squirmed, trying to get away. Why? She'd been almost glued to me nearly a week ago.

"Stop it. Just talk to me."

She stopped squirming, but it didn't get better. Instead, she glared at me. *So that's how people feel when I do it to them.* The pang of hurt in my chest fascinated me for all of a second.

"I have plans, Finn. You don't need to turn into a caveman over it."

This time, when she pulled away, I let her go. She rushed away, picked up her laptop and disappeared down the hallway.

I stared after her with a perplexing feeling of loss jabbing me in the chest.

What had I missed?

INTERVIEW X

Question: How did it feel meeting your favourite singer in Finn's living room?
Abi: Incredible. Shocking. Unreal.
Tyler, producer: full sentences, remember?
Abi: It felt incredible to meet Owen Parry. I didn't even know he and Finn were friends. It still feels unreal, like I'm dreaming and going to wake up at any moment with a smile on my face.
Tyler, producer: how do you feel about Finn pulling strings for you?
Abi: I never would have asked him to arrange that meeting. I can't remember even telling him that I love Marable. I'm not sure how I feel about the personal aspect though. It's not like he took me backstage at a show. He brought Owen freaking Parry into our living room. There's something insanely privi-leged about that that I can't quite wrap my mind around yet.
Tyler, producer: *Our* living room? So you've accepted your part in his life?
Abi: I meant his. Slip of the tongue.

CHAPTER TWENTY-NINE

FINN

After a week of script reading and Abi dodging me at the strangest of moments, I'd reached my limit. Something had changed.

Something had upset Abi. She needed to confide in me so I could fix it, but I'd barely had half an hour alone with her in days. I needed to take drastic measures.

"Did you know there's a helicopter in the backyard?" Abi asked. She stopped in front of me, her brow furrowed as she glanced between my perfectly calm expression and the patio doors.

I sat at the breakfast bar, drinking my second cup of coffee of the morning and trying to ignore the nerves twisting my gut.

Just taking my wife out on a day trip. No need to worry.

"It's our ride." I pushed a to-go cup towards her. She picked it up, the furrow deepening. "It's hot chocolate."

"Thanks." Uncertainty stretched out the word. "Where are we going?"

"You've been in LA for two months now and I haven't taken you sightseeing." I emptied the dregs of my coffee into another to-go cup while she watched me with narrowed eyes.

See? Not normal.

"I hate the place at the best of times, but it does have some pretty areas." I stood, collected my cup and rounded the breakfast bar to drop the empty coffee mug in the sink. "Figured not many people get to see it by helicopter and what use is my money if I can't give you exciting experiences?"

I eyed her, keeping my expression pleasant. Not an ounce of suspicion here. I'd overheard her telling Mona more of her reasons for joining the show and excitement had been high on her list. If she denied me now, I'd have her. How I'd get the information I wanted out of her, I had no idea.

"That sounds great," she said. To the untrained ear, her enthusiasm would have sounded genuine. I knew better. She couldn't hide that little hitch of uncertainty.

"Glad you think so. Shall we go?" I gestured to the back door as I picked up our hoodies. "The pilot's probably finished his coffee by now."

Abi followed me outside without a word of complaint. She shrugged into her hoodie and sat through the safety briefing with avid attention. I watched her surreptitiously through the visor, taking in her growing excitement.

When the helicopter lifted off, she let out a tiny squeak and scrambled for my hand. A shiver went through her and I tensed, expecting her to release her grip. She'd done it enough times over the last week that keeping my tongue had felt like slow torture.

For an hour, we flew over LA, taking in everything from the Hollywood sign to the Santa Monica Pier, and more. Every now and again she'd slap my arm, excitedly, pointing at something below us.

After ten years, LA bored me. It was a stifling place I had

to endure to be seen and rub elbows with the right people to secure roles.

Watching her bouncing around in her seat, muttering in my ear through the built-in radio system, something eased in my chest. Even when I first arrived, I hadn't enjoyed it. Too overwhelmed, too anxious, too paranoid about making the right impression. For the first time ever, I could look at the landscape below us, bathed in sunlight and see beauty in it.

When the helicopter began to make its descent over South Park, Abi tensed next to me.

"Where are we going now?" she asked, practically breathless against my ears.

"It's a surprise."

She squeezed my hand and grinned at me through the visor of her helmet. One helicopter ride and all my worries about her distancing behaviour evaporated. At last, I could breathe easily, shrug it all off as a figment of my imagination.

You did just spend a week reading psychological thrillers.

We landed on a rooftop and quickly disembarked, ducking beneath the spinning propellers. I lead Abi through a doorway and down a flight of service stairs. I'd expected a stream of questions, but apparently, Abi accepted the surprise part of the equation. Nothing but the sound of our footsteps on the concrete echoed around me.

I'd expected a gasp at least when I flung open the unlocked security door and ushered her inside. She stared around the room, her eyes wide but her lips firmly sealed. Mannequins dressed in fabrics from almost every era surround us. None of it meant anything to me, but I knew it would resonate for her.

Only that silence didn't break as she spun on the spot, and concern started to needle at me. *Had I gotten it wrong?*

"It's not Paris or Milan," I grimaced, taking in her slack-jawed expression, "but I thought you might enjoy a few hours soaking in your favourite things."

She stopped spinning. A smile slowly bloomed, lighting up her entire expression.

"I love it. Thank you." She glanced around the empty room. "Where is everyone?"

"It's just us."

Her brows furrowed and her lips flatlined. "Are they closed?"

"In a way. There are staff here if we need anything." I shrugged. "I didn't think you'd want people gawking at us or asking for pictures."

She took another look around, the tension in the air seeming to grow. Then it snapped just as quickly. Abi sank into the quiet atmosphere and began to survey the exhibitions.

"I didn't even know this was here. How ridiculous is that?" she chuckled.

"It's not ridiculous unless you want it to be."

Her blue gaze assessed me, and she sobered. Nodding, she continued down the line of displays, reading the plaques and exhibition notes.

"Why don't you do more of this?"

"What?"

"Go out. Enjoy the city." Her brows rose and she smirked. "You only seem to leave the house if it's for a job commitment or one of your friends forces you out the door." She continued down the line, her head tilting as she gasped over a piece of stitching or a button. "You haven't even gone surfing or diving since we got back from Bora Bora. Didn't you say you love doing that?"

"You've seen the line of cameras waiting at the gates." I took a seat on a bench in the centre of the room, content to let her wander and take her time. "Why do you think?"

The media circus around our marriage hadn't lessened. The band of photographers at the gate seemed to lessen each time I left, but it hadn't returned to normal levels. Cars still tailed us and I lived on edge most days, waiting for the first sprig of gossiping lies about Abi to drop. None had yet, but it was only a matter of time.

Tyler forced me out of the house whenever he could with inane outings for domestic shit that made no sense. Why would anyone want to see us grocery shopping together? My chef handled all the ordering, I didn't need to set foot in the overly lit and overly priced places anymore.

"That's no way to live surely." Abi's gaze snapped to mine, her intense focus shifting to me and only me. "Locked away, hiding from the world unless duty calls."

"I like my house." I waved it off. "Besides, I'm never usually home that much. I need to pick the next project and get a move on."

"Why haven't you?"

My brows rose. "In a rush to be alone for days at a time?"

"Of course not." Her cheeks flushed scarlet. The paranoid corners of my mind tried to convince me it was out of guilt. I squashed that. "I just... you don't need to turn down work because of me. I can keep myself company."

I noticed.

I bit my tongue.

"I'll accept one when the right project comes up." I stood, clapping my hands. "Shall we go to the next room?"

I wandered towards the door, working hard to keep my pace measured and not rushed. Desperate to push her focus away after spending days wishing for it. *Geez, my head is fucked.*

"What about all those scripts you've been sent?" she asked with seemingly genuine interest. "None of those interest you?"

Now that my reputation was on the mend, the producers and studios had started warming up to jumping on the tail end. I'd joked to Charlie that if they could make and edit a film in under a month, they'd do it just so they could release it during the airing of *Married Blind.* Every single one of them called me with an eagerness for the publicity barely contained in their voices.

Each one should have filled me with joy. It had worked. The show had put my career back on track.

Yet, it only served to drive home how fake the entire industry was.

Nearly three months ago, I'd been persona non-grata in Hollywood. No one wanted to touch me.

"None of the ones filming in LA interest me," I said at last, a frustrated note leaking through.

"But there have been some not in LA?" Abi asked, seeing beneath the lines. She had a bloody knack for it with me.

"Yes."

Abi wandered around the edge of the room, appearing more interested in the exhibitions. She couldn't fool me though. I could read every tense line in her back and the sly glances from the corner of her baby blue eyes. She'd fixed all of her attention on me. *Why?*

Five minutes ticked by while I pretended not to notice her scrutiny. Eventually, she stopped in front of me, her hands on her hips and a determined set to her lips.

"If you had no constraints and you could accept any of them, where would it take you?"

I sighed. "What's the point of this?"

"Answer the question, Finn."

"Fine," I growled. "Prague. There's an interesting fantasy film in pre-production for the winter there."

Abi nodded. "Okay. Why won't you go for it?"

I stared at her, my brows rising and a smirk tugging at my lips. *Really, dotey, why do you think?*

"Because of me?" she squeaked, pointing at her chest. I only nodded. "That's ridiculous. We —" Her mouth slammed shut and she pursed her lips.

"We what?" I asked, my tone a little harsher than intended.

She studied me, a silent war waging in her eyes. Rather than confide in me, she wandered away, pacing around the room in intense silence. I watched her, every polarising emotion and thought flitting through my head.

Confusion that my next role meant so much.

Paranoia that her odd answers and reactions meant she planned to leave me or worse.

Elation that she might want to go with me, stay with me, make something off our strange beginnings.

Frustration that she had to stew in silence rather than *talk* to me.

"We what, Abi?" I asked again. I stepped in front of her, stopping her in her tracks.

She almost walked into my chest but dug in her feet, leaving mere inches between us. Tilting her head back, she stared into my eyes with an unreadable look which deepened the claws of trepidation in my mind.

"Mona and Shaun travel together," she eventually said, tone subdued.

I studied her, keeping a careful grip on the hope battering my chest. "They do."

She bit her lip. "So, we could do that too."

"Why would you want to uproot your life constantly for my job?" My brows rose, but playing devil's advocate at that moment might have been the hardest role of my life. Elation and disbelief fought inside of me. "It's the fakest industry in the world. Every single person you'll ever meet will have an agenda. You'll never know if they're befriending you for you or to get close to me."

I couldn't keep the bitter notes from my voice. The moment I started to let it out, it took on a life of its own, digging deep into my darkest feelings. The ones that haunted me at night, the ones that made me question every decision I'd ever made.

"If I didn't already know that you love *what* you do, I'd think you were miserable," she murmured. Abi canted her head, her gaze roaming my face, taking in every involuntary twitch.

"I love it when I'm in the role."

"But not everything surrounding it."

I snorted. "Everything surrounding it is a sea of fake. Getting in front of the producers, auditions, filming." My voice hardened, remembering the way everyone handled my temporary exile. "All fake pleasantry and pandering to get you to fall into line with someone else's agenda."

"Would you ever leave LA?" she asked, her voice quiet, almost distracted.

"I'm not sure I could."

I couldn't work out her angle. She wanted me to accept a role, but we'd barely seen each other all week by her own doing. *What exactly does she want from me?*

"Why? If filming is outside LA anyway?" She stood by a display case of broaches, avidly studying each one, tracing a finger over the glass. Her rigid back belied her carefree air, however.

I bit my tongue on an instant answer and gave it some thought. Moving to LA had been a dream that, year by year, morphed into a nightmare. I meant it when I said I'd love to leave, at least some of the time. When I got to film outside the studios, I could push the fakery to the back of my mind and almost forget. Almost.

"It's hard to schmooze and be seen when you're not where they want you seen."

She glanced at me, her brows furrowed. "What does that mean?"

"A huge part of the film and television industry depends on hiring talent with name recognition." My gaze panned across the room while my mind raced to put words to a fact I'd never needed to voice before. "But when you get to the point of having that recognition, it's fleeting. You have to constantly remind the public of your existence by having more projects lined up, and being photographed with the right people at the right restaurants, parties, events."

I bit my lip, hesitating over the flood of honesty spewing from my lips. But she'd asked, right?

"As much as I despise gossip rags, you can't sell a film if everyone forgets your name."

Abi absorbed it all. Yet when she turned away from me, I could have sworn a flicker of sadness flashed across her face.

Fuck. What had I said wrong?

That paranoid panic wiggled in my chest, reminding me that the last week had not been a figment of my imagination. My wife had started to pull away from me.

We were three weeks away from the end of *Married Blind*. They'd soon be sitting us down separately to question our experiences and demand an answer to whether we wanted to stay married or get a divorce. If the response didn't match…

She'd leave me.

Or is something else going on?

That paranoid voice whispered through my mind, stroking the memories of Natalie and her strange shift in behaviour before her parting gift hit the internet.

While Abi continued to take in the museum, I let silence fall between us.

I needed the time to study her, needed to look at all of our interactions through a new lens. One where I wasn't blinded by my growing feelings.

Were they one-sided? Had I tricked myself into believing she loved me too?

Really, if she wanted me gone, I could give her that space easily. I picked up my phone and dialled Charlie.

CHAPTER THIRTY

ABI

"Are you sure this is a good idea, Tyler?" I couldn't hide the hesitation in my tone as I followed the producer through a line of massive white trailers. They towered above us, metal steps pushed up against their doors to allow access. The heat beat down on us, bouncing off the metal, intense and unrelenting. "He's up here working. I'm sure he doesn't want to have to worry about me too."

Never mind that Finn had accepted a sudden guest role in Canada literally two days after our trip to the museum. He'd knocked on my bedroom door, interrupting my sewing, and dropped the news like a bomb. No question of if I was okay with it, just letting me know he'd be flying out by the end of the week.

Of course, I didn't tell him I wasn't okay with it.

I didn't know how I felt. Too many conflicting emotions hit me at once. They were still a muddled mess of relief and guilt.

I missed him, but part of me reasoned the separation

would be good for us. Now with just two weeks left of the show, decision time fast approached. Two weeks until they forced me to decide if I could be selfish and abandon my sister for the love of my life.

I still didn't know the answer.

When Finn had said he hated LA, a flutter of hope hit me hard.

And then he tore it away just as quickly.

I knew one thing for certain.

Tyler flying me to British Columbia would not be well received. I'd just end up looking needy and insecure.

"Don't you want to be with Finn?" Tyler asked.

He almost bounced as he walked, vibrating with excitement. For the reaction he anticipated no doubt, rather than any concern for what I wanted.

I kept my mouth shut, but he didn't notice. We stopped at one of the trailers. A printed laminated sign had been tapped to the side of it denoting 'wardrobe.'

"Here we are." He clambered up the steps and through the open door. "Hello, which one of you lovely ladies is Angela?"

I followed him in at a much more sedate pace. Ian trailed me, his camera resting on his shoulder and headphone positioned over his ears, taking in every blip of my microphone. Thankfully, they hadn't recorded my constant protests. Ethan followed closely behind, holding a fuzzy boom mic over Ian.

That wouldn't be unusual, but it gave me pause.

The boom suggested they weren't mic'ing Finn up, and all of it would be a shock. Dread coursed through me, turning my stomach and making me wish I'd let Finn disconnect the doorbell weeks before so I wouldn't have opened the door and let Tyler steamroll over me.

Reluctantly, I trudged up the trailer steps. Racks of clothing ran in a line down one side while they'd left a large space open at the opposite end, bracketing it with what looked like changing rooms. A grey-haired woman chatted to Tyler quietly while another much younger one watched, her wide eyes bouncing between them and the crew.

Tyler spotted me and grinned. "There you are, Abi." He waved me over. "Come and meet your new boss and colleague."

My brows furrowed. *Boss?*

Tyler chuckled. "We got you a trainee position while Finn's on the show, isn't that great?"

Something about his enthusiasm grated across my nerves. Despite that, I couldn't deny the pang of excitement waiting for my attention. I'd always wanted to do more with fashion. Why not wardrobe for films and TV shows?

Hell, if I went back to New York, why not costumes for Broadway?

I let the excitement bloom until it thrummed through me, blocking out everything else. Tyler grinned as I threw myself into introductions, listening avidly as Angela, the grey-haired lady showed me around their on-location space.

For the first time in years, I allowed the dreams I'd locked away when my parents died out of their box.

FINN

The second the director called wrap on the scene, I let the mind of the character recede and instantly missed it. For three hours, I'd been free of all my concerns and worries. Nothing mattered but my lines and my character's persona.

Greyson didn't care if his wife left or betrayed him. He only cared about catching up with his high school friends and throwing spanners in their carefully laid seduction plans.

I wandered back to the wardrobe trailer, following a production assistant determined to get me in and out of my costume change. He understandably didn't want to be blamed for the schedule running over. If only he knew my desperation to sink back into work.

Voices floated out of the wardrobe trailer, but my battle to press down my worries captured all of my attention. The second I stepped into the trailer, I knew I'd made a mistake.

How hadn't I recognised Tyler's voice?

The smarmy asshole smirked at me from across the trailer. Ian had a camera pointed at Angela and…

"What the hell are you doing here?" I snapped.

Abi spun around, her baby blue eyes wide and her vibrant auburn hair piled on top of her head. I'd have to be blind to miss the flash of concern skittering across her face.

A pang of loss hit me in the chest and I clenched my fists against the need to sweep it all away.

Abi turned to Tyler, her eyes narrowing on him. I didn't need to hear her thoughts to know the meddling producer was to blame for her sudden appearance.

"Abi's joining you here for a couple of weeks as Angela's apprentice." He plastered a sunny fake-as-shit smile on his lips.

"No."

His smile faltered. "What do you mean no? This is a wonderful opportunity for Abi."

I crossed my arms, begging myself to stay strong.

Don't need to know if it's true, don't need to see… Fuck.

Her lips curled slightly, a minuscule confirmation. Tyler would have missed it. Hell, Ian might have too. But I'd spent months looking at her, learning her every quirk.

How dare he use her against me? He knew I wouldn't say no to her, no matter how pissed I was. I still wanted her to be happy and make at least one of her dreams come true.

What a weak fucking sap I've become.

"Fine," I groaned. Abi's shoulders sagged and Tyler

perked up. I held my hand out, warding off his next stab at meddling with my life. "But *you're* leaving now."

"What — Now, Finn —" Tyler spluttered.

"No. My contract specifically states that you are allowed to film as long as it doesn't interfere with my job." Despite all of my training, my voice shook. I pointed at the door. "There is a production assistant out there shitting himself because he has to go tell the director that I'm late. I wouldn't have been late if you hadn't pulled this fucking stunt and wasted the five minutes I had to change."

"Okay, but that doesn't mean we —"

"Read my contract, Tyler. You are not to do anything that negatively impacts my job." My gaze shot to Abi. Meeting her had been the biggest threat to my job, but I wouldn't mention that now. "Turning up here, unannounced? Definite damage. Bring the source of my... *bring Abi*? Massive distraction. How the fuck do you think I'm meant to get back into character when I'm furious at you and distracted by all of your manipulative shit?"

He had nothing to say to that, but he still hadn't moved towards the door.

"If I have to get security here to escort you off the site, I will." I stalked towards him and he took a step backwards. "Make no mistake, I will be calling my agent and you will hear from your Series Producer. Now get the fuck out!"

Distantly, I noted Abi going pale as I shouted at Tyler. I blocked it out. She wanted to use me for her own gain, and I still didn't know what hell she had planned for me. She didn't deserve my guilt.

Angela handed me my next costume with a nervous smile. Ginny, her assistant, had vanished into the racks some time ago. Lucky woman. If I could escape the chaos, I would.

"Sorry, love, I didn't think..."

"It's not your fault, Ange." I softened my tone before

shooting a look at the producer. "He's got a habit of manipulating everyone. Let me know if I need to call security."

She nodded and I closed myself into a cubicle. The fitting rooms were nothing more than some thick dark fabric on rails. I could hear every furious whisper from the main area.

The unmistakable sound of the ladder shaking under heavy feet filtered through to me and a tiny piece of my control unlocked.

I couldn't do it anymore.

I shoved my shaking hands into my hair and tugged. The pressure against my scalp both hurt and gave me something outside of my head to focus on.

Why couldn't things just go to plan for once?

I needed the space. Being trapped in a house with her, seeing her contorting herself to avoid me, it'd gutted me.

Now I'd just be trapped in rural British Columbia with her.

Somehow, I'd gone from bad to worse in less than two days.

There would be no out now. When the cameras were around, I'd have to put the mask back on and nothing had changed, but if Tyler wanted to make my life difficult, I'd make his worse. He wouldn't get past the security line again.

I threw back the curtain with a little more confidence in my step. The fury fizzled beneath the surface, but it had reached a manageable level. Once I got back to set and sank into character, it would clear.

"I told him it would be a bad idea to surprise you." Abi chewed her lip, staring at me with open worry.

"Cut the crap, Abi." I shook my head, tutting in disgust. "You've a shit poker face."

Her brows rose as I stalked past her.

"What are you talking about?"

"If you truly didn't want to be here, messing with me, you wouldn't be."

My eyes narrowed on her, shoulders slumped, teeth permanently digging into her lip. Where had my spitfire from Bora Bora gone? The woman who faked an orgasm to get rid of the cameras? I wanted her back.

Only I really shouldn't.

"You did everything you could to avoid me in LA and you had an entire house and a city to work with." I crossed my arms. "Why did you agree to go from that to a hotel room with one bed in a tiny bloody town when you've decided to hate me?"

"That's not true," she said, her voice weak.

"You don't even want to fucking look at me," I shouted. Abi flinched and that stupid pang of guilt hit me again, making it all worse. She forced her eyes to meet mine, fire brewing in their depths. I stalked towards her, forcing my face to harden when all I wanted to do was pull her into my chest and kiss her. I couldn't stop myself from getting close enough to feel the heat of her body. She tilted her head back, her gaze dancing across my lips before jolting back to mine.

Confusing fucking woman.

I stormed out of the trailer, stomping towards the set with a face like thunder.

The urge to do something reckless thrummed through me. Run off into the woods and only stop when I hit the coast. Dive off a boat in the middle of Great White territory. Something. Anything to redirect the furious pounding of my heart.

At least then I wouldn't be losing control of myself because of a woman.

Question: What are you playing at Finn?
Finn: I don't know what you're talking about.
Tyler, producer: That's a lie, but I'll play. Why did you accept a job in another country without consulting the production or Abi?
Finn: It was a last-minute thing.
Tyler, producer: That part I can believe. Lucky for you the show's exec has connections to the wardrobe mistress. Two weeks in British Columbia without your wife wouldn't have been good.
Finn: Okay.
Tyler, producer: What's changed?
Finn: I don't know what you mean.
Tyler, producer: Hate me. Hate the show. That's all fine and expected. But you and Abi seemed to be hitting it off—and don't tell me it's an act. The little moments I've seen between you two, they're too pure to be faked.
Finn: If you want answers, Tyler, I'd suggest you talk to my tight-lipped wife. *stands* and when you find out, do me a favour and keep it to yourself. I've learnt my lesson.

CHAPTER THIRTY-ONE

ABI

"I'm sure it's not that bad," Eva said, her voice calm. Usually, talking to my sister would be enough. I'd take a deep breath and look at the thing bugging me all over again.

"You're not here, Eva. You didn't see him." I shuddered remembering the hardness in his eyes. "He's never looked at me like that, not even when we first met and he wanted to get out of the show."

"Have you asked him about it?" She smiled when I shook my head, both amusement and pity in her eyes.

I hated the pity, but I couldn't deny I deserved it.

Three months ago, I would have called Finn on his shitty attitude and been done with it. If I didn't like his response, I would have shrugged it off and left it as his problem.

Now, my strength had vanished on me.

Of course, I had my suspicions about why it had abandoned me. None of them good. All of them tied up in guilt and my conflicting feelings.

"You can't keep walking around on eggshells, Abs," Eva said, her soft tone tugging me from the edges of a guilt spiral. "Talk to him. Maybe it's all a misunderstanding."

Only what if it wasn't, and talking to him made the quiet simmering tension between us explode?

Avoidance, of him and my decision, would only make it worse though. I had to decide which I wanted more. If I choose Eva, there'd be no point fighting to get through to him.

Could you live with him truly hating you?

Probably not.

Eva grimaced and I braced myself for the question I'd hoped she'd never ask. "Is there a chance you're unintentionally pushing him away?"

I bit my lip as the truth tried to bubble to the surface and shook me. Evading Eva, with more than four thousand miles between us, was easy. Lying to myself… well that would be pointless because I already knew the truth. I'd set it in motion.

I'd been telling myself for two weeks to make a decision. My every waking moment had been dedicated to agonising over it.

But I'd made the decision, hadn't I?

I could pretend all I liked that avoiding Finn gave me space to think and process my feelings without clouding my judgement.

Unconsciously, it seemed I had chosen Eva.

Only I hadn't expected to be in a hotel room with the man when our relationship unravelled.

FINN

"This had better be good, Finn," Shaun drawled as he answered the phone. "I thought you went to Canada to stop being a moody bastard. That face," he pointed at me, "says you've graduated to irruption alerts."

"She's here," I ground out.

Every muscle in my body had drawn tight the moment the director called a wrap for the day. Now, sat in the back of a transport vehicle waiting for the driver, I couldn't ignore the disaster Tyler had dropped in my lap.

Shaun's brows rose, but he shook it off quickly. "Okay, so maybe take it as a sign that avoidance isn't the best move."

"No, avoidance would have protected me."

From seeing her hurt expression every time I bit at her. From feeling the stab of guilt because in nearly three months she'd softened me, made me complacent, made me love her.

I had ten minutes to shake all of that off. Ten minutes to find the Finn who sued Natalie and made sure she felt the sting of her betrayal as hard as I had. But I'd never been delusional.

"Fuck knows I've said this before, and you haven't listened." Shaun sighed, dragging a hand across his face before narrowing his eyes on me. "Abi isn't Natalie. That woman doesn't have a devious bone in her body."

I ground my teeth. "I'm not fucking imagining it."

Shaun held his hands up. "Okay, but remember how you feel about her, man?" At my stubborn nod, he continued, "Maybe giving her the benefit of the doubt *until* something happens, will make you happier."

"Happier?" I snorted. "Happier playing pretend, waiting for the axe to fall on my neck? No fucking thank you."

"I thought you'd say that." Shaun pressed his lips together, his own frustration shining in his eyes. "Just... think before you do something stupid, okay? I'm not blind, I can see how you feel about her. You've got two weeks, maybe if you're straight with her, the pair of you can patch up the holes before it's too late."

Shaun hung up and the fizzle of restrained anger and frustration hadn't abated.

"Jesus. I'm a fucking mess," I groaned into my hands.

I needed to exhaust myself before I faced her. If I channelled the burn of this anger into a boxing bag at the hotel gym, I might stand a chance of keeping my head. Might.

ABI

Hours had passed since I'd left the set. I'd paced circles in the carpet of Finn's hotel room, mindlessly flicked through channels and sat staring at the wall for more minutes than I'd care to count, chasing the threads of my wants and feelings, struggling with the knowledge that I'd chosen my sister over the man I loved.

I'd also expected Finn hours ago.

With the mood he'd been in on set, he wouldn't appreciate my checking up on him. Even knowing that I couldn't stop worrying my lip.

Fuck. I'm a mess.

Just as I reached for my phone, the door locks disengaged and in walked Finn, dripping sweat.

It glistened on his face, arms and shoulders. He wore a loose-fitting vest that did nothing to hide the definition of his abs and pecs from me. Dark patches coated it, sticking the thin material to his skin.

Every doubt and pang of guilt I had whirling around inside of me went silent for a couple of glorious seconds. My body forgot we weren't exactly talking — something I no doubt had caused.

He tensed when his gaze landed on me. His jaw ticked and I braced myself in the leather armchair. My fingers curled around the arms, gripping them tightly.

Time to put on the best show of my life.

Here's hoping I learned a few things from him.

"How was work?" I asked, the words sounding utterly ridiculous considering the stifling tension surrounding us.

He dropped his duffle back on the sideboard and grunted. *Grunted!*

"Sorry again about Tyler."

Grunt.

"When he hijacked me, I said it would be a bad idea, but you know what he's like."

Grunt.

My brows furrowed as I watched him move methodically around the room. He emptied his duffle bag, placing items in a laundry bag. Then he repacked it. All without glancing at me.

"Did he leave the set like you told him to?"

"You can stop with the pleasant conversation attempts," he muttered.

Did he roll his eyes?

With the sun setting, casting the room in shadows, I couldn't get a clear read on him. He tugged the vest top over his head, momentarily distracting me. I'd hoped we'd have two weeks to make more memories, something to hold on to when it all came crashing down. Then he scrunched it up in his fists and waited.

When our gaze finally clashed, he stared at me with a sardonic brow lifted. Heat burned my face at the realisation that he'd caught me ogling him. Then the guilt kicked in because despite us being legally married, I'd chosen to throw it away. I needed to get my head and heart on the same page and fast.

"Why are you even here?" he asked, tone dark. "You could have asked for another room."

Had he expected that? No, he couldn't have. There hadn't

been an ounce of surprise in his expression when he walked in.

But he was right. I could have. I should have.

"I didn't—" I swallowed, giving myself a second to find an explanation other than the truth… *I'm selfishly soaking in our last moments.* "I didn't think you'd want to deal with Tyler's questions."

Finn snorted. "I'm dealing with Tyler's fucking questions daily." His eyes narrowed and his entire demeanour shifted. His hands shook as he shoved them into his sweatpants pockets. "What's it going to be this time? Fetishes? Did you record me spilling industry secrets?"

"No." It came out too breathy, too panicked. Instead of reassuring him, it only made his eyes narrow.

"What are you waiting for?" I opened my arms. "Drop your bloody bomb. Don't wait for the show to end on my account."

I stared at him, confusion a twisting, living thing in my gut.

He tutted, cutting me off. "Don't waste your breath. I see you now." He reached for the hotel phone. "I'll get you another room."

"No!" I should have kept my mouth shut. A separate room would have made my life easier with him in such a volatile and confusing state. But I only had two weeks left with him. I wanted to savour them if I could and sharing a hotel room would give me room to do that without losing ground. *Maybe I can talk him down.*

"No?" he asked, incredulous. He dropped the phone back into the cradle. "You avoided me like the plague at home, you've a bomb hanging over my head, and now you want to spend time with me?" His brows rose at my silence. "Un-fuck-ing-believable. I did not peg you for a mindfuck, Abi, but you're doing a stellar job."

"We only have two weeks left together… maybe we could…?"

I had no clue what I was asking for. Sex? Companionship? Pretending nothing had changed but keeping our emotions off the table?

Either way, the moment the words fell from my lips, I knew I should have left.

Finn's expression turned thunderous.

"You want to pretend to be a happy family?" he roared. He visibly shook and his face turned red.

I tensed, forcing back the flinch that would have given me away.

"I am not a pushover, Abi." He stalked towards me and it took every ounce of self-control I had to stay rooted to the ground. His face loomed over mine, seething and hard.

Then it all shifted, gentled as he leaned closer. With gentle fingers, he pushed my hair back over my shoulder and lowered his face. His lips grazed my earlobe, and my eyes fell shut. I clenched my fists, fighting the urge to reach for him.

You're getting what you want. Just hold strong.

"I hope the payday was worth it, dotey," he whispered, sugary sweet. His voice hardened again as he continued, grating across every nerve. "Because you've got all you're going to get from me." He stepped back, glaring at me.

Payday?

He backed away. I needed to mask the confusion, but my bravado had evaporated at the brush of his lips against my skin. We'd reached the point of no return. He seemed hell-bent on hurting me, why the hell couldn't I return the favour?

"You're being such a dumbass right now." I shook my head, warring with myself.

Finn's brows rose. "Ready to tell the truth?"

"I'm not betraying you. There is no bomb." I spat the word at him, my lips curling in disgust that he could even think that of me. "I can't stay with you after the show is over. That's why I've withdrawn."

I stopped short of telling him exactly why. No need to drag Eva into our fight. He didn't speak, just stared at me with unrestrained loathing. He didn't believe me. Why did I care?

"I love New York. I don't have to worry about being tracked by photographers whenever I leave the apartment." I stepped towards him, fuelled by the burn of my anger finally turning up to the party.

"You want the attention. No one signs up for a show like this if they want to hide from the world."

"No one so much as looks at me twice. It doesn't matter what state my hair is in. No one gives a shit and they certainly wouldn't snap pictures of me to plaster all over the covers of gossips rags with big red circles highlighting all of my faults."

He crossed his arms. "Then you won't have any problem telling Tyler *you* want a divorce, and *you* want to be put on a flight to New York immediately."

Suddenly, the reality of it all crashed into me. Had I really made a decision? My indecision must have flickered across my face because his turned thunderous.

"Don't look at me like that, Abi." He pointed a finger at me. "You did this. I bet you couldn't believe your luck when I fell in love with you." He shook his head, his tone dripping with self-loathing.

How could a few words freeze time? I'd known before. Of course, I had. But somehow I'd been able to blank it out, put it to one side and pretend that my love was a one-sided thing.

I'd been prepared to lock my feelings away in a box, but for him to… Faced with him throwing the words at me like they were no better than dirt on his shoe, the first stab of pain, the first inklings of regret hit me.

You chose this.

"You screwed us. Now deal with the fucking consequences and get the fuck out of my life." He pointed at the door, not even an ounce of hesitation in his eyes. "Just be aware, that my feelings won't stop me from destroying you if you leak any of my secrets."

I'd agonised over how we'd separate for a week. Yes, I'd imagined something a little more…peaceful? But this would do just as well.

Yet my feet remained stuck to the carpet.

I hadn't planned for my racing heart or the pain twisting in my gut. Definitely hadn't expected tears to burn in the back of my eyes.

When I didn't move, he stomped toward the door and flung it open. "Get on with it. You've got a producer to find."

I willed my body to move but it wouldn't.

His jaw shifted as he stared at my unmoving self.

"Go!" he roared.

This time I couldn't control the flinch. It served a purpose at least. It got me moving.

I grabbed my bag and rushed past him, out the door. Tears spilled down my cheeks the second I stepped into the hallway. I took off down the hall without a second glance. One more look and I'd cave and beg for forgiveness.

If I did that, it'd make all the pain I'd caused him fruitless.

Eva would still need me.

FINN

I slammed the door the second she stepped over the threshold. Silence descended on my room, too stifling as my anger fizzled out. I collapsed onto the bed and folded over, burying my face in my hands.

Part of me reeled from how easily she'd given in. The other half reminded me of the last two weeks.

Either way, I should have felt free, and the pressure should have lifted from my chest.

Yet it only deepened.

My face and eyes burned, my head swam and I couldn't stop shaking.

She's actually gone.

The first tear shocked me.

I hadn't cried once when Natalie ducked out and betrayed me. Flown into a rage, sure. Never tears.

One led to another and then the floodgates opened until I fell back on the bed, a sobbing mess. My chest hurt like someone had reached inside and stolen my heart.

I'd sworn to never let a woman get the better of me again. When I opened up to Abi, I never anticipated that this time a woman wouldn't get the better of me. She'd tear me to pieces and leave me broken.

CHAPTER THIRTY-TWO

FINN

The next morning, the pressure on my chest hadn't eased, but no matter the state of my heart, I still had a job to do. 6 AM call time didn't wait for a man to sort through his emotions.

I opened the door, blurry-eyed and barely thinking straight. One look at the grim face leaning against the wall opposite woke me right up.

"I'm not in the mood to deal with you right now." A scowl pinched my face as I shut the door. I took off down the hall, not waiting for him to follow.

Hell, I hoped he'd leave me alone.

"What happened with Abi?" Tyler asked, his voice far too loud for the time of the morning. "She says she's quitting the show."

"I'm not her keeper." I shrugged, clinging to an unaffected air I didn't feel.

I kept waiting for the elation of finally getting my way to hit.

He stalked after me, keeping pace but not really bothering to catch up.

I reached the lifts and hit the call button. The doors opened immediately, unleashing a slither of relief. So close to freedom.

Tyler followed me in. He positioned himself opposite me, his shrewd gaze scanning my face.

I leaned my head back against the mirror and shut my eyes, too aware of the dark circles beneath my eyes, the red rims making the whites look bloodshot. Everything ached. My face, my teeth, my chest, my eyes. Yet another new experience I didn't care to ever repeat.

"Something happened between you," Tyler said, tone hard. His focus burned against my skin. I didn't give him the attention he craved. "She claims it's all her fault."

"Again," I sighed. "I am not her keeper. She—" A lump formed in my throat, choking me. I pushed past it and speared him with the attention he so desperately wanted. "She doesn't want me. I'm not sure why you're surprised."

Even though I stupidly was.

The lift opened and I stormed out. Tyler followed at a much more sedate pace. I could see my car waiting in front of the hotel and I picked up my pace, desperate for the distraction of work… even if it meant I had to spend another couple of days in Canada, away from my friends and home.

My stomach sank at the idea of going home. To a house filled with memories of Abi. Maybe Shaun would let me stay with him while I had the house fumigated.

I could sell it.

"Despite what you think, Finn, I'm not stupid," Tyler called to me, his voice echoing in the almost empty lobby.

I slowed to a stop, the doors within reach and turned, holding tight to my control. Every single eye in the hotel had shifted to us. Because who needed to be conspicuous when your life's work consisted of making drama? Not Tyler.

"There's more to it that neither of you is telling me." Tyler stopped in front of me, a smirk curling his lips. "It's more complicated than that, isn't it?"

I pressed my lips together and glared at him. He could take his sympathetic tone and shove it up his ass.

"Are you done? I've got actual work to do."

"Sure." Tyler patted me on the arm and stepped around me. "Call me when you come to your senses."

With that, he disappeared through the doors, leaving me with a blossoming headache.

ABI

I'd never been the type of person to wear sunglasses indoors. That changed when I walked into Vancouver Airport.

Maybe should have put makeup on before leaving the hotel.

But then Tyler would have more time to try and weasel information out of me and I couldn't risk it. He'd barely agreed to do a final interview from New York. It was the only option I gave him, not trusting myself to sit in front of a camera and keep it together without letting the truth slip out.

Something told me if he found out I'd chosen the pain of losing Finn, he'd dig at me until nothing made sense. I couldn't have that.

The damage was done.

Even if Finn could forgive me, he wouldn't leave LA, and I'd be right back to choosing between him and my sister. I couldn't do that. Not after he'd given me the perfect out. I didn't need to choose between them anymore.

I should have been happy.

Why then did it feel like my heart had been split in two?

The plane took off and I waited, my breath held, for the moment it would all fall away.

A hundred miles. Three hundred. A thousand.

It never came.

FINN

"Finn McCarthy, get your ass out here right this second!"

Distantly I heard the front door slam open and shut, heard Mona shouting for me. I couldn't muster the energy to care that she'd barged into my house. Instead, I rolled over and buried my head in Abi's pillow.

Christ, I'm pathetic.

Two weeks since she left.

Since you forced her to leave.

I'd allowed myself to sink into work, finish my scheduled filming and not *think*. It had worked to a point. I got through the shoots without shedding more tears and wallowing in what I'd lost and the fact I *cared* that she'd left me.

All the work to repair my reputation. All the manipulation. All of it would be for nothing.

And I didn't care.

Fuck.

My bedroom door slammed open. Footsteps sounded against the hardwood, stalking towards the bed. I didn't move.

"What did you do?" Mona demanded, tone hard.

"Sparky, stop," Shaun said, his voice gentle.

"No. Abi called me in tears." Mona got closer and my fists clenched in the pillow. "What the hell happened, Finn?"

"Take a second, and look," Shaun whispered.

Sighing, I rolled over and faced them. Mona gasped. Yeah, I'd elicited a couple of odd looks on the way home too.

"What happened?" Shaun asked.

Mona's eyes widened as she took me in. Sympathy flickered across her face.

When Shaun first introduced us, I embraced her friendship. The fact she'd ripped Shaun out of his shell and forced him to face up to the hard truths of his life had been a massive bonus.

To have her think that *I* had willingly hurt *Abi* stung more than words can say.

I shuffled up the bed and conceded defeat. Avoiding them while I got myself under control wouldn't work, and lying to Shaun would never sit right with me.

So I let it all out. From falling for her to the weird changes in her behaviour to the disaster that unfolded in Canada. They sat on the edge of my mattress and listened, shock and pain consuming their expressions.

Only when I got to my suspicions, Mona winced.

"What do you know?" I asked, my voice hardening. My eyes narrowed as she glanced away from me and twisted her hands in her lap. "Spit it out, Mona. If I can get in front of whatever bomb she's going to drop on me, I might have a chance to at least keep my career."

"Get real, Finn." Mona tutted, her brows furrowing. "You spent nearly three months in close quarters with Abi. You're so consumed with what might be that you haven't stopped to think!"

"What are you talking about?"

"Can you honestly believe she'd do that to you? Sweet, caring Abi?"

"What does it matter what I fucking believe?" I snapped. "Why else would she avoid me like she couldn't face me?" I stared at Mona, willing her to spill all she knew. Silence. "If you know something, Mona, share it or stop trying to make me feel guilty for protecting myself."

Mona bit her lip. Shaun studied her, rubbing her back. "Your silence isn't helping, love."

She sighed, but finally caved. "All I know is she went from

tentatively talking about a future here to dodging it at all costs."

"Which doesn't reassure me that she's not a snake waiting to bite," I ground out. "Natalie played sweet and loving at first too. I refused to believe she'd plant cameras in my bedroom until the security team found them."

Mona's eyes widened and her head whipped around to get confirmation from Shaun. At his nod, she turned back to me, my pain mirrored in her gaze.

"I'm sorry, Finn."

"That lapse in judgement resulted in every gossip rag in the world sharing a sex tape." I crossed my arms and my voice hardened. "Abi spent the last couple of weeks dodging me, just like Natalie did. Whenever I asked her where she'd been, she got cagey. Whenever I tried to make plans, she ran away."

Mona shook her head, tears shimmering in her eyes.

"Alright. That's enough." Shaun stood, dragging Mona up with him. She glanced at him, her brows furrowing and her lips pursed. "Give us a couple of minutes, Sparky."

When the door shut on her, he turned back to me, his disbelief plain to read. "You're hurting, so I'll give you a pass for talking to my fiancée like that, but don't fucking push it, Finn."

I dragged a hand across my face, scrubbing hard at my eyes. "I know. I'm sorry."

"She won't hold it against you." He sat back down on the edge of the bed, gaze softening.

"I don't want to believe it, Shaun." I stared at my friend, letting the pain come through in my eyes and voice. "But how can I not? She's gone. She knew I suspected her and she took the out." I winced. Rubbing my chest, I continued, "Fuck, if you truly loved someone, wouldn't you fight to stay?"

Shaun nodded, every inch of him tense and watchful.

"She kept her mouth shut. If she's innocent, why do that?" My voice cracked.

"We've built our relationship on never pandering to each other." Shaun eyed me, hesitation mingling with determination in his gaze. "So when I say this, understand it's because you're one of my best friends, and I don't want to see you hurting. Okay?"

I nodded, my gut twisting with dread.

"You're a fucking idiot."

"What?" I sat up, my eyes widening and my body bristling.

"Mona's right. Abi would never sell you out to make a quick buck." He grimaced, then glanced at the bedroom door.

"You don't know that for sure."

"Seriously? Why would someone who *willingly works three jobs to help her sister* take the easy route?" His brows rose. "She didn't have a personality transplant in the last month, man. She's still the same hardworking, caring woman who married you with a tremor running through her hands."

I stared at him, mouth opening and closing as words evaded me. *Could he be right?*

"Despite her line about the attention, she's brave and strong-willed. She could have handled the paps better than any of us." Shaun tilted his head. "So the real question is, what actually drove her back to New York?"

Maybe nothing did, but I'd rather believe his version than mine.

Shaun stared at me, his expression hard, urging me to listen. "It's okay to change your mind. It's okay to love her, even though she's hurt you."

My insides churned and my face burned at the reminder. *The first woman I hand my heart to in years, and she turns on me. What were the chances?*

"No. It's not," I ground out. *Christ, I sound like a child.* "I can't trust my judgement, Shaun. I fucking *chose* to let her in. She didn't force her way. If I'd wanted to I could have stayed detached and escaped the entire fiasco without a scratch." My voice rose the more I spoke, dripping with self-loathing.

"I made a choice and it blew up in my face. That is not okay."

Shaun stared at me, sympathy clouding his eyes. "I made a choice that backfired on me once too. Do you remember how I dealt with it?"

"You didn't apply for a green card to spite Mona. Don't even compare our situations."

"You're right, but I didn't sit around feeling sorry for myself." Shaun patted my leg and stood. "I knew she might never forgive me, but I went after her and I brought her home."

"Yes, you were brave, but our situations are not the same." I plucked at the duvet, resolutely fixing my gaze on the material. *Or are they?*

"Just because Abi fucked up, doesn't mean you can't be the bigger person here."

My head snapped back, eyes drilling into him while sudden anger made my hands shake.

"Don't even say it." Horror filled my tone. "Don't you dare tell me to forgive her when she could be on her way to destroy my career."

"What would it matter?" Shaun shouted, towering over me. "You hate it here. You're constantly complaining about how fake LA is. Why would it matter if she destroyed your reputation?"

I scrambled out of bed. "Because she'd have betrayed me," I roared, the sound tearing from my throat painfully. "Because she'd be just like every other piece of shit in this town, using me for the money and the fame and I…" My anger fizzled out and my gaze dropped to the ground. "I loved her because she was nothing like them."

Shaun placed his hands on my shoulders, holding me still and forcing me to focus on him. "If your career went away today, would you still want her? Would you move for her?"

Yes, my heart screamed.

But my head spoke louder.

I would have altered everything for her if she'd asked. I would have given her anything.

Instead, she chose money over me.

Even if everything Shaun described happened, and by some miracle she still wanted me, I'd never trust her again. So no, it didn't matter what I wanted. We were fucked no matter what.

CHAPTER THIRTY-THREE

ABI

I'd experienced my fair share of breakups, some of them devastating, some of them a blip in time that had very little impact on my life. None of them plagued me.

For two weeks, Eva and Ros tiptoed around me, letting me wallow as I pleased. Neither of them asked questions and I loved them for it.

That all changed when my final paycheque from the show hit. The notification lit up on my phone, reminding me why I'd put myself in the position to fall in love in the first place.

I pulled out my laptop and loaded up the billing site for Eva's medical loan. If I ticked that massive goal off the list, maybe I'd feel better.

"What the…?"

The balance read zero. I blinked at it for a second, before logging out and back in again, certain an error had occurred.

Nothing changed.

Two hundred thousand dollars down to zero.

"Eva!"

"What?" She rushed into my room, breathing hard from the scramble. "What is it? Are you okay?"

I glanced at the screen again. Just to be sure. Still zero.

"Did — did you pay off your debts and not tell me?" Even as I said it, I knew it would have been impossible. We didn't have that kind of cash.

"No, of course not." She joined me at my desk, glancing over my shoulder. "Holy shit. I didn't do that."

"Then how...?" The question died on my lips. I knew how.

I rubbed at my burning eyes, overwhelmed. Disbelief, relief, indignation. It all rolled through me, a tsunami of emotions I had no idea how to deal with.

"You don't think Finn did it, do you?" she asked, her voice shaking.

Why would he do it? Especially after I...

Tears slipped down my cheeks. I couldn't tear my eyes away from the screen.

"Abi?"

I shook my head and brushed at my cheeks, desperate for the waterworks to stop. Instead, I choked on a sob.

"Oh my god, Abs. What's wrong?" Eva knelt beside me. "It's huge, I know, but I should be the one crying, not you. Talk to me."

"Why would he do that when I..."

"When you what?" Suspicion hardened her voice and her eyes narrowed on me.

"I..." Words failed me, and I sobbed harder.

I needed to stop crying. This didn't change anything. I'd made the right choice. Eva's debts being paid off didn't make it okay for me to abandon her.

"We've left you moping for days." She smoothed a hand down my cheek. "We've kept our questions to ourselves." She gripped my chin, the gentle edge to her tone fading out. "Time's up. Spill it, Abi."

I released a slow breath, willing myself to get it together. She was right, I couldn't keep it all in forever. It would only fester.

"I couldn't stay there, but I couldn't figure out how to tell Finn," I whispered.

"What did you do?"

"Avoided him. Made him think I didn't want him." I shut my eyes, squeezing them tight as I admitted, "Made him think I didn't love him."

Silence.

"Why would you do that?" she eventually asked, her voice hoarse but quiet.

I frowned at her. Why didn't she get it?

"I have to be here for you."

"Just so I'm clear, you love Finn?" She took a deep breath when I nodded, releasing it slow and measured. "And he loves you?"

"Probably?"

Only he had said it, hadn't he? The first time those words fell from his lips and they were in anger. I couldn't help but feel the burn of regret that I hadn't gotten to hear it in a softer light.

"And rather than stay with him and let him love you," she grimaced as she spoke, "you chose to lie to him, break his heart, and come home because of me?"

I nodded, my gaze roaming her face as confusion stuttered through me. Why did she sound disappointed?

Eva shook her head, a tiny smile curling her lips. "I love you, Abi, but you can be such an idiot sometimes."

I spluttered at that. "No, I'm not."

"Oh, you definitely are." Eva stood, her grim, shocked expression gradually lifting as she chuckled.

"Why are you laughing?"

"Because for once, I'm not the fuck-up."

I followed her into the hallway. "You were never the fuck-up."

She snorted. "Your memory's not that shit, Abs."

"No, it's not. You were always the quiet, unadventurous child." Eva glanced over her shoulder grinning at me.

She walked into the kitchen, pulled out a bottle of red and gestured for me to sit down while she poured it.

"You didn't know about me being grounded for most of my teens." Eva sniggered when I continued to stare at her in confusion. "Mom was ready to tear her hair out. Friday nights, I crawled through my bedroom window reeking of alcohol."

Eva had to be joking. I'd left a shy, sixteen-year-old behind. She'd been a virgin in more ways than one.

"I'm deadly serious, Abs." She pushed a glass of wine towards me and sat down, her eyes twinkling with amusement. "They were very happy when I moved out and became your problem." Then her smile faded, and she shook her head. "Why the hell would you give up a man like that for me?"

"How can you ask me that?" I cried before gulping down a fortifying sip of wine. "What if you relapse and I'm on the other side of the country? What if you relapse, and I'm on the other side of the world? I couldn't live with myself, Eva."

Eva's smile returned. It softened her face and made my heart ache for some reason.

"Babe, nothing in life is certain. We, of all people, should know how fast it can change." She reached for my hand, squeezing it. "With our parents and my diagnosis, it taught me not to take anything for granted." Her head tilted as she took me in, sadness creasing her brow. "I thought you'd learned the same thing."

My chest ached. I guess in a way, my decision to do the show had been exactly that… Life had gotten stagnant and I had started to take it all for granted. I needed a shake-up. I just hadn't been prepared to fall in love along the way.

It made sense, but it didn't change anything. Even if she didn't need me right now, I couldn't live with myself if I couldn't be here for her if and when she did. The fear that her cancer would relapse would never leave me.

"I appreciate the perspective." I smiled at her, moisture brimming in my eyes. "But it's too late. I pushed him too hard. He'd never take me back."

Eva leaned towards me across our small dining table. Her gaze softened as tears rolled down my cheeks unchecked.

"Do you know how many times Mom and Dad fought?" she asked, smiling again.

"I *never* saw them argue."

Eva scoffed. "How? They went at it like cats and dogs every couple of months. Huge blowouts."

"How didn't I…"

"Not the point." Eva brushed it away with a flick of her hand. "I'm trying to make you see some sense here. Stop interrupting." When I zipped my lips, she continued. "They never separated, Abs. Sure Dad slept on the sofa a couple of times, but they *always* made up, no matter the size of the fight."

I dragged a hand across my face, swiping at the tears. "What are you trying to say?"

"Only one person is stopping you from fixing this." She lifted my hands and pressed my palms to her cheeks, grinning. "And that person, dear sister, is you."

For a second, I let the possibility take root. I imagined what it would be like to take it all back. We'd renew our vows. I'd travel with him whenever he got a job outside the city. Maybe invest the time I'd lacked for years into building my own career in fashion.

Then Eva's smiling face swam back into focus.

I'd still be leaving my sister behind. I'd still live on the other side of the country.

Nothing would change.

"Thank you for the pep talk." I tugged my hands from her grip, smiling softly. "But it doesn't change anything."

FINN

"Mr McCarthy, I'm sorry to disturb you, but there's a lady at the gate without an appointment," the guard said when I answered the incessantly ringing phone

Why hadn't he turned her away? I'd put a hard do not disturb on my house expecting a media-feeding frenzy. Even Charlie had started preparing for every eventuality.

The guard cleared his throat. "I've told her no one gets in without an appointment," he continued when my silence stretched. "But she's adamant she needs to speak to you today. What would you like me to do?"

"Who is it?"

"She says her name is Eva Johnson."

Abi's sister. *Fuck.*

Before I could think too hard about it, I gave my okay.

Why is she even in LA?

She'd refused to visit while Abi lived here, but decided our split would be the perfect time for a trip?

The bell rang, echoing through the house and booming in my ear with my proximity to the door. I should have taken a moment, composed myself, maybe found a brush to tame the dreadlocks my unwashed hair had become.

Instead, I threw the door open, startling the woman who looked like Abi but not at the same time.

"Why did you fly to LA to shout at me?"

She blinked at me, startled.

"I didn't." She winced. "Much. Can I come in?"

After a moment's deliberation, I gave in to my curiosity. I stepped back, gesturing at the hallway. She edged inside, taking in the marble floor and black ironwork I barely noticed anymore.

I led her in and stopped at the breakfast bar.

She sighed. "I'm not here to shout at you. I'm here to talk."

I pressed my lips together. I had nothing to say to her.

"I'm serious, Finn." Her blue gaze fixed on me as her hands landed on her hips, just like Abi.

Something in my chest squeezed tight.

Eva gestured to the sofas. "Can we sit?"

She didn't wait for my okay, just breezed past me, expecting I'd follow. Just like—

Stop with the fucking Abi comparisons!

"I know you paid off my medical bills," Eva said as she settled gingerly on the sofa.

"Okay."

What else was I meant to say? She already knew I'd done it. Denying it would be pointless, and she hadn't asked for a justification.

"Considering the way things ended between you and Abi, that was both a surprise and an incredible gift. Thank you." Her head tilted as she considered me. "There's no easy way to say this, Finn, so I'm just going to word vomit all over you and let you do what you please with the information."

My brows furrowed and I leaned forward.

"Abi's the best person I know. Not many people would work themselves to the bone to keep their family afloat, but that's her, through and through. She's loyal."

I waited patiently for her to make her point. Inside, I squirmed. Over the last two weeks, I'd started to let Shaun's words and my memories of Abi merge. It hurt, conceding that he might have been right, but reality agreed with him.

No story had dropped. No unflattering videos. No irate phone calls from my agent about leaked voice recordings.

I couldn't deny the truth anymore, but if she hadn't betrayed me, she'd actively chosen to leave me.

"And that's exactly why I'm here," she said. "I don't fully understand what she made you believe, but my idiot sister decided that staying here… in LA, with you… would be as close to abandonment as she could get."

"I'm not following you." Even so, my stomach dropped.

She chuckled. "Yeah, I had a similar reaction." She studied me, probably seeing far more than I'd like. "Do you love her? A bold question, I know, but it's important."

"Why does it matter?" My brows rose, daring her to spew some fanciful lie. "She left *me.*"

"And I'll say it again, she's a bloody idiot." Eva shook her head. "But it doesn't change the fact that she loves you. So I'll ask again. Do you love her? Answer the question and I'll try to explain."

"Explain and then I'll answer the question," I countered, my tone hard and unyielding.

"Fine," she sighed. "Abi loves you, but she's terrified. Afraid I'll relapse, that she'd be off living her life to the fullest for once and too far away to get to me."

I cleared my throat, my brow furrowing as I tried to make sense of it all. "What are you trying to say?"

Eva glanced over my shoulder, taking in the sprawl of LA beneath us. "I think she believes LA is too far."

"It's a six-hour flight."

"I know." Eva shrugged. "You don't need to tell me. I know she's not being rational, but she won't listen to me."

The penny dropped and I shook my head.

"She pushed *me* away, Eva. If she hasn't changed her mind by now, what makes you think she ever will?" I took a deep breath, suppressing the stab of pain that fact caused.

I refused to latch on to the hope she dangled before me. Oh, I wanted it. Badly. But Abi had made her decision. She'd unwittingly used my fears against me, forcing me to lash out at her and presenting the perfect out for her to leave me without a spec of guilt.

"Only because she thought she had to."

She stared at me, her hope blaring at me from a far too familiar face. Every muscle in my body strained at the idea of jumping on a plane and forcing her to see reason. If I were the fanciful optimist, I would have already been in New York days ago. As much as I'd wanted it, one thing stood in my way…

"She wouldn't forgive me."

Eva smiled. "I think you're wrong."

"Why?"

Eva leaned forward, her voice dropping. "You didn't hear it from me, but she's a mess. She's never allowed a guy to reduce her to a moping mess before. You, though? She can't shake you off."

"I accused her of using me for money, fame, and hatching a plan to destroy me in the process." It hurt to admit it, but it needed to be said. "She might be upset, but I drove her away just as much as she ran. If the guy you loved couldn't see through your lies, knowing you had a shitty poker face to begin with, and blew up on you, would you take them back?"

Eva chewed her lip, her shoulders slumping slightly. "Okay, so we might need a bigger grand gesture than I thought."

My mouth dropped open. "I'm not making a gesture when she doesn't bloody want me."

Disbelief flickered across Eva's face. "Stop being a stubborn asshat and listen to me." Her jaw shifted and her cheeks reddened. Just like Abi. "She loves you. She made a stupid, misinformed decision and I've corrected it."

"Then why are you here but not her?" My voice echoed around us, snapping in frustration.

"Oh, give me strength," Eva growled, pinching the bridge of her nose. When she refocused on me, her eyes narrowed.

"Clearly, you both have issues, Finn. Abi's dealing with hers. Now you need to fucking deal with yours and grow a pair. She seems to think you wouldn't take her back even if she begged." Her brows rose. "Is that true?"

I considered it, let the possibility wash over me.

If I hadn't been blinded by my past and eager to mistrust…. Instead, I sank into the betrayal I expected and focused on nothing else.

Abi might have needed money, but she didn't once ask me for it. I'd had no idea what medical debt equalled in the States.

It would have been easier for her to manipulate me into giving her the money than finding dirt and the contacts to sell it for the right price.

"What does that look mean?" Eva asked, wiggling her finger in my face.

"She never intended for me to pay off your debt, did she?"

"Of course not," Eva snapped, indignation pinching her lips. "We're used to being on our own. Asking each other for help is hard enough."

"Okay."

"Okay?" Eva squeaked, sitting taller. "Does that mean…?" She grinned, somehow reading the answer on my face.

"I hope you have ideas for this grand gesture," I muttered.

"As a matter of fact, I do." She pulled a notebook out of her, brandishing it like a trophy. "I made a list on the flight."

CHAPTER THIRTY-FOUR

ABI

"Thanks for coming in today, Abi," Tyler said, waving me into the apartment with a smile. "We'll make it as fast as we can, but like I said on the phone, we just need you to wrap things up for the show."

I nodded and followed him into the plush penthouse suite. Floor-to-ceiling windows dominated the living room wall, framing a gorgeous view of the Empire State Building uptown. I knew the show had money, but I'd always assumed they reserved it for celebrities.

"Okay, so it's been a month since you gave up on Finn," Tyler said once they'd mic'd me up and messed around with the lighting. "Tell me how you feel right now."

I drew in a breath. It pinched. No amount of breathing exercises would shift the ball of tension in my chest. I'd tried meditating every single day. With Eva's debt paid off, I'd quit my third job and taken an extra couple of weeks off from the travel agency.

The free time allowed me to spend more time doing the

things I loved, hanging out with my sister and Ros, scouring thrift shops, going to yoga classes, and working on designs.

All of it used to feed my soul. I'd expected at least one of them to ease the ache of loss. They never did.

Tyler watched me, that easy smile curling his lips. He held himself with ease for once, no tension whatsoever. He leaned back in his chair, patience wafting from him in waves. I found the change startling.

None of that helped me decide how to answer his question.

"I didn't expect it to hurt this much," I said, at last. "Sure, I joined the show hoping for more, but I don't think I expected to find it. I definitely didn't consider the consequences."

"That's great, Abi." He grimaced. "Not the pain part, of course. Before we go further, I have something to show you, if you wouldn't mind."

"Sure." What else was I meant to say?

Tyler nodded and Ethan pressed a button on a remote. The TV flickered to life, displaying the apartment surrounding me, down to the armchair I sat in. I snuck a glance at Tyler, confusion hitting me hard. He just smiled and tilted his head towards the screen.

My brows rose as Finn took a seat and went through the setup. I drank him in. He looked good, but something about the sight of him screamed tired... like me.

"Talk to me about how things ended with Abi," Tyler said, his voice echoing from the screen. I side-eyed the producer sitting behind the camera in front of me.

It felt rather meta to be watching part of the show while someone filmed me for the same show.

"Maybe we could back up a bit?" Finn asked, his voice surprisingly tentative. Usually, he'd dictate the direction and breeze over Tyler's suggestions. My brows furrowed at the change. "I haven't exactly been open with my feelings for Abi on the show."

"You're right. We've seen glimpses, but …."

Finn took a deep breath and rolled his shoulders, then he looked directly into the camera. For a second, it almost felt like he saw me.

"I took on this project expecting to walk away unaffected after three months. I've realised recently that my past relationship history set me up to expect the worst from women," he said, his voice gravelly. "Every single one of them wanted one of two things from me, and in my experience, they didn't care how they got it. So I just wouldn't take the risk."

He sighed and the sound rushed through me. I couldn't believe my eyes or ears. Finn had spent months working to keep even a grain of his true self from the show, and he blew it all on an exit interview?

"That all changed with Abi. Despite my best efforts, she snuck beneath my defences and then bulldozed them to the ground."

I soaked in every word like a dehydrated woman.

"With her, I got a glimpse into what a relationship should be, two people equally caring for and loving each other."

He did?

"She made me laugh, she made me burn in all the right ways…" He swallowed hard, hesitation flickering in his gaze for all of a second before he stared at me once more, determination blazing in his eyes. "She made me *feel*, for the first time in seven years. I can't tell you when it happened, but I fell in love with her."

I sucked in a breath.

Finn shook his head, chuckling. "The irony in that, right?" He sobered, wincing ever so slightly. "As much as it hurts right now, I wouldn't take a moment of it back."

He wouldn't?

"I'm not proud things fell apart for us, but I guess it was

inevitable. We were incredible together… until we weren't. Abi started pulling away and it felt like my fears were coming to life. It all mirrored my ex's actions right before she leaked a sex tape I had no knowledge of making."

"Oh no," I whispered. Why did he say that? He'd worked so hard to keep himself separate from the show.

"For a week, I stewed, believing that Abi would betray me in a similar fashion. I didn't want to be trapped in a house with her, waiting for the evidence to drop. So I escaped, accepted the first job I could, and got the hell out of LA. For a couple of days, I could pretend my life wasn't about to implode." His eyes narrowed on someone beyond the camera, probably Tyler. "And then you dropped Abi in my lap in Canada, which by the way, was a shitty move, even for you."

"Yes, it was," I agreed in a low murmur.

Tyler handed me a box of tissues with an apologetic smile. I accepted the offering, but forgiveness would take a while. Without him, Finn and I could have coasted to the end of the show. Avoiding each other would have been easy. No explosive argument, no gut-wrenching pain.

"It took losing her for me to realise how much of an idiot I'd been," Finn said. His jaw shifted and his eyes burned into me, a promise in their depths I couldn't understand. "I expected everyone to want me for my money and fame. I was terrified of it, in fact, and refused to let anyone put me in the position of making the same mistakes again. When you introduced me to Abi, a woman in debt, agreeing to disrupt her life for months for money, how could I think anything else?"

A lump formed in my throat at the watery glimmer in his eyes. I'd done that. I'd known about his ex, he trusted me with that, and I'd used it against him.

I pressed a tissue to my eyes, willing myself to pull it together. He would be better off without me.

"But you weren't using me, were you, dotey?" Finn asked, startling me.

His voice hadn't come from the screen. I lowered the tissue, glancing around the room with pinched brows.

Finn stood a couple of feet away from me, devouring me with more interest than I deserved. His curly black hair was perfect, and his beard was finely trimmed, but he didn't look perfect. No, the tiredness I'd been unable to place in the recording clung to him.

"It's time to admit the truth, Abi. Time to tell me how you really feel." Finn took a step, then another and another, until he stopped at my side and knelt with a smile. "But first I need to apologise to you."

"No, you don't." I shook my head hard, reaching for him before my common sense could scream at me. My fingers smoothed along his bearded jaw and he captured my hand, holding it there as his eyes fell shut. "You didn't do anything wrong."

Finn's eyes popped open, spearing me with an intensity that made me want to squirm in my seat.

"I believed you'd willingly hurt me, even though you'd never given me a reason to expect it." Finn's brows furrowed. "I'd say that was wrong. I let my fears control me, blind me, when if I'd taken a moment to remember who you were, I'd have seen right through it all." He grimaced, his hand dropping from mine and his focus skipping away from my face in shame. "I said some pretty nasty things I wish I could take back too."

"But it doesn't change anything," I whispered. I gripped his chin, forcing his gaze back to mine. "I pushed *you* away. I made you feel all of that. It's not your fault, but it doesn't change my choices."

Finn studied me, assessing and then he bit his lip, holding back a smile. "So does that mean you forgive me?"

"I don't need to forgive you." I frowned.

"But if you did, you would?"

"Yes."

"Good." He grinned as his hands landed on my arms. He shuffled me around to face the camera again. "Tell them you don't want a divorce."

"I can't, Finn." I shook him off and stood.

Ian huffed but scrambled out of his seat and rushed to unclip the camera from the tripod.

"Yes, you can." Finn climbed to his feet, determination shining in his eyes. "You love me, I know you do."

"Of course, I do," I shouted. "But it can't..." I dragged a hand through my hair, tugging at the auburn strands. "It's not that simple."

"If being in LA full-time is too much for you, we'll live here."

I stopped dead, sure I'd misheard him. Heart pounding, I slowly turned to face him. "You don't mean that."

"I do."

"No, you don't." I stomped back towards him, suddenly angry. "You said you'd never leave LA because you had to be there when you weren't working. You can't just decide you're moving to New York on a whim and expect me to..."

To what? Cave? My god, I wanted to cave so badly. Elation worked through me, robbing me of breath and sense.

"I told you I hated LA too, dotey." Finn's voice softened.

His hands smoothed over my shoulders, gripping tight enough to demand my attention. I glanced up, meeting his gaze and forgetting how to breathe for a second. He smiled at me and I swallowed hard at the conviction in every line of his expression.

"You mean it?" I asked shakily.

He glanced around the room with a smirk, then nodded. "Yes, I mean it."

"You won't change your mind?"

Finn leaned forward until his face hovered inches from mine grinning at me.

"You didn't think the production could afford to rent this

apartment for one interview, did you?" He chuckled as my eyes widened and a glimmer of an idea took root.

"You… you bought it?"

"Do you like it?" he asked instead.

I bit my lip and concern trickled into his gaze.

"I'll sell it if you don't, and we can go flat-shopping together."

I glanced around again. How had he realised…

"I don't understand," I finally admitted.

Finn kneaded my shoulders, smiling despite my hesitation. "Your sister came to see me."

"You don't mean she…" My eyes widened when he nodded. "Eva. My sister. Took away off from work and went to LA?" Disbelief dripped from the words.

She wouldn't take a day off to visit me, but meddling was perfectly fine?

"I was shocked too, but she had some convincing arguments." He tugged me towards him, his expression turning serious. "Like the fact you thought you'd be abandoning her if you stayed with me." His brows rose, daring me to lie and disagree.

"Yes, that might be true." I winced as he speared me with a sardonic look. "Definitely true. I started to try, but…"

"I told you I couldn't leave LA, and you gave up."

"Yes," I groaned. "I'm sorry."

"Our relationship is still fresh, Abi. You didn't — neither of us knew how I truly felt about the city." He pulled me into his chest, wrapping his arm around me.

I'm ashamed to say my first instinctive reaction was to breathe him in. Between his spicy scent filling my lungs and the delicious heat of his body wrapped around mine, the ache started to ease, and I relaxed for the first time in weeks.

Weeks of pain that I'd brought on myself and inflicted on Finn. I didn't deserve his comfort or forgiveness.

"No, it's not this simple." I pressed my hands to his chest

and pushed. Finn refused to loosen his grip, so I leaned back and stared into his grim expression.

"It is this simple."

"No. It's not." I shook my head hard. "I hurt you. I left you, even though it hurt us both." Tears rolled down my cheeks again. "How can you forgive that?"

He released me to brush them away. "Because I need you more than I want to live without you, dotey," he whispered, his tone softened but sad as he peered at me. "I love you. Don't make me live my life without you, please, Abi girl."

"You would move to New York for me?"

"I still need to be in LA sometimes." He pulled me back into his chest. "My next project is mainly in LA, so we'd have to spend some of the year there, but the rest, yes we can spend here if you want. We can go to Milan, Paris, wherever you want." A devious glint entered his eyes and I'd lost all will to resist him. "You just have to talk to me, Abi. I want you to be happy." He grazed his knuckles across my cheek. "I can't make that happen if you don't tell me what you want."

"And if I never want to leave New York again, or I want my sister to travel with us?" My voice shook as I asked the question.

"Then your sister would travel with us." He lowered his face towards mine, the sadness filtering back into his gaze. "I missed you. Please don't make me experience that again."

"Okay," I whispered before sliding my hands up his arms and into his hair. "Under one condition."

"Name it," he said without pause.

"I get to keep working. I'd like to keep learning and keep pursuing fashion."

A smug smirk curled Finn's lips. "Your final stipulation is that I get you jobs on my projects?"

"Not necessarily. I just—"

"I just told you I don't want to be separated from you. If I got you a job on someone else's film, how would that benefit me?" Amusement shone in Finn's eyes, and I could only stare at him as the realisation hit. "Done, dotey. Now fucking kiss me."

His fingers drove into my hair, tugging me forward but also stopping me from dodging him again. His lips pressed against mine, coaxing but insistent as he took control. I didn't need the gentleness.

I bit his lip, silently begging him to speed things up, and he pulled back, grinning like a maniac. He started into my eyes, desire darkening his expression as the fun and amusement drained away.

"Your time's up," he said, confusing me. Then I realised his focus had shifted to Tyler and his crew.

I shriek-laughed as he scoped me off my fit and into his arms, bridal-style.

"See yourselves out," he called over his shoulder.

Finn carried me down the hallway and through an open bedroom door at the end. This room at least had a bed. He lay me down on it and stepped back, his gaze devouring me.

"Stop teasing me, Finn."

"Why? I'd say a little punishment is in order, wouldn't you?"

I groaned, but collapsed onto my back, wholeheartedly agreeing with him.

He could do anything he wanted to me, as long as he never let me leave him again.

CHAPTER THIRTY-FIVE

FINN

Three weeks later, I'd say we'd finally settled into our New York apartment. Some things were still a work in progress, like our schedules, but the important things were in place. I had Abi with me at all times.

Between my parents and my friends flying in, I had a matter of hours left before I lost my coveted alone time with Abi. And the woman had decided she needed to go to the corner shop instead of spending it with me.

Abi wandered towards me with bags of groceries hanging from her arms. The sight of them gave me pause.

"I thought you were going down for a bottle of wine, not to buy out the shop." I rushed towards her, freeing her of every single one of them. "You should have asked Chris to go if you needed all this."

With things starting to get back on track with my career, Charlie insisted that I hire an assistant. I missed a couple of auditions and forgot to read a script or two while I focused on Abi. So I conceded defeat.

"I'm not used to having an assistant, Finn." She stole a bag back before brushing past me, into the kitchen area. "Besides, he's your assistant, not mine."

"It's the same thing."

I placed the bags on the island in front of her and started unpacking. I still didn't understand why she needed to go to the shop when we had caterers turning up in less than an hour.

"It's definitely not the same."

I hummed, refusing to agree but tired of arguing over it. She'd get used to the lifestyle change eventually.

"I just thought your mother might like the chocolates we talked about, and your sister was desperate to try a cronut."

I stopped with a pack of marshmallows dangling between my fingers and eyed my wife. "You didn't just go to the corner shop, did you?"

She snorted. "Of course not. I would have been back hours ago."

Ordinarily, I'd use this as an opportunity to remind her why she needed a bodyguard. *Married Blind* had officially aired and half the country now knew her and her connection to me on sight. But with our home being invaded by the people who mattered most to us in a matter of hours, I took the high road and decided *not* to add more stress.

Once we'd packed the groceries away, she turned her attention to the rest of the apartment. She narrowed her eyes on a set of chairs she'd already repositioned five times.

"Leave the furniture alone."

"But maybe they'll look better over there." She pointed to a corner framed by windows.

"You tried them there yesterday."

"I know but—"

I tugged her into my arms and slanted my lips over hers, ending the argument. She moaned, clutching my chest for a second before she pushed me away.

"Don't get me all hot and bothered when we don't have time." She pouted and I couldn't help but grin.

"I'm pretty sure I could blow your mind in under an hour, dotey."

"Doesn't mean I want to rush."

My brows rose. A month in and she turned down sex. *Unfucking-believable.*

"You dragged me into the bathroom at your sister's for a quickie last week." Incredulity screeched through my voice. "Why is this any different?"

"Because Eva didn't care if my hair went into a bun." Abi crossed her arms and glared at me.

"And I do?"

"No, but your mother will."

I couldn't help it, I laughed.

"That's not helping, Finn."

"Sorry, it's just hilarious." I bit my lip, struggling to stem my amusement. "My parents can't keep their hands off each other, dotey. Never have been able to. I guarantee you, they'll disappear into the spare room after ten minutes of making nice."

Her mouth dropped open in shock. "You're joking?"

"Nope." I grinned as her face turned a lovely shade of scarlet. "Well if we're not going to fuck, how bad's the heat out there?" I nodded to the window. "Will I die if I go for a run?"

I had no intention of setting foot outside the air-conditioned apartment. People could say what they liked about LA, but at least there was a breeze. No, I wanted an argument. It had fast become my favourite way to equally get my way and get Abi off.

She's stressing out over something inconsequential? Start an argument, we fuck, Abi has an orgasm, bye-bye stress.

I eyed the tension in her shoulders. If she didn't ditch it

before the caterers turned up, she'd get in their way and make her life more difficult than necessary.

"It was fine."

I frowned. "My fine, or your screwed-up fine?"

"My fine is not screwed up!"

"So it's not forty degrees outside masquerading as twenty-nine, and I won't collapse the second I leave the building?"

Abi's brows furrowed. "Jesus, Finn, speak American. It's only eight-three."

"But is it actually?" I barely contained my smirk. "I'm Irish, love, we don't do humidity, remember?"

A growl of frustration fell from her lips before she launched herself at me. I silently congratulated myself on a job well done and then focused on getting us to our bedroom before Abi decided she wanted it on the kitchen counter. Something I'd ordinarily get behind but with caterers coming in, I had to draw the line somewhere.

I rushed into the room, lay her down on the bed and started hopping around to remove my clothes. Abi laughed at me, a glorious sound that echoed around the room.

"Stop laughing and get your clothes off, woman." Naked, I reached for her arms, tugging her up before I gripped her dress and tore it over her head.

"I can't help it." She hiccupped, her eyes streaming with tears of amusement. "You just look so serious while - while… Oh!"

I dragged my fingers through her folds and she swallowed her laughter. Her head fell back on a moan as I circled her clit.

"Now do I have your attention?" I grinned as I lowered myself to my knees.

"Yes," she moaned.

Satisfied, I ducked my head and focused on teasing an orgasm from her. I might have promised a quickie, but I had no intention of rushing. Her thigh muscles twitched at the scrap of my beard against her sensitive skin and her hips jolted forward at the first lap of my tongue.

I catalogued it all, enjoying her loud moans and cries for more, but driving her higher and higher only to pull back, time and time again.

"Please, Finn," Abi eventually begged. Her fingers drove into my hair, tugging hard enough to lift my head. "I want to come."

"Since you asked so sweetly." I smirked as I lowered my head again.

My lips latched onto her clit. Sucking. Nibbling. Caressing. Her hips shifted restlessly until her cries for more soon turned to release.

She smiled at me when I climbed onto the bed, a look of pure bliss. I moved her into the centre of the bed and sat back on my hunches, stroking myself. There was something addictive about seeing her boneless and flushed after an orgasm. I'd never get enough of it.

Abi reached for me and I gave in happily, lowering myself on top of her. I dragged the tip of my cock through the folds of her soaking wet pussy, torturing us both with the smallest flickers of pleasure.

"Finn," she gasped as her hips jolted forward, trying and failing to draw me deeper. Her fingers clutched at my forearms with desperation. "Please. We don't have—"

We both groaned as I sank deep into her tight heat. For a second, I froze, clambering for control and patience as her body squeezed and pulsed around me.

I'll never get enough of her.

Her nails dragged across my back, urging me on. I slammed into her again and again, eliciting a chorus of moans from us both, driving us to the edge fast.

Just as the tingling started in my back, I slowed and rolled us until Abi sat on top of me, gasping and groaning at the sudden position change.

My fingers dug into her hips, encouraging her to rock against me. One jolt and she whimpered, collapsing against my chest.

"That's not helping." I chuckled, the sound muffled by her hair in my face.

I continued to rock up into her, dragging an endless stream of noises from her.

"Do I need to reconsider putting you on top?" I asked, half joking.

"Yes," she groaned against my neck, the vibration sending a shiver down my spine. "Please."

I grinned, accepting her admission as permission to take control. Just as I liked it. Flipping us back over, I tucked an arm under her knee and lifted her leg. My cock slid deeper inside of her. The walls of her pussy fluttered around me, pushing me closer and closer towards the end. I ground against her clit with every thrust, determined to make her boneless and incoherent as I picked up the momentum once again.

This time when I felt the edge coming, I didn't slow down. "Tell me you're close, dotey."

"Fuck, yes," she panted.

Her fingers dug into my biceps, clinging to me as she shattered on my cock. I buried my face in her neck and shuddered through my own release.

Satisfaction and gratitude coursed through me as my heart pounded and our bodies settled down from the high. Abi's fingers grazed up and down my back, caressing my heated skin and making me wish we had all day and all night.

I lifted my head, smiling down at her, absorbing every detail—her flushed face, her pleasure-drunk glazed blue eyes and her auburn hair sprawled over my pillow.

Her lips curled as I caressed her jaw. "What?" she asked.

I shook my head, lost for words for a moment as gratitude overwhelmed me.

"I love you, dotey," I said after clearing my throat.

Her smile grew. "I love you too, Finneas."

For a second, I gawked at her, not believing my ears. "That is not happening."

"Why? You call me dotey. I need a nickname for you too." She pouted at me.

"And you can have one. Just not *that.*" I shuddered, amusement in my tone.

The movement caused my hips to press harder against her. Her eyelids fluttered as she groaned and her pussy squeezed me once more.

"Fuck," I groaned. "Do we have to get out of bed?"

Abi chuckled.

"Why am I not surprised?" Nathan's voice cut through the silence.

Abi startled beneath me, squeaking slightly at the surprise. Her pussy tightened around my half-hard cock and I barely suppressed a groan. I grabbed the sheet and dragged it over us before pulling out of Abi. I shifted to the side, making sure she stayed covered by the sheet, while I glared at my friend.

"I knew I shouldn't have given you lot the code."

"Nah, you're not. You'd be grouching at us for interrupting you, otherwise." He chuckled. "You two might be worse than Shaun and Mona."

"Hey!" A high-pitched Scottish voice shouted from down the hall. "I resent the implication."

Nathan's brows rose and he shook his head. He had a point, but did he have to make it standing in our bedroom doorway?

"It's not an implication if it's the truth," he shouted back at Mona. Then he grinned. "Plus, aren't you lucky we turned up early and could let your caterers in?"

Abi stiffened against me. "Who's out there?"

"Oh, just Shaun, Mona, Jackson..."

She blew out a relieved sigh and sagged against me. "That's okay then."

"And Finn's family of course."

"What?" She sat upright, clutching the sheet to her chest. I grabbed her before she could jump off the bed, leaving me naked in her panic. "You're joking, right?"

Nathan smirked and sauntered away without responding.

"He's joking, isn't he?" She turned to me, her eyes wide with panic.

"Probably not."

"Finn! I told you we shouldn't have." She slapped my chest, then scrambled out of bed, her eyes wild. "I can't believe I let you talk me into a quickie. What will your parents think?" she hissed.

I chuckled and didn't move an inch. "I guarantee they won't care."

EPILOGUE

NATHAN

Four Months Later

The things I do for my friends. No one else could have convinced me to wear a baby blue tuxedo and walk down a flower-strewn aisle with a woman on my arm who wasn't Catrina.

Technically, I shouldn't have been going *anywhere* with Catrina, but the dick wanted what it wanted.

"Smile," Isla whispered, barely moving her lips as she side-eyed me. "Better." She pinched my arm and I just about held back a glare.

"What was that for?" I hissed.

"For potentially ruining my sister's wedding photos." She smiled sweetly at an older woman off to our right, tears streaming down her face. "I don't care how you screw up your love life. Keep it away from my baby sister's special day."

The side door opened, and in stepped Catrina, almost like she'd been summoned. Her golden-brown hair curled into perfect waves tricking people into believing her soft-hearted image. If not for her pinched lips and narrowed eyes, she'd pull it off.

Of course, those eyes narrowed on me.

What have I done now?

"Stop," Isla growled. She pinched me again and nodded towards the fast approaching alter and my perplexed best friend. "You're an actor. Act."

Cowed, I blocked out the burn of Catrina's gaze against my neck and focused on Shaun. The lucky wanker looked normal in his black suit and tails compared to the rest of us. The only patch of blue on him came from his bow tie.

Isla left me with a parting warning look before stepping up onto the dais to Shaun's left. The moment I stepped into line beside him, he swayed towards me, a flicker of concern in his gaze.

"I'm fine."

His brows rose. "That's why your lawyer's crashed my wedding? Because you're fine?" He nodded to where Catrina leaned against a wall, her arms crossed as she watched me.

"I don't know what she wants." The lie slipped off my tongue with ease.

Well, partial lie. I had no idea why she'd followed me to Edinburgh. A simple email would have sufficed.

Finn and Abi reached the end of the aisle, clinging to the other until the very last minute.

A couple of months ago, I would have sneered at the sight. I would have had immense fun ribbing Finn for his sappy moments.

Now, things had changed. My gaze tracked to Cat again.

At least, for me they had. The damn woman had far too strict a sense of propriety for my liking.

All the more rewarding when I finally fuck it out of her.

"I don't want drama at my wedding, Logan," Shaun said, a warning note in his voice. "This is a drama-free space. Do not stress Mona out today."

"What are we talking about?" Finn asked, joining us with curiosity painted plain across his face.

"Nothing," I grumbled.

I eyed Finn. Somehow he pulled off the baby blue suit. How? I bit my tongue on the whine of frustration dying to get loose. *Hollywood royalty does not whine.*

"Nathan's brought his drama to my wedding."

"Oh, did he, now?" Finn grinned, his brows climbing as utter delight skittered across his face. "Are we taking bets on how long it takes for them to fall into bed?"

"Don't waste your breath." I turned to face the crowded hall.

Ornate, antique chandeliers hovered above their heads. The Assembly Rooms barely needed decorating with their decorative walls and original features. The place looked like a fairytale come to life.

Shaun had to pull some serious strings to get the venue for New Year's Eve but he'd managed it. Despite the chaos of the annual Hogmanay street party outside, they made the entire space over into their very own Winter Wonderland, with ice sculptors, faux furs and every white, blue and icy-looking flower on the planet.

They'd even dressed us to look like Jack Frost. Every single one of our protests fell on deaf ears and honestly, we'd do anything for Shaun, and we owed Mona for rescuing him.

Once Jackson and Mona's friend Tilly had made it to their positions, the orchestra switched pace and the room collectively held their breaths. All eyes turned to the door, ready to watch the bride make her way down the aisle.

Mine didn't make it. I got caught up in the shimmer of moisture in Cat's.

For a second, I thought my mind deceived me, but no, the Ice Maiden had melted. For a moment at least.

A fanciful dream crashed into me, stealing my breath. One

where I got to watch Cat walk towards me in a flowing white dress and a soft expression of utter joy on her face.

Fuck.

I never thought I'd be the commitment guy, but for her, maybe I could be brave enough to feel what Finn and Shaun did towards Abi and Mona. Pure, endless love.

The thought of it both terrified and excited me.

There was just one problem. We were still client and attorney and Cat — my beautiful, fierce and rule-follower Cat — had resisted my every seduction attempt thus far.

Time to up my game.

Turn the page for a bonus epilogue with Abi and Finn. I usually reserve this for my mailing list but this is easier in print. Plus, it's just nice to have it all together, right?

If you enjoyed *Married Blind*, please consider leaving a review on your preferred platform.

ABI

I woke to the rush of release, muscles tensing, hands clenching around the silk rope wrapped around my wrists…

Forcing my eyes open, I stared at the rope pulling my arms taut above my head, giving me zero movement. For a second, absolute confusion filled me.

Then I felt the tickle of his beard against my inner thigh before the culprit dragged his fingers through my soaking folds. His tongue circled my sensitive clit, making my back bow and gentle aftershocks coarse through me.

"Finn," I moaned.

He chuckled. "Took you long enough."

His lips latched onto my clit, sucking hard, without giving me so much as a moment to process anything other than the need for more.

"What time is it?" I gasped as he pistoned his fingers in and out of me. They dragged against a bundle of nerves over and over. My hips jolted, chasing him as he removed them.

"Finn," I cried, whether for an answer or for him to keep going, I don't know.

"We've got loads of time." His lips ghosted over my hip and my gaze snapped to his.

His sapphire eyes burned with need and unrestrained excitement. A feeling of absolute contentment flooded me. *Who cares if we're late?*

Five months had passed since Mona and Shaun's wedding. One feature film under my belt, one trip to Paris and a month spent in our New York Penthouse. Whenever we could, we formed routines. Waking the other with sex had fast become one of them. It didn't matter where in the world we were, or how ridiculously early our call times were, we could rely on each other.

The sun streamed through the windows of the penthouse, both blinding and enlivening.

"How much time is loads of time?" I asked.

Couldn't let him start thinking he just had to give me an orgasm and I'd let him be late all the time.

"It's only seven." He smirked, his eyes lighting up with mischief. "Plenty of time for me to make you scream."

"Promises, promises." I forced myself to relax, though I felt anything but.

The need to reach for him and *make* him move faster thrummed through me. Instead, I bit my lip and eyed him, my husband.

How could one word have the power to set butterflies free in my stomach?

If someone had told me a year ago, I'd end *Married Blind,* hopelessly in love with my surprise husband, I'd have gotten giddy over the thought, but I'm not sure I would have believed them. Too many things had clouded my mind for me to truly believe it would come true.

But it had. I no longer wished for a person to lean on, to

make me laugh when I didn't think I could, and to love me unconditionally.

I had Finn.

Finn shifted, moving up my body until his teeth grazed my nipple. I sucked in a breath when his mouth suctioned around the taut nub. His fingers continued to work me, the combination reducing me to mindless sensation.

My head rocked back and forth while his name slipped from my lips in a string of gasps, pleading for him to stop and for him to never stop.

Another orgasm crashed into me, reducing me to nothing more than moans.

How had I gotten so lucky?

"You're so bleeding responsive," Finn growled into my neck. Then he shifted over me, dragging his cock against my pussy with teasing strokes. "Are you ready for me, wife?"

I'd never get tired of hearing him say that word. He'd barely used it in our first three months and now he couldn't stop.

I grinned. "Always."

Finn leaned back on his hunches and then threaded his arms beneath my knees, lifting me until I had absolutely no control. Knowing Finn, he'd edge me for an hour before letting me come again.

He grinned at me as the realisation hit. "Sure about that, *dotey*?"

His hips shifted, just the tip of him slipping into my pussy. My eyes fluttered shut at the tiny stretch.

"Eyes on me." He thrust forward, filling me to the hilt and stealing the air from my lungs.

I fixed my gaze on his, absorbing every twitch of his features as he pounded into me. The pressure built fast and hard and, for one glorious moment, I thought he'd let me go over…

Then he slowed, driving himself deep before dropping one

of my knees to lean over me, that amused twinkle in his eyes. He pressed a forearm into the mattress beside me and lowered his face to mine. The change in position applied toe-curling pressure to my clit as he rocked against me.

"How does it feel to be completely mine, Mrs McCarthy?" He brushed my hair back, his fingers lingering on my jaw.

"Perfect," I panted. He might have let go of one of my legs, but I was still at his mercy. He held me off the bed with his thighs under my ass and his body crowding mine. He caged me in and it felt incredible. "Wouldn't want to be anyone else's."

His expression shifted, hardened. "Too right."

He kissed me, invading my mouth with his tongue, teeth nipping. It was all-consuming, just like him.

"You're mine, Abi," he whispered as he pulled back, his breath caressing my lips. "Say it."

With my eyes fixed on his, I smiled. "I'm yours. All yours."

"Good girl."

Finn shifted back. His hands gripped my hips, urging me to turn over. The silk rope tugged at my wrists, reminding me he had complete control. Once he had me on my hands and knees, he leaned over me, grazing his lips along my neck to my ear. "Remember that when you're wearing that pretty gown and have a room full of Hollywood royalty lusting after you."

He thrust into me from behind, driving hard and fast until I couldn't form words. The pressure built and built, pleasure thrumming through me, making my eyelids heavy and my muscles tense.

Then he eased off again. "Finn," I cried. My fingers clutched at the sheets, desperate to touch him in return. "Let me fucking come."

"Nope." His lips twisted while his eyes devoured me. His fingers danced over my clit, circling and teasing while he continued to rock into me. "I've got an hour before either of us needs to leave this bed, and I'm going to make you come so hard you can still feel it while we're at the altar."

For all of a second, I wondered if he was serious.

FINN

For the second time in a year, I stood at the altar surrounded by my friends. Except this time, my eyes weren't fixed on the emergency exits. Nervous excitement twisted in my stomach.

We were already married, and we didn't need this ceremony to prove it.

I'd argued against it for weeks and then Abi had rightly pointed out that my sister lit up every single time she suggested it. My parents never joined the chorus, but I'd have to be blind to miss their sly glances on our video calls. Beyond her initial visit, my mother hadn't said another word about missing the wedding… but once I saw it, I couldn't unsee it.

So here we were. Trussed up once again with hundreds of eyes fixed on us.

I glanced across the huge room, taking it all in. Abi had said our first wedding overwhelmed her with the number of people; this one was much larger. Once word got out, it grew and grew. The who's who of Hollywood congregated in this room, all of them watching me and all of them no doubt judging one detail or another.

I didn't care. Particularly not when the doors opened and Abi's sister led the charge of bridesmaids down the aisle outwards me. Ros, Saoirse and Mona followed her, all of them grinning from ear to ear and all of them wearing lavender Grecian bridesmaid dresses. A detail my sister insisted she would not have stolen from her a second time.

Then the music shifted and my wife stepped through the door, her hand tucked into the crook of my father's arm and a massive smile on her face. Like last time, her dress hugged almost every inch of her.

I bit back a groan at the sight of it hugging her hips, thighs and torso. The low cut of her dress showed off her cleavage, making me ache with the want to drag her into a room away from prying eyes.

Abi stopped before me and handed her bouquet off to Eva, who had tears shimmering in her eyes once again. Even my mother looked close to blubbering.

"Take good care of her, son," my father said, handing me Abi's hand with an amused quirk of his lips.

"Always."

And I meant it.

Abi smiled up at me as we took our positions before the officiant. This time, she stood before me, without the slightest tremor in her hands.

The officiant began and I couldn't stop myself from grinning at her like an absolute fool.

"A year ago, I didn't think I would ever fall in love again. But then you crashed into my life and refused to let me be," I said, when the officiant asked for our vows. I smirked as everyone around us chuckled. "I was an idiot, so focused on my past that I couldn't see the future in front of me. I should have known the moment I laid eyes on you that escaping with my heart would be impossible."

"Didn't stop you trying," Abi muttered.

My brows rose. "Didn't stop you trying, either." My eyes narrowed on her as the room laughed. She zipped her lips, her eyes twinkling, and I continued, "When Charlie forced me to join *Married Blind* I thought he was an absolute eejit. Now, I think I owe him a bottle of scotch."

"Better be expensive bloody scotch," my agent shouted, eliciting another chorus of laughter.

I didn't break my focus from Abi. "The point is, it turned out I could handle a little pain when you were beside me. I can't imagine my life without you. Thank you for seeing beyond the grumpy, distrusting actor. I love you."

I slid a new ring onto her finger, one I'd put thought into purchasing, rather than letting someone else handle it like the last time. The engagement ring stayed. Whoever picked that out nailed it, and I couldn't imagine any other rock on her finger.

"You didn't make it easy, Finn," Abi said. Her brows rose as she shook her head at me. "I'd never experienced emotional whiplash before, but you mastered it. I guess it's fortunate for me that you lacked control."

She smirked at me and my eyes narrowed. *Speak for yourself.*

"The soft glimpses you let me see were just too good for me to forget." She grinned at me and my heart jolted. I'd never get tired of seeing the love in her eyes. "I think I fell in love with you the moment you stepped in to help a woman you didn't know. No matter how hot and cold you were with me, I knew there had to be a great man beneath your show mask. I'm glad I didn't let you push me away. For years, my life was focused on nothing more than making ends meet. I had love, but our family had dwindled and neither of us could patch the holes." Tears simmered in her eyes and mine began to burn.

"You gave me back colour, excitement, joy," she continued. "The thrill of never knowing what tomorrow will bring, and the comfort of being supported no matter what. Thank you for loving me as much as I love you."

She slid the ring onto my finger and air whooshed out of my lungs. Something final settled in my chest and mind. All the talk of vow renewals had unearthed a fear that she'd realise she'd made a mistake and leave me.

Logically, I always knew that wouldn't happen. When she told me she loved me, I believed her wholeheartedly.

But this moment, with all of our family and friends watching, not a single camera in sight, it felt more real than the first time.

Add in the room full of blabber-mouth Hollywood stars and producers and I knew that within minutes, the entire world would know we belonged to each other.

The officiant pronounced us husband and wife (again). The room exploded in applause and I tugged Abi into my chest, wrapping my arms around her. I claimed her lips, getting lost in the feel of her pressed against me, just like the first time and every time since.

CATRINA

*B*right and early Monday morning, I rolled into the office with a noticeable bounce in my step. I'd worked hard trying to prove my worth — weeks and months of late nights, early mornings, and endless briefs — and they'd finally taken notice.

Today, I started my first solo case: acquiring an LA film studio for one of the most popular actors in Hollywood. Not that I could put a name to the face if a celeb walked past me.

Even if I couldn't care less about the celebrity goings-on, one thing remained: I was one step closer to making partner.

At some point, I'd stop grinning like a loon each time the thought cycled through my mind.

It wouldn't be this week.

If my colleagues saw me, they'd blame my unusual pep on my boss's decision to trust me with the Starlight Studios acquisition, and I didn't care if they did.

Only I knew the truth.

Only I could feel the ache of disused muscles as I walked, reminding me with each step how I celebrated my step up.

I'd never been the one-night stand kind of girl, but I have to admit, it was exhilarating.

"Knowing my luck, I'd get swept out to sea and eaten by something."

"I could teach you, if you're up for the challenge."

"Are you going to stop a sea monster from eating me?"

"I'll keep you safe from any sea monsters." He grazed my cheek with his nose. "Besides, I'm the only one allowed to taste you."

Nathan.

I could feel the ghost of his hands mapping every curve of my body, leaving marks I wished would never fade.

Mike knocked on my door. Thankfully, I'd completed all of my preparations for this meeting and got myself as caught up as the sparse notes from my predecessor allowed.

"Catrina," Mike's voice boomed from the doorway, snapping me out of my thoughts. "I hope you're ready for a big day."

"Good morning, Mr Nelson. As ready as I'll ever be." I set my coffee cup down on the desk and stood, pasting a bright but confident smile to my lips. "I've been preparing all weekend."

"Good." He stepped inside, his tall frame taking up much of the space in my modest office. "I told you she was my best, Mr Logan, and I never lie."

A tall, blond man followed Mike into my office. My heart lodged in my throat.

Nathan. Those piercing blue eyes instantly found mine.

Two days. It had only been two days since I kicked him out of my apartment at dawn, banishing him from my home and my thoughts. Yet here he was, conjuring up memories I'd spent days savouring.

Nathan strode in casually confident as if he owned the place — and perhaps a part of me too, after a single unforgettable night. His blond hair was tousled, a reminder of tangled sheets and roaming hands. That knowing look in his eyes said he recalled my bed as clearly as I did.

"Cat," Nathan mouthed, his eyes widening briefly before a sly grin spread across his face.

Panic surged as the ramifications hit me. If he said the wrong thing, my career could be over before it truly began.

"Catrina Sinclair, meet Nathan Logan," Mike introduced us with a wave of his hand, completely missing the tension in the air. "Nathan is purchasing Starlight Studios. He's agreed to get you up to date on any additional details you might require."

"Nice to meet you, Mr Logan," I said, extending my hand for a firm handshake, but keeping my desk between us.

His gaze dropped to the hard surface, flaring with a look I recognised far too well. My breath caught as Nathan's heated attention raked over me, reminding me without words of how thoroughly he had explored my body. I fought the impulse to squirm under his scrutiny, composure wavering.

"Please, call me Nathan," he insisted with a warm smile, his eyes locked onto mine.

That accent. For a moment, I'd forgotten, but oof. I'd always had a weakness for a good English accent.

The memory of it whispering into my ear while he hovered above me sent a shiver down my spine. *"See, it's not so bad giving up control, is it, Icy?"*

"It's a pleasure to meet you too, Catrina," Nathan said, his lips quirking as he clocked the flush of crimson trying to break through my foundation.

I nodded, my voice trapped. I forced myself to release his hand, hyper-aware of Mike's eyes on us, and I refused to give him any reason to doubt my abilities.

Mike cleared his throat, clueless as to the cause of the tension thickening the air. "I need to make a call. I'll leave you two to get acquainted. Be back in a jiffy!"

The door clicked shut behind him, silence ringing in his

wake. I stared at Nathan, his knuckles white on the back of my guest chair, as a slow grin curved his lips.

"Surprised, Icy?" His gaze bore into me, hinting at pleasures we had shared mere days ago. "Did you miss me?"

I swallowed hard, searching for some cutting reply. But the sight of him left me tongue-tied.

Nathan rounded the desk. "No need for shy glances — we're well past that, aren't we?"

His cologne filled my senses as he leaned in too close, intent eyes catching me in their snare. He reached out, fingers grazing my flushed cheek. I stiffened as warmth sparked beneath his touch, threatening my composure.

"Mr Logan, this is highly inappropriate." I said sharply, putting space between us. "I'm your legal counsel, nothing more."

"You can drop the act. It's just us, Cat." His gaze softened, that charming smile fading as a glint of awe filled his blue eyes. "I never thought I'd see you again."

I faltered, caught by the earnest longing in his voice. His hand rose again, slow and questioning, giving me time to pull away this time. Instead, I found myself leaning into his touch, palm against my cheek as memories rose unbidden.

Nathan smiled, thumb brushing my lower lip. "There you are. I was hoping you'd come back to me."

I caught my breath, stunned by the tenderness in his gaze. His words slipped past my defences, hinting at something vulnerable inside of me.

"Don't look at me like that."

"Like what?" he whispered.

"Like I'm the only woman in the world."

Nathan smiled, free hand tangling in my hair as he tilted my chin up. "You are, for me."

His words struck a chord deep within me, prodding an ache I hadn't felt in years. The promise of being someone's centre. Actually caring about one another and not in the 'Oh good, you're still breathing' way my mother had me. It was a pipe dream I'd forced myself to stop living for.

And I won't start now.

I blinked, scrambling for a response that wouldn't reveal how much his unexpected appearance had shaken me. "I apologise if I gave you the wrong impression." My fingers caught his wandering hand, tugging it away from my face. "Friday night was a mistake and I have no interest in repeating it. Especially not now that I'm your attorney."

I stared up at him, all six-foot, five glorious inches of him, willing him to believe the lie. If only the complications of my job and the firm's rules against client relationships didn't stand in the way, I'd happily go back for a repeat of round two.

Nathan's eyes darkened, a spark of challenge in their depths. "Is that so? Because your body tells a far different story." His gaze tracked down the length of me, leaving tiny fires in its wake. "Admit it, Cat. You felt the same spark... and you want more."

My pulse leapt but I tilted my chin up, forcing an unaffected air. "My personal feelings are irrelevant. I'm here to represent your legal interests, nothing more."

Nathan's gaze dropped to my mouth, a slow smile curving his lips. "Your lips say one thing, but your eyes confess the truth. You want a repeat of Friday night... and so do I."

He reached out, knuckles grazing my cheek in a touch that momentarily wiped common sense from my mind. I swayed toward him before catching myself, panic setting in at how easily my body responded to his.

Nathan had slipped past all my defences with unfair ease, leaving me on edge and struggling against the pull of desire. I couldn't afford a single mistake if I wanted to achieve all I had worked so hard for, but part of me yearned to close the scant distance between us, regardless of the consequences. His tempting smile might just prove to be my undoing if I didn't find the willpower to resist.

I took a shaky step back, desperate to put distance between us before I did something I would regret. "I insist we remain professional. My career is at stake here, and I can't afford any... distractions."

Nathan's smile faded, expression sobering. "I didn't expect to see you here. But now that I have, I'm reluctant to let this go." His gaze bore into me, more serious than I had seen him. "Friday was more than just physical for me. I haven't felt a connection like that in a long time. Did you feel it too?"

I looked away from the intensity of his gaze, at a loss. I had told myself it was merely lust and impulse, refusing to consider anything deeper. But there were moments when we understood each other with no need for words.

"It doesn't matter." I straightened my shoulders, adopting a brisk tone. "We can't do it again, Mr Logan. My career depends on maintaining a proper distance from clients, and..."

"Nathan." His gentle rebuke gave me pause. I glanced at him to find a small smile curving his lips, but a hint of vulnerability in his eyes. "When we're alone, it's Nathan. And your career won't suffer, Cat. I want to do this right."

I stared at him, unsure how to respond. Doing this — whatever 'this' was — would go against everything logical.

"Have dinner with me tonight. No distractions, just two people exploring whatever this connection between us might become." He smiled, coaxing and genuine. "Give me — give us — a chance. I dare you."

A knock on the door interrupted us.

"I can't do that." I turned away from him, smoothing down my skirt. "From now on, I'm your attorney. Nothing more."

His smile faded before he nodded. "If that's what you want."

While Nathan rounded my desk and assumed a more natural position, I walked to the door, willing my hammering heart to settle down. *He's just a gorgeous but pushy man who gave you the best orgasms of your life–but he is now off limits. It's okay, he'll get bored soon enough.*

I opened it to find Mike waiting, breezing into the room with a thick folder under his arm. "Sorry about that." He sat in his usual seat without hesitation, missing the tension between Nathan and me. "Shall we?"

Nathan's expression smoothed into polite professionalism in an instant. "Of course."

"Absolutely," I agreed, settling into my seat and forcing my focus back to the task at hand. "Please have a seat, Mr Logan."

The sooner we got started, the sooner I could prove my worth to Mike and cement my position in the firm. I was prepared to do whatever it took to make this acquisition successful, even if it meant resisting the undeniable charm of Nathan Logan.

Nathan took a seat across from me, sprawling into the chair with a roguish grin. His expensive suit did little to hide the muscles beneath. I tried to focus firmly on my notes but felt his presence like a gravitational pull.

"Let me give you a bit of background on the acquisition," Mike began, leaning back in his chair and tapping a pen against the papers he held. "Starlight Studios is a major player in the industry, and they've been seeking a buyer for some time. Mr Logan," — he gestured towards Nathan — "is prepared to make that purchase."

I tried my best to concentrate on Mike's words, but I couldn't stop glancing at Nathan.

His gaze slid to mine, blue eyes smouldering with a heat that threatened to make me squirm. He masked it in an instant if Mike glanced his way. But in that fleeting moment there was a promise of passion waiting to ignite again, if given the chance. Nathan leaned forward as if riveted by Mike's words, but a sly quirk of his lips said his thoughts mirrored my own.

"This case is of the utmost importance to our firm," Mike continued, his voice firm and authoritative. "Our reputation is on the line, so we need to ensure that we handle everything impeccably."

"You can count on me." I forced myself to maintain eye contact with my boss.

"Good." He nodded approvingly. "Let's dive into the specifics of the deal."

I could feel the weight of Nathan's gaze on me, and I struggled to keep my composure under the pressure of his attention. Every time I looked at him, our shared secret seemed to shimmer in the air between us like an electric charge.

"Catrina," Mike's voice brought me back to reality. "Do you have questions about the agreement terms?"

"Uh, yes," I stammered, racking my brain for something relevant to ask. "Mr Logan—"

"Nathan."

"Right. Nathan." I forced a weak smile. "You've spent some time working on this deal. Besides the misfortune with your previous attorney, why do you believe the process has been so drastically delayed?"

"I believe the shareholders cannot separate fact from fiction."

"That's quite the accusation."

"Hmm. Is it an accusation if it's true?" He held up his hand before I could answer. "That was rhetorical. The gossip rags have made a sport of portraying me as a ladies' man, and the shareholders have used those rumours as an excuse to question whether I'm truly serious in my bid."

"I... see." I frowned, sorting through this new information. "And this perception has directly impacted negotiations?"

"To put it mildly." Nathan's smile turned wry. "My 'moral

failings' have been cited more than once as cause for concern in handing over the reins of their studio. As if my personal life has any bearing on my ability to run a company."

"That does seem rather absurd." I hesitated, unsure how much to reveal of my own opinions. "Tabloid gossip is hardly evidence of poor business sense or judgement."

"Exactly." Nathan threw up his hands. "Now, I'll be honest, once upon a time, some of them might have been true, but that hasn't been the case for some time."

His tone was sincere, and it left me feeling weak in the knees. We held each other's gaze. I'd never been one to shirk eye contact, but I might have had to start before I closed the lid on this purchase.

"Now the sad truth about Hollywood is that scandal sells, so where the lies about me weren't legitimately harmful to my reputation, I let them slide." He winced. "Unfortunately, the image of me the tabloids used to drive their site traffic does not lend itself to a level headed businessman." He paused for a moment before continuing, his gaze still fixed on me.

"My priorities have changed, and I have instructed my agent to shut down any further rumours before they take root." He bit his lip and smiled at me, the sight of it making my core tense. "I believe that once the shareholders meet me, I'll be able to ease any of their fears."

His voice wrapped around me, low and intense as he focused all of his attention on me.

"I can understand why that would be aggravating." I met his gaze, pulse skipping at the glint of approval there. "Well, you can rest assured I have no interest in tabloid gossip or moral judgments. My only concern is representing your best interests in acquiring this studio, and ensuring all parties come to an equitable agreement as swiftly as possible."

Mike started to respond, but his words were lost on me. I stared at Nathan, feeling as if he had just let me in on something far greater than the acquisition of Starlight Studios.

"Have you ever been on a studio lot?" Nathan asked suddenly, his voice warm and inviting. The sudden change in topic caught me off guard.

"Uh, no, I haven't." My fingers nervously tapped on the table. "I've always been a behind-the-scenes kind of person."

"Ah, that's a shame. It's quite an experience," he said with a charming grin, then added softly, "Perhaps I could show you around one day? You know, purely for professional reasons."

My heart skipped a beat at the thought of spending time with Nathan outside the office. "That sounds interesting. Thank you for the offer, but I think we should focus on the acquisition right now."

Mike cleared his throat. "Exactly right, Catrina. You only have two days until the shareholder's meeting and it's taken nearly three months to get them to agree on a date."

When we finally finished, Mike shook Nathan's hand eagerly. "A pleasure doing business with you. We'll have the contracts ready for signing next week, hopefully."

Nathan smiled. "Likewise, thank you both for ensuring a smooth process." His eyes met mine briefly, regret flickering through them. "I appreciate your efforts on my behalf."

I nodded. "You're welcome, Mr Logan. I'll be in touch."

With a nod to us both, Nathan left. An odd mix of relief and disappointment filled me. I had done right... so why did it feel like I had let a once-in-a-lifetime chance go?

Mike chuckled, gathering his papers. "Quite the charmer, that one! But don't worry, you handled yourself well." He stood, smiling. "This was a big day, Catrina. The partners will be very impressed."

I returned his smile. "Thank you. That means a lot."

Mike headed for the door and my smile faded, doubts crowding in. This deal was everything I had worked for, yet Nathan threatened my ability to stay focused. Ten minutes in an office with him and I could barely ignore his draw. Our history — however brief — left him a distraction I couldn't ignore.

As difficult as it was, I had to be upfront with Mike — he deserved my unbiased best, and if that meant stepping aside, then objectivity demanded it. Even if the thought of losing all my progress stung.

"There's something I should tell you," I said to Mike before he could leave my office. "Regarding Nathan Logan —"

He turned, waving a hand and dismissing my concerns. "You worry too much. I know you've got this under control."

I frowned, thrown by his nonchalance. "No, that's not — there are complications —"

"Don't you start second-guessing yourself now!" Mike interrupted with a laugh. "You were born for deals like this." Mike smiled, placing a hand on my shoulder. "I never doubted for a second you were right for this." He chuckled.

"Mike, please listen— "

But he swept on, buoyed by enthusiasm. "You have my complete support, Catrina. Keep your eye on the prize. We'll make a partner out of you yet!"

Despite my misgivings, I couldn't help but smile at the praise.

"Before I forget…" Mike shuffled through his suit pockets, patting himself down with a look of pure concentration on his face. He reached into one and his expression smoothed out. "This is Mr Logan's agent, Maisy Michaels. Give her a call if you need anything." He handed me the card and spun away. "Keep up the good work, Catrina."

The door clicked shut behind Mike, and I sank into the luxurious leather chair at my new desk. I had to hand it to him, he knew how to motivate me when it mattered. His confidence in my ability steadied my nerves.

If Mike trusted I could handle the negotiations, who was I to argue?

Nathan's intoxicating cologne still permeated the air, tickling my senses and threatening my concentration. His confident voice lingered in my ears as I considered the high stakes of this case and my precarious position.

"Get a grip, Cat," I muttered to myself, raking my fingers through my hair, messing up my carefully crafted curls.

Focus on the promotion and the shiny new office.

Still my heart raced at the memory of Friday night, threatening to dismantle my carefully constructed facade of professionalism. I needed to get a handle on it. Letting the attraction run unchecked would not only jeopardise my ability to do my job but also my position at the firm.

Although with Mike's confidence in me, maybe it wouldn't affect my position as much as I'd first assumed.

You might as well give up now. You'll only fail in the end, and end up right back where you started: trapped here with me. My mother's voice echoed inside my mind, a replay of her goodbye before I left for law school in the States.

Growing up in a small town, the pressure to succeed and excel had been intense. Even with my mother's apathetic expectation that I would fail no matter how hard I tried, I had an entire town fixated on my smallest wins, pushing for more and more.

Moving thousands of miles away for law school had been the best thing for me.

I couldn't go back to that.

"Is it worth the risk?" I whispered, staring intently at the gold-lettered nameplate on my desk, Catrina Sinclair – Associate Attorney.

It had taken years of hard work, sleepless nights spent buried in law books, and countless hours to get me to this point. I was so close to making a name for myself. Was I willing to jeopardise everything for a tantalising yet dangerous attraction that might be one-sided?

Exactly.

No reason to believe Nathan actually wanted to see me again. Hotshot Hollywood actors probably had women offering themselves up to them on a platter.

Except he outright asked you out and just spent the better part of an hour eye fucking you with your boss in the room...

That meant nothing. It could have been nothing more than a game.

"Focus, Catrina," I chided myself, forcing my gaze away from the nameplate and onto the thick stack of Starlight Studios documents cluttering my desk. "You've got a job to do."

As the swirling storm of doubt and desire threatened to consume me, I replayed the meeting in my mind. Nathan had been nothing but professional in front of Mike, answering my questions with honesty and openness. The perfect actor with nothing on the line if his inappropriate interest ever came out.

Unlike him, I had everything on the line, and I had to find a way to ignore him. For the sake of my sanity and my career.

If you'd like to know what happens next, *Acting Counsel* is available on all platforms and can be requested by most bookstores. Check it out here: books2read.com/ActingCounsel Or request it from your local library.

ACKNOWLEDGMENTS

Just as *Between Takes* was very much a book of my heart, *Married Blind* wiggled its way into my head and refused to let go. Let's be honest, Finn McCarthy hijacked me and refused ransom. The man was determined to have his story told and what a story it was.

Without certain people, you wouldn't have met Finn and Abi and I need to thank them.

To my amazing editor, Dayna, a massive thank you for… well, everything. We had a hell of a time getting to the finish line on this one. Thank you for filling me with confidence, fiercely cutting words, asking the hard questions and powering through a terrifying twelve hours of technology failures. You're the best.

Big thanks to Janey for your endless support, daily encouragement and hilarious comments whenever I left you hanging in a spicy scene. I'm still not sorry, but you're the best critique partner a girl could ever ask for. Thank you.

Also thank you to my brilliant cover designer, Kirsty, for surprising me every single time you hit my inbox. The way you inadvertently craft perfect scenes for this series is incredible. You're incredible.

To my ARC team and reviewers, your support and love of my books will always be incredible to me. Thank you.

To the readers, thank you for reading this book and joining me for Abi and Finn's story.

ALSO BY MORGANA BEVAN

True Platinum Series (Rock Star Romance)

(Rhiannon)

Chasing Alys–Ryan (Resistant to Love)

Charming Daphne–Matt (Force Proximity)

Winning Nia–James (Second Chance)

Enticing Mel–Dan (Secret Baby)

Needing Emily–Emily (Accidental Marriage/Runaway Bride)

Defying Ella - Jared (Close Proximity / Snowed-in)

(The Brightside)

Braving Lily - Lily (Opposites Attract)

Daring Ceri - Alex (Second Chance)

Marrying Olivia - Lewis (Accidental Marriage)

Lovers Knot

Rockstar Regret - Nick (Forced Proximity)

Kings of Screen Series (Hollywood Romance)

Between Takes (Enemies to Lovers)

Married Blind (Marriage of Convenience)

Acting Counsel (Close Proximity, Forbidden)

Fashionably Fake (Fake Dating)

Lights, Camera, Baby! (Accidental Pregnancy)

ABOUT MORGANA

Morgana Bevan is a sucker for a rock star romance, particularly if it involves a soul-destroying breakup or strangers waking up in Vegas. She's a contemporary romance author based in Wales. When Morgana's not writing steamy celebrity romances with gorgeous British rock stars and movie stars, she's travelling the world, searching for inspiration.

She enjoys travelling, attending gigs, and trying out the extreme activities she forces on her characters.

Find Morgana online at morganabevan.com.

Morgana's Facebook Reader Group: facebook.com/groups/498919364708263